(previously published as *Kelly*)

THE **PALOMINAS PISTOLERO**
SMOKE-WAGON KID
NELSON NYE

ZEBRA BOOKS
KENSINGTON PUBLISHING CORP.

PALOMINAS

ZEBRA BOOKS

are published by

KENSINGTON PUBLISHING CORP.
21 East 40th Street
New York, N.Y. 10016

First Printing: November, 1978

THE PALOMINAS PISTOLERO

1

If there was one thing Happenstance Kelly couldn't abide, it was this damn soft streak his ma had bequeathed him that every so often outcropped to kick in the teeth his most diligent promotions—things he'd put a heap of hard thought to, like that widow at Brayfass or this goddam dude off the El Paso stage!

Kelly—still fuming at the offhanded treatment his generosity had garnered—stared after the flow, more than half minded to have another go at it.

Fat-ass puke had been just crying to be took, flashing around a wad of dough like that, then getting off by God to leave it laying on the seat! Must of been at least ten thousand in that bulging gold-stamped wallet, judging by them three five hundreds he had glimpsed when the addlepated chump had paid for his meal at Bisbee!

Watching the bowler-hatted Britisher in outlandish tweeds toting his fancy leather luggage across the hoof-tracked dust toward the doorway of the Drovers, Kelly shifted the heavy saddle on his shoulder and cursed bitterly.

Half the way coming back here from Texas he'd stood off the jolting tedium with elaborate schemes for parting this scissorsbill from some of that wealth. Some of the cons he'd dreamed up were brilliant. But when the chance of a lifetime lay right there in the flat of his hand, off he had jumped like a damnfool Samaritan to give the thing back—even running to do it!

There was times he just couldn't figure himself out.

Course a man had to be a plumb idjit these days to expect any gratitude for services rendered. This wasn't what rankled, but the la-di-da way the coot had blinked, said "Oh . . . quite!" and shoved the wallet back into his buttonless pocket, picked up his bags and gone ambling off.

Like it wasn't no more than just so much waste paper!

Kelly guessed, by God, he should be bored for the simples.

His long, solid lips pinched in at the corners. Impatience lifted the burly shoulders and swung him about toward the stage office doorway and the gaggle of loafers always on tap each time Trotter's team was due in from the east.

Like a sweep of cloud shadow crossing a field the smirks fled their faces as the heel of that glance touched one and another of those looming nearest. He chucked a black scowl at them, more disgusted

4

than mollified, though deep in his bones it loosed a stirring of pride. Damn grunts knew better than to laugh at Hap Kelly who could put three slugs out of five dead center and do it, by grab, in the blink of an eye!

It was all that kept his countrymen at bay, and he took pride in that, likewise. No one else could have kept all those miles of tall grass inviolate to a greaser the way things stood today. Couldn't last, of course—not without more killing.

Sooner or later, if things rocked along, one of the old man's white trash neighbors would likely get up the spunk to make another play. No damn gun, no matter how watchful, was going to hold off their encroachments forever.

He'd tried to tell Don Ambrocio this, wise him up, show that one of these days—if nothing else worked—that mangy pack was going to get tired of being stood off and fetch in some younger, brasher hand from outside. Good breath wasted. All this had got from the old man was grins. It was like he figured hiring Hap Kelly's gun had thrust an unbreachable barrier between his possessions and the fate that had overtaken most of his friends.

And all he'd bought, Kelly knew, was just a little more time.

Irritation clanked from each spin of his spurs as, again shifting saddle, Hap struck off for Claine's livery. Rough as a cob was no good against ambush. Man had to have eyes in the back of his head, and this was but one of the needs Hap was lacking. Being good with a gun and reasonable quick wasn't the same thing at all as being a gun*fighter*—if he'd had half the brain God give to gophers he wouldn't have took on this job in the first place!

What good was money if you weren't going to be around long enough to spend it? Back there in El Paso he'd been well out of this and had told himself so a couple dozen times. He'd gone to pick up some help but word had got ahead of him and the pair he had counted on had turned him down flat.

Climbing back on that stage had been his own doing—no one had forced him. It was just that, having put his hand to this, he had to see it through. Pride took over from judgment every time. Having nothing else it was all he'd got to cling to. Without pride a man was no better than a cur.

Just the same—

As he was passing the Bon Ton Ladies' Wear & Hat Shop an amused voice jabbed through the prop of his conceit. "Well! Look at who's back in town," it said, and when he doggedly chose to ignore this, "Cat got your tongue again?"

It brought his head sharply round.

Melanie Scott, seamstress and milliner, was enough to strike sparks from any man—not excluding the local preacher, who wasn't above sneaking a look when chance offered. Trim, assured, and the most courted piece this side of the mountains. Horse-colored hair—a kind of stawberry roan, high-piled and shining, set off the green eyes to perfection. It was the rest of her though that toned up Hap's blood to match the dark flag of the flush on his cheeks.

She always could get under his hide and was no more abashed about riling him than usual. In that mocking contralto she conceded, "Looks like you've done it again."

She never had liked him and by God it was mutual! "Done what?" he growled, drawn into speech despite not intending to bandy words with her.

Head to one side she considered the look of him braced in his tracks like some huge badgered bull. "Disappointed those barflies and loafers up yonder. Been making book—odds five to three you'd cleared out for good—but I took up for you. Told them you didn't have sense enough to quit. Said the only way they'd be rid of you was to bury you."

Like as if not enough of them thought so already! "Thanks," he grumbled, showing his teeth in a grimace. "Maybe I can do as much for you sometime." He tugged the rim of his hat down across one eye and struck off, hot and glowering, swearing under his breath. He was glad, by God, he'd never let himself by jockeyed. Imagine being teamed in double harness with *her!*

Just the bare thought put sweat across his lip.

Thinking disgustedly back over women he had known did little to disabuse him of cherished convictions. He wasn't one who claimed with a sack over their heads you couldn't tell one from the other. One thing you could damn well count on, though. When the chips were down and all the gab peeled away marriage was the goal of every last conniving one of them!

Still stewing about the things an unwary man could let himself in for he passed Claine's big stacks and strode into the stable. The comparative gloom cut down his vision till Claine spoke from a stall he'd been shoveling out. "That fancy moro you been ridin' ain't here."

Kelly eased the heavy saddle off his shoulder, put it down. He was aware that Claine—like most of these townsmen—had been considerably chafed

7

having to do business with a man they regarded a bunch-quitting bastard some ten foot lower than a belly-crawling sidewinder. Hap said with quick suspicion: "You turned him loose?"

"Girl took him off with her—"

"Girl! What girl?" Kelly growled, fists opening and shutting like he couldn't hardly wait to get Claine's neck between them.

"Here—hold on!" The scrawny stableman, cheeks blanching, backed off with a nervous hand thrown hastily in front of him. " 'Twa'n't none of my doin'— she come in here yesterday. Mouth shut hard enough to bust her nutcrackers. Caught up a leadshank, snapped it onto him an' took him away. As Gawd is my—"

"*What* girl?"

"I dunno what her name is—that Palominas filly, the black-haired one—Tiodosa is it?"

Kelly stared.

"Why would she want to do a thing like that?"

"Look," Claine said, "my job's tendin' stable. I don't read minds. I don't give that bunch no argument neither. She come from Palominas. That moro had their brand on his hip."

Kelly stood a moment longer like he was turning it carefully over. "All right. Rope me out a renter."

"Ain't got a spare horse in the—"

Claine looked like a gopher that had run out of wind a jump short of its hole. Kelly puffed out his cheeks. The stableman's eyes, getting bigger and wilder, began jumping round like he'd got a call from nature. "What I mean—only nag I got back there you wouldn't be seen dead on."

"Try me."

The feller, eyeing him slantways, scuttled out the

back door.

Kelly spent the time wondering who had put him up to this. Not that it made any great amount of difference. Man who'd turn against his own kind for money could tote up his friends on one hand. And not have to move any fingers to do it! Even Rankin Bridwell that Hap used to shoot pool with could walk past him now without blinking an eye.

Claine returned with nothing but a knot at the end of his leadstring. "Guess," he whined nervously, "one of the boys musta turned him into that upper—"

"No sweat," Kelly said. "I'll find something here I can get a leg over," and starting down the row of stalls, came to a stop beside the fidgeting hind end of a powerfully put together flea-bitten gray.

"Here—wotcher doin'?" Claine bleated when Hap backed the horse out. "You can't have him!"

Kelly—paying no attention—got a saddle blanket down from where it had been spread hair side out to dry and reached for the bitted bridle. When he had them fixed in place he went back for his saddle, Claine staring bug-eyed. Settling his hull atop the blanket Kelly reached underneath to catch hold of the girths and was yanking the flank strap through its ring when Claine, jumping round and wringing his hands in a great show of lather, cried, "Chrissake, Kelly—that's the *marshal's* horse, dammit!"

"That so?" Kelly said, and finished cinching up.

"Goddam it," Claine yelled, "that's flat out *stealin'!*"

Kelly, grinning across his shoulder, stepped into the saddle. "If he wants to press charges I guess Rankin knows where to find me."

Without further words he rode from the stable and looking edgily mean put the horse up the street,

9

ignoring turned heads, peering stonily before him like he didn't give a damn whether school kept or not.

Rankin Bridwell was standing with Bryce Murgatroyd by the Drovers porch as Kelly leisurely came abreast, seeing the ranchman's gaunt look tighten like the puckery mouth of a miser's purse as he gripped Bridwell's arm. The marshal's cheeks darkened under the battery of eyes but all he said—and very casually—was, "Nice horse, Hap."

Kelly nodded. "Figured you knew how to pick 'em. Obliged for the loan. I'll send him back straightaway."

And that was all there was to it. For now, anyway.

How Bridwell might feel about it later was anyone's guess with Bryce at his elbow to stir up whatever hell he could slip a chunk under.

Rankin repped for the law at Friendly Corners and most of the time could be got along with, but Murgatroyd swung a good deal of weight and had no love for Hap at all. By his way of figuring, except for Kelly, Hacienda Palominas would by now have been securely annexed to those broad jags and parcels he'd diddled other Mexkins out of.

The town marshal, Kelly thought, was reasonably honest and had all the guts you could hang on a fence post. But pressures had moved stronger gents than Bridwell. With an election coming on, how much of Bryce's spleen the man would stand up against looked a mighty poor reed to lean on.

Kelly, putting Friendly Corners behind him, loosed an irritable snort. This could turn out to be the worst damn bind he had ever got into.

Now that it was hot in his mind he could see how Tiodosa, used to being deferred to and being spoiled rotten, might have got her bowels in an uproar on being told Hap had climbed a stage and departed the country.

Should have told her, he reckoned, he'd be gone a few days, knowing what a hair-trigger temper she had. But he hadn't known himself till he'd happened on signs of how far Bryce Murgatroyd would go to be rid of him. Tiodosa, confronted unexpectedly by those bets Melanie had mentioned, most likely figured he had run out on her.

Kelly blew out his cheeks. By God a man had to watch himself! If her father ever got onto the truth—or even suspected what was going on between them. . . .

The bare thought was enough to run the blind staggers straight up a man's spine! A Mexkin, maybe, the old Don might of swallowed. But a gringo fooling round with his daughter could damn sure get someone killed in a hurry!

He couldn't think why he hadn't thought of this sooner.

A Mexkin's honor wasn't one of them things you could stamp and yell *boo!* at. More especial the way things stood at the moment with all his friends, skinned, that cur pack yappin' and snappin' and him believing gringos was blood brothers of the Devil. Hell could pop any moment, Hap thought dourly.

If he'd any sense at all he'd cut loose of this right now.

It wasn't that hundred a month that held him—nor even Tiodosa. He knew what they'd say, all them loudmouths around here. They'd say Murgatroyd had put the Injun sign on him, and pride wouldn't hand the man that much satisfaction.

He rode with an easy swing of the shoulders, not hurrying through the black mealy shadows or across silvered playas where bright shafts of moonglow turned the surroundings iridescently blue.

Irascible, impatient, still caught in a morass of conflicting emotions, Kelly sat on his temper and held the horse down, too wise in the ways of concocted trouble to risk being trapped with its energies squandered. Turning over his prospects countless times, he cursed the pigheadedness that kept him committed to a course which held no conceivable future.

He'd a good piece to go, for it was all of ten leagues to the nearest claimed part of Don Ambrocio's holdings and most of another to the headquarters ranch where he ruled in feudal splendor what was left of his inheritance.

Hacienda de Palominas was an old Spanish grant dating back—if you could believe—to some pre-Napoleonic Alfonso, the ony grant left at this end of the cactus which conniving gringos hadn't managed to liberate. Since the metes and bounds of these kingly gifts were seldom precise, Don Ambrocio had lost a few acres along the way. But the old fox had swiftly caught on to the trends, cut his losses without quibble and took on Hap Kelly to stave off the inevitable, a departure hardly calculated to win many friends or sit at all well with the chin-strapped hombre who bossed his peons for him.

Loco Rufino, Number Two at Palominas—a queer combination of majordomo and range boss—was wedded to his job and quick to resent the slightest infringement of what he considered to be his prerogatives. Jealousy, inflamed by unpleasant apprehensions, burned back of his stare with all the white heat of a four-alarm fire.

Kelly, trying to ignore this, had been at some pains to avoid open clashes and wherever he could he sought Rufino's advice in the hope of escaping some more drastic collision, a practice which Hap suspected furnished Don Ambrocio with considerable amusement.

Every notion stomped around through Hap's head while the marshal's big gelding took him over the miles, adding its ant's sting of festering annoyance. He had to be about ready for a string of spools ever to have let this situation get on top of him. What graveled him worst was the folly of allowing that ache in his groin—the old Adam in him—to give over the whip hand to a nizzy in petticoats, particularly one as fiercely unpredictable as Tiodosa!

How could he have been such a knuckleheaded fool! Yet how could he have guessed from either age or actions so fiery a piece would turn out a goddam virgin!

A man had to be the worst kind of chump, Hap thought bitterly, to hang and rattle after being hit with a discovery like that. Goddam pride would be the death of him yet!

None of these frustrated ponderings, however, quite took his attention off the need for constant vigilance. He rode, eyes sharply scouting the way, aware not every *norteamericano* would be laboring under such a load of class as himself. Why, you could find in these parts galoots with less scruples than a blue-tailed fly, codeless two-legged snakes caring no more about niceties of conduct than a long-horned bull at rutting time.

13

Forty miles of constant watchfulness put considerable strain on a man's capacities and the sun, when finally it clawed above the rimrocks, gave him the look of having squirmed through some knothole, eyes like scars left by burns in old leather.

He felt like old leather, too—stiff and ganted, with a good three hours of riding still ahead of him.

He got down, as he'd been doing all through the night, to give his horse a blow, himself stamping round to shake the worst of the cramps from cocked muscles, sagging with weariness, grim about the mouth as some Covenanter preacher.

Off there in the shimmering middle distance lay the patrolled sprawl of land that was Don Ambrocio's coveted empire, a patchwork of duns and dust-powdered blues, darkened with umbers where deeper smudges of foliage bordered the wavy greens of new grass. Another handful of miles would see him inside the boundaries that set it apart from gringo encroachments, faced again with dangers every bit as explosive as drygulcher rifles in the hands of his compatriots.

Distrust of his own abilities had little to do with the strange mood of reluctance which had fastened upon Kelly almost from the moment he'd got onto this horse. Call it a hunch, some grim foreknowledge about this ride and what would be at the end of it. It was like an unliftable curse laid on him, a conviction of disaster that hung round his neck with all the unbudging weight of a millstone.

He searched the terrain with red-rimmed stare, quartering each facet with lips skinned back, twice peering behind to consider the maze of buttes and gulches he'd come through in the dark. From here it was just a jumble of roughs. No trace of dust or signal smoke hung above those towering bastions, and again he bent frowning attention on the purplish twists of folded hills flanking the trail a man would normally take if impatient to tuck his boots under a table.

In his head he could see every inch of the way, including some fine possibilities for ambush. Getting back in the saddle he kept turning these over, scowling as he read gringo brands on the heads-down cattle browsing nearest.

Some bits of newest graze "preempted" by Bryce Murgatroyd touched in several places off yonder lands still held by Don Ambrocio, but Bryce's weren't the only cows Kelly saw.

This was still, officially, more or less open range— "free grass" these Texicans called it in their loud and blustery fashion. Since the intrusion of Hap into the Palominas setup Don Ambrocio's vaqueros refused to recognize these claims, throwing back foreign brands wherever come upon. As Hap had told the old man, "You can't make friends with a bunch of damn coyotes. Giving in ain't going to buy you a thing. Way to back off trouble is slam right into it with everything you've got."

Up till now this had worked with but a single demonstration of what Hap Kelly could do with a pistol. Shock had spilled most of the wind from gringo sails.

But Murgatroyd, biggest and boldest of these range-hungry pirates, was too sharp a hand not to know which end of the snake to put his boot on. The unbending backbone of Palominas resistance was Happenstance Kelly and Hap had little doubt the man would try some way to bury him. Drop enough hints and one of those Texicans with or without the crutch of Dutch courage was going to be pushed into some kind of play.

Could happen to anyone. Happen today.

There'd been plenty of time since he'd got off that stage to get tempers heated and lay out the props. Time enough, certainly, to stash men with rifles at any number of places overlooking this trail.

He put his mount into motion, forward moving again, still turning it over behind hard-shut lips.

From Bryce's point of view all the signs must look favorable. Six months of having everything his own way would have turned most men overconfident, careless; this was how Kelly in Bryce's boots would have figured. Forty horseback miles, eyes skinned for trouble and nothing untoward lifting even the ghost of a ripple around him should have dulled the keen edge of his vigilance, especially as he approached his own bailiwick. That was how it stacked up.

In this brightening light with the air full of bird calls and nothing anywhere showing that could put a man's back up how could a gent with the gall of Hap Kelly seriously expect to find a slug winging toward him?

Couldn't, of course—but nevertheless did.

It was the hunch crying out from deep in his bones, and Hap wasn't one to ignore his hunches. Just the same, by God, he was bitterly tempted! He led away several horse lengths with sardonic fantasies of biters being bit. For he was one who believed in an eye for an eye if he couldn't get an arm or a leg thrown in also.

But he was practical, too, level enough in the head to realize after a night in the saddle he might not be up to that kind of dido. He continued to dawdle with his horse in a walk, shoulders slumped, head tipped forward and spasmodically stiffened to the rhythm of the gelding's wholly indifferent gait.

With an unpleasant prickling between broad shoulders Hap followed the wheel ruts onto higher ground, around and through these sugarloaf hills that bordered the patrolled Palominas.

One place up ahead for half a mile was a long twisty pass between sheer walls which would effectively screen his progress from any watchers Bryce had posted. Likewise out of sight, just this side of that pass, was an almost forgotten badly overgrown trail angling off to the left. This ancient trace, Hap had discovered, was the original mulepack route Don Ambrocio's dad and grandpap had used before Kearney'd opened this country to gringos.

Briefly pausing to bend an ear Kelly put his indignant mount into the thorny growth of mesquites that over the years had grown up to obscure the slitlike four-foot entrance.

Having checked this out when he'd first got the job Hap knew what to expect and was not turned back by the brush and cacti which for several hundred feet just about choked it shut. The trail improved when they got past this, rimmed mostly by cholla and a variety of pear sprung up between rocks that had washed from the slopes; fortunately there weren't too many of the latter. Thing he had now the most to watch out for was the strike of shod hoofs which, if heard, could very well fetch unwanted attention.

Kelly breathed somewhat freer now he'd got off the road, halfway wondering, even, if the dread he had still not completely shaken wasn't only in his noggin. Murgatroyd certainly would be tickled to be rid of him but would the man court the

17

risk of instant reprisal should Hap someway manage to evade Bryce's intentions?

Murgatroyd wouldn't be out here himself you could bet, but personal involvement wasn't required and—if he figured things were right—there were plenty of disgruntled fools running loose who could easily be steered for the price of a bottle. Man wouldn't even have to show himself to them.

Just the kind Bryce liked for his string, Hap thought, remembering the fellow's coolly calculant stare, the confident assumptions by which—carpetbagger style—Bryce Murgatroyd generally got his way. A foxy conniver who could give the rest of this Texican rabble the cards and spades in whatever was afoot and still coming up with the winning hand.

Not that he didn't have plenty of gumption. He was just too cagey to stick out his neck when, using his noggin, others could be maneuvered into most of the risks. A twister. The sure-thing kind of gambler who, after figuring the odds, insured his luck by coppering all bets.

The kind who smiled while twisting the knife.

That was Bryce. Pure-quill polecat.

Slicker than slobbers.

Still riding the flanks of these humpbacked hills as he followed the dons' old roundabout route, Kelly's scratchy glance continued to quarter, darkly alert for the least sign that this trail, too, might be under surveillance. Both ears alert, he grew gradually aware of an increased depth in the silence about him and pulled up suddenly to sift this again.

He found nothing to hear but the chorus of insects, no bird sound at all—not even a twitter.

Yet birds were in sight. He could see three or four brightly eyeing him from cover. Cowbird, two

18

mockers. A black-and-white specimen that looked like a magpie.

His stare narrowed grimly, he peered round again without discovering a clue that might reduce this hush to understandable dimensions.

Scowling, Kelly got off his borrowed mount.

The magpie, head to one side, watched alertly. The others took wing, flapping away upslope in noisy pretense of fright.

Hap got the carbine off Rankin's saddle and—still with that considering look on his cheeks—levered a cartridge into the chamber. The magpie squawked, quit the twig he'd been clinging to, beating his wings upslope like the others.

Kelly's glance swung back across the trail ahead. Something up there or off in that scraggle of brush farther down. Why else would those birds have all gone the same way?

If Bryce's dupes had outguessed him. . . . He stood stiffly listening.

How would this crew of Johnny-come-latelys know about a route so long abandoned? He hadn't learned of it himself until the old man had whistled that siren's tune in his ear.

Hap looked around again.

No flutter of motion. Nothing even vaguely hostile for ranging eyes to fasten on. Just brush, rocky slopes, and down below, more of the same with the weight of this uncanny quiet over everything.

He got back on the horse, and rifle across pommel, nudged the gelding ahead. Within two hundred feet the trail began to curl about the precipitous bulging flank of the next-to-last convolution of these flattening hills.

Hap was partway into the sharper corner of this

bend when sound stopped him short.

The whole turn of him peered hard into the north. Off yonder that way, maybe four or five miles, he could see the huddled shapes of another clump of hills. Brush, hat high, was directly before him, but off and beyond, scarcely more than half a mile, the land dropped into a kind of shallow basin. The sound had seemed to come up from there, but sound can be deceitful, the more so when bounced off a rocky slope.

Kelly stared thoughtfully, ignoring the nudges of apprehension. Unless he'd been seen he felt sure that the sound could hardly have been raised for his benefit. Brief and choked off, it wasn't easily definable, but to Kelly's experience it had seemed uncommonly like the bawling of a cow. And this was what held him.

Cattle often bawl when driven hard or about to stampede. But there wasn't any rumble of hooves coming up to him. There was, however, a faint smell of wood smoke, smoke he couldn't see but which painted in his head several well-remembered pictures.

Kneeing his horse off the trail, holding it carefully in check, he began a cautious descent, carefully picking his way between fractured boulders, wary of loose shale and talus, utilizing the brush to keep himself hidden. In this way he came off the slope, presently dismounting where the ground flattened out.

The fire smell was stronger. Still without smoke this consolidated the suspicions that had fetched him off the trail. Tying the gelding to a bush, still carrying the rifle, he moved through the brush with all the stealth of an Apache.

Up ahead the growth appeared less dense. Where

it began to thin out mixed with pear and Spanish bayonet he stopped once more to listen, hearing now the definite sounds he had expected. In pain or terror a cow bawled just as he started forward again and a grim twist of smile crossed Hap's tightening lips.

Pushing through a final thicket of mesquite the whole ugly business was exposed to his sight.

He saw the horses first, some forty feet ahead, glad the fitful breeze was blowing toward instead of away from him. Half a rope's length beyond where the nearest horse stood braced Kelly saw the two men, gringos both, one anchored to the head of the struggling tied-down steer, the other stepping gingerly away from the fire with a cinch ring gripped between two smoking sticks.

Their intention was plain, but just to make sure doubly certain Hap glanced again toward the steer's exposed flank, and confirmed his reckoning. These were no ordinary ambition-bit ranch hands attempting to maverick their way into the cow business. That brute in the rope was already marked with the "fluidy mustard" brand of Don Ambrocio.

With surprise on his side, carbine in hand, Hap could have stopped this right where it was; but this didn't suit his notion of what the old man had hired him for. So he waited, silently watching, for this down-at-heels pair to proclaim themselves thieves.

He stood, tight of cheek, still as a doorpost, with an almost Indian patience, while the hot ring seared the animal's hide as the "iron" man drew his confident alterations. It was when he straightened, about to step back, that Kelly called: *"Hold it!"*

He could have shot without warning such self-convicted thieves but figured even waddies as stupid as these ought to get some kind of chance for their chips—that soft streak from Ma cropping out again, he reckoned while waiting for shock to let go of their muscles.

Caught flat-footed with the evidence tied and still struggling between them, this pair certainly hadn't much margin of choice unless they honed for a cottonwood send-off.

The man on the steer's head reacted quicker, perhaps because he'd got both legs folded under him. Springing up with a snarl he grabbed for his pistol, had it halfway from leather when Kelly's slug cut him down. The other, running hard, was within two jumps of his dancing mount when Hap, firing from the hip, knocked him sprawling.

The only thing Kelly felt, considering those prone shapes, was the somber satisfaction of having done what he'd been hired to do, providing the rest of this Texican riffraff with a memorable demonstration of the high cost of tampering with Palominas property. They might sneer at gab and boundaries but death wasn't lightly shrugged aside.

Kelly allowed them ten minutes of unrelieved quiet—mostly to make certain he wasn't dealing with possums—before moving nearer. Those slugs may not have prettied them up much but at least this pair was taken out of the play. Both were strangers, birds of a feather, hounds to anyone who would throw them a bone—and a glance at their mounts confirmed this conviction for neither, by its brand, belonged around here.

He went over to the bawling steer to see what the iron man's artistry had added, for—generally speaking—Mexican brands were not easy to alter. Frequently, like this one, they covered the whole side of an animal's hide and appeared to outlanders more like a skillet of snakes than a brand.

Even so, Kelly found the pair's genuis hard to take in.

With lips skinned back he softly swore.

He'd intended to kill the brute to leave with these bastards but their use of that cinch ring made this impractical. What the brand spelled out now was an H K connected—and H K, by God, had to stand for *Hap Kelly!*

"Drop the gun, Kelly."

He didn't have to look round to know he had put his foot right into it. There, burned into that hide, was all the evidence Bryce could want—plain as the smug, taunting gloat in Bryce's voice. Caught red-handed was what that tone said. No one had to tell Hap he'd been sewed up right.

With this hoot in his gut, while he stood there frozen, the rest of the picture—the ever widening implications—came in bits and gouging pieces like chain shot winging from remembered gun emplacements outside Matamoras. They wrapped themselves about his mind till he nearly went out of his goddam skull.

He could feel the watching stares digging into him, sifting every scuttling thought that flapped against the rip of this knowledge, knowing the only chance he had left was to whirl and fire. Kelly saw too well he would never make it, realizing this time it was give up or go down.

There were words on his tongue with the taste of

23

brass. He stood like something chopped out of stone, too bitterly outfoxed even to curse.

"Drop the rifle," Bryce said, and Hap let it go.

Bryce said viciously, "We'll see what that old fool thinks of you now! Unlatch that belt."

Hap released the buckle, felt the holstered pistol slide down his leg.

"Now back away from them."

Kelly did that, too.

Bryce Murgatroyd chuckled. "You can turn around now."

Kelly let the clogged breath filter out of his throat. He could see, having turned, how the cards had been stacked from the time he had put Rankin's horse on this route, from the moment he had passed Murgatroyd back in town. He'd been guilty of the oldest mistake in the book, selling the man short, and now it had caught up with him.

Bryce grinned nastily, as neatly hemmed, Kelly watched four of Murgatroyd's rifle-packing crew step out of the brush with reflections of their owner's sardonic amusement.

"All right," Bryce said when these fellows had joined him, "I guess, George, you better pile on a horse and go take the good word to that sonofabitch greaser."

The rancher's words were directed at his range boss, George Dunn, Dark high-boned cheeks and the uncreased ten-gallon hat set squarely atop that stiff brush of black hair gave the man's solemn face more than passing resemblance to that scourge of the border, Geronimo, lending credence to the whispers some of George's forebears may have worn moccasins.

When Dunn's head came round to lift a widening

green-eyed glance, Bryce Murgatroyd said, "I know that's not quite the way we had this figured, but draggin' Kelly over there with a chunk of cut-out hide won't be near as convincin' as paradin' the evidence right here where we nabbed him."

Dunn wheeled without comment. Shortly thereafter Hap heard hoof sounds departing in the direction of Don Ambrocio's headquarters, and warned himself this could get a heap worse before it got any better.

Bryce, looking at him, laughed. "Don't think you're goin' to wiggle out of this," he grinned, and set a couple hands to fixing up the signs.

Kelly, watching these brush out his tracks along with some of those left by the pair he'd shot, cursed himself for a fool. Time they got done they'd have things fixed to where nobody that wasn't crazy as popcorn on a hot stove could ever doubt for a minute Bryce's version of this business.

The big hell of it was that Don Ambrocio, with his bent conditioned to gringo trickery, was ripe to believe any yarn Bryce might spin. And Rufino, his *segundo*, who'd been claiming all along that Hap couldn't be trusted, would make short work of any doubts Don Ambrocio might have.

Hap had no one to blame for this fix but himself. He had known Murgatroyd was out to clobber him; he hadn't reckoned to be led by the nose.

His six-gun and carbine were still where he'd dropped them six feet away, but in his present state of despair and confusion he couldn't imagine Bryce had overlooked this. He wasn't about, by God, to play Murgatroyd's game again if he could help it.

He presently said, "You mind if I set a spell?"

"Don't try it," Bryce gruffed. "You're stayin' right on your toes till that greaser bunch gets here."

"Chrissake, man, he's liable to be a while—might not even be home when Dunn gets there!"

Murgatroyd grinned.

Nobody had to translate that for Hap. The longer Don Ambrocio took getting over here, the less chance Kelly, kept for hours on his feet, would have of twisting anything around to his advantage.

He was in a forked stick, no two ways about that.

As the long-dragged-out minutes lengthened into quarter hours he began more frequently to slanch looks at his arsenal. Pistol and carbine still lay bright in the dust hardly one good jump from cramped legs and aching feet. Yet he knew that with four men watching he would be shot into doll rags if he started any move to get them.

At the end of the first hour Bryce spoke again to him. "Get out of them boots, Kelly."

Hap blew out his cheeks. "I don't know if I can."

He got no answer to that.

"Perhaps if you'd have someone give me a hand . . ." and got no change out of that one, either. So he bent, grumbling, grunting. Hopping around he finally tugged off the first one, and when Bryce held a fist out, tossed it across to him. Bryce passed it on to the man standing nearest. Hap, trying to think how to make of this business some kind of advantage, dismissed the temptation when he saw the tightening look of Bryce's face. Yanking the boot off he tossed that one, too, and saw it passed on to the same galoot. "Get into 'em, Dude. It's got to look like you've handled this critter without no help but what you got from the horse."

Dude, considering the boots, pronounced them too small.

"Get into 'em anyway. Nobody else in this outfit

can wear 'em."

After Dude, grimacing, had stomped his feet into them he said, still scowling, "You want this done right you better git Johnson's sign rubbed out an' git these tracks started from aboard Rankin's horse."

Murgatroyd, chewing his lip, nodded darkly and the one hope Hap had spied in this frame went down the bleak trail his other notions had traveled.

"Smart thinking," Bryce said, and while Dude was taking the marshal's horse through its paces and dropping a loop over the tied steer's head to give him something to pull against, he put two of the others with greasewood branches to dusting the terrain to fit this new concept. The fourth man, both hands wrapped round his carbine, kept Hap in line with a gimlet stare.

When this exercise was finished to Bryce's satisfaction the boots were tossed back to Kelly who got into them without argument to stand, sagging with weariness, where he was told.

Experience urged him to ride with the punches, to appear resigned to this load of bad luck and wait for the break which, sooner or later if a man doesn't panic, almost invariably shows up. Hard part was the waiting, sweating it out, but the hardest of all was being able to recognize the chance when it came.

It still hadn't come when, two hours later with all shadows lengthened and the sun scarce minutes from dropping back of the rimrocks, approaching hoof sounds tightened Hap's jaws. There was too much clatter for this to be just Dunn.

Ten minutes later half a dozen horsemen, Dunn in the forefront, cantered round the far slope to filter out of the brush and bear down on the scene of Murgatroyd's coup. The Palominas contingent, besides the old man, included Loco Rufino, Tiodosa—black-haired and supple—plus a pair of vaqueros riding with lifted rifles across the comforting "apples" of five-inch horns.

Knowing this could be that break he was hunting, Hap's darting look discovered Murgatroyd's crew ogling the stimulating jounce of Tiodosa's curves—all but Bryce who flashed a cold grin when Kelly grudgingly relaxed.

"That's about far enough," Murgatroyd pronounced when the advance of new arrivals approached the far edge of his carefully readied stage. "Don't want you screwin' up the sign before you've had a chance to read it."

With admirable insight he singled out Rufino as the one to be invited to step down and have a look. "Rest of you stay put," he said.

Although nobody added anything to that, hostile stares picked at Hap like angry claws while the Number Two man from Palominas assayed the evidence manufactured to cut the backbone from Palominas resistance.

It did not take him any great while to reach the conclusion so painstakingly laid out for him. He seemed to Hap's searching stare to be just a mite astonished but wasn't going to fault a gift so sought and cherished. The bright, malicious burning of the look he fixed on Kelly held a hot and steaming pleasure.

"Well?" said Don Ambrocio, impatiently pressed against the horn of his saddle.

But Rufino wasn't to be hurried through this business. The unwanted presence and interference of this gringo had been too long in his hair to be shortchanged. He inspected the altered brand at some length and with narrowed glance followed the trailing rope to where Hap's hull was strapped to the marshal's horse, savoring the prospect with patent satisfaction.

"*Andale!* What passes?" called Don Ambrocio harshly.

Rufino studied the sign again, took a long hard look at Hap's boots. Approaching, he ordered Kelly to back off. When Kelly continued to stand, the Palominas *segundo* gave him a shove, and, eyeing the fresh marks made by those boots, called the *patrón* to come see for himself.

Murgatroyd, grinning, seconded the invitation. "Go ahead," he said with open relish. "Your steer. Your man. You got a right to know what he's done to you."

George Dunn said, "You been howlin' about gringo cow thieves. Ain't every owner can afford to be payin' one!"

Don Ambrocio, tight-faced, stepped off his horse. Tiodosa did, too, her stare bright as glass.

Well, Hap thought grimly, here was her chance to even things up with him if she still nursed the notion he had tried to duck out.

He couldn't tell from her look which way her thoughts ran. When her father came up to stand glowering beside her, all she said was, "I guess you're satisfied now," looking at Rufino.

The Palominas *segundo* appeared, slanch-eyed, to

be turning this over before with a snort he cried, *"Sangré de Dios!* Any child could read what has happened here! Those tracks—" He said, half strangled: "Look at the face of him!"

She said thinly, "How would *you* look in those boots stuck where he is?"

Rufino spat in the dust. They all heard the chuckle bubbling up out of Bryce. The *segundo* growled, "If those boots haff not made what I see in thees place let him *say* so!"

When no one replied Rufino's brown fist was flung out irascibly.

"These are bad times," he cried, harsh with the things stored up in his head. "Too much we lose cattle and now we see why!" He spat again for good measure. "You would let thees man go?"

Don Ambrocio did not answer, the somber burn of his stare reaching round to come back, still hot with betrayal, to the man he had hired to prevent rustling, seeing the sheen of sweat spread across Kelly's locked cheeks.

While the hidalgo stared, flushed by temper, his daughter said with curled lip, "Did you hire this man because he looked such a fool?"

Murgatroyd's face tightened as Don Ambrocio stepped back to consider his daughter, astonished. "What is this?" he exclaimed, hand to ear, eyes wide sprung as they went from Tiodosa to Kelly and returned, darkly narrow. "In the affairs of men . . ." He let that go, rather gustily sighing. "I am becoming old," he grumbled in the tone of discovery, "and have lost many things I once took for granted. A son, my wife . . . unwatched pieces of my patrimony and, obviously it seems, not a few of my faculties." Then he said, still regarding his daughter, "But I have not yet lost all of my wits."

That sharp black stare wheeled on Bryce, while affront turned darker the roan planes of the hidalgo's cheeks. "We are not all senile at Palominas, you know!" He waved a gloved hand at Kelly. "Bring this one along," he growled at Rufino, and strode back to his horse with his wrath wrapped about him, not too blinded though by the churn of his thoughts to miss the dull gleam of rifles held by his vaqueros naked and ready across the bows of their saddles.

This was all that kept Bryce Murgatroyd in check, yet the only good thing Hap could see in this turn was the frustrated rage behind the man's hooded stare.

When Rufino's hand roughly fell on his shoulder Kelly dug in his heels to twist a look at Don Ambrocio, aboard his horse now, anxious to be gone. "What about my guns?" Hap growled. But the old man would not open his lips.

Tiodosa, lifting foot to stirrup, bade Rufino fetch them and he gave Hap a shove before picking them up. "Tie his wrists," the *patrón* told Rufino when Kelly was mounted. "Tie them good," he said, a hard black stare on his daughter.

5

All the way back to Palominas headquarters Kelly tussled and tugged at the harrowing problem of how far along the old man had got with the inevitable suspicions blown into flame by Tiodosa's bold words. After quitting Bryce's presence, neither had called up further gab to fling at the other but rode in grim silence, building up in their heads God only knew what foolishness.

It was the girl, up ahead, that worried him most.

She might look as if butter wouldn't melt in her mouth but he knew her cool and deceitful exterior hid a volcanic temper and a rash of mad notions.

There was no gauging which way she'd fly if the old man lit into her . . . as he probably would once he got her inside those thick walls out of hearing. Hap didn't like the stubborn look of her back, that suggestion of defiance in the cant of her head. Sufficiently goaded she might throw any manner of thing in the Don's teeth—including intimacies shared with her father's hired gun.

Christ! Hap thought, shivering.

In this kind of fix you could look, with a gringo, for a shotgun splicing; but with a Mex proud as this one a man would be lucky just to get his damn throat cut!

Yet, much as he was tempted, Kelly put no pressure on the knots that held him prisoner. Might as well beat his head against a brick horn as scrape himself raw on a task so futile. When this bunch got to wherever they were bound for he was going to be with them whether he liked it or not; you could mighty well bet your last centavo on that! The spurs off his boots had joined pistol and carbine and trying to stampede a borrowed mount without gut hooks looked likely as scratching your head with an elbow. No horse was going to get more than three jumps before Rufino's *reata larga* got jerked tight about somebody's windpipe.

In this hard state of mind Hap had nearly forgotten the bind Bryce had put him in by the time the homeplace lamps began to shimmer and wink through the night's purple shadows.

Sentries Kelly himself had insisted be posted stopped the entourage well short of the yard. They were held in their tracks until the *patrón*, impatiently striking a match, had identified himself and each horsebacker in his party. Even then, so thoroughly had Hap drilled it into them, the head guard wasn't satisfied till one of the others got a look at every face.

They were stopped again just inside the gate and put through the same procedure despite Rufino's fuming. In the yard, the *segundo* dismounted and hauled Hap from the saddle with a roughness wholly deliberate, then maliciously kicked him onto his feet. "Bring him in," Don Ambrocio grunted, following Tiodosa already passing through the rifle-guarded doorway letting into the vine-hung patio.

The whole main house was built around this enclosed central court. Open to the stars it was bright with light from lamps in brackets high in sheltered niches. Prodded forward by the *segundo*, the first thing to catch Hap's notice as he came out of the cobbled passage into this garden of flowering shrubs was the man comfortably benched by the fountain.

In casual *dueña*-attended conversation with a younger blonde version of Tiodosa was the redheaded Johnny Bull in the continental suit Kelly'd chased after last night in town to hand back the stuffed wallet he had left on the stage. Nothing Hap's supsicious mind could latch onto held out any clue to the fellow's presence here.

The man stood up to bow with an elegant flourish in Tiodosa's direction and that white flash of teeth

33

in the burnsided face heaped additional coals on Kelly's distrust. "We'll take care of him later," Don Ambrocio rumbled in an aside to Rufino, and the *segundo's* shove sent Hap stumbling toward a line of closed doors.

Locked into a storeroom, Hap bitterly swore.

The place was black as a dungeon and without fumbling round Kelly knew there'd be nothing among these stored odds and ends of horse tack and put-away pieces of brocaded furniture that would help him get out. The door was held shut by a two-by-four dropped in strap-iron slots he couldn't get at. The room had no windows, being aired by a grilled vent over the door he'd have been hard pressed even to get his head through.

He felt around for a chair, disgustedly plopped into it, and sat there wondering what fate Rufino would be cooking up for him. Harsh thoughts tramped through his head. Intermittently he considered the unlikely presence of that ruddy-cheeked Britisher and eventually dozed off still wondering about him.

Suddenly roused from restless dreams, he couldn't figure for a moment where he was or what had wakened him. Bolt upright, he sat listening into the opacity around him. But it all came back when his name was pronounced in a jumpy whisper.

He fought himself up filled with aches from cramped muscles, precariously teetering from a stance on the chair to get nearer the grill, now almost as black as these black depths about it. He'd no idea what time it was but reckoned from the lack of light in the opening that all those outside lamps had been snuffed.

She was taking a chance just the same to be out there.

"We could talk a lot better if you'd open the door."

No discernible activity followed this overture. He could picture her standing in that parcel of silence chewing her lip while pondering the probable consequence should her father by any chance discover her part in it. But she'd come, anyway, which was more than he had looked for.

He tried to curb his impatience. "You think I'd look pretty staked out on some anthill?"

He heard a sharp catch of breath, said: "Is that what you want?"

"Why would they do that?"

Kelly said, rudely jolted, "That you, Strawtop?" and scowled in frustration when all he got was a continuing silence through which nothing came but the groan of roof timbers. The kid was easily frightened. Had he scared her away?

He smoothed some of the gruffness out of his voice, saying guardedly, coaxing. "Listen—you wouldn't want that kind of thing on your conscience would you? Look—you don't have to *open* it . . . just lift up that bar. . . ."

She'd crept off, he reckoned, and couldn't honestly blame her.

There were several years' difference between the two sisters, and at least superficially, not much resemblance, though age he supposed might have something to do with Carmen's appearing so mousily quiet in contrast to Tiodosa's more impetuous personality. Both were lookers but this younger one seemed inordinately shy, swift to blush and easily embarrassed, painfully unsure of herself in mixed company, more like a child though he guessed her to be in her middle teens. She had all the equipment if the way she filled out her clothes stood for anything.

35

He was bitterly sure she had gone when abruptly she whispered, "I do not believe I had better. Papa's terribly angry. What did you do?"

Hap pulled in a deep breath. "Depends who's doing the talkin'. I was only doing what I been hired for, trying to look after your father's best interests. I got caught in a bind."

He told her about it, the words tumbling out. About the trap Bryce had baited and how they had used his own foolish carelessness along with that steer to deceive Don Ambrocio into getting rid of him. "You mean," she exclaimed when he'd finished, "Papa really believes it? That you, of all people, have been *stealing* from him?"

Hap, in his own mind, felt this was exactly what the old man believed, but doubted the conviction had much to do with the spot Murgatroyd had maneuvered him into.

He said even harder, trying to curb his impatience, "Why else would he have me locked into this place? You said—"

"I'm not sure."

"What's that supposed to mean? And who's this dude you was gabbin' with out there? What's *he* doin' here?"

"His name," she said, obviously impressed, "is Percival Wetherington-Forsyth the Third. He's from England—the son of an *earl!* I must go now."

The sound of bare feet fled away with her voice and Kelly, still scowling, got down off the chair to spend a fruitless half hour sorting through the litter bundled round and about in search of something that might facilitate escape, by this time convinced he was not likely to get any help from Tiodosa.

He reckoned she was bent on grinding him down

for presuming to go off without bothering to drop any words in her ear. Could be, of course, her old man had got his back up enough to have locked her in—put a guard on her, even!

Carmen's visit, if it had done nothing else, had certainly proved no guard had been out there watching Hap's door. But this, in the circumstances, appeared about as advantageous as a .22 cartridge in a twelve-gauge scattergun.

Too worked up by now to get back to sleep he was fretfully wearing a groove in the floor when the bar was lifted out of its slots, the door hauled open, and Don Ambrocio gruffly ordered him out.

Though no cocks had crowed and dawn was still some while away the patio, after the black of that storeroom, appeared almost as light as if the moon were illumining it. Through this ghostly haze Kelly looked for Rufino but the master of Palominas had come by himself.

"Well?" Hap said grimly, giving him back stare for stare. "What's on the docket? You figurin' to handle this all by yourself?"

The *patrón*, fully dressed, held up a shushing hand, and not wasting any words, strode off toward the iron-bound portals that, locked through the night, closed off the eight-foot passage that was the solitary exit and entry to this huge feudal fortress the old man called home.

Following bleakly Hap stood at his elbow while Don Ambrocio, still silent, unfastened and pulled open one of the heavy gatelike doors and stepped through.

Someone yelled from the roof and two peons with carbines came up on the double to back off, apologetically knuckling the dark roll of sombrero brims, when the old man curtly waved them aside.

In this gray half-light Hap, tramping behind him, followed the *patrón* past the clutter of pens to pull up where he'd stopped, grimly scowling, by the near shore of the great dug pond where animals held at headquarters were watered.

"Now you can tell your side of it, Jank."

But Kelly hadn't picked his way past a dozen words when Don Ambrocio cut him off with a down-chopped hand. "Discussing this matter gives me much pain, but I did not come so far from my bed in the middle of the night to speak of gringos and *vacas.* We will talk, instead, about yourself and my daughter." He said on a sharper note, eyes suddenly baleful: *"Andale,* hombre! I await the connection!"

6

Regardless of warning or how well one is braced, the shock of confrontation leaps past every barrier, paralyzing thought, leaving words trapped in conflicting emotions behind laggard tongue in a throat parched and rough as the striated surface of some dried-out lagoon.

The *patrón's* bloated face swam before Kelly's stare like some fragmented monster half glimpsed across the shoulder when a man peers backward through the deceptive closed-in corridors of nightmare. And that was how Hap's mind felt, no longer part of him but something outside, beyond control. Frantically he tried to dredge up some reply which might—at least partially—deflect the *hacendado's* wrath.

Too well he knew the man's fierce pride, the depth of his prejudice, yet in his extremity the only words to come blurting out—sounding unlikely even to himself—were: "I don't know what you're talkin' about."

Don Ambrocio's stare stayed pinned to his look through what, to Kelly, seemed forever and six days before the old man wheeled with a snort, clamp-jawed and shaking, as crammed with indignation and loathing as that Hebrew lawgiver must have appeared the day he uncovered the golden calf.

The first tide of relief that came surging through Hap to uncoil aching muscles and release hard-held breath didn't last any longer than a June frost at Yuma.

Looking after the *patrón* as he went stomping off it was borne in on Kelly he had not heard the last of this—not by a jugful. With no idea what the man meant to do he could see mighty well there would be a hereafter, and direly suspected the best he could do was throw a leg across one of these nags and take himself away from here. Quick!

But even as he turned through the grip of his confusions another notion seized him and he stopped to peer again. That old man was no fool.

The longer Hap brooded the more convinced he became an attempt to clear out might prove the worst move imaginable. As things stood that old settler didn't *know* a damn thing, but let Hap get mounted . . .

Kelly swore in his throat. Flight, invariably taken for guilt, could put the noose right around a man's neck, confirming every suspicion that old man was hugging.

He'd be smarter to stay, try to brazen this out.

39

Kelly saw two things now he hadn't looked at before.

In a jackpot himself with them wolves yapping round him Don Ambrocio had no one else he could lean on. This, plus no proof, was why Hap was out here—the man's need to be sure before chopping down the last hope he had of keeping his holdings out of gringo hands. The other thing Hap saw with tightening mouth was the good probability that escape, if managed, would send him leaping into worse trouble.

Bryce Murgatroyd, you could bet your bottom dollar, would be only too happy to open a quick grave for him and would damn sure have men staked out for that pleasure.

These notions opened another door which, from where Hap stood, looked sufficiently worse to anchor him, scowling, right where he was. *No man could survive long enough to yell "calfrope" that found himself wedged between two feuding factions.*

When the first pink streaks of the new day showed above blue-black peaks Hap climbed down from his perch on a corral pole with some pretty hard conclusions tucked away beneath his hat.

He ate with the vaqueros, as was his usual habit, though as much to himself under slant-eyed scrutiny as during his initial appearance among them something over six months ago. Two or three of these boys vouchsafed him a nod, but that rumors were rife could be seen from their expressions. Most of them found other things to be looking at whenever Hap's glance chanced to stray in their direction. Conversation did not appear to be in large supply and the few quips passed seemed more subdued than usual and did not invite his put-in.

When the hands went off to the chores assigned them the mustachioed Rufino, after saddling his horse, left it ground hitched to lounge against a corral post in obvious sight of where Hap was hunkered with a cornhusk cigarillo, back to the cookhouse wall. Not a word had he tossed in Kelly's direction but the unwinking stare of that brown jowled face suggested this restraint had been put under orders.

Hap ignored him.

When the sun got high enough to make it feasible Kelly cuffed back his hat and headed for the house, finding no sign of Tiodosa in the patio where the Britisher was breakfasting in solitary splendor.

Looking round, the man observed after commenting on the weather, "I say, old chap, are you a part of this establishment?"

"You'll have to take that up with Don Ambrocio," Hap growled shortly, and sent off a mozo to find out at what time the *patrón* would be available. And while he was standing there fingering his hat Carmencita came in from the door off the kitchen, stared wide-eyed, and like a gopher popped back out of sight.

The big Britisher, continuing to put away the grub set before him, took in this departure with a grunt of astonishment. "Seemed rather in a bit of a hurry, what?"

The servant returned to say Don Ambrocio would receive the *Señor* Kelly in his office. *"Immediat-amente."*

Hap found the door open and shut it behind him. "I've come for my guns," he said bluntly.

The *patrón* with raised brows, eyeing him through the smoke from his thin Spanish stogie, asked, "What

41

gives you to think I would arm you, hombre?"

"A couple dozen people. Among them Bryce Murgatroyd."

"Do not speak of pigs in this house, Jank!"

"Maybe you'd rather speak of countrymen swindled? Friends of Palominas who pass no longer through its portals, having been buried account of damn carelessness and stupid assumptions?"

A darkness came into Don Ambrocio's cheeks. "Watch yourself, hombre." He said with the lips pulled away from his teeth, "There are limits to how much of your insolence I'll take!"

"You find it insolent to be reminded there are assassins in these hills?"

"A hired *pistolero* with nothing on his hip is in no position to fling jibes at a man with half a hundred guns—"

"Most of whom," Hap snorted, "couldn't hit a barn door if it was propped up in front of them."

"A few inches of steel—"

"Yeah," Kelly jeered. "That would be just like Christmas! But you ain't about to do nothin' that loco an' both of us know it! You had your chance. Common sense talked you out of it so let's quit sparrin' and talk sense."

Teeth showing coldly through the curl of lips Kelly continued, "this time that puke outsmarted himself but he ain't goin' to leave it there. Keepin' this place, as you've damn sure discovered, depends on the combine you already got—a tough, loyal man. You got no time to be horsin' around. I want them guns an' *I want 'em right now.*"

The old man's face showed the conflict inside him but against every instinct he finally gave in. A clap of the hands fetched one of his servants. "Pito," he said as if he grudged every word, "bring the *Señor* Kelly his carbine and pistol. *Andale,* pronto!"

When the mozo returned and departed looking back across shoulder and Kelly had strapped the shell belt around him and stood with the carbine hanging from a fist, Don Ambrocio said, "Is it permitted to ask what is in your mind, hombre?"

"Sure," Hap nodded. "We're going to change things—change the whole shebang. I made a mistake figurin' that bugger for another of these bullypuss Texicans that reckoned roughshod would get him what he wanted. The man's got eyes. We got to quit doin' things by the clock."

To the puzzled look of the old man's face Kelly said, "We got to quit doin' the same things every day at the same time and places—got to keep that sonofabitch guessin'. Now what's this belted earl doin' here?"

When the *patrón* appeared to be even more bewildered, Hap snarled, "For Chrissake! That goddam dude—that *Johnny Bull* by the fountain!"

"Mr. Wetherington-Forsyth is a guest—"

"What I mean, what I want to know is, *why?*"

Don Ambrocio looked considerably affronted, but Hap looked right back at him and the old man said as though explaining to a child: "He wants to invest some of his money—"

"Well, well!" Hap snorted, staring down his nose. "So he's hunting for suckers in them high-button boots!"

His tone made the gist of this plain enough for anyone. It brought Don Ambrocio's chin up. "You surely can't imagine . . . The man has papers! He has a letter from his bankers—"

"Yeah. I betcha. He's got other things, too,

includin' all the earmarks of a gent bein' paid not to muddy the family doormat!"

Something turned over in Kelly's head then and he growled, eyes narrowing, "Get rid of him. I don't want him around underfoot."

Incensed, the old man rose up out of his chair to lean forward angrily on the flats of his hands. "I will thank you to remember whose house you are in!" Turned stubborn, he said, furious: "You do not order all things in this place, hombre!"

Hap stared a while, but the old duffer meant it. Reminded he was standing on thin ice, Kelly shrugged. "Okay," he grumbled. "Just don't make no deals with this bugger without I sit in on 'em."

He clamped the hat on his head and, wheeling, went out.

7

Passing Rufino in the patio conversing with the dude, Kelly's scowl deepened but he did not stop.

Finding blanket and saddle on a pole at the day pen he roped out a horse, a big grulla gelding. Strapping on his gear he picked up the carbine and stepped aboard, turning the animal back through the yard to catch sight of a mozo and wave the man down. "That black stud I come in on," he said, speaking slow so there'd be no mistake. "Get someone to fetch him back into town and don't turn him over to no one but Bridwell. The marshal—savvy?"

When the man jerked a nod, knuckling an eyebrow, Kelly put the gelding into a lope and set off to locate the patrols supposed to be riding that part of Palominas which bordered gringo holdings. Some better kind of system was clearly indicated and—in light of the coup Bryce had almost pulled off—it wasn't a thing that could stand much postponement. Give his kind an inch they'd grab a mile every time!

According to the arrangement Hap had set up both teams should be passing each other at the vicinity of Apache Leap around ten o'clock, and a glance at his shadow told him he was going to have to push right along to make it.

Despite all the worries that rode in his company the remembrance of that big foreigner in the continental suit had been rubbing Hap raw in the place he did his thinking.

He had always been prone to consider obliquely anything that smacked of coincidence and saw no cause to change his notions now. It was too much to swallow that this button-booted dude should just happen to pop up to sample Palominas hospitality at this particular time. To put the case more bluntly he had a pretty strong hunch Bruce Murgatroyd was behind it, and if that trap Bryce had suckered Hap into was any indication, this Britisher's presence under Don Ambrocio's roof could prove about as salubrious as trying to ride out a sun-fishing bronc with a case of thawed dynamite tied behind your cantle.

Hap blew out his breath with a growl of disgust. A man needed eyes in the back of his noggin to cope with the way this deal was shaping up.

The Leap—a bald outcrop sticking up like a butte—took shape in the distance with no curl of

45

dust from either patrol. Kelly, sending the grunting gelding up a hogback, took a sharp look around, still without discovering any sign of horses or men.

He rode up to the butte and suddenly swore.

There were plenty of tracks the shape of shod hooves but all of them blurred from the dust wind-whipped into them, none newer than sometime yesterday. Not one horse had gone past today. "That goddam *segundo!*" Kelly growled in his throat.

He sat around for an hour; then, tightening the cinches, got back in the saddle, figuring it useless to wait any longer. It was clear enough in Hap's seething mind their absence could be charged to Loco Rufino, that diplomacy was wasted and tact could be reckoned too heavy a ballast to be lugged through the reefs this outfit was caught in. The sooner he got down to locking horns with that moose, the longer Palominas might be able to stay afloat.

But first he had better take a look along this boundary, Kelly decided, not imagining for a moment such a beautiful opportunity had passed Bryce by unnoticed.

Nor had it.

Two miles west he found tracks aplenty where a considerable jag of cattle had been chased toward Palominas acreage set aside for winter feed. Hap, knowing where they'd take him, pushed on to check the rest of the line, suspecting after that business of yesterday that Bryce hadn't called it a day and gone home.

The sun climbed higher, the horizon shimmering in this blast of heat, and he had nearly reached the westernmost edge of Don Ambrocio's range when

Hap came on more of Bryce's doing. Here a second herd had been thrown across the *patrón's* unfenced boundary and left to integrate with Palominas cattle.

Hap, looking like the wrath of God, pointed his horse for the home place, swearing.

Coming into the yard in the frying heat of mid-afternoon he spotted Rufino over by the breaking pen with Don Ambrocio watching a peeler working over some broncs. By this time most of Hap's spleen had been wedged in behind a tight-lipped control, yet the glow from its smolder plainly colored his stare as he got off the horse and strode up to the pair to demand of them bluntly: "Whose bright idea found other uses for those patrols I had out?"

The two men swapped looks. The *segundo* drew up his heavy shoulders and spat within half an inch of Kelly's left boot before he said flatly, "Mine. What about it?"

"You better get out there and do somethin' about what's come of it. You got two jags of gringo cattle helpin' our cows eat Palominas grass."

The stillness grew electric while blood surged into Don Ambrocio's cheeks and Palominas' Number Two looked shaken enough to confirm Hap's guess that this was something the *segundo* had done on his own without bothering to consult the *patrón*.

While Rufino stood like a caught fence-crawler, Don Ambrocio growled in a voice thick with phlegm: "These *vacas*—where are they?"

"One bunch—mixed stock—have been chivvied deep into that batch we had out in those hills along Riachuelo Granito. The other—probably belonging to Bryce—is feeding off your winter range."

The *patrón* snapped savagely in the direction of Rufino: "For what are you standing there? Get together a crew! *Andale!* Pronto!"

Hap spoke before the *segundo* could haul himself out of shock. "This ain't no time to go off half-cocked. With your permission, Don Ambrocio, I think some of this deal might be turned to our advantage."

"Speak, man!"

"You won't find no hands with either bunch," Kelly said. "Give me back the patrols Loco busted up and put his boys to roundin' up that mixed stock."

The *patrón's* angry look crackled round the *segundo*. "You hear? Get at it, hombre, and go yourself! Take personal charge of this!"

And Hap pinned on: "Run all the weight you can off them buggers. But before you do anything send back here the boys I had riding line."

Rufino looked mean. Don Ambrocio said, "You heard? Go do it."

The *segundo,* dark of face, took off to find his rope, and the old man proposed with worried look searching Kelly, "Would it not have been better to have had your patrols sent *muy* pronto—"

"To the prado sabroso? Nope," Hap said, grinning. "That Texican sonofabitch up to now has been stackin' this deal pretty much as he pleases. Time he learned a knife cuts both ways! With them steers on our grass he's set himself up for a kick in the ass."

"But my winter range!"

"What he's figurin', I reckon, is to keep us so busy we'll be wide open to some other skulduggery. But that's where he's wrong—we're goin' to twist this around. Let's get over to your office," Hap said, leading the way, the old man at his heels looking bewildered.

Kelly waved him into the chair at his desk. "We're goin' to shake that coyote's teeth loose! Grab a pen. You'll know better than me how to put this, but here's the guts of it: 'Please inform Bryce Murgatroyd that herd of Flying M cattle he drove onto my winter grass will be held for feed and damages at one dollar per head per day until the account is paid in full. If this compensation ain't forthcoming before I reach the end of my patience I will not be accountable for the loss of his property.' Put your name to that, get somebody mounted an' have it delivered hellity larrup to Rankin Bridwell at Friendly Corners."

Not too happily Don Ambrocio sanded the letter. "Suppose this gringo *chingao* refuses to pay?"

"No danger of that," Kelly chuckled. "He'll pay, all right. He won't have the gall after gettin' this straight from the hand of the marshal to do anything else. He'll paw an' beller, sure, but he'll move 'em. And pay you a handsome profit for the privilege."

The *patrón* said uneasily, "The marshal's a gringo—"

"That's why we're gettin' him to pass on the word."

"But he has no jurisdiction—"

"He ain't got much and that's a fact, but every last lick of it's in the right places. Any charge brought by Bryce ain't goin' to be filed out here in the catclaw and to get his case into court at all he's got to go through the local law. Bridwell ain't one to bend rules for nobody."

Don Ambrocio, stifling a sigh, considered Hap slantways. "It is on my mind that black horse you sent back by Pablo looked remarkably like the black twin of your marshal."

"Yeah," Kelly scowled. "Only horse I could get. Bryce had the livery keeper backed in a corner." He shrugged, spread his hands. And, on a fresh breath, was thinking to switch to some less sticky subject when the old man, reflectively fingering his goatee, said: "Since you and the law are such *buen amigos*—"

"You can get off that trail right now. Horse belonged to him. The law—way he looks at it— grinds just the same for a bum as a *rico.*" Hap grabbed a new breath. "Now about this Wetherington-Forsyth dude—"

Don Ambrocio said, "That's a closed trail, too."

8

Kelly, out in the yard again, reckoned a man could wear himself right into a nubbin trying to pound sense into some people's heads.

Only thing he could hit on to account for the *patrón's* shut-eyed stubbornness in the face of the fix he found himself in was the bankroll paraded by that ruddy-faced puke. If the old man was hard up for cash—and damn well could be with the mouths he had to feed around here—something was sure going to have to give quick, and it might be the stipend Hap was risking his neck for.

In no mood to peer too carefully at this, Kelly angled over to the cookshack where he badgered the *cocinero* into digging up a handout.

Having wolfed this down he stopped to pick up a rope, after which he climbed through the poles of the day pen to snag a fresh mount. Hacienda Palominas kept a good stock of horses but, expecting to be in the saddle half the night, he passed up the steppers in a hunt for a mount with endurance.

He had his loop built and his eye singling out a wiry *trigueno* in the bunch that was jostling the far side of the pen when someone said back of him, "This what you're looking for?"

"You tryin' to get me killed?" Hap growled without turning.

"Hoh! *Yanqui* joke!"

Sure beat the trains, Kelly thought, how a man could be so carried away by fresh looks and a figure—the pulse-pounding way a girl cocked her head at him—then get to hate even the sound of her voice.

He turned around. "Your old man," he said harshly, "might act like he's mislaid most of his buttons but he's got enough savvy to see through a window after it's been wiped for him!"

"Oh, Kelly!" she grinned with a tinkle of laughter, "you must not let Papa's bark put you off."

She had the big blue Hap had ridden when he'd set off to town to catch the El Paso stage, and held out the reins she'd snapped onto the halter with a smile that made light of his evident alarm. "Never has he bitten any gringo yet."

But the look of black eyes did not precisely match the half-mocking twist that had hold of red lips. He found a threatening edge to the cant of this stare plainly heralding fireworks if she wasn't kept happy in their relationship.

He crawled back through the poles, took the reins from her hand, moved the horse and his rope several yards away to pitch down the latter and reach for the blanket draped over his saddle. He shook this and smoothed it to the back of the horse and settled his hull behind the moro's withers, knowing she had followed him, angrily aware he'd have to step around this carefully.

"Your father," he said quietly, "ain't a heap pleased with the way you spoke out in front of Bryce and that trash he had with him. He run me over the coals this mornin' in no uncertain fashion." Cinching up he said almost as galled as he sounded, "Expect we better watch our Ps and Qs—"

"I can handle him!" Tiodosa said, her head flung up like a stallion bronc's.

"*I* can't," Hap growled, thrusting boot toe in stirrup, and hand gripping horn, swinging up to look down. "You know how Rufino feels. Be a little patient till I get this worked out. Damned if I'm hankerin' to find a knife in my back!"

Instead of the tantrum he thought she'd throw, Tiodosa rummaged his face with a taciturn stare, finally nodding, "We'll see."

Kelly, tight-mouthed with her eyes on his back, would have kicked a hound had there been one available; he loosed his spleen in muttered imprecations while the big moro carried him back to the cookshack. "You forget somethin'?" Coosie called, wiping fists on a floursack apron.

Hap shook his head. "Just waiting for the cock-a-doodle-doo to get back with that bunch of loafers we had ridin' line."

"What's up?"

"Murgatroyd's fattenin' a herd of market steers on the old man's winter range."

"Jesus an' Mary!" the cook exclaimed, staring, then sheepishly grinned. "You pull my leg, eh?"

Kelly, knee round the horn, got out the makings

and rolled up a smoke.

"Es verdad?"

"That's only half of it. There's another bunch all mixed to hell with them cows we spread out along the Granito."

Coosie's eyes looked as if they would roll off his cheekbones. "Chihuahua!" he gasped. "The *patrón*— what he say, eh?"

"He's on the way over here. Why don't you ask him?"

The cook, with a startled look, ducked back inside.

Don Ambrocio, coming up, considered Hap darkly.

When lack of conversation and that continuing stare had about rasped Hap's tolerance down to the quick the *patrón* said gruffly: "You heard from Rufino?"

Pitching away what was left of his smoke Kelly, squinting morosely toward the darkening west rim, shook his head. Direly certain whatever the old man had in his noggin would not be found in the realm of glad tidings he set about taking his mind off the subject.

"I been thinkin'," he said, pulling in a fresh breath. "He was sure as hell right about one thing anyhow—ridin' that line won't keep 'em out of our hair. Bryce, just by watchin', could of made his drive when there wasn't a one of those boys within earshot."

Under the burden of that silent regard he said, hurrying on, "I've hit on a better insurance. We got enough hills through that part of your range to lay out a system he'll find hard to beat. And it won't take half the crew off their chores."

The *hacendado's* unblinking scrutiny was no help

at all but Hap kept the words coming. "Put a man on each high spot with a big pile of firewood. He sees somethin' funny he sends up a signal. Every hand seein' smoke gets his mount rollin' pronto. If it's night them flares can be seen for miles."

He was still uneasily waiting for an answer when shod hooves were heard coming out of the south. Don Ambrocio, grunting, swung his head for a look. Though the light was deteriorating fast Hap reckoned these riders were the men Rufino had pulled off patrol.

"Guess that's them," he said edgily. "You want I should try it?"

The old man's look found his face again, hung there. "Go ahead," he said grimly, "but you watch yourself, Jank." He walked off toward the house.

It was no easy chore, even with wagons and twelve hungry hands scrounging round in the dark, to get hold of sufficient dead wood for his purpose. Hap was compelled to accept whatever was available, piecing this out with bundles of flammable greasewood cut loose by shovel.

Mexican vaqueros, not unlike their *norteamericano* counterparts, held in low esteem any chores done afoot and this, along with being driven to such labor on empty bellies—and by a gringo at that—soon filled the air with vigorous complaints.

"Gripe all you want," Hap advised bluntly, "but the sooner you finish, the quicker you'll eat. Any slob caught without assigned station come sunup will keep right on sweatin' till this job gets done."

He got several side-glances and a disgruntled muttering broke out, but though they turned surly and no one looked likely to strain any muscles, there was no open mutiny. Hap's gun-handiness was too well established for any of this crew to risk a demonstration.

Drifting back past Coosie's outfit Kelly ordered him ahead to set up camp on the flats midway between where the two herds had been crossed. "I want your fly right out in plain sight, an' don't feed *no*body till I give the order personal."

He got more hard looks when the men saw the wagon pull out and vanish. He suspected that the peon drivers of the ox carts into which the wood was being piled were the only hombres present likely ever to have a good word for him. But the sun had scarcely cleared the horizon before he was leading the crew at a lope toward the *cocinero's* Dutch ovens. Every vantage he'd picked, including the butte called Apache Leap, had its quota of firewood ready to throw up its spiral of smoke.

When guts were stuffed Kelly dispatched his riders, apportioning two men to each lookout. His only remark before turning them loose was the sober suggestion, "Should I happen by and find both of you asleep, don't be surprised if you never wake up."

After seeing them off, each pair provided with a sacked assortment from the half-Tarahumara cook's store of edibles, Kelly hung round while the man packed up, surveying the terrain through an ancient brass telescope borrowed, via Carmencita, from Don Ambrocio.

Though he did not catch even the glint of a rifle he felt reasonably certain the activities hereabouts had not escaped Bryce Murgatroyd's notice. Nor had he intended them to, having put this deal together in the firm conviction that an ounce of prevention was worth several pounds of cure. He didn't want the Texican laboring under the assumption that mounting an offensive would get back his cattle.

9

Back at headquarters, Hap tended his horse and went into the trapped heat of the empty bunkhouse. He pulled off boots, shirt and hat and spread himself out to catch up on lost sleep. He felt so damn drained he didn't think he'd be able, but next thing he knew the long barracks-like room was blacker than ink and aclank with the sounds of hungry men eating.

Hap lay there a while, half lost in the shadows, then pushed himself up with sundry curse-mingled groans to clamp on his hat and stomp into boots before going out to splash face and chest with tepid water from the horse tank.

When he felt sufficiently alive to navigate he went back and climbed into his dried-out shirt, tucked in the tails and strapped on his shell belt, wondering what tribulations *this* night would fetch. Though they had Murgatroyd by the short hairs right now the man wasn't one to take a hiding without at least some attempt to hit back.

With the shirt buttoned round him Kelly stepped out again, bound for the butter-yellow shine from the cookshack. It wasn't fifteen strides from the door of the bunkhouse. Yet before he had gone two yards a shape materialized at his elbow and Carmen's nervous voice said, "*El telescopio, señor, por favor.* Papa—"

"Yeah . . ." Hap growled in a poor frame of mind, and with a snort of disgust, went back inside to dig the spyglass out of his saddlebags.

He could have sworn he'd shoved them under his bunk. When his reaching hand struck nothing but air he got down on all fours to peer under the frame. Still not satisfied he popped a match in cupped fist before he'd believe the leathers weren't there.

Right and left he looked with no better luck and presently discovered them just over his chin in the bunk above and couldn't think why he would have chucked them up there.

He got them down, and hunkered beside them, put a hand first in one then sent it scrabbling through the other while a stampede of notions flapped around in his head. With no real hope he went through both again before he got to his feet empty-handed. He went outside to tell the blonde-girl, "I don't have it."

In the refracted gleam from the cookshack lamps he watched her eyes turn big with fright. He said, "I had the thing stuffed in my saddlebags. It's not there anymore."

While they were grimly eyeing each other Rufino stepped out of the cookshack door, paused, took a second look, and dragged his spurs toward them.

The girl gasped, clutched her skirts and incontinently fled.

The burly-shouldered *segundo* with chinging rowels came up thinly smiling to stop, rock solid, squarely in Hap's path. "So!" he sneered. "You are too much hombre for one woman, eh?"

Kelly stared back, knowing this wasn't going to look any better no matter which way he jumped. To mention the telescope he no longer had wouldn't help Carmencita if reported to her father; and he had of a sudden a pretty strong hunch Rufino knew all about the *patrón's* vanished spyglass.

Far worse, however, in the whirl of Hap's thoughts was the threatening implication couched in Rufino's snarled words.

The *segundo* tapped Kelly's chest with a finger, the brown-jowled face in the chin-strapped hat an indecipherable blob against the shine of the lamps. "I theenk," he rasped, finger hardening, "one gringo *chinagao* better—how you say? start putting down the farapart tracks."

All sound fell away but the slap of wind coming off the peaks to tug and flutter the ends of the neckerchief tied at Hap's throat. Back of this the quiet piled and grew, block on block, like a wall building round him, shutting him in with the man's echoing words that kept shouting themselves through the corridors of thought in a repetitive roar like the pound of an angry sea against rock.

Black though and sharp as the count on a tally sheet stood the guts of the threat and the choices left—really no choice at all if a man took the trouble to wade through the lot. *Run,* the words said, *hit a lick for the tules or the* patrón *will have you chopped into doll rags.*

Seeing this pulled Kelly's lips off his teeth and he shoved his way past Rufino without bothering to answer. Nothing he could say would change the *segundo's* intention. The man would not rest till he had Kelly out of this, but in his blind hate Rufino had not counted the solitary trump still left in Hap's fist.

He went into the cookshack and filled his plate,

found a seat at the table and sat himself down to wait out the explosion Rufino's accusations would be hand-tailored to provoke. For Kelly had little doubt the man would straightaway carry his load of spleen to where he figured it would get the best hearing.

In twos and threes the vaqueros at table took swabbed plates to the wreck pan, drifting off to resume conversations suspended by his presence. He could hear the muted rumble of their talk outside and from time to time felt the cook's covert scrutiny. When he dug out the makings Coosie picked up his empty plate and brought back the pot to fill Hap's mug again.

"How long," Kelly said, "has Loco been Number Two around here?"

Coosie, eyeing him obliquely, shrugged.

"You been a cook all your life?"

That one got him a shake of the head. "Three year."

"You here before that?"

"Sure. Born on this place."

"You find the *patrón* a good man to work for?"

The man looked at Hap's gun where it lay in the leather that was thonged to Hap's thigh.

"Si. Poco bueno."

"How does Loco get along with him?"

The cook took the java pot back to the stove and appeared to have become a sudden prey to ambition if that shuffling of pots and pans stood for anything.

Kelly scowled at him awhile, fired up his Durham, and presently rising, tugged down his hat and went outside.

Sauntering past the silent hands he scrutinized the corrals, almost tempted to take the *segundo's* advice. At least he might have pushed it around some had he felt at all sure those hombres hunkered behind burning smokes weren't squatting there on orders concerned with his departure. There looked a better than even chance they were.

Also, it had passed several times through the restless drift of Kelly's thoughts that, for as long as it could be made to last, no other job he was like to encounter would provide the fifth part of the handsome stipend he was pulling down here. Both were things a man ought to bear in mind.

Taking a squint at the stars overhead Kelly made his decision and headed for the house. Any gent hoping to stay half a jump ahead of disaster had damn well better know where he stood. A guy could stay dead a powerful long time. And get that way mighty fast around here.

Hap stopped for a spell in the deep-blue shadows outside the portals with that narrowed miss-nothing stare, peered into the patio with its shrubs and fountain and rustic seats all butter-yellow bright from the cat's-tongue flare of two dozen candles butt-stuffed into bottles. Because of the cobbled passage much of the patio could not be glimpsed from where he stood, but the Britisher's florid and animated countenance was plainly visible, jaw busily wagging like a spinster's needles.

Hap could not see who the fellow was talking to nor catch from her the gist of his words, but from the way the dude was laying it on he reckoned, disgusted, whoever was on the listening end almost certainly had to be one of the girls. With sudden startled astonishment he wondered why this should make any difference to him.

It didn't, of course, he told himself fiercely,

craning his neck like a goddam fool. When he still couldn't see, filled with the gripe of inexplicable resentment, he pushed on in, made even more graveled to find it was Tiodosa hanging on the fellow's every word with a benignly smiling Don Ambrocio seated nearby like a fond and witless *dueña.*

The smile disappeared and the *patrón's* chin whiskers bristled at the uninvited intrusion of his hired *pistolero.* "Have I sent for you?" he demanded, rearing up in his chair.

But Kelly, despite the turmoil inside him, was not turned aside by a shout. "I have come," he said grimly, "to report a theft."

"A theft!" cried the old man, staring. *"Carai!"* he exclaimed, cheeks darkening. "You dare thrust your *insignificantes* on the master of Palominas? You go too—"

"Your pardon, Don Ambrocio, but the theft I would speak of concerns no trivial matter but a cherished possession—an heirloom, perhaps—handed down in your family."

Don Ambrocio registered shock and bewilderment. Then his teeth clacked shut, his eyes blazed with temper. "Who is this thief and what as he taken? Don't gape that way—speak out, man!"

Hap spread his hands. "I had no right—I can see that now—but at the time I thought it was in your best interest—"

The *patrón* impatiently waved that away. "To the meat, hombre!"

"Well," Kelly answered, shifting his weight, "it concerns your brass telescope which I took—"

"El telescopio!" Astonishment overrode the promptings of outrage. *"You* took my telescope?" His look

61

said the gall of this gringo went almost past belief. But there was something else, too, behind the glint of that stare. "When did you do this?"

"In the evening of yesterday. While I was waiting for those vaqueros your *segundo* took off the patrols." Hap rasped his cheek with the palm of damp hand. "I thought it would help if we could find out what Murgatroyd was up to."

"But my telescope, hombre. What did you do with it?"

"Took it with me last night when I posted those men on the hilltops with firewood."

"You did that, eh? *Muy bien,*" Don Ambrocio nodded. "And what did you learn with the aid of my glass?"

"Unfortunately, nothing."

"So now you bring it back with your apologies."

"Well, not quite. This morning when I returned with the cook it was in the alforjas I shoved under my bunk. Guess I slept like a log. When I woke up the bags were on the empty bunk over me and your spyglass was gone."

10

Not a few extra worries got their teeth in his attention during the extended quiet clamping down on the heels of the stares produced by this blunt pronouncement. Feeling uncomfortably like a leper, Kelly watched the *patrón* suck in his cheeks, knuckles tightening white about the arms of his chair.

"Whom do you accuse, hombre?"

Hap shook off thoughts wheeling round like spooked broncs. "Ain't up to no pot to be callin' the kettle black, but was I in your boots I'd have Loco clean that shack out with a fine-toothed comb."

Anger brightened Don Ambrocio's stare. In tone sharp-edged with offense he began: "No man of Palominas—"

"No loyal man, sure," Hap agreed, cutting brashly into this flow of indignation. "But what's to say all men are loyal with Murgatroyd bent on wrecking your outfit, come he can't grab it no other way?"

"That devil has no—"

"You got both eyes shut? Cash money'll move mountains if you're willin' to chuck around enough. You ought to know by this time nothing's impossible to his kind of bugger. For a bottle of tequila—"

"*Basta*—enough!" cried Don Ambrocio fiercely. "Pito!" he shouted, and when the mozo came running: "Find Rufino—*andale,* pronto!"

The Britisher said, "Are you seriously suggesting that man would—?"

"That galoot," Kelly growled, "would feed right out of the same plate with a skunk! If you aim to stay healthy take my advice and pack that wad you been flashin' straight to a bank."

While Wetherington-Forsyth III thought about that the Palominas *segundo* came clanking his spurs across the flags of the patio to throw a hard look at Hap before removing his hat to learn why he'd been sent for.

Don Ambrocio immediately ordered a search of the bunkhouse. Rufino, startled, looked again in the direction of Kelly who said inscrutably, "Someone's made off with Don Ambrocio's telescope. I'll help you look."

The heavy-jowled face of Rufino tightened but he turned without comment to head for the yard. As Hap wheeled to follow he saw the younger girl, Carmen, step through the door from the kitchen. At the sight of her, Don Ambrocio, who'd been fingering the whiskers at the end of his chin, abruptly stood up, and excusing himself with a courtly bow, left the dude with the girls and strode after Kelly.

Kelly stuck so close to the heels of Rufino that the old man almost had to run to keep up. As Rufino was about to step into the bunkhouse the old man, puffing, gasped, "Wait!" and caught hold of Hap's arm.

In the lamplight shining through the wide-open door the *segundo's* turned face with its craggy brows peered sardonically at Kelly. "What kind of *Yanqui* trick do you think to play on the *patrón?*"

"I'll have no tricks," Don Ambrocio said sharply. "Call out the men, Rufino."

When the *segundo* had them all lined up before him—all the vaqueros presently available—the *hacendado* said somewhat grimly, "I regret the necessity which has brought me before you, but the matter is urgent." He went on to explain that several of their fellows had gone with Kelly last night to be stationed at high points with brush for signal fires, to be lighted in the event of further devilry inspired by the gringo Murgatroyd. Saying furthermore that Kelly had later done some looking of his own—"with the aid of my telescope which most of you have seen. When Kelly this morning lay sleeping in this place someone removed my glass from his saddlebags."

His sharp old eyes considered them. "Would anyone care to speak out concerning this?"

Though his stare was unnerving none volunteered.

"Very well," he sighed; and jerked a nod at Rufino. "Search every bunk and each man's belongings," he gruffed, following the *segundo* and Kelly inside.

The grumble of muttered conversations could occasionally be heard behind the racket of Rufino's activity. The *segundo* appeared to be enjoying his task, stripping blankets, scattering each man's sacked belongings with a heavy hand, leaving these contemptuously wherever they fell or rolled.

It began to bother Kelly. If his hunch had been right and the burly cow boss was indeed the culprit Hap had hoped to unmask, there was no evidence in the man's look or manner to suggest it.

Midway through his search Rufino came to Hap's bunk and paused to throw a look at the *patrón* across his shoulder; and it was this that sharpened and gave focus to Hap's growing uneasiness. "Yes, his too," Don Ambrocio nodded.

With a half-hidden grin Rufino reached for Hap's blanket and Kelly—realizing now that the wily range boss had outmaneuvered him—stepped back to get both men in front of him. Rufino, bent forward with predictable relish, whipped the covering aside to expose in a hollow of the corn-husk mattress the *patron's* missing spyglass.

Though mightily tempted to lay hold of his shooting iron, Hap stood still. On the balls of his feet, eyes narrowed, bitterly sure of the end result but grimly awaiting the old man's opprobrium, he kept both eyes on the burly *segundo,* knowing if violence was on the agenda it was dollars to doughnuts Rufino would trigger it.

"Carai!" gasped the old man on the heels of Rufino's astonished *"Chihuahua!"* But when the *segundo* straightened, eyes bright with malice, Don

Ambrocio oddly enough did not follow the pattern laid out for him but said instead, peering hard at his range boss, "Only fools measure others by the folly of their own acts."

Rufino looked cheated. "I—I don't understand. . . ."

"Do you imagine a man of Kelly's persuasions would report the theft after hiding this glass beneath his own blanket? He is not such an idiot. Nor am I so easily misled as to believe he is. Give me the telescope. We—"

"But, *patrón*," Rufino cried with his stare black as thunder, "who else in this place would—"

"Who else, indeed?" the old man asked dryly.

The *segundo*, confounded, could not leave it alone. "You sound like a child!" he exclaimed in a passion. "Will you stand back then and let this gringo make mock of you? This snake you have nourished and taken to your bosom?—this defiler of women!"

Don Ambrocio drew back his arm, then dropped it, trembling. "Put a hobble on that tongue or I'll have it cut out for you. I will hear no more of this—not a word! Understand?"

The *segundo*, cheeks livid, stalked from the room.

"These are surely hard days," the old man muttered as though to himself, and heaved a huge sigh. Thrusting the telescope inside his jacket he eyed Kelly bleakly, and then stepping past him, prepared to take his departure.

But in the doorway he paused to mutter under his breath, "I think you had better watch yourself, Jank," and went off moving tiredly in the direction of the house.

When Hap stepped outside, the burly *segundo* was

66

nowhere in sight but Kelly thought it unlikely the man would either forget or forgive the way his stratagem had been turned against him.

Kelly deemed it better to give heated tempers a chance to cool off. He bent his steps toward the dark slats of the horse pen, and saddling his moro, struck out for town. He felt sure of one thing. If any of his lookouts had occasion to fire brush, Rufino in his present situation would certainly be vigilant to answer the call. For the moment, anyway, Hap reckoned he could afford to put his mind on problems more personally urgent than the machinations of Bryce Murgatroyd.

It did puzzle him somewhat that Tiodosa appeared to have made no further effort toward tightening her hold. Devoutly thankful he put this down to a possible awakened interest in Wetherington-Forsyth III and fervently hoped — if this were so — it might continue and ripen.

Hap wasn't fooling himself into supposing her father's reactions to the attempts of Murgatroyd and Rufino to discredit Don Ambrocio's hired *pistolero* indicated either friendship or trust. The old fox, gnawed by intolerable suspicions, would have turned him off this spread in a hurry if so. It was the measure of the old man's need that Hap was still on the payroll.

He put the horse around twice over the same stretch of ground, eyes sharply peeled and pausing frequently to listen, without detecting any evidence of surveillance. But this, Kelly knew, was hardly conclusive. If the bedeviled *patrón* and his disgruntled *segundo* didn't care what Hap did while away from the ranch — a supposition not proved — one could scarcely feel such would hold true for Bryce Murgatroyd.

67

That grabby sonofabitch gringo was out to take over this whole goddam country and had already shown a pretty fair flair for it. Sure, he preferred to have the law on his side but a few more killings wouldn't upset his appetite.

Hemmed on all sides Hap had reached out to bolster his stance with a right and left bower — it was this which had taken him in vain to El Paso. With his need hourly growing ever more acute he was forced into finding what help he could locally.

A pretty grim prospect.

And since he was in no position to put the need to Don Ambrocio, the pay for such help — should he manage to secure any — would have to come out of his own pocket.

All this, on top of his affair with Tiodosa, was more than enough to turn any man edgy.

The presence at Palominas of Wetherington-Forsyth could damn well be reckoned as more of the same, appearing highly suggestive in Hap's harassed state. Why would the old man even for a moment put up with having that dude underfoot unless he was perilously short of ready cash? And if this were the case, where the hell was the point in Hap's sticking his neck out?

11

Kelly considered the yellow wink of lights in the deep dark below him. Leaning forward against the swell of his saddle, he tried to figure if what he'd intended was really worth the risk.

It was well within current possibilities that Murgatroyd—surreptitiously or otherwise—had put a bounty on Hap's scalp. There was more than enough as excuse for this in the tale he could tell, backed up by his understrappers, about that business of the Palominas steer with the worked-over brand. He could say, furthermore, that he had summoned the owner to have a look at the evidence with the caught cinch-ring artist still standing red-handed right where they'd nabbed him; that if he'd steal from his boss, given the opportunity he would steal from anyone. Once Hap was dead Bryce could build quite a case, and the fact that he'd been turned loose wouldn't stand in the way of anyone.

It wouldn't surprise Kelly if the Texican had had the brand cut from that steer to wave in the face of any objections. To the law it would look like an airtight case—not that any law was apt to take issue over the demise of an obstreperous gun fighter.

If he stepped into trouble he would get no help from anyone, and even if Bryce hadn't slapped a tag on him there were those round who'd be glad of the chance to drill Hap's brand of gringo for nothing. It was that kind of place. Friendly Corners.

Kelly swore.

It was the sort who would just as lief shoot him for free that Hap was going to have to draw his support from—if any. Thinking about it, sitting his blue horse up there in the timber, he felt more than half minded to thumb his nose and light out of this while he was able.

But the soft streak in his makeup handed down by his ma wasn't the only chink in Hap's armor. There was also his pride—the real bane of his existence—which along with his flinty temper made him stick his neck out, more particularly when things shaped up to get sticky. It just plain wouldn't let him quit under fire, and no matter how crazy it looked Kelly knew this.

Still gnashing his teeth, he kneed the horse on again, letting it take him down the tortuous twists by which this trail reached the desert floor. The trees fell away as they left higher reaches and cacti reared grotesque sentinel shapes through the lesser dark brightened now by the paling shine overhead and that dim band of light beginning to break behind the Red Elk peaks to the east. The false dawn came early in this kind of country.

A new day would be on him before he got properly into the town.

Some twenty minutes later, in a strengthening light that was still bullet gray where it hedged deeper shadows, he came off the last slope and saw the town's single street opening up dead ahead.

Silent and ghostly, it looked deserted at this early hour, abandoned as Galeyville the last time he'd been there. Not a single lamp showed—no sign of life anywhere—yet behind the blank panes of those dust-raddled windows more than one gent had probably thrown back the covers to grope for his hat while stomping callused feet into the cold stiffness of boots.

Hap was still moving the horse at a walk, just breasting Kronski's freight yard, the yellow ricks of stacked hay at Claine's livery up ahead on the right, when the shot ripped a ragged hole through the quiet. The slap of its wind drove Kelly from the saddle.

He hit rolling as the snorting horse took off with reins flying. Without cover, gun-fisted, Hap came lounging erect to fling himself toward the gray blobs of parked wagons.

Twice more the hidden rifle punched out lethal cargo, this racket chopping through the echoes of that first sneak shot, one blue whistler slamming off stone in screeching ricochet as Hap threw down to drive away lead through the spokes of a wheel outline in the muzzle flash.

Then he was there, plunging through acrid shadows permeated with powder stink, to find the bird flown, leaving nothing to shoot at but the pound of panicked boots.

Hap tore after these in vain, bitterly swearing when he finally gave up to retrace his steps for another scowling look beneath the wagon. One brass cartridge case was all this scrutiny netted; and he was straightening with this clenched in a fist when the yardmaster came loping up crammed with questions only half heard through a rattle of shale as a horse was hauled to a sliding stop very nearly on top of them.

From the saddle Rankin Bridwell said sharply: "What in hell's name you tryin' to pull now, Kelly?"

"Just trading shots with a bushwhacker, Marshal," Hap said dryly, and reached up to drop the empty brass in Bridwell's palm.

"Sharps," Bridwell grunted, peering down at Hap with no great enthusiasm. "See who it was?"

Hap shook his head.

"Well," Bridwell said, "you're not the most popular gent I could name."

"How's Bryce Murgatroyd stack in your rating?"

The marshal considered him through a grim silence. "What you do out there on the range is not my concern. But shooting at folks inside town limits is something I don't have to put up with." He added, curtly civil, "Leave your guns home next time you brighten my day with a visit."

"You takin' sides?"

"You know better'n that."

"How long you figure I'd last empty-handed?"

"If I have to point out a few truths I can do it. Nobody herded you into this bind. In a free grass country—"

"The rules your Texican friends lay down don't change the fact Palominas was here when this was still part of Mexico. Palominas don't come under public domain."

Bridwell shrugged. "You reckon the courts will sustain that claim?" He looked at the darkening shape of Hap's cheeks. "When you impound a man's cattle, then clap on a feed bill, add insult to injury by saying what happens to 'em depends on the speed with which this blackmail is paid, you're not layin' up many hugs or kisses. You made your own bed when you set yourself up to buck a sure thing."

"So you've joined the carpetbaggers," Kelly said.

Bridwell flushed. "Think what you like. Now hand over that pistol or get out of town."

Hap said through tight jaws, "You don't leave me no choice," and snatching the reins of his held horse from the yard master, he swung up hot with temper to knee the blue gelding back onto the street.

He hadn't gone twenty yards when a voice called behind him, "I'll ride a ways with you if you'll hold on a shake."

Hap didn't have to look round to know whose hail that was. He didn't wait for her, either, but she reined her claybank alongside him anyway. "Looks like someone's put your nose out of joint. Rankin been giving you trouble?"

"Somethin' like that I guess," Hap grunted sourly, not bothering to look at her.

She studied his expression. "Well, we've all got our jobs to do. You can't hardly expect him to go against the whole town." She added soberly, "Why don't you start using your head, Hap?"

Hard looks didn't bother her.

"If you're doing this for spite on account of Bryce getting you fired off—"

"Why don't you give that jaw a day off?" Hap growled at her testily. "Look—I'll make a deal. You tend to your hat shop an' sew up them dresses an' I'll take care of what *I'm* paid to do."

Melanie Scott was aggravating enough without that goddam smile on her face. Seemed like every time their paths crossed she went out of her way to stir up his dander. Kind of talk she threw at him would have got a man smacked hell west and crooked.

He tried ignoring her but she was too bull-headed to take the hint. "Do you figure," she asked in that slow drawl of hers, "five hundred a month makes that job you've latched onto worth getting buried for?"

"I ain't buried yet," Kelly growled. "Nor about to be."

"What kind of blinders have they put on you, Hap? Haven't you sense enough to see you can't win?"

"Says who?" Hap snarled.

That didn't put her off. She said, sounding earnest, "I'm not arguing the rights of this rumpus. Your boss has a right to any help he can get. But if they can't run him off that good land and water, they'll bury him there—and you along with him!" She took a new breath. "Sometimes I think this whole

73

country's gone haywire. Everywhere you look it's crookedness and villainy that are yielding all the dividends. No man can stem the tide single-handed!"

Eyeing his lumpy face, she cried exasperated: "You're not hearing a thing I say!"

12

"I'm hearin'," Hap growled, "but it ain't changin' nothin'."

"Getting yourself killed won't change anything, either!"

He looked round at her then, caught perhaps by something in her tone that seemed at odds with previous notions he had held about this woman.

Both horses had stopped.

A rider, coming out of a draw, said behind him, "Got a match, mister?"

Kelly turned without hurry to consider the dusty look of the speaker. His lips were stretched thin and tough below the hooked beak and near colorless stare that returned Hap's inspection above the clump of tobacco bulging one cheek. It was a face that was new here, revealing the hardness that had been ground into him and showing, additionally, both indifference and amusement.

The glance slid to Hap's waist and returned more remote to wait out the silence through which Hap regarded him.

Narrowly watchful, Kelly held out a match fished left-handed from the snakeskin band of his horse-thief hat. "Figurin' to heat up that chaw a mite are you?"

"Lot of things could stand a little heat around here," the fellow grunted, boldly taking in the salient points of Hap's companion, a kind of aggravation a man could be sure was furnished deliberate. Coolly grinning, this proddy galoot let his rummaging stare fetch a flush to her cheeks before sliding it round to say in patronizing fashion, "Got a a man wants to see you 'bout a matter of mutual interest."

Kelly, doubting it was mutual, said if anyone nursed a real craving to see him they could come take a look whenever it suited.

"You're Kelly ain'tcha? Might turn out this is the best piece of business ever knocked on your door."

"This jigger got a name?"

"You'll have that when we get there. Mine's Frayne—Shiloh Frayne."

"That supposed to mean something?"

The man's pale stare ran over Hap coldly. "I ain't got all day to set round palaverin'. You comin' or ain'tcha?"

Melanie Scott said abruptly: "Don't go, Hap."

That tipped the scales against him, having put him in a position Frayne was quick to make the most of, asking with an unmissable sneer, "You takin' orders from a petticoat, bucko?"

"What are we waitin' on?" Hap growled, knowing he was being maneuvered but unable to throw up any kind of defense that would not further undermine the roughshod rep he'd been chucking around as Don Ambrocio's hired *pistolero*.

And without looking back, lest that too be considered a weakness, he set off with Frayne toward the crib and saloon part of the town Rankin Bridwell

75

had just run him out of.

He was not too furious to suspect he was putting himself in double jeopardy by ignoring the marshal's tight-lipped warning to accompany this hooligan into what showed most of the earmarks of a baited trap.

What galled him worse was their use of his own stiff-necked pride and necessity cunningly yoked to a hard-cased understanding of the tightrope he walked as all that stood between this rabble and the ranch they were busting to carve up between them.

It was a bitter hard pill for Hap to swallow and harder still to know he had to, yet he dared not show hesitancy here lest the whole façade so painstakingly built come tumbling down to envelop him in gunfire.

If there was any one lesson twenty-three years of roving these backlands had ineradicably etched upon the screen of his knowledge it was the oft-demonstrated and inescapable conclusion that no man survived his rep as a gunfighter who would not meet every test thrown at him and kill where he had to, regardless of anything.

He had no choice but to go with this fellow with no guarantees but his own constant vigilance and a roughshod readiness to prove hard-nosed no matter what odds had been set up to trip him.

None of this showed in the slant of Hap's cheeks as he got down with Frayne and tossed his reins across the peeled rail fronting Gallagher's deadfall, a notorious den called the Aces Up.

Kelly followed the man into a near-empty bar-room dimly illumined by two unwashed windows. Tense as a cougar behind the hard shine of a reticent stare, he stayed close on Frayne's heels to pass back of the mahogany and pause in braced stance when the fellow hauled up to pound a closed door and then throw it open.

"After you," Kelly smiled, and stood in his tracks till Frayne with a shrug strode in ahead of him.

Two men were there waiting, seated back of a table that was cluttered with papers. George Dunn was the closer. The other was Bryce Murgatroyd, dressed to the nines, his teeth clamped about the back butt of a stogie. "Take off," he told Frayne with an easy assurance, and "George, you go with him and close the door after you."

After both men withdrew Bryce settled back comfortably to look into Hap's face with his pale hooded stare. "Grab a chair," he said finally, "we've things to go into, and Rome wasn't built in a day I've been told."

Hap settled shoulders against the closed door, and returned look for look above folded arms. "You got something to say, get it off your chest. The smell in this dive would embarrass a polecat."

Murgatroyd chuckled. "Guess it takes one to know one. That last move of yours sort of caught me flat-footed. In the long run however what good has it done you?"

"If you want those cattle you better pay up. That what you figured to see me about?"

Bryce smiled affably. "Way it looks like to me we got a Mexican standoff."

"You're doin' the talkin'."

Murgatroyd rolled the soggy length of his stogie across grinning lips to say with grim relish, "You've got the cattle but I've got you."

Hap showed some teeth, too. "Never pays to count chickens till you've got 'em all hatched."

"If you take comfort from that, lap up what you can of it. There ain't but two ways out of this place. One's on my say-so, other's on a shutter. Now let's get down to cases."

" 'Fraid I left my tradin' pants to home, Bryce."

The hooded eyes showed their fish-belly whites as Murgatroyd, leaning closer, pinned Hap with a malevolent stare. "We're not talkin' about trades, I'm givin' you a chance to get out of this jackpot—"

"Damn if that ain't what I like about you, Bryce—all that milk of human kindness bubblin' up out of you. Unfurl your flag and kick up the breeze so's I can give you my 'no' and get out where there's air that's still fit to breathe."

"Blast you!" Murgatroyd shouted. "You know goddam well that loco old zany you been proppin' up ain't got a snowball's chance in hell of comin' outa this on top of the heap. Only thing you can do is drag this on an' get a passel of fools killed—"

"If that's how you see it why not sit back and wait for the chestnuts to drop in your lap?"

"Because it's costin' me money I got better use for!"

"So?" Kelly chuckled.

A ruddier color washed across Bryce Murgatroyd's Yankee face. Intolerant anger flashed from his stare, goading the arrogance that ripped through his scowl.

But he controlled himself. "I'll have that spread no matter what. But short of futzin' around with this all summer I'll give you ten hundred dollars to get out of the country. Cash in hand. Paid here and now!"

"That's what you got me over here to say?"

Murgatroyd jerked an impatient nod. When Hap

still hung fire as though turning it over, Bryce growled in a thickening irritation: "Are you on?"

With a wintry quirk of the lips Hap told him, "You couldn't lay hands on enough ready cash to make me sell that old man out."

13

The rancher gave him a prolonged attention, actually appearing more curious than angry. "If you're saying that just for the sake of your pride we can reckon it said and get on with the counting."

He dug a packet of bank notes out of a drawer, plopping it onto the table in front of him. "I've found that money usually has the last word," this Yankee said cynically as he dropped a second packet down alongside it. "Two thousand. That's high as I'll go and it's the last chance you'll get to stay above ground."

"You got it all said now?"

"Anything else—" the amused mogul began, and had the rest of it chopped off as Hap, diving forward, upended the table, driving it hard against Murgatroyd's chest. The man spilled out of his chair to strike the floor spread out, the table on top of him.

He heaved it off but as he lunged to his feet Kelly prodded his gut with the snout of a pistol: "Hold still or you'll not bother anyone again."

Malevolence incarnate shone from Murgatroyd's glare but he was much too cagey to tempt Hap, and froze. "You won't get away with this!" he snarled.

"We'll soon enough see," Kelly muttered, looking around the room. His stare lingered fractionally on the door to the alley before it came back to Bryce's face with his mind made up. "Just open that door I come in by and step out ahead of me. And pray, while you're at it, no one gets in our way."

You could see by his look this was bitter tea to Bryce, but without too much choice he pulled the door wide and stepped gingerly through, very conscious of the gun in Hap's white-knuckled fist.

George Dunn, the man's foreman, stared hard from the bar, and was beginning to fidget when Bryce said harshly, "Stay out of this, George!"

Two more of Murgatroyd's bootlickers sat with bottle and glasses between them at one of the tables not far from the batwings but these, too, stayed put, anchored by the go-to-hell look on Hap's face as he prodded his perspiring prisoner abreast of them.

"Out!" Hap said thinly when Bryce started to stiffen. "And the rest of you jiggers stay right where you're at unless you're hankerin' to scrape this galoot off the doorstep. One yip and he's had it."

And that was the way they went though the half-leafs, Murgatroyd shaking, Hap with his cheeks looking chopped out of stone.

"Now just hand me them reins," Kelly told him, "and don't make no pass to get under that coat 'less you want bits of bone stickin' out of your brisket."

Murgatroyd, looking like a man with the palsy, carried out the hateful orders to the letter, too caught up in dread to risk any tricks.

With the reins in left fist, fist wrapped round the horn, Kelly said, "Shove both hands deep into your pockets and keep 'em there—savvy?"

He jammed a foot in the stirrup and was on his way up when motion to the left of him twisted his head to discover a horsebacker moving up from around the far side of the building.

"Get back!" Kelly shouted.

But with a mind of her own, Melanie Scott neck-reined the big claybank between scowling Hap and those louvered doors, ignoring as well—or perhaps not aware of—the look on Murgatroyd's face as the rancher, freed of Hap's scrutiny, wrenched his hand from his pocket and dug for the pistol under his coat.

Hap in a passion raked his mount with bright spurs but the mule-headed girl slammed her horse in behind him, directly in the path of the gun Bryce had drawn and now did not quite dare to use.

"Frayne!" the man bellowed, red-faced with frustration, and the lantern-jawed leather-slapper who had set Kelly up came stiltedly sprinting from between store fronts to fling a brace of shots after them as Hap and the girl tore off out of range.

Half a mile out of town Kelly twisted to snarl, "You ain't got the sense God give to a gopher! You *tryin'* to get dirt throwed over you?"

The seamstress tossed the roan mop of wind-disheveled hair back from whipped cheeks, her eyes bright with an inner excitement. But her voice showed something less than its usual cool reserve. "I might ask you the same. Those were real bullets, Hap." Then she chuckled, eyes disconcertingly locked with his own. "What did you do—jab a pin in him or something?"

Disturbed and edgy, Hap pulled his glance away. "Bugger tried to buy me off!"

"And you told him where to head in at, of course."

"I don't turn loose of a thing I've took hold of just because the goin' gets rough!"

"I'm sure of that," Melanie Scott replied. She considered the darkened look of his cheeks. "I don't suppose," she murmured, "when you work for a gent known to raise fast horses and black-eyed fillies there would be much choice for a mark with the proclivities of Happenstance Kelly."

He slanched a hard look at her. "If you think for a minute—"

"Just surveying it for size," she came back, and said, looking thoughtful: "Those girls *are* rather provocatively packaged. Any desperate father shrewd as your boss would be quick to seize any hold that came handy with a fellow like Bryce breathing down his neck."

Kelly yanked up his horse. "If you're tryin' to make out," he growled at her, glowering, "Tiodosa delib—" He broke off in confusion, cheeks angrily reddening as he glimpsed how neatly she had slipped that skid under him. "By grab—" he snarled, but Melanie Scott had already turned her horse round.

"Afraid I'm going to have to leave you here," she said. "After all," she smiled, "it's no business of mine how you spend your time or get pushed around by conniving people."

And before he could get loose of that she was gone.

"Women!" he muttered, and half turned to peer over his shoulder. Then, twisting around, he put the horse in a lope, striking out for the south to put a few hills between himself and whatever skulduggery Murgatroyd might have laid on as counter-measure to the deal Hap had scorned. Feller was damn sure to come up with *some*thing.

But though he cudgeled his wits trying to foresee

what possible new move the man might throw at him, sundry visions of Melanie interlaced with Tiodosa too frequently intruded for him to keep his mind on it.

He just couldn't figure that Scott girl at all, but turning over what she'd said he put some more scowling thought on that slippery old man who was paying his wages. Yet nothing he got hold of quite seemed to add up.

He couldn't honestly believe that Don Ambrocio was the sort who deliberately would trade a daughter's virtue even to secure such insurance as he presumed to have bought in Hap's growls and gun. However, the old man certainly wasn't above using a suspected relationship to strengthen his hold on a hombre who might tend to get out of hand.

Surly and fuming Kelly shelved the whole confused caboodle of unwanted thoughts and prospects, sharpening his glance to scan bitterly the rock- and cacti-cluttered landscape rimming his passage through these tumbled hills. A man in his boots could be mighty soon dead with so little to shield him from the thump of a bullet and so many jaspers honing to dangle his scalp from their belts. The one thing Bryce Murgatroyd could and sure would do was sweeten the bounty with some of that loot Hap had heaved in his face.

In this hot glare of sun bearing down from the west the swing of his restless stare went beyond his surroundings in probing search of the far lifts of land where he'd stationed those cowhands with their piles of gathered brush. Through the gray smoky haze filming these peaks not a sign of their presence could he manage to detect. No puffs of woodsmoke showed anywhere against the bowl of that brassy sky.

But how much grace a man had in the meantime could be shortened immeasurably by one wrong move, one overlooked bet or unguarded second of preoccupation with the worrisome whirl of uneasy ponderings. Vigilance was the price a man paid to stay alive in this country, and none knew it better than Happenstance Kelly.

14

So he wasn't taken aback or even mildly startled when a handful of miles from Palominas headquarters, screened in a clump of shaggy junipers, he considered the approach of a dawdling horseman apparently bound in haphazard fashion toward the sand flats flanking Apache Leap.

He'd been curiously watching the rider's antigodlin progress for the past several minutes, but now, with the fellow at last in plain sight, Hap *was* a mite surprised by the fact of his identity.

A day with the red in thermometers well over a hundred was hardly the sort that any gent with a bankroll, in full possession of his faculties, would pick to go hacking unfamiliar country. Nor was this likely to have been any whim born of boredom with two fillies as handsome as Don Ambrocio's daughters practically hanging on the feller's every word.

When the man wasn't more than half a rod from his covert, Hap put the gelding squarely into his path.

"Well! I say, old chap, what in the world are you doing out here with half of the outfit pulled from their jobs to go scouring the brush for you?"

Slicker, by God, than a handful of slobbers! Kelly thought, noting the man's benign florid countenance. "You still packin' that bankroll you left on the stage?"

Wetherington-Forsyth III flipped up his brows, blinked a couple of times and good-naturedly chuckled. "I say! You *do* appear to take a rather staunch interest. It's only money, you know. Just bits of paper—"

"Yeah," Kelly said. "You act like a guy that ain't got half his marbles. Keep packin' it, Johnny, it's you we'll be hunting for one of these mornings. Who worked up the lather to launch this 'find Hap' deal?"

"Don Ambrocio—"

"When?"

"After dinner last night."

"Sure it wasn't Rufino?"

The Britisher considered, presently shaking his head.

Hap rasped a hand across unshaven cheeks. "All right, let's get back. No sense worryin' him none."

"If it's all the same to you, old chap, I think I'll just get on with my ride."

"Think again."

The dude said bewildered, "I beg your pardon?"

"You've already come as far as you're goin'."

"Now see here—" the man spluttered; but Kelly, twisting sideways, reached for the horse's cheekstrap, and just as he did so, a rifle banged somewhere, sending its screech like an angry rattler not a hand's breadth above that dropped shoulder. Hap went flatter still as a second shot crashed through the echoes of the first, and fisting the horse back onto four legs, slammed it full-out at a haze of black

85

smoke hanging over some brush not far from the rim of the nearest slope.

The big blue stretched the stride of pistoning legs as Kelly fed it the steel, flattening his ears as the carbine flushed another burst of black powder. But the man was panicked and proved it a second later by abandoning his advantage to break cover in a snorting lunge for the rim.

He had a fifty-yard start and dropped out of sight on the ridge's far side just as Hap breasted the covert whence the drygulcher had fired. Five seconds later the blue crossed the hump and Kelly, quitting the saddle, flung rifle to shoulder, and leading the target, squeezed off a shot.

The horse ran on but the man it had carried stayed spraddled out where Hap's slug had dropped him. Kelly went stilt-legged through shale and talus, eyes never leaving that crumpled shape. When he stopped above it he could tell by the blood and the rent in his shirt the bush-whacker wasn't going to show up for breakfast.

Kelly whistled for the blue and the moro came up just as Wetherington-Forsyth, white and shaken, reined his mount to sit goggle-eyed, staring.

"Stay with him a minute," Kelly growled, swinging up, and wheeled the blue after the downed man's horse. When he presently returned with the skittish animal Wetherington-Forsyth did not look to have even so much as shifted his weight.

Kelly said, getting down, "Ain't you never seen a dead man before?"

The Britisher licked at colorless lips. "Wh-Who is it?"

"We'll have a look," Hap grunted, and toed the corpse over. The face of George Dunn stared sightlessly back. Hap said, "Guess Bryce will have to find a new range boss."

The dude turned away, bent over sideways to retch uncontrollably.

When he faced around, still green about the gills, Hap had the dead man doubled across his saddle. When he got the loose weight securely tied down he caught up the reins and plopped them into the Britisher's flinching hands.

Kelly said with a flint-hard stare, "I guess after all you might just as well finish out that ride. You can take this carrion with you, and tell your friend Bryce Murgatroyd if he wants his account marked *paid in full* he ain't got a hell of a ways to go!"

It was dark when Hap rode into the yard and flung off the blue horse before the wide-open doors of Palominas headquarters and tramped without challenge over the cobbles flooring the passage and into the shine of the patio lamps to find the old man alone by the fountain.

Though the angry ching of Hap's spurs plainly reached him the *patrón* did not turn at Kelly's approach but continued the morose regard of the liver-spotted hands lying still in his lap. "Old man," Kelly said in the harsh grating tones of one fed to the gills, 'I've just killed George Dunn an' sent that lap dog of his you been entertainin' back to Bryce Murgatroyd where he belongs. You hear me?"

Without looking up Don Ambrocio nodded.

"In case you ain't got the picture, I'm talkin' about that phony in the continental stuit you been huggin' to your bosom. I don't expect he'll be back, so you're figuring to fire me right now's your best chance."

The old man's chin looked to have sunk a little lower but at last an escaping breath came out of him and, turning his head, "I know," he nodded, peering up at Hap glumly.

When Hap kept staring the *hacendado* said, "I suspected when he came here that Murgatroyd was back of it but I needed that money he spoke of investing—"

"You'd have let him buy *into* this spread?" Hap exclaimed.

The old man shrugged. "I hoped it would help me keep hold of this place. I thought with your gun we could handle him, Kelly."

He sat there awhile, shrunken into the ashes of all his endeavors, a man without hope.

"For Chrissake," Hap grumbled, "we ain't finished yet!"

"You don't know," the man answered. "I'm worse off than you think. The gringo bank holds a mortgage—"

"An' Bryce has that bank?"

"I'm afraid so. I can't meet the payments. Even scrape up enough to take care of the interest. I can't pay you, either."

"To hell with that," Hap scowled. "I ain't never run out on nobody yet."

The old face showed life, the brightening last flare of a come-apart rocket, soon gone, falling back like the stick that's fit only for firewood. "You might as well go . . . clear out while you're able. There's nothing for you here." He grumbled after a moment, "Palominas is finished."

"Not while I've still got my hand on a gun." Hap stared at him hotly. "You put me in charge—"

"I can't do that, Jank. Not over my Number Two.

He was born on this place."

"An' part of your trouble! Jesus an' Mary, when you goin' to wake up? I rode in here tonight, straight through the yard and right into your house without a hand or a shout bein' lifted! What the hell kind of system is that?"

"I had out every man we could spare trying to find you. I thought you'd been shot, thrown into some barranca."

"You weren't too far off but I'm still in the runnin'. With that dude out of here and Bryce scrabblin' round to get hold of a foreman we might cut this yet." Hap briefly described what he'd run into in town, never mentioning Melanie Scott but bringing in Marshal Bridwell and the gun ultimatum, tersely sketching the attempt made by Bryce to syphon him out of the Palominas setup.

The old man put on a different face when the bundled-up bank notes came into Hap's story. And when he quit talking, Don Ambrocio tipped forward and cried, "There—that's it! There's our way out of this!"

Hap, blankly staring, pawed at beard-stubbled cheeks when the *hacendado* said eagerly: "Take him up on this, Jank! Say you have changed your mind, that you can't work with Rufino countermanding every order behind your back. You can say I won't get rid of—"

"It won't wash. Not after the way I handled the bugger."

"You have seen how this gringo *chingao* has robbed and bullied his way to importance and you think a little pride will stand in his way? Jesus in his Sacred Name, hombre! That one will do *anything* to make himself master of Palominas!"

"I don't think he'll do that."

"We'll find out. Tell him about that brush on the hilltops; he'll remember it was you who impounded his *vacas*. Say you came back here and walked unchallenged straight into my house, that all the guards were called off. Curse Rufino. Say I won't back you to stop his interference. Tell him about my *telescopio*. Chihuahua!" the old man exclaimed, jumping up. "Do this, Jank! You come back with that dinero and I will make you *mi socio*—my partner!"

15

Kelly pushed it around, trying from different angles to see this stratagem as Murgatroyd must view it, hackles up, hating Hap, suspicious and still smarting from all his festering frustrations, not overlooking what had happened to Dunn and the bogus Britisher they'd planted on Don Ambrocio.

He couldn't see Bryce buying it.

Yet the prospect opened by this proffered partnership was not an easy thing to put out of mind for a galoot who had nothing but his appetites and pistol. Like the flare of a match abruptly struck in pitch blackness it colored all his thinking, hauling him headlong past each glimpsed obstacle, warming cold corners with its roseate glow.

It even made the old man seem different, more a father figure than the cantankerous despot Hap had judged him.

Pawing his face Kelly rasped stubbled cheeks with

an uncertain hand, afraid of this almost, reluctant to believe the old fox was sincere yet unable for all this to kick shut the door. He wondered if Murgatroyd's dude might be got at.

When Hap first had caught sight of him the feller certainly had been heading toward Apache Leap, and it was from that direction George Dunn had opened hostilities with those sneak shots. It sure was not out of line to suppose Wetherington-Forsyth had been on his way to some prearranged rendezvous with Murgatroyd's range boss. If this would wash it almost certainly followed, as Hap had suspected, there was a definite connection between the dude and Murgatroyd's outfit.

Cutting over to the cookshack Kelly badgered the *cocinero* into fixing him up with a meal of cold snacks, after which he roped out a fresh mount from the day pen.

On top of the risk there wasn't much sense in heading for town. Wetherington-Forsyth, saddled with dead freight, would strike out directly for Murgatroyd's headquarters; which was hardly a place Hap hankered to visit.

But no other arrangement he could focus his sights on looked likely to accommodate present needs. At this stage of the game any attempt to set up a safe contact would be taken by Bryce as proof that Kelly wasn't nearly as tough and uncaring as he'd managed to seem; and if this were even so much as suspected, Hap's life was worthless.

After putting Palominas behind several hills, Kelly lined out for Flying M headquarters by the shortest route. Poking his head in the lion's mouth this way did hold out several important advantages. Even if Bryce didn't go for this deal Hap might find a chance to work on the dude. Or at least sound him out.

It had been a long while since Kelly had been welcome at Bryce's end of the cactus and this figured to be a good chance to look around and maybe get a better picture of the strength of Bryce's defenses. He wasn't like to get a better one.

But the risk was there—no getting around it. The only question was whether Bryce wanted Kelly dead bad enough to chance having him killed on Bryce's doorstep.

This was still wild country, well removed from any tangible contact with the mainstream of badge packers. Bryce had enough pull and power around here that what Bridwell thought wouldn't slow him a particle so long as this gobbling of other men's range didn't fetch in one of those boys from Fort Smith.

This was likely well out of their bailiwick; still Bryce Murgatroyd, despite his predilection for running roughshod over Mexicans, might be cagey enough to figure killing Anglos wasn't quite the same thing. At least locally Hap had a kind of standing as the personal representative of the largest landowner at this end of the territory.

Notwithstanding the myriad pros and cons that steadily whipped across his thoughts, Hap kept ears cocked and both eyes quartering each patch of shadows that flanked his path. For the moon, though up, wasn't yet high enough to thin the thicker shadows enough to see through them.

But nothing untoward delayed him during those first few hours. He was less than a mile from Murgatroyd's headquarters when the cramp of taut muscles dropped him into a walk. No use telegraphing his presence.

It didn't look reasonable for Murgatroyd not to have at least a brace of men staked out someplace with eyes peeled for trouble. Although he supposed himself well entrenched, he would almost certainly set up some means of dealing with the occasional victim seeking revenge.

Lack of any visible evidence of this was beginning to turn Hap edgy when the lamps of Flying M broke through the dappled shadows.

Kelly stopped the horse for a lengthy inspection of the layout.

He reached for tobacco and the wind for a moment took enough of a rest for him to hear the sharp click of a gun being cocked. The smell of trouble, that quick, was all around him, biting into locked muscles as he watched a distant rider pass between himself and the shine of lamps.

Motionless, Hap said, "Bryce around anyplace?"

A gruff voice growled back of him. "Who wants to know?"

"Just tell him Hap Kelly's had second thoughts about that offer he made and has come to talk turkey."

"All right, Flick, bring him in," the rider up ahead of Kelly called, and the man behind closed in to prod Hap forward.

The horseman ahead swung in from the left, and flanked on each side, Hap passed the huge red-painted barn and a sprawl of pens to pull up on command a couple of horse lengths from the gallery of Murgatroyd's much older, weather-grayed house.

In the spill of light from the uncurtained windows the man on his left said, "All right, Kelly. Unlatch that shell belt and let it drop."

With no satisfactory choice Hap complied.

"Move away from it," the tough-faced straw boss grunted, then told him to stop. "You can get down now," the man said in the tone of one who had looked for something better.

As Hap unhurriedly got off his horse the screen door squeaked protestingly open and the he-wolf himself stepped out onto the gallery to look over Kelly with a jaundiced regard.

"You show more guts than sense," he scowled, "but I reckon by God you always did." With bright flecks of suspicion in that smoldering stare he presently grumbled, "What changed your mind?"

"I can't lay out any worthwile defense with that sonofabitch Rufino all the time pullin' men off the job behind my back. If that nizzy old coot would of—no matter! I guess in this world a man's a plumb fool to expect any different from a pack of zanies like them. We got to talk out here?"

Murgatroyd grudgingly stepped away from the door. Kelly pulled the sag of it scrapingly open and Bryce, following him in, said over a shoulder: "Leave that nag where it is and keep your eyes peeled for trouble."

In the gear-cluttered main room Hap sat solidly down at one end of a battered horsehair sofa and looked contemptuously about. "Ain't changed a heap. Man would think with all you've stole you'd be above livin' in this kinda boar's nest."

The ranchman waved that away. "I'm surprised you would come here after killin' George Dunn."

Hap said roughly, "I didn't come out here to swap a lot of gab. You got a foreman's job open and I'm available."

Murgatroyd's face showed a vein-netted redness, the thin lips trap-tight as he considered the Palominas *pistolero* with a freshening distrust. "Maybe that job's already been filled."

Hap slapped both thighs with wide-open palms as though preparing to get up. "In that case," he said, "I might as well be on my way."

"You don't listen no better than you ever did. I said *maybe*—"

"Well, make up your mind."

"The deal I offered you," Murgatroyd growled, "didn't include ramroddin' this outfit—"

"It does now," Hap smiled.

16

In that second of silence before Bryce could get enough loose of his temper to hitch together a coherent rejoinder, a small, slim girl stepped into the room to throw Hap a look and a red-lipped "Oh!" before twirling to say, "Bryce, I'm sorry—didn't know you had company."

Dressed in fashionable East Coast clothes with hair the color of ripe wheat put up in a gleaming knot at the back of her head, her face in profile had a cameo's perfection. In contrast, green long-winkered eyes considered Kelly again with a flattering interest that was almost flirtatious.

Something sliced through Bryce's glare too swift to be read as, shaking his head in irritable impatience, the Flying M owner reluctantly grumbled, "My sister, Marcie . . . here on a visit. This is Hap Kelly, from Palominas." A harder edge came into his voice. "If you'll excuse us now we'll get on with what brought him here."

She turned with grace and a toss of her head to show Kelly that behind those bright red lips a quick flash of teeth, something more warmly suggestive, was there. "I trust we'll be seeing more of you . . . neighbor."

"My pleasure," Hap smiled, staring after her.

Her hands touched her hair in an expressive way, and provocative mouth still faintly smiling, she passed through a draped arch toward the back of the house.

"Don't get any wild ideas about her," Murgatroyd growled, thrusting forward his jaw, his stare sharply intent as it searched Kelly. "When Marcie puts out no fly-by-night saddle bum is going to have either foot in the stirrup. She knows which side of the bread gets the butter."

"I'll keep it in mind. Now, you buyin' or ain't you?"

"I'll sleep on it."

"Just a minute," Hap said as Bryce wheeled toward the door. "I got my own trail to cover—"

"Don't tell me your troubles."

"You offered a deal."

"You passed up that deal—remember?"

"I'm not going to stick around this place all night!"

"Is that so?" A mean grin twisted half of Murgatroyd's face and his pale hooded stare looked Hap up and down. "You'll play hell gettin' out of here without no gun. You don't think so, just try it."

Hap got out the makings and spun up a smoke while the cold of disquiet nipped with sharp unseen teeth. He said through the prod of a thickening anger, "Got a match?"

The rancher stepped back to set one down on the table. "Don't try to teach an old hand how to suck eggs." Still keeping his distance he moved toward the door, wary, thin-smiling, one hand drifting beltward as Hap abruptly stood up. Eyes cold, malignant, behind that cocked pistol, Murgatróyd said, "Don't push your luck, bucko."

When the door closed Hap's cool fell apart and he cursed hot and vividly under his breath. The way this thing was shaping up did not augur well for any profitable conclusion. Bryce was too angry for any of the things suggested by Hap's boss to make a particle of difference. He just wasn't in a listening frame of mind. And with all that hate boiling round inside him a few winks of sleep wasn't likely to change anything.

He began looking around for some way to get out.

Two windows let into this room, both facing the gallery and of no use to him with the bunkhouse across the churned dust of the yard and Christ only knew how many notch-cutters hungrily waiting to take a crack at him.

He blew out the lamps and stood for long moments peering at the draped arch, trying to recall from the last time he'd been here what arrangement of rooms lay beyond. Near as he could figure it led into a hall that went straight to the kitchen but with doors opening off it to bedrooms and Bryce's office.

He wheeled back for a look through the curtainless windows, glance quartering the moonlit stretch of empty yard, studying the shadow shapes of bunkhouse and barn, the forge shop beyond and the shed crammed full of useless junk. Not a lamp burned anywhere within this vista.

Where the hell had Bryce gone? Someplace out

in that yard you could bet! It wouldn't be like that sonofabitch to go riding off leaving Hap in the house with that willowy wench he'd claimed was his sister—a relationship never before even hinted at.

Both windows were open but nothing came through but the night sound of insects and the occasional quick flutter of swooping bullbats.

Bryce was out there all right, and not alone by a long shot. Any number of hands could be concealed in those shadows waiting in grim silence for a chance to chalk up that promised bonus and be known evermore as . . .

"Shit!" Hap snarled, the sweat coming out on him.

If they were watching the windows they would damn sure be hunkered round every other way out of this place. The only deal Bryce figured to make was the one most likely to get Kelly planted quickest!

Having reached this conclusion he stretched out on the sofa, still with boots and all his duds on, to wait out whatever the morning might fetch.

It was a prospect a heap of folks couldn't have stomached, but despite all the things churning round through his mind, he must eventually have dozed because suddenly he found himself wide awake and waiting motionless, every reflex cocked, for whatever had alerted him to catch at his attention.

The moon had taken its light from the window, leaving the dark of the room strewn with shadows. Listening into these Hap heard nothing but the thump of his heart. With much care and considerable trepidation he managed to quit his berth for the floor where some moments later he got up on one knee, twisting his head for a look at the sagging screen of the door to find it still shut and no shape crouched before it.

He looked next toward the cloth-hung arch that let into the hall and the rooms opening off it. No one showed there, either, and if there had been anybody besides himself in this room he reckoned by now he would surely have known it.

On hands and knees—not wanting to present a larger target than he had to—he moved, frequently pausing, in the direction of the hall.

Something, some small indefinable splotch of paleness, on the floor just this side of the arch aburptly caught his notice to hold him for a motionless eternity.

When still nothing happened he took in a fresh breath, moving forward again with infinite caution, presently to reach out and set down a hand on the smooth feel of paper.

A vision of the girl—that taffy-haired Marcie— blossomed fullblown on the screen of his mind. Every instinct told him the paper had got there through no other agency but he was damned if he was going to risk a light to read it.

He slipped it into his shirt unexamined, and presently stood up to pull the cloth aside and step, now bootless, into the black of the hall.

Damn little to see and nothing to hear, though he stood a long moment to be certain of this. Not satisfied then, but accepting the risk, he moved forward edgily to listen at the first door he came to. He tried the latch then and eased the door open the merest fraction of an inch, leaving it that way when convinced the room was empty.

Grimly aware the whole point of that note may have had no other purpose than to have him scratch a match, there was always the chance she'd meant to help him out of this. She just might be proposing to create a diversion — *he had to find out.*

He stopped again beside a door, put an ear against its panel, knowing at once there was someone behind it; fully cognizant, too, this might be Bryce waiting gun in hand.

Nothing ventured, nothing gained, Hap reminded himself, and moved a hand toward the latch, stopping just short of it to do some more listening.

If this was a trap he could damn soon be dead.

But persuading himself Bryce had no need for such complicated maneuvering, Hap brushed the flat of his hand gently over the panel and drew instant response in the sound of a gasp followed almost at once by a whispered command. "Come in."

A dozen thoughts clamored warning but he lifted the latch and shoved open the door, stepping back as he did so.

He even felt a little foolish crouching there in his socks with nothing hostile apparent.

The girl hissed impatiently, "What are you waiting on?"

Gritting his teeth Hap stepped into the room. Through the ripping of cloth he heard the door slam behind him. Straightaway the girl started screaming her head off and Hap knew right then that he was buzzard bait.

One intolerable moment Hap hung locked in blind outrage, transfixed by the seething tangle of passions unleashed by this bitch and the slick way she'd placed him where Murgatroyd would have all the excuse a man needed.

She had the shift half torn off her—still screaming her yells fit to wake the dead—when Kelly, lunging, caught her a cuff across the side of the head, sending her crashing into the wall, all the breath spilling out of her.

Through the roar of hot blood Kelly heard running boots, and seizing her fiercely, spun her about, propelling her violently toward the pale rectangle of the one open window.

But halfway there he saw the folly of that and savagely dragged her back to the wall. Bare-lipped he snarled, one arm round her throat, "Keep right on coming if you want her neck broke!"

"Wait—" Bryce cried flatly; and a vacuum of silence closed over the hall with a last thump of boots quitting outside the window, leaving nothing to hear but the girl's ragged breathing.

It looked for a second like a Mexican standoff, Bryce plainly aware that with his life on the line Hap had little to lose, until the unseen hooligan outside the window put in his oar. "She's only a dancehall floozie fer Chrissake!"

Through the mutter of whispers that came from the hall Kelly, tightening his grip, said cold as a well chain: "You can blame it on me but somebody'll talk—somebody always does."

He could picture the hate that must be twisting Bryce's face to be balked so near to accomplishing his purpose, almost *feel* the fellow hefting the odds, countering one set of weights with another, trying to bring them in line to where the edge that he had would look worth the risk.

"I'll trade the girl for a pistol," Hap said, and heard someone guffaw, under cover of which sundry scuffings and scrapings outside the back wall made it ominously likely that whoever Bryce had out there was preparing to put a lot more than his jaw in this and hadn't no great way to go to be heard from.

Still with that elbow lock round the girl's windpipe, letting her know by the pressure put on it he was more than half willing to make his threat good, Hap said with his mouth hard against an ear, "Keep out of line of it but edge toward that window."

He guessed Bryce was right when the rancher had told him Marcie knew which side of the bread got the butter. She didn't test his mood, and when they reached the back wall, disregarding the feel of her half-naked hide, he forced the girl down onto hands and knees, and having no trust in her continued docility, struck her behind the ear with his fisted free hand.

He let go of her when she slumped, swiveling his head for a squint at the window just as the galoot outside looked in. "Go ahead," this one said with the boldness of knowing Hap wasn't heeled, "break her neck if you want—I'm comin' in anyhow," and—not seeing Kelly nor very much caring with that pistol making him ten feet tall—he thrust a leg over the sill.

A startled squawk was ripped from his throat as Hap, reaching up, got both hands round his boot and savagely twisted. Leverage brought Bryce's man off his perch in a crashing fall that, shaking the shooter out of his grip, sent it skittering into the wall. Turning him loose Hap jumped for the pistol but the girl, much closer, got there first, had it wrapped in her hand, finger on trigger, and was bringing it up when Kelly stomped on her wrist.

The gun fell out of it. Hap snatched it up and the other man drove his weight violently into Hap and smashed him back in a staggering sprawl.

Normally Kelly could have taken this joker but the man's savage rush had caught him off balance, slamming him shoulder-first into the window ledge, leaving that side of him wrenched and nearly paralyzed. With bursts of light lancing through the kaleidoscope whirl of his senses—further hampered by the punishing fist that was pounding his kidney— Hap in a desperate heave got the hand with the pistol free of his weight.

The man almost instantly shifted his attack. Holding Hap pinned with this smothering weight he got one strangling fist locked around Kelly's throat, reaching out with the other in a panting attempt to immobilize the gun. Right there Hap got lucky.

Striking out with a last spurt of guttering strength the flailing six-inch barrel of the captured Colt slammed solidly against the fellow's hunched head and he collapsed onto Hap like a dropped sack of feed.

Kelly wriggled free, found the doorway filled with the snarling shapes of charging men. From this prone position he drove three slugs into that surging mass. He staggered erect, then half fell through the window. Wild yells and cursing tore through the bedlam he left behind.

Without waiting to ascertain what might come next he lurched to his feet, breaking into a run for

103

the black of a slope that loomed dead ahead. Twin bursts of handgun fire followed him with a screech of blue whistlers and then he was into the chest-high brush, scrabbling his way toward the crest of the ridge, the heat of this effort burning his lungs.

Clear at last, he looked back with a catch in his side and the agony of breathing almost obscuring the pain from lacerated bootless feet. He could see lanterns bobbing down below where men churned through the brush.

When this first frantic search failed to turn him up it was dollars to doughnuts Bryce would mount the whole crew to scour every inch between this ridge and the Palominas boundary they'd be expecting him to make for, and he knew in his present near-exhausted state he would not be able to cut it.

The safest alternative was to head for town, get as far as he could before some bright gook latched onto this thought, hole up someplace through the nearing day and try when he could to get out of this country.

But Hap could be stubborn, too, and he wasn't the kind to run out on a man.

While he fought for breath he hunted alternatives and hit on one sure thing none of that bunch would be likely to look for.

In pursuance of this, with more wind up his gullet, Hap began to worm his way back cautiously, watching those lanterns. He kept clear of the places where the rattle of brush would be most apt to betray him.

Disregarding aches and the stabs from torn feet, he listened to the frustrated growl of Bryce's voice and watched the bobbing lanterns disappear round the house.

Hap stretched flat on his belly and waited this out, Murgatroyd's tricky dodges too fresh in mind to risk mistranslating any more of Bryce's intentions.

Even when the crew reappeared in a rush of horse racket Kelly stayed where he was, seeing them wheel past in a thunder of hooves, bound sure enough to head him off. He found a little satisfaction in having outfigured them but knew mighty well he wasn't out of this yet—not even temporarily. He hadn't been able to guess in the dark if Murgatroyd had pulled the whole works out of here, but he had to assume it wasn't too probable in view of Bryce's caginess.

So he didn't court peril by exposing himself; time enough for that when he knew how the wind blew. Meanwhile, still making like an Apache, he wormed his way nearer the room he'd recently escaped from, inching along till less than fifty feet lay between himself and that open window.

He learned nothing from stretched ears after watching the room the better part of ten minutes. He was about to get up when he remembered the girl.

It was considerably unlikely that Marcie had ridden with them. Bryce wouldn't have wanted the bother. If she was still in the house a man would think he'd have had some sign of her—unless she had stopped one of those blue whistlers.

He began to sweat when that thought caught up with him. No matter what, the killing of a woman was about the quickest way to a damn short life in this stretch of catclaw. You could drop any number of gun-handy galoots, rob a bank—even steal a man's horse—without incurring anything like the wrath kicked into a white-hot fury by the violent demise of a woman. If that fool bitch had got herself clobbered, the sooner Hap knew and got whacking the better!

Surging erect, still in poor light, he moved alongside the window for another hard listen. But though he crouched there, edgily hearing the fading night voices, open vest stirred by the wind coming down off the peaks, he found no sign at all to suggest that anyone gave a damn for his presence.

He shivered.

He stood a while longer, cursing under his breath. Then, pushed—turned reckless by the roweling pressures—he snapped a match in cupped palm and hunched forward, holding this while he had his quick look.

Nobody in there. Not even a stiff.

If he'd tagged anyone in that wild exchange of shots he hadn't hurt them bad enough—*or had he?* They could have been moved into some other room.

He probed this thought a bit further. It might pay him to know. Even in his need to get away from this place he dared hardly depart without finding out what had happened to the girl.

Which brought him grudgingly over the sill. The shadows inside were a lot thinner now—dawn would soon be upon him, hastening his need to find a horse and get clear.

On lacerated feet that were now mostly bare he slipped into the hall, every sense cautious and alert.

The rake of his stare grimly fastened on the strip of yellow light showing beneath the draped arch that shut off the front room.

Tiny rustles of motion came from beyond it to root him. The sound of water splashing shaped a picture in his head of wounded being cared for but no grunts or groans accompanied this—no voices at all, not even a whisper was he able to catch. A stealthy retreat was certainly indicated, but a half-shaped plan and the need for knowing what had happened to the girl drew him irresistibly forward till his hand was on the door.

Gun raised, he threw the door open with one quick shove of that levering hand. And stood, arrested in mid-stride by the sight of Marcie naked, wet and startled, in a battered tub half filled with water.

He saw that the girl was completely alone.

"Damn if you ain't a cool one," Hap growled, looking her over with a man's appreciation.

The fright dropped out of her face with a sniff and she went on with her washing, lifting one leg to slosh the soap off it.

"Where's the rest of them?" Hap said, still bemusedly staring. "The ones that got hit."

"Don't flatter yourself—if you hit anyone it sure didn't show."

"Where's the cook?" he said suddenly, mouth turning grim.

"I haven't lost any cooks." She grinned at him, gamin-like. "Come scrub my back—"

"Get into your clothes," he said harshly, stepping into the room to put a wall at his back, nervously scanning the black gleam of the windows; but Marcie, ignoring both him and his growls, went on

107

with her ablutions.

It would be less than honest to say that Hap was immune to these paraded gymnastics. With so much sensuous beauty bouncing around—all shiningly wet in the lamp's yellow light—he'd have hardly been human had the sap not begun to churn up a definite ache in his crotch.

But stirred along with this was a fierce anger that drove him across the intervening eight feet to yank her savagely out of the tub. Beset by this fury he snarled with his jaw not an inch from her own: "If you don't hanker to get roasted you'll get out of this rat's nest like the heel flies was after you because I'm goin' to burn it plumb down to the ground!"

And with a shove that pretty near sent her sprawling, he was grabbing for the lamp when an amused voice said behind him, "Don't touch it."

Wetherington-Forsyth.

Harrowed by things more urgent, Hap had forgotten that sonofabitch! Now the tables were turned, and Kelly knew without looking that the fellow's tweedy shape would have a shooter whose trigger would get squeezed with considerable satisfaction if the bastard were given the merest hint of an excuse.

But in the same flash of thought one other fact was equally apparent. To throw in his chips would no more than postpone briefly the inevitable. Even if the Britisher held him over for Bryce the end result would be just as unpleasant; for all the face Hap had cost him, Murgatroyd could not afford to let him go.

Dropping into a crouch as he came spinning round Hap fired from the hip, the sound of it lost in the double-barreled roar of the sawed-off Greener that fell from the dude's loosened grasp as the man, toppling forward, folded convulsively. A bad egg come to the end of his rope.

The churn of Hap's mind held no room for regret, his attention loping to matters still urgent, chiefly the natural inclination to look out for Number One.

A solitary cartridge was all he had left unfired in that pistol. It was imperative to survival that he turn up more immediately. The corpse regrettably had neither handgun nor shell belt.

Swinging back toward where the shaking girl was white-faced and staring, he caught up his boots and stomped himself into them. "God!" he growled, hurting; and grabbed up the lamp to pitch it, flaring, against the handiest wall, shattered glass sending flaming oil voraciously racing over the sofa and other stuff Hap heaved after it. Marcie, not stopping to snatch up her duds, went pelting ahead of him through the rusted and sagging screen of the door.

He forgot her, too, once he reached the yard. A loose mouth might do twice the harm of a bullet, but bullets were now uppermost in Hap's head, hurrying him toward the frame bunkhouse and cookshack. At this precise moment, warsack on shoulder, the limping hand who cooked for Bryce's outfit wheeled into sight between the two buildings, stood rooted for perhaps two parts of a second and with a frightened squawk fled in jackrabbit jumps for Hap's ground-hitched horse.

Kelly let him go and plunged into the bunkhouse that was still half filled with the departed night's shadows. He got a bracket lamp lit and found no sign of his confiscated shell belt. Rummaging the crew's belongings he presently turned up a box of loads that would fit and stuffing these into his pockets after replacing the spent shells in his captured Colt,

109

he threw the lamp under a bunk and got out of there.

Sprinting across to the cookshack he filled a towsack with edibles, tipped over the stove with its bed of hot coals and ran into the yard now dappled with light from the roaring flames leaping out of burst windows and through the roof of Bryce's tinder-dry ranchhouse.

No time to waste. Murgatroyd's crew—even if they failed to spot those towering flames—would mighty soon catch that woodsmoke smell and discover the glow so luridly painting the overcast sky.

Kelly ran for the pens, caught up a rope, and dropping his sack, headed for the pair of nickering horses excitedly circling the five-foot posts of the bronc-stomper's domain.

Two minutes later, without saddle or blanket, he piled aboard one of them and dug in the spurs with nothing but a twist of rope round its jaw and a fistful of mane to give it direction. Towsack bouncing against its flank, Hap took off for the hills in the same kind of haste the cook had shown.

19

The only regret Hap took into the graying light of false dawn had to do with the money he'd been sent there to fetch. He had been too driven by the press of events to ransack the house even had he figured Bryce fool enough to keep any sizable amounts of cash on hand. This past year the man had been too firmly dug in to lean on the need of getaway caches.

Those two bundles of bank notes he'd dangled before Kelly that night in town would have been put away into somebody's safe—that saloon's more than likely.

It was grimly obvious to Hap's scowling thoughts that the most he'd accomplished had been to raise hell and pop a chunk under it.

Sure, he'd lost Bryce more face—a mighty good pile of it; he'd proved the man vulnerable but he hadn't really hurt him—except, perhaps, a little in the pocket—and not even there had he been hurt badly. Murgatroyd was still very much in the saddle and would be wilder now than a goddam March hare!

Hap wasn't fooling himself about that.

Away from Palominas he'd reduced himself to the status of an outlaw. Bryce still swung a heap of weight in this country and every last bit of it was going to come down on Kelly. He wouldn't have a friend left when Bryce screamed. Hap's one best chance lay in reaching Palominas.

But wasn't this what Bryce reckoned he might do? Right now, this very instant, the man with all his fire power was streaking hellity-larrup to get between the fugitive and the doubtful haven of Don Ambrocio's protection. Unless Hap cleared straight out of the country he'd be bottled up proper and sooner or later—even at Palominas—would get his come-uppance no matter how vigilant and careful he might be. Money spoke around here and Bryce would pile enough on his scalp to make a burro flinch.

A new ploy, outlandishly peril-packed, was beginning to gnaw at the back of Hap's thinking—a stratagem in concept so preposterously unlikely no one but an idiot would figure to look twice at it.

But desperation sometimes has its compensations. By riding a large enough circle around Bryce a man could probably reach Palominas. But Hap with time in short supply was in no mood for jouncing around on a half-wild horse for another week of Sundays with no better prospect than climbing back into a half-sunk ship.

The old man—if Hap could get his hands on that dinero—had said straight-out he would make him a partner and the glint of this notion still colored Hap's wheels. Not even Bryce would imagine that Hap could be so damn loco as to cut out for town. But town was where the money was and the partnership pull too strong to resist.

Hap kept off the skyline wherever possible. He came as near to Friendly Corners as he dared before holing up in a thicket of mesquite to wait out the rest of the daylight hours. He didn't think that with all the care he'd employed, antigodlin around through ravines, barrancas and occasional dry washes, he'd been spotted—at least not close enough to have been identified.

Wolfing a cold snack from the grub he'd lifted from the Flying M cookshack, he quenched his thirst from a tin of tomatoes and dozed away most of the day. Cowhands traditionally think first of their mounts but Kelly, case-hardened through long years in the saddle, was inclined first of all to look out for himself. The horse, tied by a foreleg, could lunch on mesquite beans and if these didn't hold him he could skin a few branches.

It was almost night when he roused himself to take a squint at his surroundings. Finding no sign of movement he hacked open another tin of tomatoes, feeding the horse a large part of the pulp. To counteract the discomfort of aches and bruises, he felt the need of tobacco but wisely refrained from giving in to this urge.

Not till full dark did he come out of hiding. By this time, he reckoned, Murgatroyd would probably have discovered what had happened to his headquarters.

It was some satisfaction that the only law Bryce could appeal to was Marshal Rankin Bridwell whose jurisdiction was too circumscribed to be of any real help. Bryce would doubtless send someone in with the horrendous tale of what Hap had done to him, if only as cover against public opinion should Hap turn up with a hole though his bellows.

It was a leadpipe cinch that Bryce would prodigally spend whatever it took to get Hap off his back. And in the shortest time possible. He had to! Otherwise every poor sonofabitch the man had climbed over to get where he was would be out to get back some of his own. Which could pull Bryce down in mighty short order—not that anyone had to tell *him* that!

Way this shaped up Kelly had two choices, both harebrained and plumb loaded with risk. He could ride straight in, hit the saloon and dig for the tules, shooting down anyone who got in his way. Or he could try to get hold of Melanie Scott and hole up at her place till chances looked better.

Impatience inclined him to opt for the first but plain common sense nagged him into the latter, which in its way seemed just as studded with potholes. Women could gum up the best-thought-out scheme. If she put up an argument he'd plain have to use force because no other refuge he hit on could match hiding out in a dressmaker's shop. It

113

was not only handy but about the last place Bryce would think of to look for him.

He approached with as much stealthy care as could reasonably be managed. It took some doing and twice on the way he very nearly was spotted, even though scouting the place through back lots. First time, in the dark, he almost barged into a line hung with wash. Then a dog started yapping about the heels of his mount, but the horse settled that with one well-placed kick. Just the same Hap got down and turned the bronc loose, feeling a heap too conspicuous perched on its back. Besides, he told himself, it was straining credulity to imagine Melanie Scott had room for a horse among the frames of her clothes dummies. To leave it outside would be a dead giveaway.

So he went on afoot.

The goddam street was filled with knots of gabbing townspeople; it looked from where he stood that the word had got around about that bonfire he'd started. And there was Rankin, too, he'd have to watch out. The marshal had said flatly to leave his gun at home.

At last Kelly found himself at the dress shop's back door. There he stood for long minutes, trying to be sure no late customer was getting herself a fitting.

The old man really needed that dough but it was more than this and his proffer of partnership which had dropped Hap into this impossible bind. Money and power were the things Bryce worshiped, and snatching those bundles of long green at gunpoint with folks enough watching to get the word round would hit that bugger right where he lived. This might just be the straw to break Bryce's grip on this country.

But daydreaming buttered no parsnips. When the peril of exposure became more than he could stomach Hap gave up listening for gab he couldn't hear, and trying the handle, found the door unbarred. He stepped quickly inside and shut it behind him.

Kelly stood in the shadows of this untenanted back room and heard Melanie Scott call "Yes?" with the same offhand composure that had always been the basis of his discomfort when around her. Nothing ever ruffled that calm and Hap with his brawler's rep and rough ways found her frequently glimpsed amusement a little hard to take.

He pushed through to the front room to find her fitting a frock to one of her frames without even peering around at his intrusion. This put an edge to his voice when he said, "I need a place to hole up for a couple of hours till that pack of fools on the street clears out."

Intent on the work in hand she said through the pins in her mouth, "What have you been up to now, Kelly?" but not as though she gave a damn really.

Irascibly Hap answered, "I've just burned Murgatroyd out of his home place." He looked for the shock this ought to have given her.

She took the pins from her mouth to look up with a grin, "I've been wondering when you would get around to it."

"That all you got to say, for Chrissake?"

"It's done now, isn't it?"

The smile still hung on her lips but he found harder to read the look that considered him from wide-open eyes. He was more bothered by it than what she said next.

"You've been bound for the owlhoot as long as I've known you. It's not too surprising to hear that

115

you've got there."

Hap snorted, then growled, "I'm goin' to pin back his ears if it's the last thing I do!"

She nodded. "I know. I figured you'd try when Bryce pressured Rob Raymond into firing you out of that job you had with him."

Hap said, surprised, "I hadn't reckoned it showed."

It was her turn to flush, and this was so out of character he stared like a ninny. She turned back to her work, saying over her shoulder like it didn't much matter, "What brought you to town?"

"You remember that galoot put the finger on me when we was sparrin' out yonder last time I rode in—"

"Shiloh Frayne? That hired gun Bryce imported?"

"Yeah. Well, it was Bryce wanted to see me. Found him waitin' in the Aces Up. Had the gall, by God, to set there back of two bundles of bills an' say I was on the wrong side of the fence!"

Melanie nodded, searching his face. "I know all that—so where is this leading?"

"I figure to take them bundles away from him."

The sudden change in her complexion astonished him. She said, wholly still: "You plan to stick that place up?"

Kelly grinned. "I'm goin' to fix that bastard's clock. But *good!* When these mealy-mouthed knuckle-heads round here learn he bleeds just as quick as anybody else—"

"Hap Kelly, you're a fool!"

"You'll see," he sneered, too het up to listen. "All you got to do is hide me awhile till some of them waddies pack up to go home. Then you'll see how a chump you wouldn't have round to wipe boots on can whittle Mister Big right out of his brass collar!"

She said with an asperity he took for contempt, "I can see by the way that jaw's sticking out I might's well try to pound sand down a rat hole—but I'll say it anyway. You want to know why that talk makes you out to be a fool?"

He looked into that glare and returned it, compounded. "All right, dammit. Go ahead an' tell me."

"Because it simply won't work."

"Why not?"

"Because he's already here. Rode in from his place not a half hour ago and told what you did. It's all over town. He's put a price on your scalp—says you've—"

"I've heard the wind blow before! I don't care what he says—"

"You better care about this. He's told everyone you're going to stick up Gallagher's, make him open that safe to get at the money you think he's been keeping there."

Had the girl suddenly climbed up a chair to bite him, Hap couldn't have looked more taken aback. The sound that came out of those livid cheeks was the growl threatening lift of an arm—his whole stance—predicated action. The coppery glint of that steel gray stare appeared to be holding her personally responsible.

Melanie Scott's own glance, though unreadable to him, remained coolly sober, with nothing about it to indicate fright. "Don't burst your surcingle," she said without moving. "If you're bound and determined I certainly can't stop you—"

"Damn right!" Hap muttered through the clench of white teeth.

"I can't stop you," she said, "but you'll not hide here if you intend to do anything crazy as that. I'll be no party to suicide."

An explosive snort came out of him. "That crew never saw the goddam day any one or ten of 'em—"

"Kelly, why don't you get onto yourself? Palominas surely can't mean that much to you. It's going to fall regardless of what you do."

When he continued to glare she said with those eyes seeming to dig hard at his face, "Is that girl—Tiodosa—you're so anxious to die for?"

A flush welled up past the scarf that was knotted tight round his throat. The big fists clenched. Cheeks darkening, furious, he spun with a bellicose clank of spur rowels and stomped from her sight.

The slam of the back door shook the room.

Hap strode unheeding in his frustrated fury through the night's stove-black shadows. Not till the dapples of the lamplighted street lay directly before him was he able in his rage to think clearly and realize the enormity of the odds stacked against him.

It was preposterous to suppose, forewarned as they'd been, that he could even come near to getting into Gallagher's. Too many loafers were still standing around. And, though he saw no sign of them, it stood to reason—when the rake of his glance crossed that line of hitched horses—that Bryce would have enough of his own crowd inside to make certain that Hap came out on a shutter.

He backed off a bit to consider this soberly.

One thing for sure. He'd never be expected to come in by the front. Not with all that bunch of nuts standing round.

And he damn sure wouldn't get in by the back!

It was the bounty Bryce had posted that made this so sticky. Any fool might be tempted with so much on Hap's scalp to try a sneak draw, or think to pot him from ambush.

Which reminded Hap to take a hard look at the rooftops. From any number of these a sniper with a rifle could command the whole street. This was a worrying thing for a man in Hap's boots to contemplate. Smart thing to do was get rid of this silver-buttoned twenty-dollar vest and pick up another hat. That way, maybe, whoever Bryce had posted to keep an eye out for him might take a little longer to make out who he was.

Backing into deeper shadow Hap emptied its pockets and pitched away the vest, sent his hat spinning after it. Might turn out to be considerably more difficult getting hold of another—not that he expected to latch onto one that fit. He was looking around for something to make do with when he spotted Rankin Bridwell, shoulders hunched against a post not scarcely a rope's length from the unplastered adobe front of his objective. Of all the places for that buzzard to roost!

This didn't stack up to be any happenstance. The marshal, of course, must have been regaled with the comments Bryce had been passing and obviously intended, if there was any truth in the rancher's claims, to be where he could deal himself in.

About the time Kelly's churning mind hit paydirt, his glance picked up the town drunk, old Prognosticatin' Pearley, poking through two barrels of

119

trash set out by the general store's lazy clerk. A fresh inspiration took hold of Hap's figuring.

When he was sure he wasn't focused by anyone's attention Kelly went back, and carefully folding it inside out, retrieved the vest he had just thrown away. Tucking it beneath an arm he bided his time until old Pearley, scratching the sag of his bloated belly, began to move off at a staggering lurch into an across-lots hike for the place he called home.

By dint of careful timing Hap intercepted him about a hundred yards short of his packing-crate shanty and swung into step beside him. Hap laid out his propostion. In the starlight the old codger blinked at him owlishly. "Do I know you, sir?" he inquired with vast gravity.

Though it had long since ceased to be a source of amusement, it was still generally true that the more drunk the old fool got, the more flowery were the two-dollar words he took out of mothballs to induce further charities.

Hap, gruff with impatience, growled, "Know me? Jumpin' Jehosophat! You don't remember Tillicum Benton what was master's mate that time you was pilot on the old *Dakota Belle?*"

Without waiting for an answer, Hap said, "I want to trade you this here vest for your hat."

The old reprobate hauled off his headgear for another look at it. Carefully setting the bowler back on his noggin, with drunken dignity he loosened his belt and felt around in his drawers as through to make sure he still had his possibles. "May I ascertain for what dubious purpose this trade's been initiated?"

Hanging onto his temper with considerable effort Hap dug out a cartwheel from his pocketful of change, held it a moment in front of Pearley's stare, plopped it onto the folded vest and growled in a take-it-or-leave-it tone, "You swappin' or ain'tcha?"

"I dislike doing business in such precipitate fashion—"

Depositing vest and dollar in the trembling hands Kelly collared the bowler and made his getaway, too screwed tight and jangling to waste more time. But instead of retracing the route he had come by he struck off at right angles on a roundabout course which presently fetched him past the dilapidated ruin of what—before the volunteer fire brigade wrecked it—had been Friendly Corner's most profligate honky-tonk, behind which he paused for another hard look toward the Aces Up.

The marshal was still propping up his post and at least half the loafers, despite the cold gusts swooping down off the rimrocks, were still hanging around waiting out Hap's appearance.

Kelly set about the task of moving them. Muttering under his breath, he ducked into the broken-walled palace of pleasure and found, as expected, a motley array of wind-funneled trash.

Moving into a shielded corner where the combustibles were thickest he struck a match in cupped palm and tossed it where it would do the most good.

He was halfway back to where he had first spied Bridwell when the cry of "Fire!" went up hysterically. Electrified havoc engulfed the wooden-frame cowtown as every man on the street broke into headlong motion. While some ran for buckets and three or four to get axes, most raced directly for the scene of the blaze. They burst out of buildings like aggravated hornets from a prodded nest.

But Bridwell, after the first couple of jumps, pulled up to stand peering beneath the brim of his hat like a shipwrecked sailor hunting for land; he was still at it, swearing, when Hap caught him a clip behind the ear with his pistol.

Not waiting for any rooftop commotions Kelly dived for the batwings, hurtling into the saloon as though flung from a catapult, gun up, eyes slitted. Every chair had been emptied. The lone pair of customers leaning against the bar made haste to show their peaceful intentions as Hap growled at the goggling proprietor, "You know what I'm here for—get busy."

Gallagher's prominent Adam's apple jerked like the float on a fishline. "Come on," Hap snarled, "it's not *your* dough I'm after. Get that box opened up before I run out of patience!"

With shaking hands Murgatroyd's banker knelt before the iron monster. After two fumbling attempts which his nervousness aborted Kelly said sharply, "Next try's your last," and the safe's door swung open.

"Them two bundles," Hap grinned, "is the ones with my name on 'em. How come Bryce ain't takin' care of this *personal?* He run out of guts after shootin' his mouth off?"

The aproned man, getting up with the bank notes, kept his face shut.

"Just tuck them under my arm, friend."

Gallagher, looking like he was walking on eggs, had pretty nearly got to where he could do it, with an arm half extended, when that mean-eyed glance snaking over Hap's shoulder sent Kelly into a lunging spin. A gun—pounding back of him—ripped its slug into the yelling apron but Hap's return fire, taking the shooter high in the chest, smashed him backward through the wrenched-open doors.

Kelly, grabbing up the nearer bundle of bank notes, with head tucked in arm, dived straight through the window in a shower of shards.

He lit on a shoulder but was up in an instant, charging the horse line hitched to the tie rail. But the terrified mounts, squealing and pitching, tore off with the rail before he could grab one. Hap, blocked by the straggle of shouting shapes running toward him, whirled to slam full-tilt into Bridwell, getting up groggily from where Kelly'd dropped him.

Both men went down in a racket of gunfire.

Kelly, desperate now, rolled back of the horse trough, came onto a knee, and firing over its rim, sent the howling pack diving for cover. He was up straightaway, plunging into the welcoming black between buildings.

"You damn fool!" Melanie cried, reaching out to lay hold of him. "Here—" she gasped, panting, thrusting reins over the hand still clamped to the bundle of bank notes, "get out of here quick!"

Kelly hauled in the horse, jabbed a boot in the stirrup and was gone in a thunder of hard-running hooves.

21

Because of the roundabout course he was forced to pursue to elude far-ranging units of the crew Bryce had hunting him, it was late afternoon before Hap sighted Don Ambrocio's headquarters. Twice after crossing onto Palominas range he was compelled to duck again, turned back on both occasions after he'd thought to have clear passage. The first time, coming up out of a wash, he had run point-blank into a trio of hard cases put on his trail by Murgatroyd's bounty. This surprise, being mutual, was all that had saved him. He had gone shearing off to the banging of carbines and used up most of an hour trying to shake them before wearily managing at last to get clear.

The second time, zeroing in from the west, he wasn't three miles from the headquarters buildings when two of the Palominas crew, waving arms from their lookout, hollered for him to join them. Dead tired on a mount that was just about finished, Hap climbed floundering up the hill to find out what they wanted. He wasn't thirty feet away when the suddenly grinning bigger one, jerking up the hand that had been hidden behind his leg, tried to blast Hap from the saddle. Only by rolling out of it, Apache style, did Kelly get under that lethal hail.

From flat on his back, reins locked in left fist, Hap fired under the horse. The man dropped from sight. Jumping up, Kelly plunged round the nervous animal just in time to see the man's scar-faced companion trying frantically to board a fractious skewbald mare.

"Better quit, Romero, while you're ahead."

Instead the man whirled to snap off a shot and Kelly countered, square between the eyes.

Hap leaped past his buckling shape—letting go of his own mount—grabbed the mare's reins and dug in his heels. She tried for all she was worth to get loose but Kelly hung on, and presently, trembling, eyes still wild, she let him come up to her.

When he reckoned the worst of her fright had

subsided Kelly tied her reins to a scraggly bush and went back to see what had become of the swarthy breed. He found him face down, unconscious but still a good way this side of the grave. It was the measure of Hap's mood that he considered giving him the "coo de grass"—the paisanos' name for what they did with unwanted prisoners.

He knew a hurt snake was twice as mean as a well one, but shaking his head at this latest example of the soft streak he had picked up from Ma, he took a knife and a single-action pistol off the man, kicked the carbine out of reach and went off to fetch the breed's browsing gelding. He roped the fellow belly-down across the saddle, then took the reins off the horse he'd got from Melanie and turned the animal loose.

Kelly climbed onto the mare without another look at the dead man. He set out for the ranch with the lead horse in tow. Both of these jaspers had been Rufino bootlickers and he kept a sharp watch lest others of their ilk succeed.

The afternoon sun was pretty low above the rimrocks when Hap and his entourage trekked into the home ranch yard. Except for the vaqueros' cook, and somebody possibly at the line of mud huts the old man had let the peons build for themselves, at this time of day there shouldn't have been anyone around to witness the arrival. But the way things had been going Hap was not too surprised to observe four of the majordomo's more favored partisans strategically posted at inconsequential tasks, looking round with hard stares as he stepped down and dropped rein.

"Que pasa, hombre?" the stocky favorite called, striding toward him while Hap rather curiously

considered their placement. The nearest of the four stood with a rifle at the casa's main gate while the farthest from Kelly lounged against a porch post in front of Rufino's quarters.

"And what are you doing here with old hens and roosters?" Hap asked insultingly. "The old man made a mozo out of you?"

The vaquero had the grace to flush. Then his widening eyes, passing over the mare, almost popped from their sockets when he got close enough to recognize the bloody freight lashed to the lead horse's saddle. "Jesus and Mary!" he gasped in shock.

"Yeah," Hap said grimly. "Weren't you supposed to be watching that border herd?"

The man snapped, "I do not work for you, gringo!"

"Well, by God, you do *now* if you stay on this place. Cut that pig loose an' look after him. *Andale— pronto!*"

Two of the other three were starting toward them as Hap, his bloodshot stare still pinned to the vaquero, said, "It could happen to *you,* man."

With a convulsive swallow and an obvious reluctance the big *paisano* got to work on the ropes. Kelly gave a last scorching look at the fellow, and headed for the majordomo's quarters in the little mud building that stood next to the barracks where the cowhands slept. Midway up the yard he passed the curious stare of the man who had been propping up the porch post. "Look after those *caballos,*" Hap growled and went on.

The mud building given over to Palominas' *segundo* had two rooms, the one off the porch fixed up as an office with a butt-scarred rolltop and a rickety wooden filing cabinet where the ranch ledgers customarily slept. The back room held nothing but the *chimayo*-covered cot and a miscellany of horse gear.

There was nobody in the office but the sounds muffled panting interspersed with grunts and groans drew Hap, narrow-eyed, to the sarape-shrouded arch. Thrusting aside the blanket Kelly stared with mixed feelings for perhaps half a minute before letting it drop with a look of disgust.

Backing off to the desk he called gruffly: "Rufino!" and the place went as still as though he stood in a vacuum.

"*Quien es?*" the man growled through sundry rustlings of garments.

Hap grimly said, "If you've got your clothes on, you better come out here."

Shoving the blanket roughly aside Rufino appeared, flushed of face, to demand angrily, "Has the sky fallen, gringo, that you—"

Hap said, fed up with a whole heap of things: "Couple items out here I think you ought to have a look at." He wheeled, dragged his spurs across the porch to strike off toward the now-swollen group circling the spotted mare and gelding. He was just as well pleased to see that both mounts were precisely where he'd left them.

Coming up to the group he sent one of the gaping peons to fetch the *patrón*, hustling the man on his way with a shove. Hap found the dark-faced *segundo* suspiciously eyeing the bulge in his shirt.

On the ground between horses the man Hap had packed in across the saddle, though still unconscious, was beginning to groan. A fiercer look suddenly narrowed the stare of the big majordomo. "*Que pasar?"* he growled, adding in English as the peons fell back to make way for Don Ambrocio, "What happened to this one?"

"Glad you asked that," Kelly said, nodding. "Seems he got in the way of a bullet—inspired, I suppose, by some of your spleen. Made the mistake of taking a few shots at me."

The boss Mexican's stare fanned out like spider legs, chucked a side look at the *patrón's* rigid face and loosed a harsh guffaw at so preposterous a tale.

But the old man, peering from one to the other of the restive mounts, said to Hap, "Pedro never put a leg across a mare. And what are you doing in that *Yanqui* hat?"

"In carrying out your orders, *señor*, I was compelled to make a few hurried decisions—"

"The *patrón* wants to know," Rufino broke in, "what Pedro was doing on that skewbald mare."

"He wasn't on the mare. That was your friend Romero—"

"And what has happened to Romero?" Don Ambrocio inquired.

"He was misled by the same evil companion that overtook Pedro—"

"You shot him, too?" Rufino said nastily.

"What would you do," Kelly asked the *patrón*, "if two men you'd placed on a hill to keep an eye on Murgatroyd's beef called to you urgently, and when you approached, never expecting such duplicity, tried to fill you full of holes? Certainly I shot them."

In a half strangled voice the majordomo snarled, "Anyone who'd believe this fornicating gringo—"

Hap's short laugh cut him off in mid-sentence. Pulling the bundle free of his shirt, Kelly's left hand roughly thrust it against the *hacendado's* chest. "You believe this don't you?"

Under climbing brows Don Ambrocio stared down his beak of a nose at the offending prod of that thick sheaf of currency. Before he could speak, Rufino, who knew the old man a lot better than Hap, asked in cold scorn, "Is this how a gringo buys indulgence?"

The quiet that followed this masterly stroke closed around Hap like the rise of a wall, block on block, holding him fast for the eagle's claws. But the old man, though his brows drew down above the darkened look of wrinkled cheeks, blew out a great sigh, and instead of demanding the expected explanation, peered thoughtfully at Hap.

"And now you have come for your reward, I suppose."

"Well, you said—" Hap began.

"I have a long memory," the ranchman assured him, rolling the cigar across his mustached mouth. "It reminds me there were two of these packets according to what I was led to believe. Where is the other?"

Kelly started to explain what he'd run into in town but the *patrón* cut him off with the look of a man who brooks no excuses. With his *rico's* stare bleakly rummaging the face of his hired *pistolero* he remarked with a smile that did not extend above his teeth, "The offer I made was based on two packets. Since you brought but the one I will do what I can with it; but even an hombre as ignorant as you could hardly expect a slice of Palominas for a job that, at best, was no more than half done. I suggest you get rid of that offensive hat and clean yourself up."

On this note, with a final hard stare, the master of Palominas, the bundle of bank notes tucked under an arm, strode off toward his casa.

22

With the incessant *chert-chert-chert-chert* of a builder bird mocking him, Kelly's livid face snapped around to survey the hard teeth so gleefully displayed by the malicious grin of Rufino. With the *patrón* not yet safely out of hearing the man kept his crowing carefully inside though his vast belly shook to each stifled guffaw.

He could not, however, quite resist a further jibe; and when Don Ambrocio passed beyond the *puerta* the big *segundo* gasped through his chuckles, "*Cuidado*, hombre! The promises of *ricos* are well suited to fools—as filled with wind as a sack of frijoles."

Kelly, crammed with his fury, grabbed up the reins of both horses and without looking back wheeled off toward the pens like a sore-backed bull.

In a towering rage he stripped off their gear, slammed it bitterly into the manure dust and put up the bars. Too mad to cuss, he stomped over to the cookshack and glared the *cocinero* into fixing him a meal. By the time he had got the whole plateful inside him, the last trace of his mood had been wiped from lean jaws.

Back at the corrals he roped out a fresh mount and kicked it into a lope as he rode out of the yard. Soon as he'd put a pair of tall hills behind him Kelly pointed the horse toward the place where Murgatroyd's cattle were turning the *patrón's* winter range into cow flops. With no room for a plan in his seething thoughts he reckoned he would hit on something!

A man didn't put in the kind of work he had to be fobbed off with the sort of gab that sonofabitch Ambrocio had handed him!

After that run-in he'd had with the pair he had posted to watch Bryce's herd, it was doubtful that anyone presently was keeping those critters under surveillance. With any kind of luck he could run the whole goddam bunch across the border.

And no questions asked! This kind of thing—on a less grand scale—was being done all the time. And it was one way—the quickest—of getting back some of his own.

Yes, lifting Bryce's herd held considerable merit from where Hap sat still nursing his wrath. Since Murgatroyd's bounty had all but given him the name, he might as well have the game to go with it. Sale of those cows would set him up with a stake—not so big a one maybe as he'd been led to hope for but good enough probably for a start someplace else.

There was nothing for him round here but a first-class chance to catch a fatal dose of lead poisoning!

And the theft of this herd, once Bryce knuckled down to paying that feed bill—with nobody smart enough to keep him in line—would damn sure put Don Ambrocio out of business. And in mighty short order.

The more Kelly pushed this notion around, the more he vengefully liked the look of it. Though he might lose a few, under cover of the not-too-far-away night he should by sunup have the great bulk of those critters within shouting distance of the

131

Mexican border. Not able to uncover any insurmount-able drawbacks, he did come up with a small bit of business that, so far at least as Bryce was concerned, should go quite a way toward speeding things up, besides hanging the responsibility squarely around that old skinflint's neck.

In pursuance of this Kelly tossed away his disreputable headgear to arrive bareheaded at the bottom of the hill where he sent up a call that, after he'd hallooed a couple more times, fetched a face into view to find out what he wanted.

Kelly shouted, "Come down here, goddammit!" He waited impatiently while the vaquero, afoot, scrambled over the rocks with a number of oaths not in everyday use. Kelly growled when the man had at last come up with him: "Any chance of the loan of your hat for a spell? Sun'll be up before I get to the ranch and with this color skin and no bonnet some damn fool might mistake me for one of them Texicans."

The fellow didn't exactly wriggle with enthusi-asm. So Hap dug up a peso, and when that didn't help, put a couple more with it, knowing there wasn't one of these buggers could long resist the talking power of cash in the hand. For a clincher he said, "I'll send it back with three more soon's I get there."

Having been caught up on the craziness of gringos the vaquero, more than content with an easy profit, was too smart to risk it by voicing any questions. He even volunteered the loan of his ragged blanket with its hole for the head. "To be sure no gun is turned on you, *señor*," he said gravely.

Kelly thanked him, pulling it over his ears, and put the sombrero with its blue Palominas chin string on his head and rode into the twilight's deepening shadows, not much pleased with this performance but not worried about it, either, to pass up the chance of compounding his treachery if the word trickling back stood to wrap Bryce more bloodthirstily round that old sonofabitch's skinny throat.

So why not, he decided half an hour later, twist every twig he could use to that purpose? If he could just get this thing set up right the resultant clashing confrontation might well rid the range of both those bastards—Don Ambrocio *and* Bryce too!

Revenge being sweet, Hap reckoned it worth however much risk and bother it put him to. Accordingly he revised somewhat his previous intention. He wheeled the horse at a jog toward the black line of hills along the Riachuelo Granito where he picked up the pair of copper-faced riders he had left there to send up a smoke if Bryce and his Texicans attempted to cross.

"We're moving that herd," he told these two brusquely. "The old man wants them sold into Mexico," and watched startled looks change into pleased grins. "In his hurry, however," Hap went on glibly, "the *patrón* forgot to mention where we should take them."

He let this sink in, then appealed to their vanity. "Either of you know of anyone over there who will give hard cash an' keep his mouth shut?"

He watched the exchange of swift questioning glances. Then "Don Cipriano Valdez," they said almost in unison.

"Is he a friend of the *patrón's?*"

They appeared rather dubious. The taller one said, "This one lets nothing stand in the way of a profit."

Good enough," Hap nodded. *"Andale,* hombres—

let's get whackin'!"

They took Bryce's herd across the border in the first gray light which heralds the sun's trek across southwestern skies. Both Hap's helpers wore the blue chin strings identifying them as men from Palominas and any time lost in fetching them was more than made up by the increased ease and speed of pushing these bawling lumbering brutes beyond any chance Bryce had of reclaiming them.

While Kelly and the other hombre held the cattle in a brush-fringed draw three miles south of the line, the taller vaquero—by name Gallego—rode on ahead to contact the man who would set up the deal.

A purple dusk was closing over their holding ground when through the raucous bawling of the restive herd, which had been twelve hours now away from water, Kelly heard the faint rumor of approaching horsemen. And reached for his rifle.

He hadn't risked a fire, and having been all day with nothing in his belly, he was in a frame of mind to shoot first and talk later when he caught his first look at the oncoming riders. There were only two. Hap could see soon enough the first of this pair was Gallego, followed by a narrow-eyed hatched-faced breed Hap wouldn't have trusted half as far as he could throw him.

As the pair drew nearer he could see this fellow sizing up the herd. With a rifle pointing groundward in the grip of right fist, Hap exchanged a civil greeting as the two pulled up before him.

Gallego said, "Señor, this is Pepe Cano, an acquaintance of Don Cipriano. I have his assurance the arrangement is made."

Cano grinned when Hap, nodding, asked if he

had brought the cash.

"No, *señor*. The price is arranged; the money counted. I will put it into your hands when these *vacas* are delivered satisfactorily at Tres Pinos."

"And where is that?"

"My headquarters. A village five *millas* from this place."

"Ha ha," Kelly said, not even pretending to smile. "I was not born yesterday either, amigo—and hold that horse still or I will give him something to fart about." He tipped up the Henry's snout. "These cows didn't swap the United States for Mexico to change hands on your terms."

"If they like it so well, why don't they return?"

"A real card," Kelly said to Gallego. "Does he know I'm a shoot-first talk-later?"

Cano sneered. "You speak very strong for a man without friends in this country."

"You come here to buy cattle or just exercise your jaw?"

The fellow said darkly, "I could take these *vacas*—"

"You could try."

Cano's eyes shone unpleasantly.

Hap got a fistful of cartridges from a pocket, held them out for the other to look at. "These wait on you, amigo. Better make up your mind for there are some among them not as patient as myself."

Gallego looked about to fill his pants but the man from Tres Pinos abruptly said, "Very well. If you will not put this herd where I want it, find yourself another buyer."

"Who needs your help? This Valdez," Hap scoffed, "will buy as quick from me as he would from you."

"Perhaps. If you can find him."

135

"I will wait six hours for you to fetch the money. In hard cash, hombre. United States dollars."

"Nothing was said about—"

"The rules have been changed. Bring two men only. If I see more there'll be a gnashin' of teeth an' considerable wailin' back where you come from. Ride with God, Cano."

23

After the man who had been swallowed up in the dusk was out of hearing, Gallego sat batting his eyes and shivering as though feeling the need of a hole to crawl into. "Was that wise, *señor?*" he plaintively asked, twisting about to peer after the fellow.

Kelly said, laughing shortly, "There is only one way to play cards with a bandit. Act like you got a whole army behind you an' try to keep one jump ahead of him. He'll be back, never fret."

Those cheerful words did not greatly appear to improve the man's outlook but the churn of Hap's thoughts had already left him. "Watch the cows," he bade, and swung into the saddle. "We're movin' this herd soon as I get back."

He rode east at a lope, hat pulled low and eyes watchful, knowing those critters had to have water. They would bawl all night if he didn't find some. What wind was still blowing came out of the west and had there been any streams near enough over there the cattle would have made the fact manifest.

Three-quarters of an hour later with the moon coming up he cut the horse south with an uneasy mind. If he failed to find what he was looking for he could hardly hope to gain very much by shifting the herd to another location. Cano would track them down by their racket and lose him all chance of surprising the fellow and any crew fetched with him.

For all Hap's bold talk it didn't appear likely the man would return without bringing enough hands to get the job done. So the only berry still left in Hap's bucket would be to push on and try to sell these critters elsewhere. He couldn't see much hope of getting far enough off with a herd of this size to escape Cano's clutches.

He could abandon the herd, but all the work he'd put in would be for nothing. He would still have the satisfaction of working his spite off on Don Ambrocio and Murgatroyd, but without the stake he'd been after merely getting back at that pair was poor consolation. Being flat broke in Mexico, an obvious Anglo was not a fate he would wish on a dog.

Too riled to turn back he kneed his mount west but the horse refused to answer the signal. Kelly mean-mindedly fetched him a clout in the ribs with a spur but the stubborn brute, clamping teeth round the bit, surged on straight ahead, never changing direction by so much as an inch.

Kelly, swearing, half lifted his fist, then suddenly curious, let the horse have its head and five minutes later, cresting a ridge, looked down on a tank shimmering wet in the moonshine. He had to stare twice at the mill to believe it. But there it was beside a dug tank that was big as a pond and not one building anyplace in sight.

When the horse put his head down Hap got off and tried the water himself. Then he filled his canteen, pouring out the old dregs, climbed back in the saddle and hauled the horse away from it.

By his reckoning Bryce's cattle should be due northwest about an hour from this tank, and shoving the horse into a lope, he attempted to gauge how much leeway he could count on for getting the herd moved before Cano could round up his gang and get back there.

Of course the man, with a far better knowledge of this region, would probably guess straightaway when he found the herd gone where Hap was bound for. But this couldn't be helped. Main thing right now was to get the cows moved.

He could see, though, that any plans shaped up to surprise Cano back there where the herd was now would have to be scrapped. That shifty-eyed breed would be damn well alerted before this bunch ever got within range, warned by the sure-to-be-noticed complete lack of sound. Hap would have to find some way of handling him differently. He began thinking about the terrain round that tank.

His own approach had been up a talus slope but Cano's *bandidos* would come down most likely out of the north, or maybe northeast, the way Hap was headed right now. And the going this way was pretty much the same; that water was in a shallow basin or pocket with hills dropping off—as he recalled—on three sides. What the fourth side was like he couldn't remember. The smart thing, anyway, would be to set up a first line of defense farther out.

So he looked round, examining his surroundings with more attention to physical characteristics which might lend themselves to the sort of tactic he had in mind. He wasn't aiming exactly to wipe out Cano; he'd be just as well suited to setting an example from which he could deal on terms guaranteed to insure that there would be no hang-up to prevent his leaving with loaded pockets.

Time all the brutes had wet their whistles and been settled round the windmill tank the overcast morning was well on its first lap toward straight-up noon. Since it wasn't too probable that the critters would stray, considering the way they had been hustled over here, Hap and the other Palominas vaquero wheeled tired mounts and rode out of the pocket to head back toward where they had dropped off Gallego.

At the mouth of a stony barranca they'd left him with orders to slow up Cano if he showed, to at any rate set up enough of a racket to give them some warning of the bandit's approach. Since they'd heard no commotion at all, Hap had reasonably supposed he'd seen nothing to shoot at. But now, peering round with no answer forthcoming to Hap's lifted hail, as they neared the gray rocks of this steep-sided ravine Kelly felt the first stab of an uneasy hunch.

He pulled up, with the scowling Ramirez beside him, and scanned the sign left by their earlier passage. He found, as half feared, an overlay of shod hooves almost certainly left not a half hour ago.

Ramirez got down to examine these closer, and hunkered on boot heels, looked up to say, "Maybe fifteen minutes."

"How many?"

"Six, maybe seven."

"Riding hard?"

"No, *señor*. *Poco* careful. These Cano, I theenk, she ees one damn smart coyote."

"Yeah," Kelly said, darkly eyeing the barranca. "Seem funny to you we didn't hear any gun sound?"

The man stared at him, silent, then lifted shoulders in the shrug, typically Mexican, of one who knows when to keep the mouth shut.

Kelly knew what he'd most likely find. Studying the ground, he kneed his mount into the mouth of the ravine, then wheeled the horse sharply to say explosively, "The sonofabitch ran out on us, Taco!"

Ramirez nodded. Climbed back in the saddle. "*Gallina,*" he grunted with a shake of the head. "No backbone." He waited with the patience of a man who takes orders.

"We've lost the herd," Kelly finally said flatly, and sat a long moment with the boil of his thoughts. He scrubbed the back of a hand across whiskery cheeks. "*Adios,* amigo. You better take word of this back to the *patrón.*"

"And you?"

"I've a bit of unfinished business down here."

24

Kelly headed toward the basin where the cattle had been left. He twisted round on the leather after a couple dozen strides to find the vaquero riding his wake.

"You forget where the ranch is, Taco?"

Ramirez shrugged.

"You figure to be a goddam hero or somethin'?"

The Mexican grinned around the brown-paper cigarette he'd just lighted. "No, *señor*—I leave that for you, the paid *pistolero.*"

"Go on. *Irse, marcharse!* Clear out," Hap growled at him.

"I have much hunger. When we come to the *vacas*—"

"When we come to the cows there will be the bullets."

"And after the bullets the *maletas*," Ramirez said, blowing smoke. "Even a dog should have a bone he can gnaw."

Kelly dug in his pocket. "Here is your bone." He held out a gold eagle.

Ignoring the coin Ramirez looked a long time in his face. Kelly said grimly, "There is a little time yet if you hurry, man. Use it."

"You think they weel not be watching for you?"

"They'll be watching."

"But not at Bodega."

"Wine cellar? What have you put in that *cigarro*, hombre?"

"Is waterhole, *señor*."

"They've already watered."

"But in ten *millas?*"

"They go so far?"

"The place of Don Cipriano is more—*poco mas.*"

"What makes you so sure a feller slippery as Cano has to deal—"

"He has the power, *señor*. In all of Sonora there is no other *rico* so grand. Don Cipriano stands next to the *gobernador*. Could buy him and sell him like basket of feesh."

"If he's that big a mogul why would he want to buy a few hundred *vacas?*"

"You don't know that everything is bought? Is Mexico, hombre!"

Well, Kelly thought, it figured. A boundary didn't make much difference in people. Take Cain or

141

Pilate. The galoots that got ahead in this world were those most busy looking after themselves.

"All right," he grumbled. "Which way—can you find it?"

It was south, of course, but more to the east than where they had left Bryce Murgatroyd's herd. Even on tired horses they had little trouble reaching Bodega well ahead of the cattle. It wasn't any great shucks of a place, just a handful of typical boxlike houses built of mud bricks around a tank fed by springs, a country store and the inevitable cantina. Hens and pigs roved the dust-yellow length of the hundred-yard street. Hap, at a guess, put down the two-footed year-around population—even counting kids—at something under thirty. He didn't see anything like that many.

After a first startled stare the curious few drawn out-of-doors by the spectacle of strangers found urgent chores that took them out of sight *muy* pronto. The only adult male bold enough to stand his ground and grunt back at the be-pistoled pair was the one-eyed cotton-pantalooned dispenser of liquid joy. And even this gruff citizen appeared somewhat less than happy to serve them.

Having cut the thickest of the dust from his gullet Hap left Ramirez to keep an eye on the fellow during preparation of the promised meal, stepping again outside to see how this situation might be shaped to advantage.

To meet Cano's outfit of cutthroats on anything resembling legal terms would be deliberate suicide. Kelly was not swayed by thoughts of fair play. Nor was he any longer very much interested in retrieving the herd. He reckoned, even though the fellow had probably aimed from the first to take over this godsend the cheapest way possible, he had doubtless fetched along at least a portion of the price demanded; and Hap imagined these pesos, if they weren't on his person, would still be somewhere about his horse.

Now the first thing he'd look for while the bulk of his crew were taking care of the cattle would be something to wash the dust out of his system, and to that end would likely come to the cantina.

Satisfied, Kelly rejoined his companion. They probably still had plenty of time but to be certain he loudly demanded, "Where the hell is that grub!"

The one-eyed proprietor poked his head through the ragged sarape that separated barroom from his quarters at the rear. "*Immediatamente,*" he called. "Be there in just a minute."

And true to his word he came bustling in, both arms loaded with smoking dishes. No sooner had he set these down on the table with eating tools beside them than Hap—wasting no breath on gab dressed up in polite embroidery—demanded brusquely, "Feed our *caballos* and see that they're watered—at once, *comprender?* With oats!" he growled when the man bobbed his head. "And get them off that street. I want 'em ready to go at the back door of this place uno quarta hora."

"In fifteen minutes," Ramirez said after him, slapping significantly the scarred stock of his carbine.

In a fraction of this time both had emptied their plates, washing down the fiery Mexican food with warm bottled beer. "Go take a look," Kelly grumbled at Ramirez, himself getting up to peer over the batwings.

The late afternoon sky still looked like slate, the

143

cloud cover thickest—a bleak leaden gray darkening rapidly, in the south; and a gusty wind had come up again out of that quarter, pungent with the smell of wet greasewood and the rain that Hap reckoned would soon be upon them.

There was no one in sight—even the kids they had seen were gone now, most likely pulled off the street by anxious mothers; but beyond the stock pens a low wavering smudge of dust hung in tatters like smoke against the blackening horizon. And this, Kelly reckoned, would be Cano's outfit harrying that herd to get under cover ahead of the rain.

In the turbulent whirl of racing thoughts one worry cried out above all others. He must not this time overlook anything. One mistake with this bunch could damn well be his last!

He went out through the kitchen, finding Ramirez at a shedlike addition to the back of the place supervising the care of their transport. While the unsaddled horses were chomping the grain in their nosebags the patch-faced proprietor was busily applying currycomb and brush.

"I'll stay with this one," Kelly told Taco. "Get onto the roof with that carbine and make sure none of that crew when they get here follow our friend away from them pens."

Ramirez departed.

Kelly said, speaking loud to be sure the man understood, "Get the saddles back on and screw them down tight." When this was done and painstakingly tested he caught up the reins, leading both horses to the cantina's back door where he tied them with slip knots. Afterward he led the one-eyed owner into the barroom where it was roughly made certain the man had no weapon before Hap appropriated the cut-down shotgun shelved back of the bar.

"Now a piece of advice," he said bleakly. "We're waitin' on a feller that's going to come in here— a *ladrón* with a bunch of stole cattle. If you put any store on stayin' in the quick you'll keep your nose out of this—savvy?"

"*Sí, señor.*"

"Make sure you remember it. Now get over against that far wall and stay there."

The first big drops were already pelting the rusted tin of the roof when he strode with the shotgun to where he could observe the corrals across the louvered swing doors. The oncoming herd wasn't at this moment more than a quarter of a mile from the pens.

Hap settled himself out of sight from the street to wait with whatever patience he could, as near to praying as he ever had been.

In his head he went over the possibilities again and hoped to hell he had figured this right. If Cano wasn't a drinking man he probably wouldn't have come within reach, in which case Hap would have to try something else or pass up what thin hope he still had of getting hands on a stake. He was too damn old to build one up now from scratch—a man got old pretty fast in this country. And them as didn't watch out could stay a long time dead!

The approaching downpour was still piddling round in a hit-or-miss fashion when those riders out yonder began to cramp the herd into a more malleable shape preparatory to funneling it into the pens. Almost as though this were a signal the storm broke with full force and through the windblown sheets of pummeling water one chinstrapped rider, intermittently seen, tore loose of the rest and came barreling low-bent straight for Hap's setup.

25

Hap stepped back against the bar where he could watch, grim as death, both the half-leaf doors and the black-patched proprietor hugging himself as though expecting any moment to have the place fall in on him.

In Hap's sweating hands both hammers of the shotgun were back at full cock when the sound of hooves was heard through the drumming of that wind-driven rain. These skidded to a stop. Booted feet hit the porch, the swing doors burst open. A burly shape dripping water came slamming through half blinded to freeze suddenly staring incredibly, split seconds before the blast of the sawed-off drove him, spinning grotesquely, off his feet in a crumpling fall.

With a bleat of terror the cantina's black-patched owner raised a shaking hand to cross himself as Kelly, mute with shock, peered unbelievingly at that huddled shape on the barroom floor; then, cursing, eased down the hammer on the unfired second shell, eyes looking like holes burnt through a bed sheet.

"Sonofabitch!"

This wasn't Cano—*it was no one he'd ever seen before.*

Still swearing he stepped round the man to rake with black glance through the pounding rain the rope-swinging horsebackers filtering Murgatroyd's hijacked herd onto those cedar-post pens. It was begging a miracle to hope or imagine the shotgun's blast had gone completely unnoticed; yet none of the riders, glimpsed through that wind-harried downpour of water, appeared to have been deflected from the task in hand. There was nobody coming, or even peering, this way.

Kelly's look dug into the man against the wall. "Know this feller?"

The man nodded sullenly.

"Well? For Chrissake who is he?"

"Don Fulano. *Segundo* for Don Cipriano Valdez."

Kelly chewed at a lip, staring down at the man. He had been so sure—and so goddam wrong! Had this worked out the way he had figured, Hap had never intended to go north again. It made no difference why this Don Fulano had chosen to accompany the ragtag crew who'd made off with that herd. As the emissary and spokesman of Don Cipriano the facts of his death now made it impossible for Kelly to remain in this country. The man's *patrón*—this influential buyer of stolen cattle, regardless of profit or any other consideration—could not afford to leave the killer unpunished.

Hap had got this far in assessing the situation when hoof sound again hauled his glance toward the doors. With the lips peeled off his teeth he crouched in his tracks above the single-loaded barrel. When the horse stopped outside, Kelly pulled back the hammer, butt against hip, eyes adamant as agate as he waited, sweating, for a target.

The man outside stepped onto the porch but instead of coming in backed off abruptly. On his way through the batwings Hap heard the horse grunt as the man leaped aboard, and almost at once heard the hard thudding of hooves. The slam of a carbine—even as Kelly was lifting the sawed-off—slewed Cano round and he gasped a thin cry and fell out of the saddle.

The horse ran on, covered stirrups whacking its flanks, bound with that telltale empty hull straight for the crew penning Murgatroyd's cattle.

Faced with a terrible choice, Kelly fired bitterly, saw the horse go down, and cursing, ran after it, pushed by the need of getting hands on the money which had driven him into this bind.

Three men at the pens jerked round to stare as Kelly dropped the now useless weapon and bent over the horse to snarl at discovering no saddlebags on it. Above the rain and the racket of bawling cattle he heard the harsh shouts, saw two horsebackers wheel to come pounding toward him. From the roof Taco fired and the nearer went cartwheeling to the ground. Passing Cano's sprawled shape Kelly drived through the batwings.

The one-eyed proprietor was nowhere in evidence as Hap, heavily breathing, bent over Fulano to turn out the man's pockets with no better luck. Snarling—almost crazed with impatience—he ripped open the man's shirt and found his reward in the money belt snugly strapped underneath it. Feverishly jerking the repository free, Kelly ran through the kitchen and out the back door to find Ramirez, mounted, hanging onto his horse. Hap caught the thrown reins, flung himself into leather. Both horses took off at a hard pounding run.

"Where to?" Ramirez yelled.

"Palominas!" Kelly answered, face still twisted with fury.

All of this work, this damn riding and risk—and the mockery of being forced, if they were slick enough to make it, back into country where there was bounty on his head—made Hap frantic. And the real brassbound irony banging through his anger was the suspicion—sparked by the feel and weight of the belt inside his shirt—the whole bloody lot had been gone through for nothing!

A dangerous frame of mind. And Hap knew it. What he ought to have done, said the clarity of hindsight, was to have taken off with the bundle he'd got from that safe. If he'd lit out with that instead of St. Bernarding it back to that conniving old man he'd have been well ahead of anything he'd likely get out of this now. If he *got* out!

Wild as he was—and despite the frustrations which kept his blood boiling—it wasn't long before he was noticing the covert looks his companion kept slanching at the lumpy place in the back of his shirt.

Beginning now both to think and react like the outlaw Bryce had cunningly named him, Kelly told himself that whatever was in that belt he had damn well earned. Wasn't heavy enough to be much of a stake, but if Ramirez thought he'd any part of it coming he was in for a sure enough nasty surprise!

He said, thrusting a finger up into the wind: "You want to scoot on ahead an' break the news to him?"

Ramirez, a bit dubious, scowled. "You mean . . . the *patrón?*"

"You ain't afraid of him are you?"

The Mexican, shrugging, did not commit himself. He asked, instead, plaintively, "What did you take from Fulano back there?"

Soaked and shivering from the cold gusts of wind, Hap let his horse drop into a walk while his stare

149

swept the black weeping clouds overhead. Off west a ways, maybe four miles, he saw a stretch where stars were beginning to show through. "You been a help," he said dryly, "but not that much, friend," and eyed the man darkly till Ramirez, spreading his hands, let his glance drop away.

But it lay there between them, contentious as a bone between two stray dogs. And it wasn't a thing passing time would improve. Hap foresaw that it would keep working on Taco, building up in his head an unforgettable affront, gnawing at pride like the teeth of a rat.

The time to take care of the man was right now; all his experience told Kelly this. But that soft streak wouldn't quite let the wildness inside Hap take over.

He jerked out his pistol, jammed his mount against Ramirez. But instead of blasting a hole through the fellow Kelly salved his conscience by whacking the surprised vaquero an arm-numbing clip across the right shoulder.

Ramirez' carbine fell out of his hands. The sound of its clatter among the rocks down the canyonside came metallically back through the drip and drone of the slackening rain.

"Get down," Hap said gruffly, reaching out to clamp hold of the other horse's cheekstrap. "Do yourself a favor and be a little careful."

With a black hateful look Ramirez reluctantly got out of the saddle.

Letting his grip slide along to catch hold of the reins Kelly said, grimly earnest, "If I see you again it's goin' to be just too bad, hombre," and rode off, heading north, with the man's horse in tow.

Hap berated himself through the next several minutes for seven kinds of a fool, yet felt better in the part of his head Ma controlled. Considering the risks he even felt a little virtuous about it. Whatever ultimate fate overtook Ramirez now was Taco's own responsibility. It was not a heap likely their trails would cross again. It even gave Hap an advantage because now, if he were forced to lay up a spell at Palominas, he could tell Don Ambrocio any tale he liked. And the loss of that herd was sure to make the old fool too dependent on Hap's pistol to put up much of a squawk at his return.

If he could just get back across the border in one piece, Hap reckoned he had it made.

26

It was a bright crisp morning with the air swept clean and the sun not yet even one hour high when Kelly rode out of the Mexican hills and sat his mount to scan with satisfaction the sparkling appearance of the flats stretched out before him. He had already put the international boundary safely behind. It seemed prudent now to cut loose of Taco's horse, for any man in this country traveling with two horses would almost certainly stir undesirable speculation.

To this end he got out of Ramirez' saddle and climbed aboard his own. Having chased Taco's horse a couple of rope lengths off with a few pitched stones to stand on dropped reins, Hap set out across the flats at a leisurely jog that was considerably more alert than his manner suggested.

He had not yet taken time to have a look inside the belt he had ripped off Fulano and which he now wore strapped, unnoticeably, next his skin. Hap was extremely reluctant to find just how little he suspected was in it.

Long as he didn't brashly set out to count, he could always keep hoping the fellow'd fetched along enough to set a man up in the bottled-goods business. Hap had damn well reckoned soon as he'd hefted it that the belt lacked considerable of being the stake he'd played for. Better to have taken Murgatroyd's bribe and got straight out of the country. Because with two thousand dollars U.S. a man could buy a little security.

Which brought his mind around to Don Ambrocio again and the slick way that liar had sluffed him back into the hired-hand category after all that gab about making him a partner!

Kelly, swearing under his breath, told himself that this wasn't finished yet. With Bryce even more determined now, the price of Hap's services was due to go up, and then up some more with compound interest. He still had a few shots left in the locker! When a man gets to scraping the bottom of the barrel he can't hardly go anyplace but up. And if he played his cards right he might even wind up *owning* Palominas!

Hap wasn't fool enough to honestly believe that, but like whistling in the dark, it made a chummy sound and he was at the point now where almost any sound that wasn't hostile could be counted as a comfort.

It was nearing eight by the sail of the sun when the gelding fetched Kelly onto the ridge from which he'd figured to sight the nearest of the high points he'd spent a whole night toting men and brush to.

He could see it, all right. And by standing in the oxbows, he could glimpse the bald top of Apache

Leap butte. It was nothing he saw that put the frown round his eyes; it was the complete absence of any evidence of smoke which put a cold tingling across the nape of his neck. The orders he'd given had been plenty explicit. At first sign of an approach from hostile holdings—even dust if it appeared stirred by horses—the man who saw it was to send up smoke.

Perhaps those boneheads reckoned one rider no fit cause for alarm. Yet this spur was part of Bryce's range. Had Rufino, he wondered, pulled all hands off these spy posts again regardless of Don Ambrocio's censure?

It was odd, too, Hap thought, that he hadn't run across any fresh tracks this morning. You'd have figured Bryce too cagey not to have at least one man in this vicinity, if only to keep tabs on current activity. He had a pretty stiff stake in those cattle Hap had lifted.

The more he wooled this around in his head, the more convinced Kelly became that news of Hap's exploit—at least word that the herd was no longer in these parts—had reached Bryce already.

He kicked the horse into a run, recollecting a few things he should have thought of sooner. If Bryce knew the herd was gone he wouldn't be sitting round twiddling his fingers.

Within half a mile of the place he'd been aiming for, Hap saw the buzzards and pulled up with a curse. No need to check on that pair!

He pointed the gelding straight for headquarters, and ten minutes later came into the first sample of Bryce's revenge. Murgatroyd's outfit had been here ahead of him, and far as he could see, this whole end of Palominas was shot, burned black in a fire that had utterly destroyed every scrap of forage—

grass, trees, everything was gone! And mighty damn recent he discovered an hour later when he came to the place where last night's storm had probably put an end to the fire.

There were tracks here—plenty—where Murgatroyd's Texicans, following the flames, had gone pushing on toward the old man's headquarters.

Hap still had six to eight miles to cover and kept his eyes skinned sharp, having no wish to blunder into that bunch. Three-quarters of an hour later he pealed both ears as well, edgily alert for any rumor of firearms, pulling the horse down to little better than a walk, watchfully rummaging each patch of shadow, every clump of trees offering even the vaguest possibility of ambush. He watched for dust, and smoke as well, and so came finally without seeing either to the last lift of land between himself and the Palominas home ranch.

No smell of smoke was here apparent, nor sound of shooting. Whatever had come of Murgatroyd's raid was probably past history, one way or another, but a man in Hap's boots could not afford to get careless, he reminded himself bleakly.

He maneuvered his way toward high ground, patently reluctant to have a look at what Bryce's crew had done here last night, grimly recognizing that this might be a lull with the old man's home place still beleaguered. But if this were true, it occurred to him presently, there'd pretty certainly be some of Murgatroyd's bunch holed up on the crest, if only to make sure no one got through.

Kelly couldn't think where any help would come from but this did not lessen his vigilance one whit. He did not feel any hankering to be numbered among the casualties, as he could be mighty quick if

Bryce and Company had not yet pulled out.

He got off the horse, and leaving him tied to a wisp of rabbit brush, began working his way from bush to bush until he got to where it became at once evident there was no one staked out among the stunted growth that fringed the ridgetop. And from what he could see of Don Ambrocio's headquarters, whatever had happened here was already over.

Six of the old man's vaqueros were moving about the yard in plain sight, two of them sporting bandages, all of them armed but disporting themselves with much of the exuberance one suspects the Concord farmers to have shown after chasing the redcoats off their bridge.

Hap considered the scene with mixed emotions, among which joy wore a jaundiced face. The cockiness exhibited by those Palominas cow prodders hardly suggested the prodigal's return was likely to be greeted by passed-around pieces of the fatted calf.

At least he wouldn't have Bryce to contend with, and guessed he should be able to cope with the old man if he could get to the bugger without being salivated by one of these clowns. He went back to his horse and swung into leather.

He glimpsed turning heads as he came off the ridge and did not catch one friendly hail. Coming into the yard he schooled his face to ignore scowling looks and had almost reached the casa's great gate when Tiodosa slipped through it to stop short at sight of him.

One would hardly have pictured past pleasures shared if judged by curled lip or the cut of her glance. He saw fresh bullet scars in the chipped plaster back of her and made no move to pull off the

155

chin-stringed hat he had bought for three pesos. "So!" she said in a hard, crusty tone. "You've decided to come back now that we've succeeded in driving off that rabble!"

He wondered, considering the hateful look on that face, how he could have been fool enough to have imagined she'd ever cared anything about him. But he dredged up a grin. "Is the *patrón* available?"

Hastening steps in the passage fetched the old man in view, the scowling *segundo* appearing behind him. "Kelly!" Don Ambrocio exclaimed, staring up at him. "Get down, man—get down."

"I dunno," Kelly said through the girl's hostile silence. "You seem to have got on well enough without me—"

The old man chopped that off with a snort. "We live by the grace of God," he cried, beaming. "Only the divine intervention of his saints—but enough of us! Tell me of the cattle, Jank. Did you make a good deal—did you fetch back the money?"

Kelly showed a dour face. "We were set upon by bandits. Right after we crossed the herd into Mexico. Gallego claimed to know of a man who would take the whole lot, one Don Cipriano— a *rico*, he said—and rode off to arrange this.

"He returned with a shifty-eyed weasel who called himself Cano. This *ladrón* wished the vacas delivered to his village, but having been around a fortnight or two, I refused to agree. Wanting to get you the best deal I could I insisted on *Yanqui* dollars; and when he went away, presumably to fetch them, I moved the herd, leaving Gallego to wait for him.

"Gallego, obviously knowing him better than I, disappeared."

"He has not come here," Rufino growled, scowling.

"Only his horse, eh?" Kelly said, pointing his chin toward the pens across the yard.

Don Ambrocio, attempting to get over this, snapped with some impatience: "And then? You spoke of *bandidos*, Jank—tell me about this."

"One big hombre and Cano—Taco named him Fulano—overtook us with an army of horsemen in the middle of the night. A great storm was on us. We lost the whole herd—"

"You came here to tell me that?"

"No," Hap said flatly. "I came back here for my wages."

A considerable silence closed down around Kelly, highly charged like the quiet that precedes tumultuous thunder.

"Where is Ramirez?" Rufino asked gruffly.

A very sticky question if by some chance—like Gallego's horse—the fellow had turned up here ahead of him.

Hap spread his hands in a Mexican shrug. *"Quién sabe?* I was almighty lucky to get clear myself."

"You are not clear yet," Tiodosa said.

27

Blackest hair, whitest teeth and the pear-shaped breasts so snug to his hands in visions called up from the backlog of memory had little to do with that face glaring back at him. Wheeling round on her father with fierce tones she cried, "Have we not already had enough of his lies?"

And Rufino, grumbling behind her, tucked in his two-bits worth to remind the *patrón*, "this is not the way Gallego has told it."

Don Ambrocio, peering from one to the other, like a hectored bull, blew out his cheeks, shouting, "*Bastar*—enough! I am master of this place!" and to Hap, "I make you welcome, Jank. My house is yours—"

"I don't want your house," Kelly said, cold-jawed. "All I want is the wages owed me. Now—*muy* pronto."

The old man shook his head. "I cannot do this. The money you brought was paid to the bank. But if you will stay," he said, not quite pleading but patently desperate, "and take charge of this ranch I will make you not only *segundo*"—looking hard at Rufino—"but partner besides."

Shifting round in the saddle Kelly hardened his heart. "I've heard the wind-making racket before."

"Jank, I swear it! As God hears my voice I will write you a paper!"

Kelly pawed stubbled jaws. Bryce must have hurt them worse than it looked for the old coot to go that far. And he could not deny it was some satisfaction to see the black fury on Rufino's cheeks and the disbelieving stare Tiodosa could not hide.

"Write it now," he said gruffly—"in *duplicate.*" The *segundo* stomped away in a passion as Hap stepped from the saddle to follow the *patrón* through the passage and across the flagged patio toward the old man's office.

Behind his desk Don Ambrocio picked up a quill and scratched away on handmade paper embossed with the heraldic device of his family. When this was finished he wrote out another.

"You are mad!" the girl cried, reading over his shoulder.

158

"Pito!" he called, and a mozo came running to knuckle his forelock.

Tiodosa, bending over her father, tried to get at the papers but he shoved her impatiently out of their reach. He said to the servant, "You are here to witness a bequeath I've just made—"

"Pay no mind to him, Pito! He is out of his head!" the girl cried.

Her father peered at her grimly. "Will you sign this?"

"Do I look such a fool!"

Again lifting the quill Don Ambrocio penned an addition to both papers. "Pito, call my vaqueros. And my daughter, Carmencita." To Hap he said quietly, "Will this stand in your courts?"

"With a half a dozen signatures I'll chance it."

The servant came back with the *patrón's* youngest offspring, four of his cowboys filing in behind her to stand, hats in hand, to wait on his pleasure. Much less assured than her sister—or quicker to grasp where her best interests lay—Carmen with no sign of astonishment solemnly watched her father's wrinkled old face, never once straying to the cold-jawed look of his hired *pistolero*.

"I have brought you all here," Don Ambrocio told them, "to know my intention and to bear witness to it." He read aloud what he'd written: "Being in poor health but sound mind I hereby depose and intend, for all who may read or hear of it to know, that Hap Kelly, an Anglo, is today named *segundo* of Hacienda Palominas; this in reward of services rendered. I further state and do testify that of this date and henceforward for as long as I shall live this man shall have a one-half interest in all my property and chattels—including cattle and horses—and same shall

159

be his to have and to hold. Should Hacienda Palominas still be enjoying the concern and fruits of this man's labors at the time of my demise, then and in that event all my holdings shall be divided equally between this loyal man and my beloved dutiful daughter Carmen Elodia de Ibarra y Zámora."

Glancing up from the paper to consider in turn each of his listeners Don Ambrocio asked, "Is this understood?"

Fingers curled like claws, ashen-faced with shock, Tiodosa sprang from her chair to confront the old man with blazing eyes. "You cannot do this to me!"

"It is done," the *patrón* said, and signed his name with a flourish.

On her twisted face was the look of venom incarnate as she spun in a whisper of rustling skirts to rush from the room as one blind in the grip of an all too obvious fury.

Don Ambrocio said to Carmencita, "And you, my daughter, shall be first to put your name under mine."

Carmen, taking the quill did as directed while the assembled vaqueros stood like posts in a stillness only disturbed by the sound of the pen.

After all had affixed their marks to both papers opposite the names he had written down for them, and had silently departed with never a lift of their eyes toward Hap, Don Ambrocio held out the top sheet to Kelly who, folding it, stuffed the crackling thing into a pocket.

"Okay," he growled as one given his due, "I better know just how bad Bryce has hurt us."

The old man sighed. "Pretty bad. We're not much hurt here, but after we drove them away from the casa where we had the advantage they set fire to the range and have probably destroyed both line camps. I've not had the chance to make sure of this but it's not unreasonable to suppose, in departing, they also made off with many of our cows."

Kelly nodded. It figured. "How many hands we got left that can still use a rifle an' stay in the saddle?"

"Five here, I think. At the line camps . . ." He shrugged. "None, probably."

"I'd better find out an' go after them cattle."

When the old man said nothing Hap spoke again. "Meantime I'll go look up Loco an' give him his walking papers—"

"No." Shoving his chair back Don Ambrocio looked straight at Hap. "Leave him alone. He can't bother you now."

"I won't have the man round!"

"Rufino stays."

Kelly stared at him hotly. "For Chrissake! *Why?*"

"Because I promised his . . ." The old man's jaw hardened. "This is not your affair."

"Accordin' to what you just read off this paper," Hap growled, tapping his pocket, "runnin' this operation *makes* it my affair. You better take another hard look at the facts—"

"You watch yourself, Jank." The old man, bridling, surged onto his feet. "I am still master here! What I have done—"

"Sure, sure," Kelly sneered, leaning over the desk to snatch up that second paper, "the Lord giveth and He taketh away. Now you listen to me! You can butter it up but the fact remains that unless I can put the skids under Bryce—an' almighty quick—Palominas won't be nothin' but a goddam memory!

"Only reason you see fit to put me in charge is you're in a forked stick with a half-gutted ranch, an' if you figure I'm goin' to save your bacon spendin' half the time peerin' over my shoulder to keep from being knifed in the back you're crazier'n a bedbug. Either Rufino goes or I do!"

The darkened skin of Don Ambrocio's face reflected the awful struggle inside him between what he wanted and this bitter choice. Both of them knew his only chance of survival depended on Hap, that even at best all the odds were against it.

He slumped back in his chair, all the wind going out of him. With anguished eyes he said as if the words were being torn out of him. "The man is my son, Jank."

They stared at each other while the grandfather clock ticked away in its corner. Almost anything else Hap could have taken in stride. But Rufino revealed to be the old man's bastard really tied Kelly's hands.

Before he could think of any suitable rejoinder the sound of boots coming over the cobbles twisted Hap's head for a look out the door. What he saw wiped all expression from his face.

Rufino came in shoving Ramirez ahead of him, a malicious satisfaction shining out of his stare.

28

"When this fine new *segundo,*" Rufino told the old man, "took Murgatroyd's cattle across the line into Mexico he took with him two vaqueros to manage the handling. Gallego you have heard. Hear now the other. Tell him, Taco, about the loyalty," he growled with gloating grin fixed on Hap.

When Ramirez quit talking there was complete silence. The old man seemed shrunken within his clothes.

"Well?" Rufino jeered. "What does your so-loyal Jank say to that?"

Kelly smiled above the Durham he was shaking into the fold of cigarette rice paper. "I don't reckon the *patrón* needs me to cue his thinking."

Don Ambrocio, looking ten years older than Moses, made an obvious effort to control himself. After swallowing whatever had been stuck in his throat he said with some vestige of oldtime authority, "This changes nothing—"

"Changes nothing!" Rufino shouted. "You would put this hacienda at the self-seeking whim of a gringo *chingao* who has—"

"Yes."

"You blind old bat!" the deposed range boss snarled. "This gringo bastard spits on your name! Right under your roof he's—"

"Whatever he's done, the one hurt most is that Texican pig."

"—your own daughter!"

With his face like something hacked out of wood Don Ambrocio said, "He is the only one who'll stand up to that pirate."

Swelled up big as an eight-mule baggage wagon, cheeks apoplectic, Rufino backed frothing, into the doorhole to get enough space to drive a hand at his pistol; he had the weapon half drawn and staggered abruptly, mouth stretched wide, to topple with a crash that shook the room.

"Down!" Kelly yelled through the echoes of that shot. Whipping out his own six-shooter he shoved past Ramirez to spring low-bent with vicious haste into the patio. No target showed in that sunlit court, but off in the shadows of the cobbled passage a flutter of movement drew his fire.

A ragged cry went up. Muzzle flame winked and the passage grew filled with the shapes of running men. With lead screaming round him Kelly emptied every shell in the cylinder, driving them back, seeing two fall before the shadows were still.

Ramirez with his carbine came running from the house, calling gruffly, "They've gone?"

"Not far—we better bar that gate," Kelly growled, ejecting spent shells to reload as he ran. He could hear the vaquero's boots pounding behind him, feel his back muscles crawl, but he did not look around.

Reaching the gate he dropped into a crouch, grimly raking the yard in that first hurried glance, hearing the bellow of Bryce's shouted orders, but not finding the man, throwing one shot at a shape partially hidden behind the stone trough.

Over his shoulder Ramirez' carbine cracked spitefully and one of Bryce's crew across the yard fell whimpering off the roof of the cookshack.

Two things disturbed Hap more than a little, Ramirez behind him and the unnatural quiet with which—almost like a sell-out—those Texicans appeared to have glommed onto everything but the house itself; come within an ace of doing that, too!

Where the hell were the hands he'd watched making their crosses under Carmencita's signature? Was he up against, here, another of Tiodosa's vengeful caprices? It didn't seem probable that Murgatroyd's crew could have surprised them all.

Yet they might, he reflected bleakly. Except for some fool's itchy finger triggering the slug that had dropped Rufino, Bryce might have caught them all flat-footed and taken over the ranch without firing a shot.

Kelly told himself this, yet could not believe it. More likely, he thought, Don Ambrocio's vaqueros—rather than work for a gun-hung gringo—had stood like posts and let the bastards take over! This was how it shaped up; but having worked around Mexicans most of his life Kelly was loathe to believe this also. On a place like this the *patrón's* word was law. No matter how underprivileged these *paisanos* or how hopeless their prospects a partisan loyalty was as natural to them as eating and sleeping. He couldn't believe it was in them to let Bryce take over without lifting a finger.

He said over his shoulder, "How many of that bunch do you reckon are out there?"

"No sé."

"You figure our boys are killed or captured?"

"Quién sabe?"

It was in Ramirez' voice that, while he might go along with the *patrón's* crazy notions, he was under no compulsion to agree with or like them.

Kelly made his hard choice. Bryce, as things stood—if he could keep hold of his present advantage—would win hands down. He had to be rattled, shaken loose of his confidence and whatever strategy had given him the yard.

"Cover me, Taco. I'm goin' out there," Hap growled, and straightaway lunging from the gate's concealing shadows, went zigzagging at a crouching run to drop, breathing hard, behind the stone trough, wondering afterwards when nothing ricocheted off it why the Flying M guns had so abruptly quit firing. Surely some of Bryce's crowd—even if they were all on the far side of it—should be peppering away at him.

Then he remembered. "You still there, feller?"

But the man on the trough's other side—the galoot Hap had thrown that slug at—didn't even so much as let out a grunt. *Was he dead or playing possum?*

Hap hadn't glimpsed enough to do him great damage. "Drop your shooter in the trough," Kelly said through clenched teeth.

About half a minute dragged by without answer before Hap heard the splash. Then he said, "Now the pistol—"

"You'd like that, wouldn't you!"

"Look," Kelly growled, "if I have to come after it—"

"You come right ahead, bucko."

There wasn't much else Hap *could* do, he reckoned. While this sonofabitch had him anchored out here Bryce might find a way into the house.

He eased a fistful of cartridges out of his pocket, lobbed them into the air. While still spinning over him—before the lowest splashed into the tank—someone yelled: *"Look out, Frayne!"* and right in the midst of all this commotion Kelly rounded the trough in a lunging dive to come down on the fellow in his flustered confusion with all the dropped weight of a sackful of cats. Breath whooshed out of him. Almost before the man knew what was happening Hap had an elbow locked under his chin, gun wrenched away from him and the butt of it scrambling what brains he had left.

Dropping the limp shape, Kelly—now with a six-shooter gripped in each fist—came bounding erect to plunge straight at the cookshack. With dust spurting up all around, Kelly's pistoning legs kept on pumping, incredibly fetching him nearer his goal. Something cuffed at his chin-fringed hat—you could see it jerk, but Hap kept going—even after, at one point, he was spun half around.

But Murgatroyd didn't have it all his own way. Ramirez, from the gate, was throwing lead, too, and though this may have seemed ineffective it likely disconcerted at least a few of Bryce's outfit; and from two different windows of the house rifles intermittently kept up a frenzied chatter, the heavier tones of one of these pounding like a buffalo gun.

Hap hurtled through the shack's open door, found the struggling cook tied hand and foot and stopped long enough to cut him free. Wheezing like a leaky bellows he hauled himself up the Indian ladder to crawl through the open hatch onto the roof.

There was blood on his shirt but, half doubled over, he reached the parapet overlooking the yard, dropping behind it to lay there gasping like a fish out of water. When tortured lungs jerked enough air into him, he came onto his knees to pull off the hat and take in what he could of the scene below.

This advantage of height was not as great as he'd hoped, only three of Bryce's crew being immediately visible. Two of these he knocked sprawling, but the other man ducked and got under cover.

Kelly wished he knew how many there were, and suddenly inspired, wriggled over to the back of the roof to see if he couldn't locate Bryce's horses. Not finding any sign of them he made his way next to the parapet farthest from the house and discovered them tied in brush a couple of ropelengths beyond the corrals.

Too far off to disturb much with a pistol.

He wriggled back to the hatch. "If you think you can get to the far side of them pens," he called down to the cook, "go spook their *caballos*."

Coosie rolled frightened eyes but jerked his head in a nod. Satisfied, Kelly crawled back to the edge overlooking the yard.

Nothing had much changed down below that he could see. Ramirez still crouched in the shadow of the gate, and for the moment at least, the guns had quit barking. Hap still hadn't located Murgatroyd and wondered uneasily what the man was planning. He knew Bryce too well to imagine him idle.

"Can you hear me, Bryce?"

"Sure. What's on your mind? Ready to pitch in your hand?"

"You know better'n that," Kelly answered. "What will it take to call off your dogs?"

"You and the old man and both them dames right out in plain sight! I've already got two men inside the house. In about three shakes—"

"Don't count on that."

"You're pinned down, man. You ain't goin' nowhere without collecting more holes than a goddam colander! If—"

A distant flutter like dried sticks snapping under somebody's boots leached through Bryce's talk and choked off the rest of it.

"Them sounds you been hearing," Hap called, "that kind of cork-stopper poppin', was Coosie makin' dog meat of them broomtails you tied back of the corrals."

It wasn't hard to imagine in the following silence the sort of looks swapped wherever two or more of Bryce's understrappers lurked.

Murgatroyd attempted to make light of this by saying that when they left his outfit they would be riding Palominas horses, but this fetched a jeering laugh from Kelly who was now fairly certain Bryce was inside the bunkhouse, the roof of which wasn't more than thirty feet from where he crouched.

"Trouble with you," he told Murgatroyd, "is you're one of those galoots that never gives a whoop how many hands gets killed as long as it puts a few more bucks in your pocket. Right now you've got those poor dumb bastards thinkin' you're about to take over this spread, when the truth of it is—"

"You're wastin' breath if you think that hogwash is going to lever you outa this bind. Right now," Bryce yelled, "them two boys in the house has got that ol' fool an' both of has la-di-da brats—"

A rattle of shots came out of the house and he triumphantly shouted as this racket abated: "Flip! Tanner! Drag that carrion out where Kelly can see it!"

"You all right up there, Jank?"

"You bet," Hap said. "I'm fine as silk. In about half a minute I'm going to burn that place down right over Bryce's head."

It got powerfully quiet out there in the yard. "He's bluffin'," Bryce growled. "He can't get at this place. Most of what crew he's got left we've tied up. We got him outnumbered—"

"You better count heads again," Hap flung back. And said for what effect it might have on the rest: "Three of them rannies you had round the yard didn't even wait to kiss you goodbye. Four others I can see ain't like to go noplace—not to mention that pair you slipped into the house."

"I want out!" someone hollered from the barn.

"Then pitch out your guns an' start hikin'. Anybody else for town?"

A splatter of shots made Hap duck behind the wall. He supposed it was begging a miracle to hope Bryce's all but consummated victory would fall apart this late. Hap's bold talk might scare off one or two like that bird at the barn, but . . .

Abruptly, Kelly, quiet as a tarantula, scooted back

to the hatch, lowered his length and dropped the few feet to the cookshack floor. Bryce wasn't going to be put out of business by dropping a handkerchief or calling him any rash of hard names.

Getting a lid off the stove Hap peered around for cook's short-handled shovel, then emptied the water from the bucket on the sink, wiping this out with a floursack apron. Humming under his breath, hand wrapped in wet apron, he opened the door to the firebox, scooping the coals out into his bucket. Carrying this, he climbed back to the roof.

He felt a little light-headed with the pain in his side stabbing like a hot knife, but had no time to take care of it now. Cupping mouth with both hands he ordered Taco at the gate to shoot the first Texican that offered a target. Stepping back and picking up the bucket by its more than warm bail he took a few practice swings and lobbed it over the wall.

Its arrival on the bunkhouse roof made considerable racket, rolling over and over scattering coals as it went. "They tell me you're pretty good with a fire, Bryce—let's see how you handle this one."

Someone stuck out his head down below. Taco's carbine cracked and across the sill the fellow hung face-down, too dead to skin.

"You sonofabitch!"

Murgatroyd's shout fetched a chuckle from Kelly. "It ain't the fire on the roof you got to watch out for," he advised sardonically, "but the one you'll run into when you try to get out. How's the wind feel down there?"

Nothing further was heard from Bryce or his cohorts for at least five minutes. Through a turmoil of coughing someone grumbled a question whose gist escaped Hap in the roar of the fire that was devouring the roof. A falling timber threw up a shower of sparks. The heat down there must have been fierce, he reckoned, judging by the scald of it against his own face.

He backed off with bloodshot eyes, when he recalled that the barracks-like structure's single back window was out of Ramirez' range of vision.

At this precise moment the Sharps at the house threw out two reports and Kelly, running over the cookshack roof, was just in time to see a man knocked sprawling beyond that back window.

Leaning over the parapet Hap called gruffly: "Better give up down there while we can still get you out in one piece!"

It got him a cheekful of plaster chips and drove him back, blinking, as a pair of blue gunshots opened up from the window. Pawing tear-stung eyes, Hap snarled: "Don't be a fool, Bryce! You can't take it with you!"

But apparently the Flying M owner wasn't yet convinced.

With watchful eyes on that window Hap sidestepped to where their guns couldn't reach him and yelled to Ramirez: "Look out they don't try to bolt out the front."

"I've had enough!" came a shout from the window.

Someone pitched out his Winchester and came scrambling after it, Bryce and one other clambering hard on his heels—both empty-handed—as Hap held his fire.

He could see the mouth working in that first tipped-up face but could not catch the words through the cataract roar of wind-lashed flames.

Murgatroyd focused Hap's attention by throwing up empty hands as the third fellow, whirling, whipped up a pistol, fanning the hammer in a shriek of blue whistlers.

But he was firing too fast in his frenzy to kill, and Hap, staring into that smudged, frantic face, knocked him down with a slug planted squarely between the eyes. Shiloh Frayne flopped around, gouged the ground with spurred heels and was finally still.

Twenty minutes later, with the last of his crew given a horse and advised to keep riding, Murgatroyd, disheveled and sullen-faced, stood scowling raunchily, fenced in by the silent shapes of Don Ambrocio, Coosie, the four liberated hands and a patched-up Hap Kelly.

The old man came around the still smoking fire-darkened walls of the bunkhouse to stop beside the *patrón*. "Hangin's too good for him," Coosie said, mopping the sweat from black cheeks. And Ramirez growled, "That town crowd sure won't back us against him."

They all looked at Hap.

"Hell—you're the *patrón*," he told Don Ambrocio, not much liking the old man's stare. "It's your hacienda. Your grass an' line camps. Your people—"

"But yours, also, partner. I cannot shoot this pig in cold blood."

"Then give him a gun and a ten-yard start. You know the routine."

The old man smiled slyly. "You are the one who wanted to be boss, Jank. You took on the management—responsibility for decisions—when you replaced Rufino as Number Two."

"Whereabouts on this paper," Hap asked, producing it, "did that get tucked in?"

"The postscript, *compañero.* Just over my signature."

Kelly squinted red eyes. Yes. It figured. Every deal he'd got into with this old fool had found him holding the short end of the stick. "Let's get over to the office," he growled, shoving Murgatroyd ahead of him. "You too, Taco."

Inside, with the old man sitting back of his desk and Bryce getting up more wind with each passing moment, Hap told his partner, "Put down the cost of everything you've lost—everything this bird's cost you—double it an' tack on ten percent for interest. What do you come up with?" he asked when Don Ambrocio finished.

"Twenty thousand, two hundred and forty-three dollars—U.S."

Hap looked at Bryce. "Pony up."

"You crazy? I ain't got nothing like that kinda cash," the man spluttered, glaring back at him belligerently.

"Didn't figure you had. But you can raise it—"

"You better shoot him," Ramirez said, sounding ugly.

"Shootin's too good for this sonofabitch. I want to see him squirm—an' I don't mean just *wriggle*. I want to see this bastard break out a real lather. I want all his tough friends to be watchin' him do it."

Murgatroyd looked like he'd been kicked in the groin.

"Write it up," Kelly said. "In the form of a bill, due an' payable on call. Then another just like it for me to put up in town; an' give him the quill."

"I can't raise that much on short notice!" Bryce gasped.

Kelly told the old man, "We can go into court with this thing and get a judgment, have a receiver appointed—"

"Hell's fire, man—"

"Put your name on them papers."

With bloated cheeks gone the color of wood ash, Murgatroyd signed with a shaking hand after only one look into Kelly's bleak stare and the snout of the gun pointed square at his brisket. He had no doubt how near death he stood.

"Now," Kelly said, stepping back but still grim, "you got a choice, bucko. Maybe you'd rather write out another paper—a quitclaim to everything you've got, turning over all your interests, lock, stock an' barrel, to Palominas. In which case you get a horse and directions to the shortest route out of this country."

Bryce stared at him, licking dry lips, abruptly nodding. Like a man gone blind he picked up the quill and wrote as directed.

"That's letting him off too easy," Taco snarled, glaring hotly.

"You think about it, man. It's goin' to eat on this scissorsbill the rest of his life. He'll be all the time wonderin' if he sold out too cheap."

After Murgatroyd left, a broken, cringing lump of lard, Kelly told Don Ambrocio, "When Taco's not too busy with the chores of this spread he can ride into town an' put up them two papers Bryce signed first off. That way there ain't like to be no question who takes over his properties."

Don Ambrocio asked, puzzled, "Why not you? You're the big man here—"

"Nope. I've other fish to fry." And, producing the partnership agreement from the pocket where he'd stuffed it, Kelly coolly tore it several times across and put the ragged pieces in the *hacendado's* hand.

"Thanks just the same, but I guess not. I've got a little nest egg wrapped around my middle and a gal in town I might persuade to help me spend it.

"I reckon we've reached the partin' of the trails. *Buena suerte!* old man, and *vaya con Dios.*"

SMOKE-WAGON KID

Chapter I

THE MAN THEY HANGED

Stumpy Harker's first concrete evidence that his boss was engaged in just that unlawful business for several months hinted by his neighbors, came while he was being hanged. He had been shown the telltale hide now rolled behind Stewart's cantle, and had received the Crazy L owner's assurance that this little party was by way of being first payment on Two-Pole-Pumpkin's score.

. Stretching hemp would not have been so bad, he was reflecting, had he known all along the risk he had been running. But he had not. Being himself of an honest disposition, he had taken Lothrop's honesty for granted. Loyalty to his salt, once these rumors had gotten round, had been too great to admit of any doubt.

In extenuation of Stumpy's credence and allegiance, let it here be stated that no faintest shred of evidence in support of the ugly rumors had ever come before his eyes. Yet this circumstance was scarcely strange; Stone Lothrop was a careful, close-mouthed hombre. The thing for wonder was that Stewart had gotten wise.

Someone must have slipped, reflected Stumpy. Yet he would have been willing to bet his neck against the hanging that the someone had not been Lothrop. Could there have been a defection among the riders of the Two-Pole-Pumpkin brand? Or had the slip been the sure result of overweening confidence? Stumpy wished he knew; it would have made him feel much easier in his mind.

"Rustlers," Lefty Corner of the Cinch Ring growled, "recognizes on'y one kinda warnin'—the lass-rope kind."

"This drought has been takin' toll enough without no help from cow-thiefs," was the pointed observation of Hootowl Jones. "An' said thiefs is gettin' t' be a damned sight too numerous around these parts. It's time a few of the breed was weeded out."

Lefty Corner said, "Hell, let's string him up an' get it over with!"

If Stumpy heard the ominous words, he gave no sign. Beneath the lone cottonwood lifting gnarled branches above the little clearing in the chaparral, he sat on his horse in stoical silence. Mid-summer had come to Gawdforsaken Valley, and the heat, although the day was nearly done, was stifling. Now and again, Harker raised a calloused hand to mop his sweating face.

No use kicking, he reflected. When you worked for an outfit and ate its salt you were expected to take its orders. That he had been the recipient of no such orders as he was about to be swung for made little difference; others had and, to judge by the grimness of these men's leathery faces, had evidently carried them out with fine perfection.

His mind dismissed his cogitations as the group surrounding him pressed closer. Getting ready for the kill, he mused, and an ironic humor glinted briefly in his eyes. He could almost picture the lazy grin that would tug at Lothrop's heavy lips when word came to him that these vengeful valley outfits had snuffed the light of an innocent man. Stone Lothrop would know how to make the most of such a fact.

"Got yore second crow-bait picked out yet?" he scoffed.

"You better be singin' low, fella. Yore time is nearly up," Jones told him in that solemn air that had earned for the Long H owner his "Hootowl" nickname. "You better be composin' yore thoughts in prayer—"

"I ain't never been the prayin' kind," Harker answered coolly. "I'm expectin' it's a mite late now t'start."

"Pretty perky, ain't yuh?" Corner sneered.

Stewart said, "Stumpy, you got any friends you'd like to send a partin' message to? Or any personal effects you'd be wantin' some gent t'have?"

"Shucks," Stumpy grinned, "I ain't got no effects worth botherin' with. You boys can hev anything I've got, an' welcome."

"Sure there ain't some friend or relative you'd be wantin' us t'get a message to?"

"Can't think of any," Harker answered slowly. "But was I you, I'd go kinda slow on namin' Stone Lothrop rustler. Even with that hide an'—"

"Heck," Corner snarled his interruption, "there

ain't no other outfit in these parts whose brand'll cover ourn!"

"Pity yore eyes wa'n't open t' the Two-Pole-Pumpkin possibilities when yuh registered yore brands," Stumpy hurled right back.

The jibe stung, as was evidenced by the darker tinge on Jones' rough cheeks, and the baleful glitter that flashed from Corner's eyes. Only Stewart appeared unmoved. "Two-Pole-Pumpkin," he said, "was here first an'—"

It was Harker's turn to do the cutting in. "All the more careless of you gents, registerin' brands that it could blot. But you're right. Lothrop was here first—an' he'll likely be here quite some spell after you fellas is long forgotten."

"They raise 'em modest on the Two-Pole-Pumpkin, don't they?" Corner jeered. "But talk's cheap. An' bein' so, yuh better be devotin' all the wind yuh got t'talkin yourself outa that hemp necklace yo're a-wearin'."

Stumpy Harker chuckled, knowing full well the seriousness of his predicament. Cattle had been taking wings in right large numbers even before drought had hit this valley, and the drought had proved no stumbling block to the bovine evacuation. Somehow and somewhere, the brain behind this wholesale exodus knew of a place where thirst and scarcity of feed did not exist—knew of the place, and the manner in which these cattle could be transported. The steal was slick as frogs' legs, because this range, including so far as was known all range beyond the valley's rim, was sweltering in the heat and desolation of this drought for a radius of more than one hundred baking miles. Stumpy Harker knew the futility of any plea for life; these men were out for blood—and meant to have it.

"C'mon," growled Lefty Corner soullessly; "let's swing this rustler up an' get it done with. I'm gettin' so damn hungry my backbone's rubbin' all the linin' off my belly!"

"Yeah," approved another. "Let's hang the low-down coyote an' hit the trail. Be gettin' dark 'fore long, an' I wanta see him wiggle."

The lips of Stumpy Harker curled. In one thing Corner was absolutely right: talk was cheap. But if he knew anything at all about his boss, these yapping coyotes—and only Ed Stewart was excluded from the category—would come to rue this day and the ready weapon they were getting set to place in the hand of big Sandy Lothrop.

"Go to it, you mangy buzzards. Git on with yore gory work."

Stewart sighed and shook his head. "I hate t' do this, Stumpy. But I can't quite persuade myself that you could ride for Lothrop all these months an' not be implicated in this stealin'. You must have known it was goin' on. In such a position a honest waddy woulda quit an' left for other parts. Yore stayin'—"

Stumpy's laugh rode through his words. Stumpy's tone was too sincere for the tag of bluster: "Ed, yo're gettin' soft."

Stewart shrugged and gave the order, "All right, boys."

"He won't be feelin' so darn chipper when his boot starts beatin' air!" Corner snarled, and threw his weight with that of another man's on the end of the rope where it dangled from the branch. In a twinkling they had secured it about the cottonwood's scraggy bole.

Yet even while someone lashed his wrists behind him and his neck was being strained by the tight-stretched hemp, Stumpy Harker's mind was alert and working. He was reflecting that Lothrop had never heard of Hoyle or Queensberry or any other of the tinhorn rulewriters; the only code that Lothrop played by was one of his own creation, one fashioned to suit his aims. Stumpy's great regret was that he wouldn't be around to witness the results of this necktie party.

With an abrupt movement of his arm, Hootowl Jones brought down his quirt in a whistling arc that ended on the steaming flanks of Harker's mount. With a resentful snort the startled beast lunged forward.

And then to the lynchers' ears came unexpected sound, came definite warning that their act might bring reprisal. Like an echo to the sounds of Harker's vanishing bronc, a swift rush of hooves beat out of the chaparral to the north.

In consternation the lynchers' eyes sought one another's faces, clung for a pregnant second, then swung to the north where the rolling drum of hoofbeats even now was fading to a far dim flutter.

With a curse Lefty Corner spun wickedly on his heels and went scuttling for his horse. With answering oaths the others sprinted for their own. Into saddles they swung, not one showing any wish to linger, not one failing to strike his mount with quirt and spur. Yet of them all, it was Corner with his ashen cheeks who left the clearing first.

Soon all were merged in the swirling shadows of descending night. The clearing loomed deserted save for the still and moveless figure dangling pendant from the branch of the cottonwood tree.

Chapter II

THE GIRL WITH THE JET-BLACK HAIR

Bright and hot the day had dawned, with the brass haze of heat shrouding the distant purple hills and played in shimmering undulations twelve feet above the tawny earth. In no way, the girl was thinking, was this day different from the dragging others preceding it throughout a long-drawn fourteen months. Through all those days no single drop of moisture had fallen in Gawdforsaken Valley; nothing had fallen save the burning rays of the searing sun and the countless numbers of gaunt, bony cattle, whose mournful lowing had been a constant source of irritation.

Standing in the gateway of the *patio*, she drew a weary, heat-damp hand across her aching forehead. Heat and bawling cattle had filled those awful days. But now the doleful lowing was stilled, and the whole vast world was naught but heat and silence. A stealthy silence whose presence was nearly as unrelenting as the sun's, a monstrous stillness that filled Gawdforsaken Valley to the brim—a brooding hush that pressed against one like a living thing.

Silence ... heat and silence. Heat that even darkness abated little, for the sands of the valley floor cooled slowly, and those precipitous hills rimming its blue distance kept out all but its own hot breath. And only the counter-irritant, of the cattle's ceaseless bawling had for a little time relieved its awful hush. Now that was gone, and there was nothing left but dust and heat and the solemnity of forgotten places.

Through the great gate, *la querta del zaguan*,

Yolanda's slowly turning head focused a resentful stare upon those outside things that lay within her vision: those same depressing, insensate things, those all-too-familiar things which had hemmed and sought to stifle her ever since, as a bride of sorts, she'd come to this Two-Pole-Pumpkin rancho fourteen months ago.

Those same dusty, sand-scoured adobe outbuildings were smeared against the same dun background of blistering earth, uncared for and unchanged. The sun-bleached *vigas* of the ranch-house cast the same monotonous shadows. The great gate itself stood always open, yet she had the feeling that if some poor fool had moved it, the thing would have taken voice to squeal a protest, so securely enwrapped was it in the slumbering peace of centuries. Perhaps its poles had even taken root, so heavily did they lean on the changeless customs of the land. And out yonder there the bone-white poles of the aspen corrals loomed just as bleak in the blazing sun as on the day she had come. The same hock-deep dust lay about them, hardly stirred in all these months; and the same gnarled cottonwoods stood sentinel along the curling path that led to the outer gate.

This awful quality of suspended animation held the power to shrink one's soul. Too vividly these surroundings told the insignificance of man. Her heart cried out in protest. This country drove one in upon oneself . . .

As though sensing her thoughts from where he lunged against the wall, Lothrop said with a sneer:

"An' what of it? I expect it's about time something woke you up an' gave you a slant on yore relative importance in the general scheme of things. This is a big country; a *man's* country. 'F you ain't big enough to measure up, you're better out of it."

"I'd get out of it quick enough if I had the chance."

"Ho, ho!" Lothrop chuckled. "I bet you would. But this country's all right if you're big enough for it. Why don't you try makin' yourself agreeable for a change? Fella can get a lot of fun out of life, if he's willin' to meet it halfway. Same with a woman."

She made no answer, knowing that in silence lay her greatest weapon to annoy him—to avenge the insults which he heaped upon her day after day.

Her lack of retort stirred resentment in him now, drove dull color into the bull-thick neck that bulged the open collar of his dusty flannel shirt, thinned to a tight straight line the sensual thickness of his lips, and pulled his black brows downward in a sullen scowl.

"What fool," he muttered thickly, "would believe you an innocent girl after fourteen months with me?"

Yolanda's rounded chin shoved higher. Turning, she swung into the *patio*, and from that into the main living-room in which were windows facing upon the outer yard. Lothrop followed. With an oath he dropped into a cowhide chair that creaked beneath his weight.

"Playin' the stone goddess this afternoon again, eh? I'd oughta blister yuh with a bull whip! An' I may come to it yet! A man can take just so much of this fine lady stuff, an' I'm reckonin' to hev a bellyful right now. There's a heap of things that I may be, but not one of 'em's a blasted mat for a stuck-up filly to wipe wipe 'er boots on! Hear?"

Yolanda continued without apparent perturbation her survey of the yard. The sum total of her observations was revealed in a leisurely, "You could easily improve this place by straightening the poles of those corrals. A coat of paint wouldn't hurt the fronts of the buildings, either, and could easily be applied by the crew in a day or two—even at the snail's pace your men customarily adopt when they work."

"Do you hear?" he persisted, with a softness that was ominous.

"Could I fail to hear?"

"Then answer, damn you."

"Certainly I heard that ranting you were doing. Were you calling the hogs or the ghosts of your dead cattle?" And the smile with which she curved the berry redness of her mouth whipped up Lothrop's stormy blood and drew a pronounced flush across his cheeks; curled the fingers of his hands about the chair arms with a tautened grip that bleached the skin about their knuckles. He contained his surging temper with an effort that laid new sweat across the paleness of his forehead.

"Some day—" And there he stopped, to listen with canted head. The drumming beat of sand-muffled hooves rolled in from the desert and brought him out of his chair and across the floor, to halt before the open window, from which one swipe of a calloused hand removed the curtains Yolanda had hung. He seemed to have forgotten her in the intensity of his interest in these sounds. His form loomed tense as he swept a probing glance across the valley's tawny reaches.

Looking through her own window, Yolanda beheld a distant horse and rider boiling headlong through those shimmering undulations marking the steady upward swirl of dust. The rider was crouched low down above the horse's outstretched neck, and his steady downward flogging arm bespoke a lashing quirt. What speed! she thought. The man must be mad to drive his mount so in that heat—mad or crazy with fear.

She looked again at Lothrop, attracted by his smothered curse. He must have recognized the rider. His attitude seemed to grow even more tense. The frown that crossed his brow put savage lines about his mouth, and jutted his chin with a stubborn belligerence that told of surging passions.

"Who is it?"

Yolanda hardly recognized the voice as her own; it was strained and filled with an excitement she assured herself she did not feel. What was it to her if some fool *vaquero* were bent on killing his horse? And what message—if any—could he bring that should so step up the pounding of her heart?

"Who is it?" she repeated.

But Lothrop did not notice. With determined stride he wheeled from the window and went stamping into the *patio*.

Yolanda's shifting glance discovered the rider pelting up the lane beneath the cottonwoods, and she hurried after Lothrop, stood behind him while he waited.

The horseman came through the open gate and slid down from his mount before them. She recognized him for Suggs, one of Lothrop's riders, a hard-faced man who, on seeing her, still kept his battered hat upon his head. He was breathing hard, as though he, and not the pony, had made that fearful run.

"There's hell to pay!" he blurted out in answer to Lothrop's question. "They've got Harker—hung 'im higher than a kite!"

She caught the start that stiffened Lothrop's shoulders. "Who?"

"Corner, Stewart, an' Jones!"

"Oh. them three, eh?"

"An' some of their outfits."

"What did they say—or couldn't you hear?"

"I could hear well enough," Suggs grunted, and bit off a good-sized chunk from the plug of tobacco he brought up out of a pocket. "Could hear all I wanted, anyhow. They tol' Harker it was time the rustler breed was bein' thinned out, an' that they proposed t' start on him."

Yolanda's feeling of nausea swiftly changed to one of bitter resentment. How dare anyone hang that poor old man! He was the only one of Lothrop's crew who had ever expressed sympathy for her position here; the only one who seemed to have a spark of human kindness and understanding. Why, it was ridiculous to think of that old man as a rustler!

Suggs was speaking again: "It's a laff they shoulda picked on Harker. He wouldn't know how t' run a brand if his life depended on it."

"What else did them three roosters say?"

"Wal," Suggs grunted through his chew, "they ast Stumpy if he had any las' words he'd like t' hev passed on. He allowed as how they might tell her," and he jerked at thumb at Yolanda, "he figgered 'twas time she pulled her pin. Jones said it was too bad she'd ever hooked up with a dam' yeller-bellied rustler, an' that she'd oughta had better sense."

Lothrop did not speak at once. Then he said:

"Them's harsh words to use against a man for maverickin' two-three puny dogies, seems like."

"Yeah," Suggs grinned, "it sure does," and laughed. The brows of the black-haired girl arched inquiringly at this. Then her glance betokened sharp interest as Suggs drawled: "What we gonna do?"

"Nothin' . . . at the moment."

"Huh? *Nawthin'!*" Suggs seemed startled. "Great cripes! Mean t' say yuh're figgerin' to let them valley outfits get away with this dam' lynchin'?"

Yolanda listened tensely for Stone Lothrop's reply. Surely he never would let a man of his be hung for rustling and not avenge his death.

But Lothrop just stood there, eyeing Suggs derisively.

Then finally he murmured: "What's one man to get excited about. After all, Stumpy's death ain't botherin' us, an' likely enough Stumpy *was* a rustler. I've had it in my mind for quite a spell to get rid of him. I never did like his shif'less ways. Fella that'll steal a pie will steal a bull, given the opportunity. I reckon Stumpy was a plumb bad actor an' only got what he was askin' for."

Suggs' wide mouth hung open, but Yolanda did not see. Blindly she turned away. Sickened by such perfidy, she fled inside the house with an indignant click of her heels, slammed into her own room and closed the door with emphasis.

In that room at Two-Pole-Pumpkin in which Lothrop customarily corralled his hard-faced henchmen when laying plans for some new project, the subdued sound of voices mingled with the rasp of frequent oaths and the scrape of shifted chairs. The smoke of brown-paper cigarettes, splayed from expanded nostrils, rose blue above the table and writhed its swirling bulk about the great coal-oil lamp that hung from the beamed ceiling. Drawn together before each open window, Indian blanket curtains served to bottle the humid air, that was close and reeking with the combined aroma of tobacco smoke, fumes from cheap whisky, the horsy tang of damp clothing, and the sweat of unwashed bodies.

This was the night following the one which had witnessed the hanging of Stumpy Harker, some seven hours after Suggs' arrival with the news. Till now the boss of Two-Pole-Pumpkin had been displaying a calm indifference to Suggs' fuming demands for instant action. Yet it was because of the hanging that this conference had been called.

Lothrop's range boss, Black Jack Purdin, had just returned from Rincon and he had the latest gossip on his chest; had, indeed, made several efforts to unburden himself, only to be thwarted in each instance by Suggs' blustery demands that Two-Pole-Pumpkin get immediately to horse for the purpose of upholding its honor and avenging itself on the valley outfits for their untimely snuffing of Harker's light.

Tall and gaunt, Jack Purdin ws a rawboned man with a jagged knife-scar across his left temple. A heavy drinker, the range boss had imbibed a considerable quantity of distilled cactus juice while at, and since leaving, town. He was, consequently, in a surly mood and of no mind to brook further interruption from Suggs.

"If you're all through with them suggestions," he growled malignantly, "favor me by shuttin' yore yap till I get my second breath." Suggs reluctantly subsided. "The Smoke-wagon Kid's at his didos again."

His red-rimmed eyes took on a glint of satisfaction as he beheld interest in their tautened postures.

"That fool," Mitch Moelner sneered, "is shore invitin' a window in his skull."

Tombstone, a pale cadaverous man with sunken eyes and great hollows in his cheeks, nodded gloomy agreement. "Can't no gent monkey with the gov'ment without getting his comeuppance sooner or later. Man'd think he had more sense."

"Sense—hell!" said Moelner scornfully. "He's jest a bobtailed flush with a hankerin' for a rep."

" 'F I was entertainin' them kinda notions, I'd keep 'em to myself," Purdin observed with a scowl. "First thing yuh know he'll be campin' on yore trail."

"That would worry me into a lather, I expect."

Moelner's talk was no harder than his looks. He was, like most brush-poppers of the region, tall. And he was lean with a suggestion of fibrous toughness that blended well with the lithe smoothness of each deliberate movement. At some past date, smallpox had dug several pits in a countenance whose parchment-taut skin threw into prominence the narrowness of a skull structure that gave to his features a sinister sharpness, disagreeably emphasized by a lantern jaw.

" 'F yuh had as many wheels in yore think-box as the Kid's got in his, it would," Jack Purdin said with malice. "Some day that spleen of yoren is gonna choke yore gullet."

"When it does, you won't be around to do any laffin'."

"Them that spits in the dust brews mud."

At this point Stone Lothrop's drawl cut in upon the argument. "What's the Kid done now?"

"Yanked them two greasers outa the Socorro jail an' turned 'em loose."

"Them jaspers what robbed the Rincon bank?"

"Wal," Purdin answered, "that's what they been accused of. But the Kid tol' Sheriff Hausleman it'd be a good idee to arrest the right hombres fer a change. Claimed them greasers wa'n't no more guilty of that hold-up than Tuck Harniss was of lootin' the Overland las' week."

"He's takin' a lot on himself, cuttin' in on law business thataway."

"How much dinero they got plastered on his scalp now?" Lothrop made the query thoughtful-like.

"Five hundred U.S. dollars!"

"That's a heap o' money t' stick on one man's head," Suggs marvelled.

Mitch Moelner sneered. "It's a heap to stick on *that* head."

"What's wrong with that head?" Lothrop drawled, turning his heavy shoulders toward the speaker. "Could you have done the things the Kid's got away with in the las' ten months, an' kept yourself on the loose the way he has?"

"All he's done," Moelner said, "is shoot up Del Beecher, a bushwhacker what had a yaller strip a yard wide up his back; lift the scalp off'n five-six 'Patches that was so drunk they couldn't see anythin' but double; call the bluff of that gang what runs Rincon, an' let a coupla greasers outa jail. What's worth braggin' about in that?"

"How about the time he called Hausleman a damn fool to his face?" Suggs asked. "I guess that didn't take guts?"

"No more guts than a jackrabbit hops around with. Had his gun on Hausleman all the time he was talkin', didn't he?"

"He didn't hev no gun out when he got them greasers outa jail," Purdin growled. "The trouble with you is, yuh can't stand t' see no other gent gettin' a rep that rivals yoren."

"Ah, why don't you hire the damn grandstander t' help yuh steal cattle from these valley outfits, if he's so damn good?"

"It's an idea I've been considerin'," Lothrop said, and observed the swift looks his men exchanged among themselves. Most of them seemed pleasantly surprised. But no emotion was to be detected in the leathery mask of buried hopes Mitch Moelner presented to the world.

"If you do," he suggested, "yuh better find him sleepin' quarters that ain't inside the bunk-house. I'd no more think of closin' me eyes round that glory hunter than I would of shovin' my gun-barrel down my mouth an' pullin' the trigger!"

Black Jack Purdin laughed. "I don't guess the Smoke-wagon Kid could find time t' bother with such small fry as you."

The fingers of Moelner's right hand were toying with one of the silver buttons on his vest. His bold glance was fixed intently on the high-boned face of the range boss. A sour grin crossed his lips. "Sometime, Jack," he predicted, "you'll be makin' one of them funny cracks when I ain't in no mood to 'preciate yore humor."

Defiance mingled with the caution in Purdin's heavy stare; the defiance won and routed the other. "When I make a crack I stan' behind it all the way," he snarled, the liquor in him churning up his blood. "What I said goes as she lays—an' it wasn't figgered t' be funny. Yuh wantin' t' make somethin' of it?"

"I don't wrangle with fools," Mitch Moelner sneered.

Lothrop's voice cut coldly across the tightening

silence: "I've heard enough of this yappin'—more'n enough. Leave off now 'fore the bunch of you get t' burnin' powder." He weighed the saturnine Moelner with a probing, steady glance. Smoothing down his tone, he added, "From all I've heard about him, Mitch, you an' this Smoke-wagon Kid might belong to the same breed of leather-slappers. You're both slicker'n the hinges of hell; don't see how any man could rightly say either one of you was better than the other. But it would be a smart hombre that would put the monickers of both you boys on the same payroll."

His glance was on the wiry Moelner closely, endeavoring to determine the effect his words had made. But that saturnine visage was about as revealing of expression as would be a face beaten into a chunk of lead with an axe handle.

Moelner tucked his thumbs in his gun-belt, hitched his chair nearer the wall, and tilted back, swinging his booted feet against its bottom rung with a display of cool indifference. He did not speak.

Suggs said: "What're we gonna do about Stumpy's hangin'?"

Ruidosa, a thick-set swaggerer, leaned forward in his chair. "If there's goin' to be any powder burnin', the place for it is ol' man Stewart's spread." He looked to Lothrop for approval. "Stewart's the one that worked up Stumpy's finish. Stewart or Jones."

Lothrop's thoughtful glance took in the steeple-crowned sombrero, aglint with golden spangles that was worn by Ruidosa at a rakish angle atop features whose creamy innocence advertised the amount of time devoted to their improvement. The glance took in as well the aristocratic slenderness of the well-kept hand that raised to the little black moustache whose ends were greased and pointed as those of a Spanish captain's.

Suggs was saying: "What them range-hawggin' polecats has done t' one Two-Pole-Pumpkin rider, they'll do to the rest, less'n we beat 'em to the jump."

"Keep yore string rolled up," Moelner advised. "They wouldn't have the guts t' tackle a man they thought was guilty."

Suggs gave him a queer look, then turned to Lothrop. "What we gonna do, Stone?"

"Nothing . . . at the moment."

"*Nothin'!* Why, great cripes, we can't let 'em get away with that! They ain't got no right t' string up one of our boys!"

"Nope—" Mitch Moelner's grin was sly—"that hangin' was an insult to the entire Two-Pole-Pumpkin. Stumpy wa'n't guilty of misbrandin' anybody's cattle. Stumpy wa'n't no more guilty than the rest of us righteous cowprods what slicks saddle-leather sixteen hours a day, keeps our noses clean an' minds our own dang business."

Chapter III

STONE LOTHROP LAYS PIPE

Stone Lothrop was the product of his wild environment, an adventurous spirit, and a complete lack of moral rectitude. No scruple had ever been permitted to become an obstacle in the path of his desires; no fear of possible consequence had held him back from any venture he had accounted profitable. In this rough locality, where men called each other "neighbor" who lived eighty miles apart, his rise to power and influence, if not spectacular, at least was steady. Already men were looking to him for guidance in their everyday affairs; some had been considering him as a possible candidate for office even, while a few—already holding office—were swayed considerably by his views. Of the latter was Sheriff Hausleman, a great hulking ox of a man who had never held an original thought in his forty-seven years of life.

It was in Lothrop's mind, as he covertly studied the faces of his men, that Hausleman's use—as a sheriff—had about reached its end. If the Smoke-wagon Kid had taken two prisoners out of the jail at Socorro, and turned them loose right under the star-packer's nose, it was about time Hausleman was being removed and a better man found to fill his place—at least a man better fashioned to Lothrop's ends.

Few were the men in this country who could brag of having crossed Lothrop to advantage; there had been several, but only three were still around—Jones, Corner, and Stewart. These men were the owners of the other big valley outfits. He and they had never gotten along, not from the moment of their arrival in Gawdforsaken Valley. First there had been trouble over water rights, never completely settled, and of late, political differences had aggravated the situation. Dealt staggering losses by this drought which had squatted, leech-like, upon this range, Lothrop had derived an ironic pleasure by recouping from these men's surviving herds. Other ranchers, from farther south, were driving north their stricken herds, and it was to these he had sold his rustled stock. But this practice, he was aware, could not go on indefinitely.

He spread a lazy grin across his mouth at Moelner's words. A grin that stopped the sharp retort he could see was trembling on the lips of Suggs. "Whether Mitch is right or not," he said, "makes little difference. We're not goin' to fool with this two-bit rustling business any longer. There's plenty of other things we can turn our han's to . . . things that'll net us bigger profits. This is grand large country we're livin' in, boys. A country wherein opportunity abounds—"

"You sound," Moelner jeered, "like Hausleman pluggin' for election."

Lothrop grinned. "Well, it's true. This *is* a big country, an' it'll furnish plenty of opportunities to the man that's awake to his chances—a man, for instance, like me. Look at the silver mines bein' opened up in this territory. Look at the gold an' copper. Look—"

"Are you tellin' us t' go to work?" Purdin asked. "Honest-like, an' regular?"

Lothrop chuckled at his amazement. "Don't look so pained. Work, like confession, is good for the soul, Jack. You're gettin' soft."

Purdin was regarding him slanchways. "It's a cinch that hangin' aint' responsible fer that palaver. You—you aint' gettin' *religion*, are yuh?"

"What's wrong with religion?"

"Nothin', I guess. But it ain't fer the likes of us."

"You sure told the truth that time," Moelner remarked drily. "The only religion this crew could ever go for is the creed of Easy Money!"

"Exactly," Lothrop nodded. "An' there's easier money to be had than what we're gettin' out of rustled cattle. This is a sucker's game, an' I've only been piddlin' around in it till somethin' else opened up. Well, the somethin's opened."

"Such as what?" asked Purdin curiously. "Somebody startin' a new filibuster?"

"What I've got in mind will be easier than that," Lothrop said and, leaning forward, he lowered his voice. "Prospectors have been doin' pretty good in this region for quite a spell. What I've been thinkin' of will net us better, an' without walkin' behind no burro's rump. But it's goin' to take a little time to get organized."

"Just what you got up your sleeve?" Mitch Moelner asked.

"Did you ever stop to think what a profit could be made by goin' into silver?"

"Silver? You mean buy one of these fellas' mines?"

"Buy—hell!" Stone Lothrop drawled. "Look. Some of these mines are goin' to prove steady producers. Bound to. Law of averages'll take care of that. Most of these hole-diggers passes their ore over the bar or across the counter an' takes its worth in drink or grub. But there's mines at Silver City that are goin' to pay big dividends. An' they're goin' to start payin' quick. I'd say inside two-three months. Mines like the Golconda, the Silver Dollar, an' the Blood of Life."

Mitch Moelner nodded slowly, a feline glitter in his gaze. But Purdin, not comprehending, said: "They figgerin' t'give us half their finds?"

"They don't know it, but they're goin' to give us more than that. There's only one stamp mill been put in at Silver City. The men ownin' it have got a good thing. They can charge whatever they feel like, an' it's my notion they're goin' to charge a-plenty.

Most of the outfits up there ain't goin' to be able to pay such toll, an' of the few that can there won't be many that will.

"Consequently, they're goin' to have to pack that ore to Socorro, an' to reach Socorro they're goin' to have to cross the Jornada." Lothrop's shrewd cold gaze swept the faces of his men while a sardonic grin tugged at the corners of his lips. "Does the idea penetrate?"

Black Jack Purdin wet his lips. "You mean they're goin' t' pack that ore across the Jornada on mule-back?"

Lothrop nodded slowly.

"An' that we're goin t'—" Suggs balked at putting the thing into words.

But Lothrop chuckled. "Such is the notion that's been millin' around in my head. How does she set?"

"By Gawd, it don't set so good!" Suggs said, and swore.

No definite change came over Lothrop's features, nothing a man might catalogue. Yet somehow his shoulders appeared more lumpy, hunched, and his cheeks seemed darker, harder, like parfleche-wrapped rock.

The belligerence fled from Suggs' eyes. A dampness that was not of the heat came out upon his forehead, and spread as Lothrop said:

"What?"

Suggs licked his lips. "Well, I know I ain't got no right t' be talkin' outa turn," he whined ingratiatingly, "but it looks to me like that would be a damn good way of gettin' our necks stretched—a heap surer an' quicker than rustlin' steers."

Lothrop's smoke-grey glance grew vacuous, expanded to watch each man. "Are you against it?"

The question probed Suggs softly. He gulped, attempted to speak, yet each time stopped short of words. He knew what lay behind that question, and he knew what answer was expected, was in fact demanded. The stuff of which martyrs are made had been left out of him. He wiped a sleeve across his face; the sweat was getting in his eyes.

"Are you against it?" Lothrop's repeated words drifted lazily through the smoke to spur his speech— succeeded.

"No," he almost whispered, "I ain't ag'in' it. But I sure ain't lookin' forward none."

Lothrop smiled. "There's nothing in the idea to get yore lather up. Takin' the ore from those pack trains when they try to cross the Jornada is goin' to be the easiest thing you ever did." His tone was definite, convincing to all but Suggs. "You'll find it easier than rollin' off a log. Nothin' to it. The Trail of the Dead," he savored the desert's name as another man might taste some old rare stimulating wine. "Even the name is goin' to be in our favor. I tell you, we've got this job licked before we start."

"What about the law?" Purdin wanted to know.

Lothrop's black brows rose sharply. "What law?" he said, and a tiny ripple of humor disturbed the cast of Moelner's cheeks.

The distant sound of hoofbeats checked whatever reply Purdin would have made. He stiffened, as did the others, and turned to face the door. The sound was beating nearer, drum-like in its throb. Louder and louder it grew, finally to cease with the slither of braced legs in the yard outside. A rider's boots hit dirt, came thumping down the *sala* . . . The rattle of knuckles shook the door.

"Come in," Lothrop called in a calm flat voice.

The man who entered was tall and thin, typical of that arid range, booted and spurred and belted. Held by a chin strap, a dust-covered Stetson was shoved far back on his head. He was a man Lothrop knew in Socorro.

His glance took in the gathered men. He nodded curtly and shut the door.

"What's up, Rafe?"

Rafe's eyes met Lothrop squarely.

"Hausleman," he said, "is dead."

Chapter IV

"YOU COULD EASY GRAB THE SHERIFF'S STAR"

Lothrop's eyes met Rafe's squarely. Far back in their smoke-grey depths a light of calculation kindled, but was not permitted to reach their surfaces. "Put your cards on the table where we can see 'em, Rafe. Let's see . . . when did this happen? Whose blade was responsible? Callares'? Boseman's? . . . I reckon it wasn't no accident."

"It wa'n't no accident, surely," Rafe said, tight of face. "An' nobody's knife slit his gullet, neither. He was killed deliberate . . . by the Smoke-wagon Kid."

"No!"

"Yes, by grab! An' right in the main street—right front of Melanchton Tiebalt's store. There was six or eight of us lookin' on. Damn me for a greaser if it wa'n't the quickest thing I ever see!"

"Spill it," Lothrop said. Like that.

"Well, it was like this," Rafe confided slowly.

"There was a bunch of us standin' round in front of Tiebalt's place chewin' the rag, yuh know, way fellas will? Well, some fool made a crack about all the rustlin' that's been goin' on." He stopped abruptly. "Say, where's Stumpy at?"

"Stumpy," Moelner drawled, "has got hisself a job with another spread."

"Get on with yore story," Purdin growled.

"Would, if yuh would give me haff a chance. Well, one thing led to another till some damn knothead remarks that it was pretty cute how the Kid had walked into Hausleman's jail an' sprung them greaser pris'ners. That opened things up fine, yuh bet. Hausleman, being sort of prideful-like, cuts loose a string of cusswords that woulda taken the hide right off a burro's rump. 'Lows as how he's aimin t' turn that four-flushin' Smoke-wagon hombre inside out, next time he comes sashayin' into town, an' use 'im for a rag to clean 'is gun with. An' just about right then the Kid hisself eases through the crowd an' stands there eyein' the sheriff up and down like a plug hawss he might be figgerin' to buy."

When the man from Socorro paused to scan the faces of his audience, enjoying the looks of interest they displayed, and his own importance, Black Jack Purdin—never a patient man—did some swearing of his own.

"Get on with it," Lothrop prodded. "We've got other things to do 'sides listen to yore gas. What happened?"

"Nothin' much, for a minute. The Kid just stood there real quiet-like lookin' him over. It fair give me the creeps! But when he spoke, it was worse—made a fella kind of think of hell, it was that harsh an' sinister. "What was that ag'in?" he says.

"Hausleman got whiter'n the teeth of a nigger's smile. He was startin' to back away when the Kid's left hand reaches out an' gets him by the collar. 'Fore yuh could say 'Jack Robinson' the Kid's right smashes him in the jaw. Gawd, yuh could hear 'is teeth crack! The Kid smacks him ag'in an' lets him loose. Hausleman, like the fool he was, jabbed for his gun. It was the las' move he ever made, intentional. He got his gun, all right—Kid let him, purposeful, I guess. Just sat there watchin' 'im with 'is eyes glowin' like a panther's an' that mockin grin on 'is han'some face. He never moved—I swear he never even blinked till Hausleman's gun cleared leather. I never seen 'im move then, even, but flame sorta jumped from 'is hand an' the sheriff went down with a winder through 'is skull."

For long seconds no one spoke. Then Suggs let out his breath like an old dog full of colic. Black Jack Purdin swore. Tombstone said:

"I been expectin' this. It's what comes of pickin' a scissors-bill with nothin' but air in his think-box. I warned yuh, Stone, that Hausleman wasn't the man."

Lothrop nodded. "He wasn't my choice; conditions, circumstances imposed him on me. But I'm not sorry he's out of the way." He turned his big shoulders back toward Rafe. "Where's the Kid at now?"

Rafe grinned sourly. "Yuh wa'n't expectin' him t' linger in Socorro after that, was yuh?"

"He's downed men before."

"A sheriff's a little different."

"I don't see no difference. Kid gave his man a break. That lets him out, so far's the law's concerned."

"So far's the law's concerned, yeah. But there's

public opinion to consider."

The grin crooking Lothrop's heavy lips was derisive. "Yeah?" His voice held a thin cynicism. "Public opinion's got a long way to go before it could worry me or the Kid. What did public opinion do about Curly Ives when he held Beck Colter up in front of the Rincon Bank, an' damn near beat his head in 'cause he didn't have more'n five cartwheels on 'im? What did it do about Moak when he loaded Jack Dunn with cusswords on the road between Rincon an' Radium Springs, and, seein' he wasn't armed, shot him through the head? An' this in broad daylight, right in plain view of two ranches, an' while several teams were comin along the road! Public opinion—*Hell!*"

Moelner leaned forward, and the lantern light threw dark shadows across his lean-carved cheeks, emphasizing the prominence of his narrow bone structure. "You're right, Stone. But it's due for a change," he warned. "An' it'll change quick-like an' unexpected when it does. We don't want t' get caught with our pants down."

Lothrop's sleepy-lidded eyes swung round to Tombstone's lounging posture, played upon the gunman's cadaverous face with its sunken, brooding eyes and great hollowed cheeks; upon the dark crossed gun-belts whose holstered weapons were slung butt forward for the rare and deadly cross-arm draw. He said:

"Tombstone, let's hear yore views on public opinion."

Tombstone grinned in a way that exposed his snaggly teeth, then spitted amber juice at the tomato can serving as a cuspidor. He shrugged when the shot went wild, and made a grimace. "Me," he said, "I don't waste no time figgerin' out notions on anythin' so damned unreliable. My motter's allus been: 'Shoot first an' do yore laffin after.' If follered persistent-like, it'll keep a gent above sod for a right smart spell."

Lothrop's answering grin licked a thin line across his mouth. Only last week, Tombstone, in need of money, had ridden his horse into Kelly's saloon and, flourishing a naked pistol, had tossed his buckskin purse upon the bar with the request that Kelly put two-three ounces of dust into it as "a temporary loan." Kelly had been quick to take the hint. And, to amuse himself while the saloon-man was weighing up the levy, Tombstone had emptied a gun at the bottles ranged along the back bar. So far, the episode had trailed no consequence in its wake.

Lothrop let his glance play over Ruidosa. The flashily garbed road agent was smoking with a strange nervousness, his beady eyes uncommonly sharp. A vague look of trouble lay across his cheeks, it seemed to Lothrop. But perhaps this was but a fancy born of the way the smoke and the light threw shadows.

Lothrop's gaze lay on him heavily as he asked, "What do you think about it?"

It almost seemed that the gaudy ruffian started. The Adam's apple moved behind the dangling chin straps of his hat, and indecision delayed his answer. When it came it was couched in the form of a question:

"What about Stumpy?"

"What about him?" The rancher's high blood laid a definite flush across his cheeks. Darn Harker, anyway! Was the fellow's hanging to sow rebellion among these trusted men? With harshened tone he repeated, "What about him?"

"Seems like—" Ruidosa hesitated, then plunged on—"that necktie party might mebbe 'a' been a sort of warnin'."

Lothrop said coldly, "If there was any warnin' meant, it was in regard to rustling cattle. Well, we're through with that two-bit game. No need to get the wind up."

"Well, yuh asked my opinion, an' yuh got it." Ruidosa shrugged. "Yuh have got my backin', too. Yo're boss. You make the plans; we'll carry 'em out."

"Sure," added Black Jack Purdin gruffly. "The boss ain't never let a man down yet."

Lothrop relaxed. This was better. "Anyone think to cut Stumpy down an' plant him?"

Tombstone nodded "Suggs an' me." His brooding eyes stared back at Lothrop darkly. "What we goin' t' do about Corner, Jones an' Stewart? They'd oughta get their needin's. We'll hev trouble with them gents yet, less'n we stomp 'em out while the stompin's good. Leave a rattler be an' he'll multiply considerable."

Lothrop put him off with, "They'll be tended to, don't worry," and turned his gaze on Rafe, who had been restlessly shifting his feet.

Rafe said, "About that Socorro business, Stone. You could easy grab the sheriff's star. Don't know's you'd want it, of course, but I reckon you could get it if you did."

Lothrop's breath deepened noticeably. "You think so?" Though disciplined, his tone revealed the excitement kindled by the possibilities he glimpsed with himself as sheriff. "You ain't fixin' to have me cut a big gut, now, are you?"

"Heck, no," Rafe said. "I'd never pick you t' run no sandy on, boss. What I said is straight. Two-three solid citizens was hintin' round last week that things would be a heap different if yuh was packin' the sheriff's star. If they didn't do another thing, the commissioners would sure appoint yuh t' fill out Hausleman's term."

Purdin's eyes were bright with anticipation. "Yuh could start for Socorro to-night—"

"By grab," Lothrop said, "I believe I'll do it!"

Chapter V

THE SMOKE-WAGON KID

At that eastern university honored for so short a time by his presence, it was said of Guy Antrim that had he been with General Kearny that intrepid officer would have annexed all Mexico, instead of one lone province. Native sons expressed their admiration by calling him *El Tigre*. But it was Governor Axtell who showed deeper insight when he said, "Give the rogue lead enough, and he'll rid the territory of all the badmen in it!"

Antrim was not a man to whom at first the casual observer would be apt to give great heed. He was quite boyish-looking and, at that time, could hardly have been much more than twenty-three, slenderly made, and with broad sloping shoulders that seemed a deal too large for the rest of his slender body. Lithe as a willow wand, his narrow-hipped waist held lines of speed, confirmed by the very quickness of all his movements.

Yet a closer look would have told the most casual of passers-by that here was no man to trifle with. The jaw of a fighter was slung forward beneath his long, wide, whimsical lips, and above those lips a Roman nose curved in the style of a vulture's beak. His eyes were curiously aloof, like those of some untamed animal, yet were never still an instant, perpetually probing his surroundings in a manner most embarrassing to others. His general appearance was best described as "foxy" though such a term would fall far short of doing him justice.

His face was dark from many suns, and his hair was red, like the waters of the Rio Colorado, and it—when taken in conjunction with the high, flat cheekbones and the cynical lines occasionally to be observed beneath his eyes—gave hint of violent passions and a dynamite temper not always under complete control.

He wore heavy leather chaps of the kind described as "batwings," scarred, and black in color, and the ordinary cowboy dress consisting of a blue cotton shirt, black scarf pulled tight about his neck, dusty ten-gallon Stet hat, and fancy Hyer boots with three-inch heels and silver plated gut-hooks with Texas-star rowels and pear-shaped danglers that jingled as he walked.

He was walking now, pacing the room with a nervous stride, as though deep in the complexities of some troublous problem. There was, at times, a savage light showing through the cold blue depths of his roving glance, and a cynical curl to his lips. And more often than not, the lean fingers of his ungloved hands would stroke caressingly the smooth dark butts of the heavy pistols strapped to his thighs, as though promising them swift employment should things not go to his liking.

A shadow abruptly darkened the doorway. Antrim whirled like a cat, and both his guns were focused menacingly as, stooping, a big man squeezed inside.

The man straightened up, grinned sourly at the levelled guns, but lost his grin as his eyes encountered Antrim's gaze. He frowned, then said, "Howdy, Kid. Feelin' kinda proddy this mawnin', ain't yuh?"

Antrim ignored the question. "There's such a thing as knockin'. It's a healthy habit some of these knot-heads oughta learn—yourself included. Trouble with this country is, it's raw an' crude an' primitive; it's filled with all the scum run out of better places." He paused to eye the intruder contemptuously. "It's a disgrace, Moak, to these United States."

"Sure, sure—I know it is, Kid," the big man said placatingly, "an' that's the truth. But you have got t' give us time. Yuh can't clean a country this size up in fifteen minutes—nor fifteen years. Takes time. We're doin' the best we can. We—"

"Was that why," Antrim cut in coldly, "you killed Jack Dunn the other day?"

Moak's face went a trifle pale beneath its bronze, and he eyed his questioner uneasily. "Now what yuh wantin' t'bring that up for?" he queried testily. "Jack Dunn was a hawss thief, an' yuh oughta know it. The fella was in need of killin' bad. I ast him where he got that piebald mare he was forkin', an' he tol' me it was none of my so-an'-so business. I might even 'a' let that pass if he hadn't started reachin' for his pocket. Did yuh think I was gonna stan' there an'—"

"That wasn't the way *I* heard it," Antrim's drawl ws filled with sarcasm. "But let it go. What did you want?"

"They've appointed a new sheriff t' fill out Hausleman's term. Thought mebbe yuh would be wantin' to know. Special since he's lookin' for yuh. Got—"

"Who?" the single word cut through the other's talk like a knife through cheese, arresting him with its quiet force.

"Lothrop."

"That fella that runs the Two-Pole-Pumkin?"

"Yeah. The fella some folks is callin' a cow-thief. An' he's huntin' yuh."

Antrim's brows drew down in thought. It was the only sign of reaction he gave to the information. His face showed no vestige of fear. Nor was apprehension discernible in the easy lines of his lounging posture.

The brows raised abruptly, revealing a cool determination in the blueness of his eyes. "Thanks, Moak. I'll look him up."

"Are yuh plumb crazy?"

"I've been called about everything else; why not that?"

Moak shook his head, and his hard face showed disapproval. "If I was yuh, and valued my hide, I'd get out of town as quick as Gawd an' a hawss' laigs would let me."

"An' thereby prove whatever suspicions are bein' entertained about you," Antrim said derisively. "Facin' him down will spike half an enemy's guns."

"While the other half," sneered Moak, "are blastin' windows in yore skull!"

"Antrim's cold grin fired up his youthful face and made it reckless. "Just the same, I'm lookin' him up. It's never been my style to run from trouble."

The sheriff's office was located in a large adobe shack, the rear of which had been somewhat re-modelled to serve as a jail. Behind the sheriff's desk,

Stone Lothrop sat with a gleaming badge pinned on his shirt, and a lazy smile on his heavy lips as he eyed the man who stood, fingering a battered hat, before him. This man, George Hildermin, had been a deputy of Hausleman's, and seemed to have a hankering to continue under the new regime in his former capacity. But for reasons easily guessed, Lothrop was not certain that he wanted him.

Lothrop's heavy lips were still curved in their lazy smile, his smoke-grey eyes intently probing. Hildermin was not a prepossessing man, so far as looks went. His eyes were watery, with an unpleasant habit of bulging. Because of its width, his mouth was a deformity, and the double row of huge teeth set firmly in massive jaws gave to his countenance an animal-like aspect of expression truly repulsive. No longer young, Hildermin's skull was almost bald, save for the monk-like fringe of hair about its sides. He was known to be a notorious bummer and was oftener indebted to the coarse humor at his command than to his usually empty pockets to provide himself with necessary sustenance. His favorite feat, often indulged at the Grand Hotel, was so to spread his monstrous jaws as to bite clean through seven dried-apple pies at one time. Bets with strangers as to his ability to do this had often earned him tobacco money for a week. It was whispered in the trembling of the leaves that Hildermin had removed there from some place in the vicinity of Alder Gulch, whence he had been driven by a vigilante clean-up. And it was this suspicion that finally determined Lothrop to oust him from his office.

Looking him coldly in the eyes, Lothrop said, "I'm afraid you'll have to go, Hildermin. Hausleman let this country get into pretty bad shape. It is high time someone set about cleaning it up. It will be better for all concerned if this office is completely rid of all the last incumbent's friends and allies."

Hildermin's popping eyes betrayed his reaction to such a speech. "B-But I thought—"

"Yore thoughts do not interest us in the least," Lothrop cut him off. Suggs snickered from where he slouched beside the window. And Hildermin scowled as Lothrop added: "You ever been in Nevada? Virginia City? Alder Gulch?"

Hildermin's surly shake of the head was negative, but his eyes revealed a trace of fear behind their narrowed lids.

"Ever been around Elk City? Or Bannack? . . . Haven't, eh? . . . Well, have you ever been in Rattlesnake or Brown Lodge or Cottonwood?"

Hildermin licked his lips and shifted his feet uneasily. "No," he grunted. "What yuh askin' me all them questions for, if yuh are goin' to kick me out?"

"You might say as how I was curious, George," Lothrop answered, and a grin licked a thin line across his mouth. "You see, I happen to know there was a George Hilder*man* up in that country who was connected with Plummer's gang, an' I just kind of wondered if mebbe you wasn't him."

Hildermin turned deathly pale. He began a stumbling backward movement toward the open door, one shaking hand disappearing jerkily inside his coat.

"Are you?"

Hildermin appeared undecided whether to flee or face the accusation out—for it was an accusation the way Lothrop said it. Keeping his hand inside his coat, the ex-deputy stopped. "Gawd, no!" he gasped. "I don't see why yuh should say such things. I never heard of no such man."

"Did you ever hear of Plummer?"

Hildermin reluctantly nodded. "I guess everybody's heard of him. He was hung, wasn't he—by vigilantes?"

"Was he?" Lothrop grinned as Hildermin shivered. "Well, I'm not fixin' to arrest you, so don't get lathered up. I expect you'll be lookin' for another job, now, won't you?"

Hildermin just looked at him. He seemed to be questioning himself as to what lay behind the sheriff's question. He was not left long in doubt.

"I was goin' to suggest that if you was short of funds, mebbe my foreman, Purdin, would put you on. I own the Two-Pole-Pumpkin out in Gawdforsaken Valley. If you get out that way, you might do worse than ask him." And still with that faint grin upon his mouth, Lothrop returned his attention to the papers littering his desk.

"More comp'ny headin' this way."

Suggs' comment drew Lothrop's gaze from the documents he was fingering. He watched an elongated shadow rock toward the door, strike the board walk outside and spill across it, lapping up against the step. The clank of spurs was plainly audible in the afternoon stillness. Now the scuff of boots rose from the walk and the comer's shadow slid inward across the floor.

Against his intentions, Lothrop got out of his chair at sight of the man who entered, and shoved his back against a wall. The man's features could be plainly discerned, for the room's light was good. Unlike the casual observer, Lothrop was not deceived for an instant into thinking this boyish-looking stranger some ordinary hand. In that country a man had to stand certain hard tests before being considered by his fellows as an equal; he had to have certain worth-while qualities. There was but one known court in the land whose opinions carried weight, and it was expected that a man would—if crowded—go to it promptly and settle his case. Cases settled in such a court held no appeal; they were final and irrevocable. One could see that this stranger knew that fact, and appreciated it: it was disclosed in the way he packed his guns. Lothrop discerned all this at a glance; he observed that this man had "stood the acid," and so addressed him respectfully:

"Howdy, stranger. What can I do for you?"

"You are the new sheriff?"

"Yes. My name is Lothrop—Stone Lothrop."

The stranger appeared to be studying the floor. When he looked up there was a frosty, ironical light in his eyes. "I hear you been lookin' for me."

Lothrop's heavy face showed a thin smile, and he chuckled deep down in his throat. "I'm lookin' for a number of men. But not the way I been lookin' for you—an' not for that purpose, either. Kid, I want to thank you for doin' the people of this country a damn big favor."

Antrim's red brows arched. "A favor? How was that?"

"By removin' the former incumbent of this office. That crook, Hausleman. It was a public service," he said, and held out his hand.

Antrim eyed the hand quizzically, dismissed it, and his glance sought the sheriff's face. "You ain't been huntin' me just to tell me that?" It was more like a statement, the way he put it.

Without change of countenance, Lothrop hooked

the hand in a suspender. "No," he said easily. "I want to hire yore guns."

A glint of amusement flashed from the blue of Antrim's eyes. "What makes you think they're for hire?"

"You *would* hire them, wouldn't you? If the pay was right?"

"Well, if the pay was right . . . Leastways, I'll admit to findin' you interesting. The last sheriff to hold down that chair was right anxious to see me swung. Would you mind explainin' the change of sentiment?"

"The last sheriff," Lothrop said brusquely, "was a fool. Things are goin' to be different now. This country's in bad need of law. I aim to see that it gets it."

Antrim drawled, "I see," and a grin curled his wide lips saturninely. "You figure to work on the principle that it takes a gunman to out a gunman. That it?"

"Roughly, yes." Lothrop's eyes met Antrim's squarely. "You got any objections to seein' this country cleaned up?"

Antrim's eyes met Lothrop's squarely. "On the contrary. I'd be plumb tickled to help in the cleanin'. Killin's are gettin' so common round here it's *time* someone was puttin' a stop to them—even if it takes more killin's to effect said stop."

Lothrop chuckled. "I see I ain't misjudged you none. You'll take the job, then?"

Antrim eyed the bit of metal gleaming in the lawman's hand. "A deputy's job?"

"Sure."

"What about those rewards—those bounties Hausleman tacked on my pelt?"

"You don't need to worry about them; I'll see they're struck off the records if you sign on with me."

Antrim's gaze was sharply probing. A lesser scoundrel would have flinched from it, but Lothrop met it steadily, and the bulldog grip of his heavy features was coldly earnest.

"It's Gawd's truth, Kid, I need you bad. An' I'll go any length to get you. This is a tough country, an' she'll take tough men to tame her. But she's a country that's well worth savin' for folks that will apppreciate her. Are you takin' the job or ain't you?"

"Since you insist," Antrim said, "I'll take it." And the ghost of a grin flashed across his lips.

Chapter VI

AT THE TWO-POLE-PUMPKIN

Halfway across the Jornada, Guy Antrim stopped briefly at a small rancho run by a Mexican. He was an old man, this rancher, frail and stooped of figure, and nearsighted, to judge by the squint of his peering eyes.

"Buenas dias le de Dios, señor," he greeted Guy.

With true Spanish courtesy, Antrim answered the salutation in kind, *"Que Dios se los de buenos a Usted, señor."*

"My poor house is as yours, *señor*," the old man said. "Will you rest?"

"But a moment," Antrim answered. "My way is long, and I am overdue. Do you find it safe in these troublous times living here alone in the desert?"

"I have nothing to lose but my life, *señor*, and that is in God's hands."

Antrim took the olla of water the old man handed him. It felt good as it trickled down his dusty throat. "Gracias," he said, when the rancher came back leading his horse, whose muzzle dripped moisture. "May God reward you."

"*Vaya con Dios.*" The old man waved his hand as Antrim rode off.

He stopped at noon at the Long H ranch of Hootowl Jones on the eastern edge of Gawdforsaken Valley. Only two hands were there at the time, and he ate with them and Jones. Smoking brown-paper *cigarros,* he and the rancher lingered a spell at the table after the punchers left.

"Yuh will find this country easier ridin' on a full stomach, I expect," Jones observed. "Guess the Jornada's pretty dusty."

"I reckon."

" 'Fore yuh shove off, yuh better fill yore water bags. No tellin' when yuh will get another chance. Water's scarce in this country—'bout as scarce as elephant tusks on the White Sands. Kinda bad country t' be ridin' in after dark."

Antrim smoked in silence. He could feel Jones' suspicion surging round him like a rope. It pressed against him with a wicked insistence. But no sign on his part disclosed his knowledge. Jones would ask no embarrassing questions much as he might wish to know Antrim's business and identity. He would put no questions directly because to do so might be to invite gun-play. Personal questions were not popular in that part of the world.

Jones' glance was on him intently, probing, trying

to tear the mask from his features. "Lookin' for a job of ridin'?"

"No . . . not especially. Just moseyin' around, as a man might say. Just hankerin' to know what's on the other side of the hill." Antrim suddenly grinned. "I just been broke out of the army. I'm kinda at loose ends. Isn't there a gent named Stewart runnin' a spread around here some place?"

He saw caution cloud the cold gaze of Jones. He watched Jones crush out his cigarette and take a middling-big bite from a plug of black tobacco. Jones munched, much like a heifer, and through his munching said:

"There's a Stewart, I believe, that runs a ranch some place in this valley. Fella named Ed Stewart. His iron's the Crazy L. Yuh a friend of his?"

"Nope. I don't know the gent; just heard tell of him, is all. Heard he had a real nice layout over here."

"He ain't lookin' fer no riders, young fella, I can tell yuh that," Jones grunted sourly. "He's got more hands now than he savvies what t' do with. This damn drought has like t' put us valley ranchers plumb outa the cow business fer keeps—an' it may, yet. That or rustlers."

"Wouldn't hardly think a discernin' rustler would bother with such gaunted-up critters as I've been lookin' at this morning," Antrim observed.

"No, yuh wouldn't think so. It just goes t' show how ornery a human can get. I reckon. Cow-stealin's about the lowest thing I know of. Have much of it where yuh come from?"

"Quite a bit," Antrim said; "but we aim to make it right unpleasant for gents caught so engaged. We string them up usual-like without much fussin'."

He looked at Jones squarely. The rancher's face was a taut dark mask. But not swiftly enough did Jones conceal the glint that flashed in his sombre eyes at the mention of hanging rustlers. Antrim did not ponder that glint now, but stored it away in his mind for future consideration . . . there were other things stored there . . .

"It's the only sure cure fer such cusses," Jones grunted gloomily, spat, and changed the subject. "Any news up to the county seat? Or haven't yuh heard?" he added carefully.

"I reckon you've likely heard that Hausleman was killed," Antrim suggested, and, at the other's nod, said, "They've put in a man from down this way to fill out the rest of his term. Fellow by the name of Lothrop? Know him?"

"Lothrop!"

For an instant Antrim glimpsed the steel in Jones' soul. Then Jones' lids drew down and veiled his eyes. His face was solemn. "Yes, I know him . . . as well as I figger to want to. He's a neighbor, as yuh might say. Lives over near t' other side of the valley. Runs the Two-Pole-Pumpkin brand. He—" Jones checked the sentence at its start and grimly closed his mouth.

"Not a friend of yours, I take it?"

"Not a particular friend," Jones said.

Antrim would have liked to ask Jones if he knew anything against Lothrop—anything about the rumors connecting the Two-Pole-Pumpkin owner with the rustling that was going on. But he well knew the value in reticence. This was not a land where questions could be lightly or safely put to any save one's closest friends, and even then questions were best left unasked. It was the code; a man's past belonged to himself until of his own volition he made it

217

public property. Few men in that wild country had come there of deliberate choice; many of them had arrived "two jumps ahead of some sheriff," as the saying went. They assumed a different name, and the chances were good of their remaining undiscovered. However, what a man had done before coming there was little cause for concern; it was what he did *while there* that counted.

Under the covert scrutiny of Jones, Antrim felt glad he had pinned his badge inside his vest. No telling what type of hombre this gangling rancher might be; his rough, suspicious exterior might cover either the soul of an honest man, or the warped cunning of an outlaw. Many an honest man held the law in vast contempt, and would do his best to thwart it. When one worked on law business, it was profitable to keep the fact to oneself.

"So Lothrop's got to be sheriff now," Jones' voice held a thoughtful tone, a casual thoughtfulness that did not deceive Antrim any. He knew that he had roused Jones' interest in some way by the news. "Do yuh reckon he will clean up some of this hellin' round the boys are doin'?"

"Couldn't say—I don't know Lothrop t'more than nod to, hardly. I heard, though," Antrim added, "that he's aimin' to put a stop to some of these killin's. They tell me another mine owner's been dry-gulched over to Silver City."

"Dry-gulchin's are gettin' so common over that way," Jones said morosely, "that nobody pays 'em a mite of attention any more. This country's goin' to the dawgs, if yuh're askin' me. They orta send the troops in here an' clean it up."

"This country's big," Antrim observed. "It'll take some time to smooth it down."

"Yuh goin' to hit Corner or Stewart for a job?"

"Ain't been thinkin' of it. I might, though, if the pay was right."

Jones said: "Let me give yuh some advice, stranger. No one in this valley is puttin' on men now. The best thing yuh can do is to get on yore hawss an' head back where yuh come from. I tell yuh this with the best of intentions."

For a moment Antrim sat quiet and a chill came over the room. Then he crushed his cigarette upon a saucer and pushed his chair back. A cold grin curled his wide lips saturninely as he rose.

"An' with the best of intentions," he said, "I reckon I'll stay."

Dusk was beginning to roll its sable blankets across the range when Guy Antrim came in sight of the adobe buildings of Lothrop's ranch headquarters at Two-Pole-Pumpkin. Though he had travelled across the valley all afternoon he had seen no other riders. Neither had he observed any cattle. He had seen nothing but scattered tufts of sunburned grass, parched earth, and in the distance the barrier hills that hemmed that place. During the afternoon they had been a palish sort of blue, but now they were limned deep purple against the darkening heavens.

The dark bulk of a man stepped out of a deep shadow by the gate leading to the *patio*, and blocked his path. The lighted windows of the rancho showed a glint of metal in his hand, and Antrim stopped in his dismounting with one foot still in a stirrup.

"Put it down," the other said, "an' name yorself. An' do it quick or yuh can give it to Saint Peter."

"Guy Antrim. I think your boss is expectin' me."

"Yeah? Well, we'll be findin' out about that." He

raised his voice, "Suggs!"

"That you, Mitch?"

The voice of the man with the pistol drawled sarcastically, "Naw—just one of the cows," then coldly growled, "Go tell Lothrop there's a pilgrim out here callin' hisself Guy Antrim which says the boss is expectin' him."

The scuff of retreading boots told Antrim that Suggs had departed on the errand. Standing hipshot beside his horse, Antrim rolled a cigarette. When it was made he placed it casually between his lips. "Mind if I light a coffin nail?"

"You can light a haystack, for all of me."

The cool insolence of that remark spoke volumes. It told Antrim that this man before him had a set of nerves under beautiful control—beautiful. It was the sort of thing a man might say who, unarmed, would just as lief spit in a cougar's face. It was the remark of a man who had an utter confidence in himself and whom no circumstance could dismay.

For this reason, as Antrim's right hand brought a flaming splinter to his cigarette, his glance went searchingly to this Mitch's face. He found it a hard, bronzed mask—a mask of ironic humor. And there was a cold ironic humor in the tone with which he said:

"Satisfied?"

Antrim grinned. "Sorta. You Lothrop's major-domo?"

As the match went out he saw the fellow's bold glance register cynical amusement. Mitch said, "I would be if Lothrop had just a haff ounce more of savvy." And Antrim guessed that Mitch would just as soon have said that to Lothrop's face—or Purdin's.

Approaching footsteps, and the jingle of spurs

drew Antrim's gaze across Mitch's shoulder. Two men were coming from the *patio*, the lighted windows throwing their shadows elongated on the opposite wall. One was a gangling, loose-limbed fellow who walked with a limp. The other, by his breadth of shoulder, Antrim knew to be Lothrop.

As Lothrop came up he shoved out a friendly hand. "Glad to see you," he said, as Antrim took it. "You made good time. Hadn't hardly expected you until tomorrow."

"I left early."

"Let's go inside. Can't be no hotter in there than it is out here, an' it'll be a sight more comfortable if we do our palaverin' sittin' down. We just finished supper. Have you et?"

"Consid'rable dust," Antrim answered drily. "Grub don't seem to flourish much on this valley sage. But don't go puttin' your cook out on my account. I can make out till morning."

" 'Twon't be no trouble at all," Lothrop said peculiarly. "My woman does all the cookin' here. She won't mind."

As they entered the *patio* and Lothrop turned toward an open door, over a burly shoulder he called, "C'mon in, Mitch. Suggs can hold the gate down for a spell."

Back in the storehouse of his mind, Antrim deposited the fact that the Two-Pole-Pumpkin kept a sentinel posted. This Mitch had not just chanced to be standing in that shadow by the gate. Of course the Indians in this country *did* occasionally daub on a smear of warpaint, still . . .

They entered one of the lighted rooms off the *patio*. Antrim saw in one comprehensive glance that it was well furnished for the times; it seemed almost luxurious with its Navajo and Hopi blanket rugs, its pine and cowhide chairs and settees. There was even an oil painting on one wall above the calico dado.

Lothrop called, "Yola—we've got company. One of my men from town. Fix him up somethin' to eat," and dropped into a chair, thrusting his feet out comfortably before him. He waved Antrim to a seat and began the manufacture of a brown-paper quirly. "Kid," he said easily, "this is Mitch Moelner. You'll find he'll do to ride the river with. Mitch, this here's the Smoke-wagon Kid." He watched them amusedly from beneath his sleepy lids.

Antrim, in the yellow light, could see that Moelner was a tall wiry man with a dark, lean-carved face. In each of Moelner's lazy movements was the smooth confidence of a panther. There was one gun strapped about his waist, but a bulge in the left side of his vest disclosed the presence of a shoulder gun. Antrim recognized a kind of surly strength about the man; not so much a swagger as a coldly arrogant indifference to the rights and opinions of others. He was clad in trousers of some dark material and wore a vest of the same sort with silver buttons over a blue flannel shirt.

Antrim said, "Glad to know you," but did not offer his hand.

Moelner's glance was mocking. "So you are the Kid, eh? I reckon you've teamed up with our new sheriff on the chance of gatherin' more scalps. Business gettin' bad?"

"It'll be gettin' better soon, I expect."

"That's not open to argument," Moelner said, and laid his shoulders against the wall. "Considerin' yore rep, you know, you don't look so tough. I've seen lots meaner lookin' hombres than you."

"I reckon you have. I don't go around makin' faces at folks, an' the rep wasn't of my seekin'."

Moelner said, "Well, we all have our peculiarities. I guess you had a lot of luck."

Antrim's cold grin fired up his face and made it reckless. "A gent that thinks so always has the opportunity of findin' out."

"Yeah," Moelner remarked, "I guess that's so."

What more might have been said was at that moment postponed by an unexpected diversion. A girl had entered the room and stopped halfway to the table; stopped with swiftly indrawn breath. A slab of meat fell from the plate she carried, struck the floor and rolled.

Moelner looked and a saturnine humor brushed across his cheeks.

The girl was staring at Antrim. Her face was pale. Her wide glance revealed stark amazement, as though she asked herself what this man was doing there; dread stared from it, too, and recognition. Then a film of caution whisked between her thoughts and those who watched.

"That's one hell of a place," Lothrop's voice drawled coldly, "to put a fellow's grub."

"I'm sorry," she said breathlessly, backing toward the door; "I'll fix something else."

Antrim's features were immobile; smooth as marble, they reflected no slightest fragment of his mind. His long high body relaxed at perfect ease, made a quite impressive picture of indolence; a picture calculated to lure astray any suspicion the girl's strange actions might have created in the minds of his two companions. But underneath this cool exterior, Antrim was a seething mass of chaotic emotions; question after question rose and fell without an answer. A statement of Lothrop's came back to him now and heightened that wild turbulence rushing through his blood. Yet his poise was perfect, his outer calm unruffled, and the glance with which he scanned the various appointments of the room was utterly serene and tranquil.

Lothrop's stare was sharply probing. About him, though, was an air of indecision, of unsureness, reflecting the unsettled state of his temper. Moelner had settled his shoulders more comfortably against the calico wall and his thoughts were sheathed behind a deep inscrutability. Here, Antrim felt, was the more dangerous antagonist, should these men become aligned against him.

"She's been actin' kind of queer lately, Kid. You'll have to make allowances for her," Lothrop said, completing his smoke, placing it between his lips, and crossing toward a lamp. "I don't reckon she's feelin' right, exactly."

Antrim nodded with an apparent indifference.

"You haven't noticed a leathery old coot, about six-foot-six, hangin' round town, have you?" Lothrop asked. "Fellow by the name of Harker?"

"Can't say that I have. Friend of yours?"

"One of my hands." Lothrop pulled a deep draught of smoke into his lungs, and exhaled it slowly while his brows took on a thoughtful frown. "Funny thing about that. Harker's been workin' for me upwards of four years. Good, steady, hard-workin' type. Can't understand it. He left for town about ten-twelve days ago."

"Didn't he turn up there?"

"Not that I know of. None of the saloons has seen him an' he hasn't been to the store."

"Mebbe," Mitch Moelner offered, "Lefty Corner or Stewart or that damn Hootowl Jones could give a pretty good guess where he's gone to."

Lothrop smoked moodily. At last he said, "That's what I'm afraid of. Been bad blood between 'em ever since that trouble over Salt Springs. I don't include Stewart in anything that mighta happened to him; Stewart's a pretty square-shooter. But them other two . . ." He shook his head. "I'm prob'ly wrong," he added hopefully. "Like enough Stumpy will come joggin' in one of these evenin's lookin' fat an' sassy. He mighta gone to Silver City. He seemed kind of excited like about the ore they been takin' out of some of those mines up there."

"Don't you never believe it," Mitch Moelner said darkly. "It ain't like Stumpy to stay away like this without saying somethin'. You know it. I'm bettin' one of them damn bushwhackers has put a window through his haid."

Antrim pondered these things briefly, and put them back in that portion of his mind where other things were stored.

"Do the soldiers from Fort Craig ever come through here?" he asked irrelevantly.

Lothrop looked at him with an alive interest, and then some thought laid a shadow across his cheeks. "You're wonderin', I reckon, about some of the robberies that have been goin' on. We been doin' considerable speculation along them lines, too. The soldiers ride through occasionally, yes. But I don't know's they've ever caught any road agents. Who-ever's back of these stick-ups an' the gen'ral cuss-edness that's goin' on is plenty smart. But I'm keepin' my eyes open, you can bet on that. Like the soldiers, though, I can't be more'n one place at a time."

Chapter VII

A WOMAN PLEADS

Antrim nodded. "I guess that's so," he said, and let his glance go round the room, noting the way the lamps' mellow light picked out shadows and emphasized the bony sharpness of Moelner's features and rounded the stubborn heaviness of Lothrop's face into a smooth mask of earnest determination. It was curious, he thought, the way an angle of illumination could play tricks with a man's character.

In the thoughtful silence a coyote's wail drifted out of the desert's deep stillness, one mournful drop of sound in the vast immensity of space; a long-drawn, brooding pulsation, lonely and changeless as was the desert waste itself. Used as he was to those open lands, Antrim felt a stricter sense of isolation, a greater feeling of personal insignificance in the ultimate scheme of things. Yet his reaction to the sound, as to most other things with which he came in contact, cast no shadow across the serene tranquillity of his outward appearance.

Lothrop said, "The first thing I aim to do is catch that fellow Moak, the man who shot Jack Dunn, the prospector, in broad daylight right in plain view of two ranches, an' with several teams comin' along the road. That hombre's got to go. It's gents like him that's giving this country its bad name. We can't expect to get no decent citizens into this country while killin's an' robberies are so common that folks don't even talk about 'em hardly."

"Is he still in the country?" Antrim asked. "I thought he pulled his picket pin right after the Rincon Bank was robbed."

Mitch Moelner's dark and narrow countenance hardened, and a soft oath left his lips. "So he's the saddle-blanket polecat that pulled that deal, is he? I'd admire t' meet up with him. I had five hundred dollars in that crib."

"So Hausleman knew it wasn't those two bean-eaters he locked up, did he?" Lothrop murmured.

"Can't say, as to that," Antrim answered. "But they weren't the first two innocent gents he put under lock'n key, so I shouldn't wonder but what he had a pretty good idea that—" He let the rest of the sentence trail away and, with his dark blue glance on Lothrop, said:

"Wasn't Hausleman a friend of yours?"

Lothrop fetched a wry grin. "Appearances are apt to be deceptive, but I'm beginnin' to be afraid he wasn't. I helped put him in office, though, if that's what you mean."

"Hausleman," Moelner said, "was anybody's dawg that would hunt with him."

Lothrop met Antrim's glance. "It's men like that," he declared, "that give politicians a bad name." He stared at the rafters thoughtfully. "I'm hopin' things'll be different, now. It's time this lawless element was weeded out. I'm goin' to do my best, an I'm countin' on you boys to help me. We'll arrest every road agent we catch. Them we can't prove nothing on, we'll warn out of the country. Those that don't go, we'll plant."

Antrim grinned a little wryly. "When I think of all the hell-raisin' goin' on round here, it gets me riled. This is a fine country—God's country—an' I hate to see it contaminated by the kinda trash that's been driftin' in. These tracks the Santa Fé's been layin' across the country are signs of progress. They're goin' to be a big help to the country; going to open it up. But they're attractin' a passel of mighty undesirable citizens, an' some way has got to be found to get shut of 'em."

"Seems t' me you are talkin' mighty sassy for a fella with yore rep," Mitch Moelner remarked. "How do you know but what these damn vigilante committees you are talkin' for so strong won't mebbe string you up alongside the rest of the gore-dabblers yo're runnin' down so hard?"

"Perhaps they will," Antrim answered coldly. "But what I do's between me an' my God, an' what happens to me'll be in the same category. I've never robbed any man, an' I've never driven my lead into any man's back—nor talked across gunsmoke to any man that wasn't needin' that kind of talk."

Mitch Moelner spat. "Humph!" he said with a scepticism that whitened Antrim's cheeks. "Wal, you've sure got plenty of tongue oil. Hootowl Jones oughta hire you t' keep his windmill goin'. If you go round expressin' them kinda sentiments in wholesale lots, like you been doin' here, you are goin' to be about as popular in Socorro as a preacher on payday night."

"You wantin' to make somethin' out of it?" Antrim asked with dangerous softness, laying down his knife and fork preparatory to pushing back his chair.

"Hell," sneered Moelner scathingly. "I don't pick quarrels with fools."

Lothrop said with surprising swiftness, "That'll be enough of that wranglin'. We've got work enough on our hands—an' trouble enough, too—without stirrin' up hard feelin's at home. Go on an' finish yore supper, kid. Mitch, you go out an' keep an eye peeled for the boys."

After Moelner, grinning twistedly, had gone, Lothrop said, "The Santa Fé's plannin' to lay track to Deming. Did you know?"

Antrim shook his head, and through a mouthful of food, said, "I hadn't heard. Why Deming?"

"Well," Lothrop pursed his heavy lips throughtfully, "I'd say to connect with the Southern Pacific from California. That's the story that's been given out up to the capital. May be the right one. But I've got a sneakin' hunch that the main thing them railroad men have got up their sleeve is Silver City, an' the minin' camps. That country up there is a treasure vault. But, to realize on their finds, them miners have got to have some way of gettin' the ore to where they can get hard cash for it. Tradin' in ore an' dust is all right on a small scale, but it ain't no account when it comes to buyin' a ranch, or a store, or a herd of cattle. Them things needs cash. The railroad will provide them miners with a quick way of gettin' cash for their diggin'."

"You figure the trail through the Sierra Caballos will be abandoned?"

"Not abandoned," Lothrop said, "but a lot less used than it's bein' right now. Most fellas will ship by rail, once the Santa Fé runs track down this way." He paused to regard Antrim curiously from beneath his shaggy brows. "Do you know," he said softly, "that trail is goin' to provide some enterprisin' scoundrels with the opportunity of a lifetime."

"Yeah? I expect you mean the mule trains packin' silver ore through those mountains when travel slackens on that trail are goin' to be temptin' bait for gents with easy consciences, eh?"

"Exactly. That's wild, rugged country up there in

those mountains, Kid. Kinda lonely-like an' desolate. I've got a hunch there's goin' to be some ruckuses on that trail."

"I expect your hunch is right," Antrim said. A cold humor glinted from his eyes. "One way you can make that country safe for the miners' pack trains, though."

Lothrop's glance was a question, and in it there was just a tiny trace of concern. "What way is that?"

"By sendin' me up in that country as your deputy. I'll guarantee to get those trains through for you."

Lothrop shook his head; definitely, yet with seeming reluctance. "Can't be done, Kid. 'Twould be an uproarious move, sure enough. But I can't spare a deputy up there in those mountains; you, least of all. Nope, them miners will just naturally have to take their chances. I need you too bad around here. May even have to use you in town, if things get worse. Right now, though, I'm figurin' to have you keep your eye on things here in Gawdforsaken Valley, an' out on the Jornada."

"Put Mitch Moelner to watchin' the valley."

"I ain't quite sure I trust Mitch, Kid. Some ways I do. Then again there's times when I could almost swear he's in with the toughs. Nope, I couldn't put Mitch in charge here; I want Mitch where I can watch him."

They talked on awhile longer about this and that, mostly range conditions, the price of cattle, and suchlike; then Antrim picked up his hat and headed for the door. "I'll take care of my horse, I reckon, an' then turn in."

Lothrop nodded. "Put yore bed roll in the bunkhouse. Don't expect many of the boys'll be in tonight. Anyway, Mitch or somebody will point you out an empty place. See you in the mornin'.''

As Antrim moved across the moonlit *patio*, a shadowy figure detached itself from the blue gloom beneath a pepper tree, beckoned, and once again grew indistinct in the darkness. Antrim swung aside, strode into the murk and beheld the vague, blurred figure of Yolanda.

"Well?"

He heard again the sharp, sucking sound of breath drawn through her teeth, as when she'd nearly dropped the plate in front of Lothrop. He could sense the stiffening of her slender form as she drew back. He could not make out the expression of her face, but he could guess it.

"Is that all you have to say to me, Guy Antrim? To me, the woman you swore you loved that night in Santa Fé? After all these awful months, is that all you can find it in your heart to say?"

"What else?" he asked derisively. "That tone you're usin' would have moved me once, I reckon. But your talent's wasted now. A lot can happen in fourteen months."

"You're hard," she said softly; "hard and bitter, Guy. But don't blame me too much. I was young; my head was easily turned. Lothrop came. You were away, and he seemed such a *grande caballero*. He—Do you know what it is to be born of a good family whose fortunes have been so reversed by a change in government as to leave it penniless; as to leave it owning large estates mortgaged to the boundaries? Do you know what it is to watch foreign pigs and even your own people taking advantage of your straitened circumstances to steal your birthright?" Do you know what temptation is?

"We were facing ruin, Mother and I," she said fiercely when Antrim did not answer. "Ruin! Lothrop had painted pictures for us of his verdant acres, hundreds of thousands of them, well-watered, teeming with servants, trod by countless herds of sleek, fat cattle! Can you blame me, young and impetuous as I was, for seeking to escape the ruin I saw before me? With those grand pictures of wealth and position under the new regime as the wife of El Señor Lothrop, I left my home one night—ran off with him. I was a fool; I do not deny it. But I have reaped my reward."

She leaned toward him and her almost-whispered words were seared with bitterness: "Do you know what it is to be caged on a blistering desert for fourteen months with a man like Lothrop?"

"I know what it is to be described as a 'killer'—to sleep by fits and starts when opportunity for sleep permits, with one eye always open, and one's hand curled round a gun. I know what it means to owe one's life to unceasing care and unremitting vigilance; to a quick draw, and a steady glance. I know what it is to live in the constant expectation of some mongrel bushwhackin' gun-packer drivin' his lead through my back for the doubtful glory of bein' able to boast that he's outsmoked the Smoke-wagon Kid. I know those things," Antrim answered evenly.

"But those things you spoke of—no. I have no knowledge of your life, nor of the events that may have figured in it since you left Santa Fé. When I started East for college, I too was young. Oh, yes— and filled with fine illusions and high ideals. You say you were a fool. Well, you were no greater fool than I, Yolanda. I can see that now. But I have no knowledge of those things you mention. And frankly, ma'am, I have no curiosity concerning them."

He touched his hat, bowed and, wheeling into the moonlight, stiffly strode away.

"Wait!" Her voice was like a broken bell. "Guy! You can't go like—" The taste of ashes was in her mouth. The proud head drooped as a muffled sob shook the slender form within the pepper's blue-black shadow.

Chapter VIII

"DON'T SHOOT!"

When Antrim entered the mess shanty for breakfast with the hands, he appeared completely oblivious to their presence. One brief, all-encompassing glance he vouchsafed them, then turned his attention strictly to the task of tucking away the food with which his plate had been laden by Yolanda. He was staring thoughtfully at the ceiling when she served him, and for all the sign he gave she might never have come near. Her lips curled scornfully as she moved away, but he was not watching. His manner was reserved, grimly preoccupied, forbidding.

His meal was nearly finished when a swelling thunder of hoofbeats drew his eyes from his plate. The glance he flung at Lothrop was coldly questioning. Lothrop shoved back his chair, wiped his mouth on a sleeve, and strode outside.

The hoofbeats suddenly terminated in the yard. Antrim could hear the subdued mutter of voices. Then footsteps, accompanied by the clash of spurs.

Lothrop stuck his head in the door. His eyes flashed to Antrim's meaningly. And to Mitch Moelner's, too. Then he disappeared, and those within the mess shanty could hear him go striding away across the yard with the newcomer.

Leisurely Antrim rose and as leisurely followed Moelner outside. He saw Stone Lothrop and a short, heavy-set man heading toward the corrals. The stranger was gesticulating excitedly. Antrim's glance swept the yard, came to rest on the stranger's horse. The animal stood still, head down and body quivering. Sweat plastered its flanks in gobs. Antrim's glance reached out across the yellow earth, and his eyes were squinted, thoughtful. When he swung them back to the strange rider, who was swinging open the gate of the main corral, they were kindled with live interest.

"Looks like that hombre's been ridin' hell-fer-leather," Moelner said, his glance on the stranger curiously. "That's a Broken Stirrup bronc he was forkin'. Ol' man Catling's brand—his spread's the other side of Eagle."

Antrim strode toward the corral. Moelner grimaced at his broad back and followed, one thumb hooked in his gun-belt.

The stranger had shaken out his lasso and was approaching the milling *remuda* when Antrim came up. Antrim remained silent, leaning indolently against the bone-white poles while the stranger cast his rope, missed, and swore. Antrim watched while he hauled it in and built another loop. The fellow's second cast was luckier. He snared a short-coupled blue roan weighing near a thousand pounds; with the feel of the lasso about its arched neck, the animal stopped with braced legs, big body quivering. The man walked down the rope and, slipping a bridle over the horse's head, led him toward the gate.

"What's up?" Antrim said.

Lothrop turned and regarded him strangely. "This fella," he said, "tells me Moak showed up at Catling's ranch last night while the boys was away an' attacked Catling's fourteen-year-old girl. Her yells brought the ol' man on the scene. Moak shot him through the stomach."

"That's right," the man said dustily as he led his captured mount through the gate and picked up his saddle. "The rat drove four slugs through his guts before the ol' man could aim his hawg-laig!"

"Moak? The man that riddled Jack Dunn?"

"Yeah, *Moak*—the yeller-bellied sidewinder!"

Antrim studied the man's white face and bloodshot eyes. "What happened then? When'd you find out about it?"

"Happened close on to ten o'clock, I guess. Kid told us about it when we rode in this mawnin', early. We'd been to town. Ol' man had given us our forty per the afternoon before. She was pretty much upset, cryin' an' laffin' all to oncet. Moak had pulled out a coupla hours 'fore we got there. I left the boys huntin' his trail an' come on here. Figgered the sheriff had orta know."

Lothrop and Mitch Moelner exchanged significant glances. Antrim saw, but gave no sign. He picked up the cowboy's rope and began coiling it. His jaws were clenched and his mouth was a grim-lipped line. Cold fury brightened his hard eyes. Without words he strode into the corral. He built a loop without lost motion. The cavvy swirled with a rush of dust, pressing the far side of the pen. Inexorably Antrim closed

235

the interval. His loop was twirling now above his head, growing larger with each undulation of his wrist. It left his hand, darting forward with an uncanny precision that dropped it over the arched head of a bay whose long slim legs promised speed. The abruptness of its stopping sent up little bursts of dust.

Antrim gathered in his slack and led the horse from the corral. Still leading it, he walked past Lothrop and Moelner to the kak-pole, slipped a bridle over the bay's head and removed the rope. His centre-fire saddle slapped loudly on the bay's smooth back.

"Texas man, eh?" Broken Stirrup spat.

So did Moelner, and said, "In some ways, mebbe. He *looks* the part."

Antrim shoved one booted foot against the bay's distended ribs with a force that knocked the wind from its barrel. A swift tug jerked the latigo tight. He stepped into the saddle and the bay went into the air. It struck earth on bunched feet with bone-snapping violence.

Antrim flung the plunging horse around, soothed it down with the same display of quiet confidence with which he performed the slightest chore, and sent it cantering toward the bunk-house. Dismounting, he trailed the reins and stepped inside to get his rifle, a buffalo gun with a revolving cylinder.

When he emerged, Lothrop and the salty Moelner had roped horses and were leading them toward the kak-pole. He thrust the rifle into his saddle scabbard, an affair that was slung butt forward in an almost horizontal position along the bay's near side and passed between two leaves of the stirrup leather. Gathering the reins in his left hand, he climbed aboard.

While Lothrop and Moelner were gearing their mounts, Antrim lounged in his saddle with his leg crooked about the horn, and rolled a cigarette. As he lit up and inhaled great draughts of the fragrant smoke, he watched the Broken Stirrup puncher lead his own winded broomtail to a small corral, turn it in, and raise the bars. Antrim continued to watch the man as he strode back to his borrowed roan and swung into the saddle. A black scowl on his face told plainer than any words his anxiety to be gone.

Antrim urged his bay to where the man sat waiting. He observed the impatience that marked the fellow's every movement. He said, "How far is it to your place, pardner?"

"Twenty-five mile."

Antrim considered. "You made good time."

"I figgered to," the man said shortly. "You Lothrop's range boss?"

"Not hardly. There seems to be a doubt about my official standing. Lothrop said he was hiring me as a deputy sheriff. But yesterday I overheard one of his riders tellin' another that I was his heavy artillery."

The heavy-set rider joined in Antrim's laughter. "You kinda look the part, as that hombre," he jerked a thunb at Moelner, "jest remarked. I'm called Pronto Joe—I'm top screw over to the Broken Stirrup. Don't believe I caught your name."

"Don't believe you did. It's Antrim."

Pronto Joe regarded him curiously, a light of speculation in his faded eyes. "Seems like I heard Lothrop referrin' to yuh as the 'Kid.' Yuh don't happen t' be the Smoke-wagon Kid, I don't suppose." He was right careful to handle his tone so that it did not form a question.

Antrim smiled mirthlessly. "Some gents prefer to

call me that."

It was odd to witness the homage the Broken Stirrup foreman's eyes paid the owner of that cognomen. To him Antrim seemed suddenly to become a magnetic figure, a man to look up to—a person of consequence, one might almost have said, whose slightest wish was a thing to cater to.

But Antrim, seeing, smiled derisively. "Reputations," he told the puncher, "don't mean much. They flare up overnight, an' vanish just as swift. Only a fool would call a rep like mine an asset. Be thankful you haven't got one. It's bait for ambush lead."

Pronto Joe appeared unconvinced. Then, seeming to recall his errand, he scowled across a shoulder toward where Moelner and the sheriff sat their horses conversing in low tones. "Them gents sure take their time."

"The law can't be hurried. You'll have to keep your shirt on."

Lothrop must have noted the Broken Stirrup foreman's look, for he abruptly urged his big horse forward, Moelner following suit. "Do you reckon," he asked, coming up, "yore men have cut Moak's sign?"

If they haven't, they're still ridin' herd on it," Pronto Joe said grimly. "When you figgerin' to git under way?"

Lothrop gave him a sour look. "You ain't no more anxious to catch up with that killer than I am. Let's go."

The soft, muffled pound of horses' hooves was a steady, even rhythm. Only the tinkle of clinking spur chains and the occasional creak of saddle leather gave it company. There was no talking. The time for talk had passed. These men's faces were grim, forbidding as Antrim's own.

Antrim's bay horse set the pace at a swift running walk that broke occasionally into a trot, a pace that guaranteed to put many miles behind a man between now and dark, and yet leave him with a mount that could do as much again tomorrow. The killer, if not yet captured by the Broken Stirrup punchers, or aware of their pursuit, would be overtaken in due time. There was no sense in ruining horseflesh. Determination and persistence, not speed, would run their man to earth. At least, such was Antrim's thought.

A half-hour passed, an hour, and only the soft muffled cadence of the horses' hooves, and the dust that rose behind them, gave evidence of their presence. The sun beat down with molten rays. The bits of metal in the men's equipment grew hot to the touch. The trapped heat of the valley enveloped them.

Three hours slipped behind them, and the rhythmic cadence of steadily trotting hooves still beat against the sand, drummed gently on the stillness. They rode abreast to avoid the dust that billowed up behind. Off in the distance to the left the high shoulders of the San Andres Mountains loomed pale blue against the brassy sky. To the right rose Elephant Butte. In the southwest the Sierra Caballos shimmered in the heat haze. The desert floor grew rolling.

The low adobe structures of the Long H showed off to the right against the base of the red cliffs hemming the southern end of Gawdforsaken Valley. The riders dipped down into a dry wash and the buildings were lost to view.

In another half-hour they were out of the valley and on to the dun expanse of the stifling *Joranda del Muerte*. The Sierra Caballos drew closer; mysterious and sombre they loomed above the desert, a maze of tangled light and shadow, grim and awe-inspiring.

The powdery dust rose about the riders now in choking billows. Though they pulled their neckerchiefs over their faces, burning particles of alkaline grit got into their nostrils and throats. Their eyes became inflamed and watery, and their heads ached with the awful heat.

Gradually a breeze sprang up, hot as the draft from some mighty furnace. Dust devils swirled across their path, enveloping them, drenching them with the fiery particles. Yet they kept doggedly on, nervily holding their sweating horses to a trot; the easy jog-trot of the cowboy.

About four in the afternoon they saw the bleached buildings of Engle pushing up out of the tawny earth. Lothrop turned to the man from Broken Stirrup.

"Reckon we better push straight on to the ranch?"

"Might be a good idee," said Pronto Joe, "if we stop off at town a spell. No tellin'. Moak mighta lost the boys. If he never knowed they was after him, he mighta gone to town."

Lothrop nodded. "Might have, anyway. We better see."

They swung their horses a little to the left. Slowly, as they rode, the distant false-fronted structures climbed above the desert floor, assumed their actual size. It was nearing five when the posse clopped through the dust of Engle's single street and pulled to a halt before a paintless building which

240

bore in crude lettering across its front the words:

CANTINA CABALLEROS

"We'll take a look in here," Lothrop said. "Joe, you an' Mitch go in. Me an' the Kid will wait here with the hawsses."

Moelner and the Broken Stirrup foreman swung to the ground, looked at their guns, then swiftly parted the cantina's swinging doors and entered.

Lothrop and Antrim sat their saddles in the sun. It was as hot there as in the desert; there was no difference. Vagrant breezes riffled the hock-deep dust of the street. A dust devil swirled off the Jornada, spun between two buildings, crossed the street and broke upon a store front, covering everything with alkaline grit.

"Reckon we'll catch up with Moak?"

"Sure we'll catch him," Lothrop said with emphasis. "I was appointed sheriff to cut down crime an' criminals. I sure aim to oblige." He quirked his heavy lips. "When—" He broke off with a ripped-out oath as a thunder of hooves burst out from behind the saloon. His spurs cut deep as they raked his pony's flanks. But Antrim's horse was already lunging forward.

Down the street they pounded. They could not see the other horseman, but they could see his dust between the buildings. Antrim flung a look behind. Moelner and Pronto Joe were sprinting for their mounts.

Antrim saw, as they left the town and went speeding into the desert once more, the fugitive horseman half a mile away. He was bent far forward in his saddle; his raking spurs and flailing arm were working in unison to wring the last ounce of speed

241

from a horse that looked built for endurance.

Now they were pelting directly in his wake, and all they could see of him was an occasional glimpse of his back and his horse's rump through the dust he was ripping up.

Antrim's cold eyes keened beneath his puckered brows. "You reckon that's him?"

The wind of their pace whipped words from Lothrop's answer. But Antrim gathered that yonder rider was their man.

He drew the rifle from its boot. Unless something were done swiftly, this race was going to prove a long one. Moak was steadily increasing the interval between himself and his pursuers.

Antrim rode with his rifle lying across his legs. He leaned his upper body forward, ran one hand along the bay's arched neck caressingly, coaxed more speed with gentle knees. Slowly they left Lothrop, cut down Moak's lead. But Antrim knew his pony could not keep up that pace for long. Ahead on the desert showed the squat outline of a cabin. Some two miles away it was, yet he knew that if Moak got there he would put up a fight, would sell his life as dearly as he could.

The rush and slap of the wind beat against his face as Antrim hoisted his boots from the stirrups, riding sharp-shooter fashion as he'd seen old Indian fighters do. The steady flogging gait of Moak's pony beat against his ears as he raised the rifle to his shoulder. Long experience had taught him the correct elevation for work of this sort, yet he knew that shooting from a pony's back was chancy work at best. Reckoning the windage as best he could, he squeezed the trigger gently. Sand spurted two feet ahead of Moak's sombrero.

Lips tight, eyes squinted against the glare, Antrim fired again. The fugitive's pony faltered, recovered, and went on. Yet its pace was uneven now, and slowed.

Antrim relaxed. A half-mile sped by without event, while steadily he overhauled the fleeing Moak. The fugitive's horse was reeling now, and Moak was belaboring it cruelly, raking it viciously in an effort to get from it a last desperate ounce of strength that might possibly take it to the cabin before . . .

Again Antrim took his feet from the stirrups. Again he brought the rifle to his shoulder. Three slugs jerked at Moak's sombrero, and the man shook his head like an angry wasp. Once more Antrim squeezed the trigger. The fugitive's pony dropped.

Moak landed on his feet and immediately broke into a lurching run toward the cabin, now a scant four hundred yards away.

Ramming the rifle into his scabbard, Antrim unloosed his rope from the saddle and shook out a loop. Twirling it above his head with gathering speed, he urged his pony in the other's wake. Closer and closer he drew to the runing man. Swifter and yet more swift became the wiggling loop's gyrations.

Suddenly the rope left Antrim's hand. Straight and true the singing noose sped out to trap the fugitive. Moak's right foot lunged fairly in it. The next instant he was flat on his face as Antrim's bay slewed to a stiff-legged stop.

In one smooth movement Antrim was out of the saddle and sprinting forward to where Moak struggled furiously to free himself. Moak saw him coming, and clawed for a gun. But even as the pistol's muzzle levelled, Antrim's boot sent the weapon spinning

243

from his hand. Vile curses spewed from the killer's mouth.

Coldly Antrim said, "Get up on your hind legs."

The fugitive glared. "Yuh go to hell!"

Antrim grabbed him by the collar and yanked him upright. "When I say stand, you better stand." The bunched knuckles of a hard right fist stopped squarely against Moak's yellow teeth. The sound was like a bull whip cracking. Moak sagged, but Antrim's firm left hand kept him on his feet, suspended. A muffled beat of hooves came up from behind. Antrim relaxed his grip on the gunman's collar and stepped back.

It was Lothrop. Something in the sheriff's eyes must have warned Moak. His face went pale as ashes as he thrust trembling arms above his head.

"Gawdlemighty, Stone! Don't shoot!" he cried. "I ain't got no gun! I—"

What more he might have said was drowned in the flat sharp crck of Lothrop's pistol. Moak grabbed convulsively at his chest. His knees buckled and he toppled forward in the sand.

With tight lips Antrim swung into the saddle. Moelner and Pronto Joe topped a distant rise. Antrim wheeled his horse.

"Hey!" Lothrop growled. "Help me with this carrion."

"I always make it a point to bury my own dead. Seems to me like others could do the same," Antrim said, and kneed his horse into motion. "I'll be seein' you in town."

Chapter IX

RINCON AFTER MIDNIGHT

Antrim sat in the *Cantina Caballeros* and stared morosely into his glass. Reflecting upon the ruthlessness and calculated cruelty of which humanity is capable, he came to the considered conclusion that the world was a scurvy place. His faith in man had almost reached the vanishing point. It was at this moment that a mutter of hooves outside announced the coming of further patronage. The bartender mopped a soggy rag across his counter and surreptitiously wiped a used glass dry upon his apron.

A Mexican in a steeple hat slid inside, crossing himself nervously. *"Madre de Dios!"* he exlaimed. "A dead man ees coming!"

"Huh?" The bartender stared, while a left hand automatically went beneath the bar in search of the sawed-off. "Where?"

"Down the road. Three *caballeros*. One has a dead man tied across hees saddle!"

When spurred boots clumped across the veranda, Antrim looked up. The swinging doors parted and Lothrop entered, followed by Pronto Joe and Moelner. The latter sneered and nudged the sheriff. Lothrop turned, and his eyes met Antrim's. He crossed to Antrim's table. He pulled a chair out, and it creaked beneath his weight. He rested his elbows on the table's edge, and supported his chin with cupped hands.

"In this country, Kid, when a scorpion crosses a man's trail, the man's a fool if he doesn't squash him."

Antrim regarded his still full glass in silence. When he looked up, his eyes held a steely glint like sun on sharpened spurs. "I been thinkin', Lothrop. I—"

"Now don't tell me you've decided to turn in yore star," the sheriff cut in swiftly. "This is a hard country, an' it'll take hard measures to enforce the laws an' make this territory a place for a man to raise his kids. Mebbe I was a little hasty in downin' that coyote. But what of it? He deserved what he got ten times over. You know that! If we'd brought him in, he'd never got to trial—either some damn fool woulda turned him loose, or a mob woulda yanked him out an' hung 'em!"

"That may be so," Antrim admitted. "But I been thinkin', Lothrop, an' I wasn't thinkin' of turnin' in my star. I was thinkin' that a liar was about as lowdown an article as a thief—or a killer. And I hate thieves an' killers, Lothrop, the way some folks hate work."

Lothrop looked at him intently; the smoke-grey surfaces of his eyes were hard, opaque. His manner became reserved, thoughtful, and when he spoke his voice was serious:

"I hate 'em too, Kid. A killer is like a mad dawg. No community can afford one. When more than one gets to prowlin' round it's time something was done about the situation. Now this Curly Ives hombre—I've been doin' considerable thinkin' about him. He's the fella that beat Beck Colter to death in front of the Rincon Bank after holdin' him up an' findin' Beck didn't have more'n five cartwheels on him. Smashed his head in with his pistol barrel an' rode on outa town without no one liftin' a finger. A disgrace to the Territory! The black shame of Rincon!"

He flashed a covert glance at Antrim, but Antrim's high, flat cheeks were giving no portion of his thoughts away, and his eyes were vacuous, baffling.

Lothrop said, "It wouldn't surprise me to learn that Ives is the leader of this gang, that's terrorizin' the country, that's robbin' miners an' prospectors, and raidin' isolated ranchers. It's my belief that Moak was a member of that gang."

Antrim said, "Moak might have been."

Lothrop nodded. "Well, I've a hunch that Ives is the leader. Killin' Beck Colter ain't the only piece of devilment he's done. He's boasted more than once, an' right here in this saloon, of things he's done that would hang him if folks weren't so damned busy tendin' to their own affairs an' keepin' a eye skinned for Injuns."

"What do you propose to do about it?"

"I propose to fetch him in."

"The way you brought in Moak?"

Lothrop's high blood laid a pronounced flush across his cheeks. He quit smiling suddenly, and a change of thought flung a long shadow across the brightness of his eyes. "If necessary," he said dustily, "yes."

"In other words," Antrim suggested, "you aim to fight fire with fire."

"I aim to rid this Territory of badmen!"

"The Territory, eh? That's takin' in quite a jag of land."

Lothrop lowered his voice. "The day may come when I'll be governor, Kid," he confided meaningly.

Antrim's eyes gleamed with cold amusement. "You've a deal more nerve than I figured you for. An' consid'rable more ambition."

"Why not? This country's new, it's big. There's a scad of opportunity goin' to waste round here; it's jest cryin' for a man that's big enough to grab it.

That man's me—I'm no saddle-blanket gambler. You string with me, Kid, an' you'll be sitting cozy as a toad under a cabbage leaf in Texas." His glance at Antrim was searching, and his tone grew very earnest. "You lay yore bets with mine an', by cripes, we'll show some folks a thing or two."

"I'm packin' your star."

"Yeah." Lothrop said it oddly. "Let's get a drink."

Lothrop set down his glass and turned to the Broken Stirrup foreman.

"You seen anything of Stumpy Harker down yore way lately?"

"Nope. You lost him?"

"I ain't sure. But there's somethin' right funny about his disappearance. I don't get it. Nobody's seen him. It's damn peculiar. He never stayed away like this before. He did go into town on a drunk occasionally, like most hands. But he never stayed this long. An' what's more, he ain't been seen around town."

"Which town?"

"Rincon. But he ain't been to the county seat neither. I'd give somethin' to know right where he is." He turned to the barkeep. "You ain't seen any of my riders down this way, have you?"

"Not me," the man denied. "Only man I know on yore outfit's Purdin. An' *he* ain't been here in Gawd knows when."

"Mebbe he quit," Pronto Joe suggested. "Fellas will do that sometimes."

"Not when they got a month's pay comin'," Lothrop snorted.

"Well, no; that don't seem likely," Pronto Joe conceded. "That makes it look kinda bad, don't it?

Y'u s'pose he's layin' out on the range some place, bad hurt?"

"What would he—" Lothrop began, then said, instead of completing the thought, "The blasted drought ain't left me hardly enough critters to bother ridin' herd on. I had t' let three of my boys go las' month. Anyway, I thought of that, too. Had the fellas take a look, but they couldn't cut his sign."

"Yeah, that drought ain't doin' the Broken Stirrup no favor, neither," Pronto Joe grunted heavily. "Now Catling's been killed, I dunno what'll happen to the spread. Don't seem like Gert will be wantin' to stay on after all this hellin'. Mebbe she'll sell out. Stewart made the ol' man a offer last week. Gert's got some kinfolks back East, case she decides t'take him up."

Lothrop turned to Antrim. "Kid, I want you to go to Socorro. Blanding, the deputy there, may need some help. Town's gettin' kinda wild. I'll be along in three-four days—"

He broke off suddenly as there came a rushing clatter of hooves. The sound was muffled at first, but swiftly swelled to terminate thunderously before the cantina veranda. The group inside stood silent, facing the batwing doors, as they heard the rider hit dirt and cross the boards with dragging spurs. The doors bulged and Suggs came clanking in, his hair disordered beneath his shoved-back hat, excitement sparkling in the eyes he turned on Lothrop.

"Yuh better git to Rincon quick! Hell's gonna pop!"

"What's up?"

"Some damn liars claim they caught Ruidosa stickin' up a coupla desert rats."

"Are they crazy?"

"Well," Suggs growled, "accordin' to that fella, Hildermin, who brung the news, they are some riled. He seemed t' think Ruidosa's goose would sure be cooked if yuh didn't show up right sudden."

"When did Hildermin get in?"

" 'Bout two hours after you boys left."

There was a dull gleam of anger in the glance Lothrop turned on Moelner. Dull color too, burned visibly in his heavy cheeks. "We got to have fresh hawsses. Go get us some, an' don't waste no time arguin'."

Moelner went out at a clanking run.

"Reckon I better go with you," Pronto Joe offered seriously.

"Raise yore right hand," said Lothrop gruffly, and swore him in. "You," he said to Suggs, "go on back to the ranch. I can't afford to leave it short-handed with all this talk that's goin' round 'bout Geronimo makin' medicine. Keep the boys in close."

Antrim, who was watching Lothrop at the moment, thought he saw the burly rancher lower a significant eyelash. He could not be sure, but he stored the thought away.

Ten minutes later they rode out of Engle, heading south. Lothrop had said no more about sending Antrim to the county seat. The Kid rode with them.

They swept into Rincon shortly after midnight. From open doors and windows great bars of golden radiance pooled out across the hock deep dust of Rincon's unpaved street, radiance that made the great lopsided bucket of a moon seem pale by contrast. Oil and pine-knot flares affixed to the high false fronts of the town's flimsy structures illuminated fitfully the misspelled legends scrawled unevenly across them, and served to some extent to light the rough plank sidewalks under them. Rincon was an all-night town, boasting at that time half a dozen saloons and gambling halls, one hotel, two or three blacksmith shops, two stores, and four honkytonks.

Lothrop led the way to the Coffin Bar, the town's largest saloon, and the four dismounted before the hitch pole fronting it, racking their mounts among the horses of the resort's patrons. Judging by the noise coming from the place, there were still a good many customers inside.

"This is Hodine's dive," Lothrop muttered softly. "Watch yoreselves. He hates officers like poison. Kid, you an' Mitch come in with me. Joe, you stay here with the horses. If anyone gets gay, shoot first an' *habla* about it later."

He shoved through the half-leaf doors, Moelner and Antrim following. They got their back to a wall while they accustomed their eyes to the glare of the many coal-oil lamps bracketed about the barn-like room. The place was thick with tobacco smoke and crowded with men. Cowboys and miners rubbed elbows at the three-deep bar.

Moelner said, "What's the lay?"

The smoke-grey eyes beneath Lothrop's sleepy lids scanned the crowd intently. "There's a lot of excitement in the air. These fellas know it an' are reactin' to it. They know it, but they're not in on it. They're restless, wantin' to be doin'. I reckon Ruidosa has still got his lamp lit. You fellas ease out an' circulate. See if you can find where they're holdin' him an' who is in charge. I'll wait here."

Outside the resort, Antrim let Moelner take the lead. They headed up the line, walking through the dusty road because the sidewalks were already filled to overflowing, and progress through such a mob would have been well-nigh impossible, without arguments—things to be carefully avoided at the present pitch of the crowd's temper. There had been plenty of noise inside the Coffin Bar; a sort of forced gaiety, feverish, taut-strung. But out here on the street it was different. Men moved sluggishly along the packed walks, moved in groups of twos and threes, with their heads close together. The subdued mutter of their voices was like an ominous drone, ever present; heard even through the blatant sounds flowing out from the saloons and honkytonks.

Antrim said in Moelner's ear, "It's like I told Lothrop back at the ranch. Times are due for a change. Folks have about reached the point where their resentment toward conditions is goin' to take an active expression. The toughs had better pull in their horns, or they'll get 'em knocked off."

"You ain't tellin' me a thing. I've seen this comin'." Mitch Moelner turned his head. A peculiar grin twitched his saturnine lips. "You an' the rest of the gunslicks better be huntin' new pastures. Yore days is numbered."

"Where do you figure that leaves you?"

Moelner chuckled. "Me, I'm adaptable to change," he said, and flicked a sweeping glance across the crowd. "Besides, I'm on the side of law an' order. I'm packin' a star."

Antrim, as he strode along at the other's side, his eyes restlessly probing the faces going past, considered this enigmatic remark, but could make nothing of it. He thrust it back with those other things he meant to ponder over when leisure afforded opportunity. He was packing a star himself.

There was no regular jail in this town, he recalled. Whoever had Ruidosa—and Antrim could not quite decide who Ruidosa was—in charge must be holding him either in some private dwelling, or in some store taken over for the purpose.

Moelner said, "Let's lounge over here against this buildin'. Might be listenin' would be a faster way of gettin' places than walkin'."

Antrim looked around. They were opposite the mouth of a dark and narrow alley running between a general store and a blacksmith shop. The place Moelner had his eyes on was the latter. A pair of blazing pine knots, affixed to the posts supporting the wooden awning on the store, played a murky light across the crowd. "Suits me," he said, and followed Moelner's panther-lean figure as it wove a sinuous path through the muttering groups.

Reaching the blacksmith shop, they got their backs toward the wall and loitered there, letting their gaze wander across the surging throngs. Purple gusts of smoke from the flares spread darkly over the walkers, drove alternate lights and shadows across scowling, grinning, sullen, taciturn, wooden faces, gave hints of their different nationalities, revealed and hid the covert flashes of their eyes, and mingled among them farther down the walk. Various breeds and races were among this restless crowd, but tonight their blood was one—deep black.

Antrim stole a look at the man beside him and found that the gunman had pulled his hat brim low across his eyes, shrouding his face in gloom, and that one ungloved hand lay against the holster on his thigh. That ungloved hand told Antrim something, for in that country only riders who were lightning on the draw, and hence had something of a reputation —with its attendant disadvantages—omitted to glove their hands. The low-pulled hat brim told Antrim something, too. This was *buscadero* country.

"There's plenty of tornado juice loose in this crowd," Moelner grunted. "Workin' itself into a ringy mood. Pretty soon they'll be ready to dig up the tomahawk. See anyone yuh reco'nize!"

Antrim shook his head.

"That gent that just went past with the fat man—he took one squint at you an' shut his mug hard enough t' bust his nutcrackers. Yo're getting t' be a celebrity. Better pull yore hat down 'fore some of yore dead men's kinfolks comes along an' spots you."

"I can—"

Moelner snapped, "You can shout, too! Yuh *fool!* You wanta jam the Chief's play?"

Antrim lowered the hat brim. There was logic in the gunman's words.

Three men went past abreast; big fellows, dark of garb, determined of mien, men who carried sawed-offs and appeared oblivious of their surroundings. Groups parted magically before their progress. Not once was their measured stride interrupted; not once were they forced to leave the crowded walk.

Moelner looked after them suspiciously. He touched Antrim's arm. "C'mon, Kid. Neck meat or nothin'." And he swung into step behind them. Antrim followed.

The men they tracked left the walk abruptly. Wheeling into single file, they passed through the batwing entrance of "THE GOLDEN GUN—Pecos Rourk, *Prop.*"

Up the same steps moved Moelner with Antrim at his back. He reached the doors, and there a hand stretched out to stop him, a hand whose wrist projected from the black sleeve of a gambler's neat frock coat—a hand that held a gun.

"Yore business, friend."

"Is my own." Moelner's glance flashed sharply against that chiselled countenance. "Can't a man get a drink when he wants one?"

"Not here."

"What's the—"

"Dust, hombre—make tracks!"

Antrim felt Mitch Moelner's long frame stiffen; could see the muscles swelling in Moelner's neck, and the surge of red that dyed it. He put a hand on the gunman's shoulder. "T'ell with it, Mitch. Their whisky's diluted anyway. Let's go up to the Coffin Bar."

The gunman's form relaxed, but he snarled as he turned away, " 'F I ever get another snort of Rourk's bug-juice I hope I bust a gut!"

The gambler's laugh floated after them.

Antrim said, "Never throw away the key to a door, *compadre,* till you know what's on the other side."

Moelner gave him a hard stare, said "Humph!" and swung into step beside him.

They reached the Coffin Bar. Pronto Joe still sat his saddle before the hitch pole. His eyes played over the crowded street significantly. "Sheriff's goin' to grab this brandin' iron by the hot end ef he ain't careful," he commented shrewdly.

Antrim untied his horse and stepped aboard while Moelner went inside for Lothrop.

The doors of the resort bulged outward, spilling light across the steps. Two men emerged. Lothrop's rock-like figure and rolling strides were easily recognized, though his features were deeply shadowed by the light behind. He came up to the rack, jerked loose his reins and swung stiffly to the saddle.

Moelner followed.

Without words Lothrop swung his big horse into the busy street. Antrim rode on his right, Moelner on his left. The range boss of the Broken Stirrup brought up the rear. They walked their horses through the dust. Men got out of their way. Some cursed them, but they moved.

Chapter X

FOUR AGAINST THE MOB

Down the center of the street they rode and stopped before the Golden Gun. They swung out of their saddles in unison, racked their mounts and ducked under the hitch-rail. Their long spurs chimed as they crossed the rough plank walk. The resort's steps groaned beneath their upward tread. Metal on Lothrop's vest threw fugitive, slicing sparks. The sentinel's eye was caught and he scowled blackly, but made no move to stop them. Lothrop shoved wide the swinging doors and they followed him in.

The great barroom of the Golden Gun was crowded. Men stood about the bar six deep; they packed the space between the gaming tables, and were spewed out in clustered knots upon the gleaming dance floor. Lothrop seemingly cared nothing for this fact and went striding forward, cutting a trail with his burly shoulders, shoving men off his elbows, deliberately bowling them from his path, and saying never a word, never looking to right or left, his smoldering eyes fixed grimly upon that black-clad man who stood atop the bar. Pronto Joe had left them at the door, and now stood with his grey-shirted back against it, his rifle cuddled in the hollow of his arm, his cold glance alertly roving, watchful, saturnine—almost inviting, one might have said. Antrim and Moelner strode in Lothrop's wake, their right hands swinging, brushing laden holsters at each firm step.

Men turned at the commotion and the murmurous drone of many conversations dropped sullenly. A tautened stillness rose through which the three men strode unhurried, their measured tread resounding strangely in that crowded place. Men more distant from their trail swung startled faces in the smoky shadows. Their eyes lit with the expectancy of a hasty reckoning.

Yet the last man lurched aside from Lothrop's shoulder without challenge. He stopped before the bar, got his feet wide apart and firmly planted. His arms hung akimbo, their doubled hands resting on his hips, the right a scant two inches from the smooth dark butt of the holstered pistol he had not deigned so far to draw. The sleepy lids lifted in his heavy face; his smoldering eyes peered upward and met the frowning stare of the man atop the bar.

"You, up there! What's the big idea?"

The fellow straightened; his frown grew blacker. "This is a meetin' of the Citizens' Protective Committee an'—" He suddenly stopped, his widened eyes revealing his discovery of Lothrop's official identity. "How'd yuh get in?"

"I walked in," Lothrop drawled. "I've come for the prisoner. Fetch him."

A gasp went up from the gathered crowd. The man on the bar growled, "I—I—you——This prisoner, sir, is goin' to be hanged. We're tryin' him now."

"Then where's he at?"

"We've got him under guard. He's in the back room."

"Mean to say he isn't present at his own trial?"

"What would be the use?" the man snarled back defiantly. "He's guilty, an' by Gawd he's goin' to hang!"

"You've got the gall to tell me that?" Lothrop's voice came softly through his teeth. "To my face? Mister, you fetch the prisoner here right now."

Antrim's glance revealed a grudging admiration for Lothrop then. It took real nerve to stand there in that crowded room of grim-faced men and demand the surrender of their prisoner. The chairman's face was white with rage.

"Sheriff or no sheriff, we caught the fellow, an' we're a-goin' to keep him till we're done with him. If you'd been 'tendin' to yore duty——"

Lothrop's big right fist shot out, got him by the ankle, and jerked. The chairman left the bar with a squeal like a stuck pig, crashed to the floor and lay there groaning. Lothrop stooped, grabbed him by the shoulder and yanked him upright, "If I'd *what!*"

"You dirty, schemin', yeller-bellied—!" Still snarling epithets, the chairman's hand slid inside his coat. But it didn't come out; not then! Lothrop smashed a hard right fist against his jaw, and the man reeled backward, sagging.

Oaths, shouts, pandemonium broke loose in that packed saloon—was suddenly stilled by the flat sharp crack of a rifle. A man staggered sideways, dropped his pistol and sat down, clutching at his ribs. The rifle cracked again; another man dropped. Antrim flung a hasty glance across his shoulder even as hands dragged his pistols clear of leather.

Through the scattering crowd, which was swiftly awakening to its danger, he saw the Broken Stirrup foreman crouched beside the doors, the weaving muzzle of his long gun a grim challenge to the mob.

Lothrop's voice rang out curtly above the running clump of boots. "Git up them hands an' back against the walls! The next damn man to put his mitt to gunbutt is goin' to hell on a shutter!"

That stopped them squarely in their tracks—all but three. Those were diving for the window. The rifle cracked again. One of the three crumpled across the sill. Moelner's gun added its spiteful voice to the roaring echoes; the second man fell outside the window, and the third spun shrieking, took three steps and crumpled sideways across a table, taking it with him to the floor.

The acrid tang of burned powder drifted among the stiffly rigid men who were holding their hands at arm's length above their heads, their faces blanched, their eyes appalled at the havoc ten seconds had witnessed in the room.

"Vigilantes, eh?" sneered Lothrop. "You back up ag'in' them walls an' keep them hands right where they are or you'll get a bigger dose of the same medicine. Vigilantes—hell! Not in my county, you ain't! Two of you go fetch Ruidosa in here. I'm the gent that'll decide what's to be done with prisoners."

During the interval while the two were gone, their companions regained some measure of their old belligerence. They stood more loosely along the walls. Their faces were grown more wooden, more completely expressionless, and a darker, restless light had come into their watchful eyes. Their hands, by degrees, had slipped down lower until now several pairs were hardly even with their owners' shoulders.

Antrim saw these things where he stood with his lean hands folded across his chest, and his back against the bar. He saw them, read the signs correctly, yet his face hid his knowledge well; his long wide lips retained their whimsicality, and his blue gaze appeared to be completely absorbed with the strata of wavering smoke drifting lazily just below the raftered ceiling.

Outside, the night seemed to have taken on a deeper silence, a sort of brooding hush. He could hear men moving on the walk that lay between this room and the street; their voices seemed insufferably loud by contrast with the thin tight stillness, and yet he knew their tones were cautious, filled with a kind of repressed excitement that spelled devilment. In their tread he read a stealthiness he did not like.

His broad sloping shoulders swayed a little. A chill rubbed along his back, and he looked toward Lothrop to see how the sheriff was taking it. Lothrop's mouth still showed its lazy smile, but the smoke was thickening in his eyes. Moelner's body looked taut. Pronto Joe was getting pale. . . .

Antrim sent his stare back toward the men. A ripple ran along that line from wall to wall; only their bulk in numbers, Antrim felt, was holding things even. One swift word or a sudden motion. . . . A leader was all they lacked.

The thought drew Antrim's glance to where their old one still measured his length before the bar. In moments now he'd be coming to. But there was no hope for them in him.

This thing could not last; something was bound to break. He could feel the tension like a knife. Those men still had their guns. Another five seconds of sustained inaction would surely snap the spell.

Antrim started forward. One man against the wall had dropped his hands below his shoulders; another five seconds of this would convince him of his chance. His hands would be a little lower. He would make the fateful plunge. Antrim moved straight toward him, slowly, inexorably. The man's face whitened. A tremble started up his arms.

Antrim said, "You! Step three paces forward."

The man hesitated. His chance was lost. Mechanically he moved from line.

"Go find what's keeping your friends. If you ain't back inside a minute, I'll come after you."

Lothrop said, "If that prisoner ain't here inside of a minute, it'll be too bad for the bunch of you! Git!"

Just as the man reached the back room door, it opened. Ruidosa, followed by the pair who had gone for him, stepped into the room. The last man closed the door behind him. Lothrop waved the three vigilantes back in line. "Who," he said, "next to him," and his boot prodded the chairman's outstretched form, "is in charge?"

The men along the walls looked at one another uncertainly. No one seemed to know. Lothrop's lips curled as he started at them. "A fine organization," he jeered. "Well, comebody come up here. I've got to make medicine an' I can't do it alone."

The man Antrim had called from line stepped forward sullenly.

"Where's the two burro men this fella," jerking a thumb at Ruidosa, "is supposed to have tried to stick up?" Lothrop asked him.

The man shrugged. "Damfino. I didn't see 'em."

Lothrop snorted. "Well, where's the gents that

brought him in? The fellas that claim that they caught him red-handed in the act?"

The man pointed toward the window. "That's one of them," he said. "The man across the sill. The other one is the chairman, Shane."

"All right," Lothrop said, and took an official-looking document from his coat pocket. "When Shane comes to, you tell him he'll be wanted at the county seat to testify inside two days. I'm taking charge of the prisoner on this writ of habeas corpus, in the name of the civil authorities of this Territory. Get a bucket of water and bring Shane to. The rest of you clear out."

The vigilantes stared at him uncomprehendingly. One of them said, "You mean we're free to go?"

"Yes. The next time I find a vigilance committee tryin' to operate in this county, though, it'll be a dif'rent story. If you're wise, you won't entangle yoreselves with one again. Now clear out 'fore I change my mind about lettin' you off."

Chapter XI

LOTHROP PULLS THE STRINGS

Whatever else Stone Lothrop might be, Antrim reflected as the frustrated vigilantes slunk from the place, he was neither fool nor coward. He had handled this tough situation with an unexpected adroitness; almost, one might have said, with cunning. With a minimum of bloodshed, he had taken the prisoner of the Citizens' Committee away from them, had clearly and definitely put them in the wrong, and had then magnanimously dismissed them with a mild rebuke. He had stage-managed it well, and had withal shown himself so completely master of the situation, this crowd would not be apt again to try this. He had given them an abundance of food for thought. His satisfaction with himself was revealed in the glowing good nature with which he took the bucket of water the man had brought and dashed it over the still recumbent, yet now groaning, form of the vigilantes' unfortunate leader.

Shane spluttered, gasped, blinked his eyes open, and struggled to an elbow. From this vantage point he peered up owlishly at the grinning sheriff.

"Feelin' better?" Lothrop queried.

The man gingerly felt his bruised and swollen jaw. "W—what hit me?"

"I did," Lothrop said with his lazy smile. Somehow his words conveyed the idea that he was sorry. "I had to," he went on. "You was practically foamin' at the mouth. Couldn't make out whether you'd been bit by a hydrophoby skunk or if someone had mixed rattleweed with yore smokin'. I hit you 'cause I didn't want no harm t' come to you. You're feelin' better?"

Shane peered up at him uncertainly. "I—I guess so," he muttered thickly.

Lothrop helped him up and brushed him off. Then he stood back, allowed the man to recover somewhat. When Shane's eyes appeared to be less befuddled, Lothrop said:

"I've disbanded yore Committee an' given 'em a lecture. 'F you're as smart as I think you are, you'll not try organizin' them again—you'll leave law business to them that's appointed to administer it. I been lenient to yore outfit. A damn sight more so

263

than they deserve." He gestured toward the window. "Only three of 'em got killed. A couple more was wounded, but their friends has taken them away. Remember: it costs a heap more to revenge injuries than it does to bear 'em. I'm not censurin' you. I figure you done yore duty accordin' to yore lights. I don't want no more of this vigilante stuff, though. Next time I'll smash 'em flatter than a wet leaf. That's a fact you'll be wantin' to keep in mind. You go take a coupla burnin' sensations now, an' you'll be seein' things with a calmer eye."

White and trembling, Shane was ogling the dead men by the window. Lothrop had left them as they fell, and they provided a fine object lesson—particularly since none of the lawmakers had been so much as scratched. With an audible gulp, the wilted vigilante boss wheeled to the bar.

Lothrop turned his big shoulders toward the man Antrim had called from the line. The fellow's eyes were fixed on Shane, and they were filled with scorn.

Lothrop said, "A fella that'll bed down with dawgs has got to expect t' get up with fleas."

Still looking at Shane, the fellow sneered. His glance met the sheriff's then, and he said, "I guess you're right. I'd ort to of had better sense."

"You're learnin' fast," Lothrop commended, then showed the cunning that had brought him up from nothing to his present powerful status in this border country:

"What do they call you, friend?"

"Brazito," the man said suspiciously.

"Well, Brazito," Lothrop suggested, "would you like an easy bunk as deputy?"

Brazito started, and rasped his jaw with a sun-browned hand. "Such a job wouldn't make me mad," he admitted, grinning.

"Well, I'm goin' to make you my deputy at Rincon. Raise yore right hand."

When the lawmen, leaving Brazito to dispose of the dead men inside the Golden Gun, stepped into the street, they found it darker and not nearly so crowded as it had been when they'd arrived in town. They located a horse for Ruidosa, put him on it with his hands securely lashed behind his back, and climbed aboard their own ponies. Then Lothrop turned to Antrim.

"Kid, I'm sendin' you to the county seat with this prisoner," he said slowly, as though considering something in his mind. "I've got to get after Curly Ives, an' I can't be bothered luggin' this Ruidosa around with me. An' I can't leave him here. There ain't no sure facilities for guardin' him. I don't think that bunch of vigilantes will get together again—at least not for some time—but some other gang might get their mind set on a lynchin'. This prisoner has got to have a fair trial. If we take him to Socorro, he'll get it. It's time this county got a taste of law an' order. I'll be seein' you at the county seat in a few—"

He broke off as a thick-set man who had been moving along the walk wheeled and came over. Standing by Lothrop's horse, the man looked up and said, "Ain't you the sheriff?"

"That's what I been appointed."

The man regarded him curiously. "My name's Thatcher," he said at last. "I run the Star brand, east of here a piece. I'd like to know if that rumor's true?"

"If you mean the rumor that I took their prisoner away from yore damned vigilance committee an'

265

packed 'em off to bed, it certainly is."

"My eyes told me that much," Thatcher said with a grin. "No, I mean that story that's been goin' round about Corner an' Hootowl Jones bein' on the make—rustlin' other folks' cattle?"

"Corner an' Jones swingin' wide loops?" Lothrop looked surprised. "I hadn't heard."

"Well, there's a story goin' the rounds that their outfits has been sleeperin', maverickin', an' actually brand-blottin' high, wide an' han'some. You're from Gawdforsaken Valley, ain't you? Don't you own the Two-Pole-Pumpkin outfit over there?"

"I own the Two-Pole-Pumpkin, all right," Lothrop said. "But I'd hate to think my friends Jones an' Corner was on the rustle."

"Well, yore foreman, Purdin, rode into the county seat the other day an' swore out a warrant for 'em."

"You don't say!" Lothrop looked perturbed. "I hadn't heard of this. Still—" He paused, apparently lost in thought. At last he said, "I ain't been to the ranch for more than a few hours in the last two weeks. Ain't seen Purdin at all—like enough he's been out on the range tryin' t' save what scant stuff this drought has left me. Still an' all, him swearin' out a warrant don't hardly convict Jones an' Corner of anythin', Thatcher. Anyway, I ain't seen him an' don't know anythin' about it. Far as I know, Jones an' Corner is upright gents, square-shooters. I'd hate to learn different. They've always seemed as much ag'in' rustlin' as I am."

"That's the way I've always regarded them," Thatcher said. "Square an' upright men. But that rumor was goin' round before Purdin swore out his warrant. I don't like the looks of it. I been dickerin' with them two t' buy a herd of two-year-olds they been aimin' to dispose of. But I'll be damned if I cotton to the notion of buyin' stolen beef."

"Well, I don't blame you there," Lothrop said seriously. "I wouldn't want to, either. But all I know is I ain't never been given no warrant to serve."

"When you get to the county seat, you'll prob'ly find it waitin'," Thatcher remarked morosely. "Why can't men stick to the straight-an'-narrow? Seems like this country gets into a man's blood. Either it makes a monkey out of him, or else a plain thief!"

Lothrop shook his head. "No sense holdin' the country responsible for a man's didoes. You might's well call Gawd accountable; He made the country, remember. In my experience, a man's what he is: square or ornery accordin' to circumstances, an' sometimes underneath he's a heap diff'rent than he seems. Man," he added oracularly, "is a strange mixture of good an' bad. Some is square an' upright, like a good hawss; some is lamb-like, meek as Moses; then there's them that leans towards the wolfish side; an' others is just plain two-legged coyotes. Yep, coyotes—like this fella Ives I'm goin' after. The kind that likes to catch gents unarmed an' salt 'em down without no risk."

"Well," Thatcher said, preparing to leave, "I reckon it takes all kinds to make a world. Though it does seem this Territory's got more than its share of the less desirables. Glad to've met you, Sheriff. Drop round to the ranch sometime. An' keep a strict eye on them hombres over to Gawdforsaken Valley."

"I'll sure aim t' do my best," Lothrop said.

A silent observer to this conversation, Antrim's eyes, as they rested on Stone Lothrop, held again that light of grudging admiration. The man was as smooth as a gun-fighter's gun barrel.

While Lothrop spoke with Pronto Joe, Antrim sat with one leg crooked about the saddle-horn, reviewing a number of strange things he had filed away in his mind—things, that is, which had struck him as strange at the time of their happening.

First there was that curious meeting he had had with Mitch Moelner, on the night of his first visit to the Two-Pole-Pumpkin. Why had Lothrop felt it necessary to station sentinels about the place? Because of Indians? Antrim did not think so.

Secondly, there had been Lothrop's casual mention of Yolanda as his "woman," signifying, as it did, that he had not married her.

Thirdly, Antrim's meeting with Yolanda in the *patio* was still vivid in his mind, and the things she had said about Lothrop, although he had hidden it well, had aroused in him a fierce resentment toward the man, a resentment to which little things from time to time had added fuel.

Lothrop's voice interrupted his whirling thoughts: "When you get to Socorro, Kid, see if you can find out anythin' about that warrant Thatcher was speakin' of. After all, if Purdin's really swore one out, he must have somethin' definite ag'in' them fellas. Friendship's friendship, but duty comes first. If Corner an' Jones have been rustlin' cattle, I ain't got no option but t' bring 'em in."

Nodding, Antrim dismissed his speculations.

Chapter XII

HELL ON THE TRAIL

High up in the Sierra Caballos, along a rough untrustworthy trail that tortuously wound about great frowning crags and upthrust buttresses of rusty stone, oft-times dipping crazily down declivitous slopes that only a goat—or a burro—could manage, and that rolled one's stomach nauseously as it clung to precipitous cliffs, crawled a pack train of forty burros. This outfit, owned by Craig Smith & Company, and from it taking its name of Smith's Train, had thirteen days previously left Silver City en route for Socorro, by way of Fort Bayard, San Lorenzo, Hillsboro, and the Sierra Caballos. Once they descended these, they planned to cross the Jornada just east of Elephant Buttes. Two days back Smith's Train had turned its back on the Rio Bravo's muddy waters and had this morning crossed the divide. With Smith and two smaller owners—Shinkle and Laidley—in the lead, the train now was threading its dangerous way down toward the foothills, dim seen blue smears against the Jornada's fiery sands.

Smith, Shinkle, and Laidley were energetic business men who had in the course of the past three months disposed of their stores of merchandise in the mining district centering around Silver City. In exchange for this merchandise they had received a considerable amount in gold dust, nuggets, silver ore and currency, which they intended taking back with them to Saint Louis, and with a part of which they hoped to square their accounts with Eastern creditors. True, they were not planning to take this dust and ore so far as that, but expected to exchange it at Socorro for its equivalent in currency and minted coin. Theirs had been a risky venture, and they were rightly jubilant at the successful disposal of the wares they had brought through such dangerous and Indian-infested country.

But they were wary even now. Many a chilling tale had come their way before leaving Silver City: accounts of road agents, renegades, and other desperadoes who preyed upon small parties crossing the mountains and desert, yarns calculated to curl tenderfoot hair tightly; knee-shaking stories of Apache torture, death at the stake, and the pleasant pastime of feeding a man to the ants.

These tales had some influence in persuading Smith, Shinkle and Laidley into combining forces and making the trip in one caravan. Smith's Train, they felt, was sufficiently large and strongly guarded to discourage such marauders as might obtain information concerning their prospective overland trek. Yet they had exercised care and circumspection in approaching and picking men for the journey. The ten they had finally hired were as good as money could buy, men known for their discretion, raw courage, and integrity. These men were well armed and, fully expecting to fight their way through.

Ore and dust and nuggets, amounting roughly to some eighty thousand dollars, was packed in buckskin sacks and evenly distributed through the packs of the forty burros. Besides this great treasure, Craig Smith's personal saddle-bags contained around fifteen hundred dollars in treasury notes enclosed in letters to people in the States, and entrusted to Smith's care by the friends and kinfolk of these persons at the mines.

Despite all Smith's care and caution, however,

news of his train, its route and destination *had* leaked out. Because of the fear of some such possibility, Smith's men had exercised great vigilance during the first ten days and nights of the trip. On the eleventh night, worn out by this constant expectation of unfulfilled attack, their watchfulness relaxed somewhat. Reaction set in, and on the twelfth night only one guard was posted, although relieved every hour. During this, the thirteenth day, much badinage had been passed between the members of Smith's fighting force concerning the dire peril of this journey. A complete let-down was resulting. When they pulled up for camp at five o'clock on the evening of this day, no precautions were taken beyond a cursory inspection of the juniper and pinion-dotted shelf selected as a camp-site. Satisfying themselves that one side of the forty-foot shelf dropped sheer to bed rock some ninety feet below, and that the other rose in a bald escarpment for an almost equal distance above, they removed the packs from the animals, penned the latter in a hastily-erected rope corral, and busied themselves about the more important task of getting supper.

Lothrop, Moelner, and Pronto Joe rode out of Rincon on the Engle trail almost fifteen minutes before Guy Antrim was ready to leave with Ruidosa for the county seat. Antrim had been detained by some instructions Lothrop had asked him to pass on to Brazito, the newly-made Rincon deputy. It had taken Antrim eight minutes to find Brazito and deliver the sheriff's message. Eight uncomfortable minutes, in fact, for almost any second among them might have witnessed another attempt at mob justice, or an effort on the part of the prisoner's friends or pardners in crime to release him from the grasp of the law. Evidently Lothrop's bold move in obtaining possession of Ruidosa had thoroughly cowed, for the time being, all belligerents in the vicinity, for no overt moves were made.

Just as Antrim had gotten his prisoner once more astride a horse and was himself preparing to mount another, a gaunt red-haired man in faded Levis appeared from the shadows.

"You are the Smoke-wagon Kid, ain't you?" he asked, his keen eyes probing the surrounding gloom as though desiring to make certain his conversation with the deputy remained unobserved.

Antrim nodded, watching the man closely.

"Well, look," this fellow said, reducing his voice to a merest mumble, "I got something I reckon you oughta know. You are a depity of that new sherrif, I take it? . . . Thought so. Well, what I wanta say is this: I got a small spread over near Lake Valley. Friend o' mine just got back from over there round Silver City. He mentioned that he had seen one of Lothrop's men over in the neighborhood. Been hangin' round there for quite a spell."

"No law against that, is there?" Antrim looked at the man curiously. The fellow his friend had seen was probably the missing Stumpy Harker.

"No law ag'in' it, no," the man said quietly. "But there's a right smart chance there oughta be. Happens there's been a trail outfit formin' there. Craig Smith an' Company. Figgerin' to go 'crosst the Sierra Caballos to Socorro with a big pack train of dust an' ore." He paused as though to let these facts sink in, then— "The train pulled out o' Silver City on the first of August. This here's the twelfth. Does that signify?"

Antrim's face rid itself of all expression. His glance

was cold, inscrutable. "What does it signify to you?"

"Just this: Smith's Train hadn't oughta be more'n fifty miles or so from here this minute."

"Unless," Antrim pointed out, "they've had troubles with Indians or road agents."

"Yeah," the man said dryly. "In which case we've likely heard the last of 'em."

"Just what was your reason in mentioning that your friend thought he saw one of Lothrop's men at Silver City?"

The red-haired man grinned twistedly. "That's for you to figger out. An' my friend didn't *think* he saw one of Lothrop's men; he *saw* him. An' it wasn't the one the sheriff's doin' all the gassin' about, neither."

"Just which one *was* it?"

The eyes of the red-haired man were mocking. "I'm not cravin' any plantin' yet, nor I ain't anxious to put the neck of some innocent gent in no noose. I'm tellin' you what my friend tole me. You can do as you see fit about it. I don't know yore friend there," and he shot a fleeting glance at the interested Ruidosa, "nor I don't know you, either—except by yore rep. But if you're as int'rested in seein' justice done as I hear you are, why . . . in case Smith's Train don't get through, you'll mebbe have some idees on the reason. I figger that train had oughta hit Engle day after tomorrer."

And without further words the red-haired man slid off into the shadow between two buildings and disappeared.

Antrim turned to Ruidosa and regarded him thoughtfully. "Well," he said with a shrug, "time we was gettin' on. Let's go."

Antrim and his prisoner were two miles out upon

273

the Jornada when it happened. They had just dipped into the heavy gloom of a deep arroyo where the blue-pack shadows swirled like smoke, and spread across the trail as it led between a handful of stunted trees where a humus covering veiled the earth and muffled footfalls.

"Halt," a gruff voice bade, "an' throw up yore hands!"

Body taut, Antrim peered through the sultry murk, caught the vague chill gleam of metal and, stifling an impulse, obediently raised his arms. A flexure of his knees stopped his pony. The led horse carrying Ruidosa also stopped.

Three men emerged from the deeper shadows, indistinct blurs in the heavy gloom. Afoot they were, and masked. Each man held a levelled gun.

"Been takin' good care of our friend, Ruidosa?" jeered a drawling voice.

"Well, I been takin' the best care I could of him," Antrim answered equably. "Stone Lothrop couldn'ta done better himself."

One of the men chuckled. The man who had asked the question said, "I expect that is so," at which his companions laughed uproariously. The man went on, still in that lazy drawl, "You've done yore duty as you seen it. An' we are glad to know so careful an officer. If we are ever tailed up, I'm hopin' you'll be handy t' take us in tow. But yore jurisdiction, friend, ends right here. We'll be takin' charge of this hellion right now. Ben," he said to one of the others, "be so kind as to get a holt on Ruidosa's reins . . . Now lead his horse back there among them junipers whilst we finish our business with this Smoke-wagon Kid."

As Ben led the prisoner's horse off into the black

gloom beneath the trees, Antrim tensed his body for instant action should the occasion demand it. He could not see any sense in risking his life to save Ruidosa from a fate he probably well deserved, but he was in no mood to act as target for dry-gulch guns without lifting a hand to protect himself. The chances were long against him emerging triumphant from any gun fight which might ensue; but at least he could have the satisfaction of taking one of these hombres with him.

Fortunately, perhaps, for all concerned, he was not called upon to do so.

"Kid," the leader said, "you are not goin' to like this. You have still got yore gun, but I'd advise you not to resort to it. You are goin' to have to get down off that cayuse."

"Why, sure," Antrim said, preparing to sling his left leg over the horn.

"No, you don't!" drawled the masked man softly. "You slide off the *near* side or you are apt to slide into hell."

"Listen," Antrim said coldly. "Listen. You be thankful I've let you take possession of my prisoner, an' let well enough alone." A hard gleam was coming into his dark and narrow eyes. "There's a limit to what I'll take from the sort of coyotes that hide behind masks."

"Don't try to get rough," the spokesmen jeered, and twirled his gun suggestively. "You can't cut it— not just now. There ain't no man can beat a levelled Peacemaker."

Antrim shifted his weight tentatively in the worn saddle and saw how quick and unerringly this fellow's pistol focused into black stare upon his heart. He showed a hard and instant grin. "I guess that's so." He slid down from the horse's back.

"That's better," the leader told him mockingly. "Now just step back about four paces an' turn around."

"What's the big idea?"

"You'll find out in due course, as them newspapers say."

"If I'm goin' to be shot I prefer to meet the lead head-on."

"You ain't goin' to be shot if you behave an' do like you are told. But we ain't got all night to wrangle here. Back up an' turn round."

Antrim took several halting backward paces and turned his back upon Ruidosa's new captors. Before he realized what was happening, almost, he felt a jerk at his hip and his reaching hand found his holster empty. "I'm just figurin' to take the precaution of tossin' yore hawgleg over under them trees," the drawling voice informed him. "Temptation's a awful hard driver, an' you are much too valy'ble to us alive. Mebbe we'll be meetin' some time again, Kid. *Adios.*"

Vaulting swiftly astride their horses and grabbing the reins of Antrim's and Ruidosa's mounts, the masked men spurred into hurried motion. Antrim's hand sped to his boot-top and rose spouting flame. The leader's mocking laugh floated back through the swirling shadows, and then they were gone in a rush of hooves.

Antrim stared bleakly across the lifeless arroyo. Above its southern rim the stars shone big and bright against the purple sky. He prowled beneath the trees until his foot encountered the gun that had been taken from him. He picked it up, broke it and took several cartridges from its cylinder. He snapped the hammer several times to learn if it was working right. Replacing the cartridges then, he slipped the weapon in its holster, reloaded the smaller gun and returned it to his boot. Then he climbed up out of the arroyo and turned his eyes toward Rincon. Two miles away it was; its lights were like tiny sparks.

Antrim struck a match and looked at his silver watch. Three-thirty. He broke the match in two and dropped it while the starlight came creeping back, pale and blue in contrast to the orange of the vanished flame. Between that place and Rincon a slumbrous sea of sand, shot here and there with the dagger forms of cacti, stretched faintly gleaming. He turned his head. The moon hung low above the dark shoulders of the Sierra Caballos. Somewhere in that desolate waste a lobo's howl thickened the land's deep monstrous hush. Antrim's mind rebelled against the mysteries and plain-felt currents of turbulence that the country held for him—rebelled futilely against the realization that the nearest horse was back in Rincon, that shanks' mare must carry him across those intervening miles. With a bitter oath he squared his shoulders and started walking—no cinch in high-heeled boots.

"The night of the thirteenth—an' Friday t'boot!" one of Smith's men had derisively told another as they'd sat about the campfire smoking before turning in for an early start on the morrow. "I reckon that Lothrop man we saw near Fort Bayard was just a whizzer, Jed."

Jed looked a little uncertain in the flames' red glow. "Wal, I don't know. That fella Lothrop is a heap uncertain to monkey with. Don't you reckon, Charlie?"

Charlie Shinkle shook a grizzled head. "There's folks," he said, "as calls him some mighty hard names."

"Yeah—an' which they're right careful not t' spout within his hearin'," Laidley scoffed. "No matter where yuh go, yuh will be hearin' hard things said about gents that's middlin' fair successful by other gents what ain't."

"Well," the first man remarked, "we've got mighty nigh haffway to Socorro. An' we ain't had no trouble yet."

"No—not yet," Craig Smith said grimly.

He was sitting alone now. He had his back to the towering wall that rose above them to the right of the trail. The men had long since wrapped themselves up in their soogans and stretched out, their feet pointing to the fire that now had died to a few faint embers.

Craig Smith sucked on his battered pipe and stared off into the distance, thinking of his wife and the two kids back in Saint Louis, thinking how glad they'd be and how their faces would light up when he told them of his good fortune on this trip. It had been a dangerous undertaking and a tough journey, but it had been worth it. Eighty thousand dollars was a sizable sum of money, and worth a bit of risk.

The eternal silence of that vast country wrapped the mountains round him. Naught disturbed it but the wind soughing through the dark tracery of the pines. Down through the penetrating chill of mountain air a bright moon shone, bathing the needle-carpeted shelf in an argent glow.

What startled him, Craig Smith never knew. He hadn't moved, and even now he did not bat an eyelash. But somehow a taut jumpiness had gotten into the night stillness of the lonely places. It wasn't nerves, for Craig Smith was not that kind of man. He did not think it was imagination, either; though in justice he admitted that he had not been lulled to the state of false security enjoyed by his companions. Still, his questing eyes could discern no cause for the sudden alarm that had come upon him.

He got up and stretched his legs by walking around. He skirted the sleeping men sprawled about the ashes of the campfire; got a notion to inspect the rope corral that penned the tired burros, and sauntered leisurely in its direction.

He had strolled, perhaps, to within ten feet of where the makeshift enclosure was anchored to a gnarled juniper stump against the dark outline of the towering wall. There he stopped, rigid, staring. From the far end of the corral a number of slowly-moving elongated shadows were thrusting their thin blue shapes out across the bare whiteness of the moonlit rock.

Without a sound, without even the creaking of his leather boots to betray his movement, Craig Smith lowered his crouching form to the ground, drew the pistol from his holster and stretched out slowly with the weapon held before him. There was something fierce and blazing in his narrowed eyes as, between the legs of the motionless burros, he saw the creeping legs of an unknown man.

Smith did not lose his head; he waited, watching closely as the man passed out of his vision and another took his place. This man, too, was moving stealthily. Elsewhere a swift blur of motion showed. Tugged, Smith's gaze swung edgily; he saw a man cross soundlessly the bare patch of rocky trail. He was a tall man, lean and gaunt as a timber wolf; a man whose face was masked to the eyes. Merging with the deeper gloom, this man stopped and crouched half forward, listening. Another followed, and another. Two other blurs of movement drew Smith's eyes, one to either side. Flitting shadows against the murk.

Bitter lines warped Smith's dark features. A curse rushed against his teeth. He jerked his lips apart and threw his voice across the silence recklessly:

"Boys! Bo—"

That much was heard. The rest was lost in the roar and smash of leaping guns. Their thunder bulged against the cliff, recoiled and rolled out over the chasm, shattering against the yonder rocks. Craig Smith had come to his feet as he yelled; he was reeling backward now, blood from his riddled torso daubing his shirt. He crumpled suddenly. His hat fell off and rolled a little way. But he did not move. He lay there with his yellow hair against the pinions' fallen needles.

Smith's companions and their men were scrambling from their soogans; terror stared from their sleep-filled eyes, and the hands that sought their guns were trembling. Frightened oaths were on their lips.

Up from the shadow-dappled trail the dim forms of crouching men were advancing through a fog of powdersmoke, jets of livid flame spurting from the weapons in their hands.

Panic-stricken, the guards of Smith's Train broke and scattered, striving to reach the darkness of the trees. The rip of bullets whined among them, dropping them like quail. Here a runner doubled up, and pitched forward. Dust and powdersmoke filled the murk with a pungent, acrid odor, foul and choking. It swirled up about their scuttling bodies, clogging lungs and nostrils, bringing tears. To the right of Laidley a man clutched suddenly at his middle and fell. To the rear of him another staggered, lurched sideways and vanished in the gloom. Before him was a smear of moonlit rock. He thought he swerved his steps to miss it, but the thing came up and struck him in the face. It took him seconds to realize that he was down, that something was prodding his ribs like a white-hot iron. But he wouldn't die that way. He got his weight up on his elbows, got a knee under him and one foot firmly planted. He heaved himself erect. Something struck him in the back, smashing him like a hammer. He went swaying to his hands and knees. There was blood in his sobbing voice.

Shinkle saw him from a patch of juniper; started back to aid him. Four steps he took, and tumbled.

"I reckon that's all," a calm voice drawled across the dimming uproar. "A thousand dollars a second, boys. I'd call that right good pay. Throw this carrion off the shelf an' we'll get busy packin' the burros. We wanta be off this trail by mornin'."

Chapter XIII

TO HAVE AND TO HOLD

Ruidosa, who rather fancied himself as something of a lady killer, came to the conclusion that this occasion was especially designed for a demonstration of his talent. Finding another man's woman in an empty house was a direct challenge to a man of his accomplishments. The way a slender olive hand rose gracefully to caress a greased end of his little black moustache advertised as much; and if more proof were needed, it would easily have been found in the leer of his appraising eyes.

His lips smirked a grin as with a swagger he put his black-silk-clad shoulders against the *patio* wall and chuckled, "Well, *nina de los ojos,* I had not expected the great good fortune of finding you here alone. Surely, the hand of God is in it. I shall burn a thousand candles, presently. Have you no welcome for me? Come, come—speak up. There need be no shyness between us."

He made a picturesque figure as he leaned against the *patio* wall, *cigarro* dangling from his grinning lips. His close-fitting jacket was profusely ornamented with finest lace, a bit bedraggled and dusty now, but fine for all of that; his pantaloons were a bright blue and superbly decorated with silver buttons; his boots, though dusty, were of finest stamped leather, and richly worked with silk; his *armas*—protectors— were of panther skin; while his scarf, which he wore loosely knotted about his neck, was of a lively lavender. His *sombrero*, a-glitter with golden spangles, lay against the back of his neck and shoulder blades. held there by the buckskin thongs of the chin strap passed through the slits of a great silver concha. His tousled curls, damp with sweat, were tumbled boyishly about the smooth whiteness of his forehead.

Picturesque he might be, but Yolanda's lips curled as she eyed him scornfully. "You'd best have a care how your tongue swings, hombre. These walls have ears, and Stone Lothrop may return at any moment. You ought to know how jealous—"

Ruidosa cut her off with a deprecating wave of his *cigarro*. "Somehow," he said, relapsing into English," Lothrop's jealousies don't seem to interest me overmuch. Let's make the talk ourselves—of you an' me. Let us, in fact, be sensible and not waste time in talk at all. Actions speak loud enough, an' I've a notion you can be right entertainin' if you've a mind to."

The delicate brows that overarched Yolanda's dark, full, lustrous eyes rose sharply. "You dare say those things to me? *You*—a saddle tramp? And in my own house?"

Ruidosa laughed. *"Yore* house! Say, quit the play-actin'—hell, you don't even own the dust around this *casa!* You tryin' to cut a shine? You don't like Lothrop no more'n I do. Take a tumble to yoreself, kid! Where you goin' t' find a better Don Juan than me?"

"Don Juan—*you?"* Her white teeth gleamed in a mocking laugh that matched his own of a moment before. "Bah! You make me retch! Such brazen impudence. *Mira*—you watch out or you will find your neck in trouble, *mozo.* In this country you cannot treat a woman like this with impunity; at least, not a lady. *Vamos!* an' take your love-making with you!"

"Jesus-Maria! That I should listen to such lip from your kind of baggage!" Ruidosa swore, and levelled a malignant glare upon her as he shook himself free of the wall. "For that I'll get some lovin' outa you whether you like it or not. Come *pronto,* or I'll give you something you ain't lookin' for!"

A paleness came into her cheeks as she read the purpose in his eyes. A pulse throbbed nervously in the ivory column of her throat; the full breasts pushing against the thinness of her clothing heralded the agitation that suddenly gripped her as she backed away.

"Come here, by Gawd, or I'll come an' get you!"

283

"Santa Clara! San Jose!" Still backing from him, she crossed herself. Her eyes flew wide as he began advancing. There was a slow grin on his full lips now; she watched his burning black eyes— *"Sangre de Dios!"* she cried, one hand before her as if to ward him off, the other at her bosom. "Have you taken leave of your mind?"

He sneered. "Not yet I ain't. You goin' to show sense an' be obligin', or am I goin' to have to gentle you?" While he spoke, he was closing the interval between them, not fast, but inexorably. "Well?"

"You—you wouldn't—"

"You're wastin' breath," he grinned at her meaningly. "That patter might hold off some fool dude, but not me. You're dealin' with a man what knows his woman an'—Hey! C'mere, you little baggage!"

Choking a husky prayer, Yolanda turned and fled. Straight for the hall door she ran, her skirts swishing about her legs and impeding her progress. She could hear the clatter of his boots behind her—so close! But she got first inside the house and sped panting down the hall. His thundering curses seemed almost at her ear; his foul promises spurred her on and lent her strength to reach her room. She lurched inside, her breath coming in great gasps. She sagged her weight against the door, but it would not close. Ruidosa had a boot between it and its frame. She was driven back as he hurled it open.

Her lips, as she faced him wide-eyed, were great red splotches against the alabaster paleness of her face. Her breasts rose and fell, and with each sobbing breath threatened anew to burst their covering. The sight whipped a febrile glow into the renegade's lecherous gaze. She stood leaning against a heavy table, breathing panicky prayers.

Ruidosa, sure of her now, approached with a great show of leisure, his cynical lips framing an exultant grin. His grin grew wider, mocking, as she slid around the table, placing it between them. He laid the flats of his hands against its edge, and stood thus supporting himself while his avid stare devoured her.

She tried to speak, but her words were choked with panic. She felt paralyzed beneath his baleful gaze. She saw the bunching of his muscles, beheld them swell against his shirt. She saw the gathering of his weight; but she wasn't quick enough. His hand shot across the table's barrier, caught in the shoulder of her *camasita*—ripped!

With a low cry she broke free, and she backed against the wall— What it was that drew her gaze she did not know, for there had been no sound; but suddenly she was looking across Ruidosa's shoulder at the open doorway. She went tired and limp with an excess of reaction. For the doorway was not empty, and the sun of noon that before had brightened the hall was now dimmed.

Grim and cold, Antrim stood there in the portal. His jaws were stiff, his mouth was a straight line. Never had the girl seen such fury, such cold white fury, in a man as she saw in Antrim as he stood there eyeing Ruidosa.

Frightened, she still had to watch; she could not pull her glance away until a blur of movement told that Ruidosa had read his danger in her face. Ruidosa had, and turned. He was a sullen lump against the table. His lips were sagging loosely.

Antrim rolled and lit a cigarette while the stillness thickened. And all the time his glance was on Ruidosa closely; it blazed like sun on windswept ice.

Ruidosa's cheeks were like weathered lead. The brooding silence deepened, became insupportable. Ruidosa snarled, cursing softly. A flame sprang into his eyes and his forehead showed pulsating veins.

Antrim's voice came low and dusty, "Ruidosa—this is it."

The renegade's hand flashed back to leather. Not until it touched did Antrim move. Then both hands jerked and livid flame stabbed outward from his hips. Ruidosa leaned forward as if to meet those swift twin bursts of light. He crumpled suddenly, pitching forward to measure his length at Antrim's feet.

For long moments Antrim's eyes stayed on that motionless form while Yolanda stood uncertain, silent. There was a kind of horror in her gaze, but there were other things there, too.

But Antrim did not look. He sheathed his weapons abruptly, wheeled, and went dragging his spurs down the stone-flagged *sala*.

She saw his shadow on the yellow dust of the *patio*. Then only the dust.

Chapter XIV

"YOU CAN PASS THE WORD AROUND"

"There's just one reason I've got for livin'," Antrim told Stone Lothrop that evening. He had met the rancher at *la puerta del zaguan*, evidently on purpose, for he had been lounging by the great gate for at least two hours prior to the latter's arrival.

Lothrop, accompanied by a number of his men, had just ridden in. The men, having unsaddled and turned their weary horses into one of the pole corrals, had departed for the bunk-house; Lothrop had headed for the ranch-house, to be stopped by Antrim's detaining hand and a strange agateness of glance.

Lothrop regarded him curiously. "Yeah?"

"That's right. I live for just one reason—to afford outlaws an' other hard cases the shortest route to hell."

Lothrop stopped in his tracks, and his breath deepened. Then he grinned. "That's a laudable aim, Kid, an' one I'm glad t' hear you express. It was a damn good day for Socorro County when you an' me teamed up. Our intentions—yores an' mine—sure foller the same unpopular trail; we're both a heap anxious to put a permanent end to this hell-raisin' an' general lawlessness that's givin' this great country such a bad rep. An'," he declared impressively, "we'll do it, too."

Antrim turned his shoulders toward Lothrop squarely.

"There was a time," he remarked softly, "when I had an ambition to set the world afire—for a woman naturally. Felt like I had ought to go to college an' get myself an education." He noted that Lothrop appeared to be more interested in his tone than in his words. While the rancher rolled and licked a cigarette, he resumed in the same soft evenness of voice; "I went. When I got back from the first term I found that the woman had run off with another man."

"That just goes to prove the folly of a man gettin' education," Lothrop said, but his glance swept

Antrim's face with a risen vigilance as he put a match to his smoke. "Education's got a lot of drawbacks. I say the man's happiest who follows in his daddy's footsteps, carryin' on the old job an' the old traditions."

"It may be that you are right," Antrim admitted. "However, like I said, while I was gone this woman hooked it with another man, who was prob'ly doin' what you suggest an' follerin' his ol' man's footsteps. She slipped off in the night with this fella and disappeared. Nobody much seemed to know where she'd gone—or if they did, they kep' it to themselves. With her gone, I didn't see much sense in resumin' college. I spent a deal of time practicin' with a pair of Colts. Then I took up my present career of dishin' out lead to needy hellions."

The ensuing stillness was thick with baffling, unexpressed thoughts and conjectures. Both men stood looking out over the tawny earth for several moments. Antrim's eyes turned first, and he saw how Stone Lothrop's thick wide chest made a heavy shadow against the failing light—a large plain target for a Colt's .44. And he saw that Lothrop was smoking with a strange nervousness, and that his eyes—when they swung round—were very sharp.

"Seems sort of curious," Lothrop said, "that you should have felt a hankerin' for huntin' outlaw scalps."

"My folks," Antrim said coldly, "were victims of outlaw lead."

Lothrop's shoulders made an expressive gesture. "Well, I'm sure flattered some by yore confidence, Kid, but I don't just see why you should be tellin' me all these things.

Antrim could understand that. Folks out there

seldom said much concerning their past and their personal problems. "You go and take a look in the lady's room," he suggested. "There is somethin' there you had ought to see."

When Lothrop returned from his visit to Yolanda's room there was a film of moisture on his dark face that even the fierce heat of that stifling valley could not have put there. He looked at Antrim for a long moment without speaking. Then he said, "Let me be the first to congratulate you on a damn good piece of work. Of course he should have gone to trial, an' that was what I had in mind when I started him to the county seat in yore care. I—"

"He had a trial."

"Umm, yes, I suppose he did. Still, you ain't hardly been elected judge yet, Kid. Understand, though," he added hastily, "I ain't criticizin' you for shootin' him. Like enough I'da done the same if he'd tried to escape whilst he was in my charge. One thing I can't see, though, is yore reason for bringin' him here an' catchin' him in Yolanda's room. That don't hardly seem the—"

"In her room, "Antrim said dustily, "is where Ruidosa took the plunge."

Lothrop started. Some unrevealed thought laid a strict reserve across his gaze. "You mean you shot him in her room?"

"You've called the turn."

"But you was takin' him to Socorro—"

"That's where we *started* for."

"Then what in hell was he doin' in there?"

"I didn't ask. It didn't seem important. I shot him because he *was* in there." Antrim looked squarely into Lothrop's smouldering eyes, "I'm aimin' to shoot the next skunk I find there, too. You can pass the word around."

Antrim, nursing a bitter mood, was perched on the top pole of one of the empty corrals. He was reflecting grimly on his actions of the past few hours, and in review he found them far from satisfying. It wasn't that he regretted the killing of Ruidosa; that renegade had more than deserved the fate that had overtaken him. His dissatisfaction came from something else; he had just made two discoveries that made him out a fool in his own estimation!

Turbulence rocked gustily through his arteries. It took him minutes to cut adrift of his smoky passions. He got a check-rein on his temper finally and grinned derisively as he recalled how, not so many hours ago, he'd been calling Thatcher a fool. "Well, it takes all kinds," he muttered wryly.

From that first day in the sheriff's office at Socorro he had known that some time he and Lothrop were due to clash. And he'd been made increasingly aware of it with each passing day, with each new bit of mystery, suspicion, evidence. It had been inevitable from the day someone had laid him tenderly in a cradle; perhaps before. Fate, Destiny— call it what you would—long since had cast the die and decided on his rôle in life. Just as long ago it had been decided that on some dark night Yolanda would so far forget her breeding and obligations as to drop from ken with some unknown adventurer. Just as hundreds of other things had long since been decided, such as Ruidosa's death—and the manner of it. It had not been written that Antrim's trail and Lothrop's could cross and part again without significance.

He was a fool for censuring the girl the way he had;

certainly he had been less than just. Who was he to have judged and found her wanting? Hell must have laughed at the idea of Guy Antrim setting a pace in morals!

The first of his discoveries that had placed him by the side of fools had been the realization that he was still in love with Lothrop's woman! Still in love, that is, with Yolanda, who *now* was Lothrop's woman! As a discovery it was distinctly undesirable. His affairs were far too complicated now to afford a new entanglement.

But the second of his discoveries was worse. The first had betrayed him into the second, and the second concerned Stone Lothrop—that man of keen perceptions, that fellow of iron nerves. The damage might not be irreparable, but the fact remained that he had placed a trump in the rancher's hand. The next move was up to Lothrop, and that it would be speedily forthcoming Antrim did not doubt.

It came even sooner than expected. Suggs' voice whined across the yard:

"Hey, Kid! *Kid!* The boss has work for yuh!"

Antrim lowered his lean form from the corral, headed cautiously toward the voice. He made out the rider's figure, a deeper shadow against the murk. He halted ten feet distant, and each hand rested on a gun. "Yeah?" he said it softly.

"That yuh, Kid?"

"Well, you can start oratin', anyway."

"Listen: The boss says fer yuh t' hit the trail fer Socorro—pronto."

"How come?"

"Wants t' make sure things is running smooth an' easy with a scarcity of violence. Says fer yuh t' get there quick an' hold the lid on, no matter what yuh find. He'll be along with extra deputies inside two days. Got it?"

"Yeah."

"Git goin', then."

In that room at Two-Pole-Pumpkin where Lothrop customarily gathered his hard-faced supporters and retainers when laying plans for some new project, the great coal-oil lamp that hung from the beamed ceiling was lit again. The door was closed, and the curtains drawn across the windows. Much smoke from slender *cigarros* was being splayed through divers nostrils; rising and drifting, it lay in layers between the table and the lamp. At the table's head stood Lothrop, coldly surveying the gathered company from beneath his sleepy lids. Apparently content with what his gaze had taken in, he pulled up a chair and sat down, resting his massive elbows on the table's edge.

"Well," he said, "let's get to business, gents. Suggs, were you—"

"Just a minute, Chief," a dark-faced man with a close-cropped black moustache and heavy sideburns said. "Have you heard anything from Ruidosa?"

Lothrop said drily, "Not directly. But he won't be riding with us any more."

"The damn bunch-quitter!" Mitch Moelner sneered. "He—"

"He didn't quit from choice. He's been shot."

"Shot!"

"Yes, Keldane, shot."

"Was he bad hurt? He ain't dead, is he?"

"He ain't never said he was. I found him in 'Landa's room. The Smoke-wagon Kid claims he potted him

292

there. There was two bullet holes in Ruidosa's skull—one through each eye-socket."

Keldane gasped, "By juniper! That guy could shoot the buttons off a caterpillar's belly!"

Moelner said, "Where's he at?" and got up out of his chair.

"No sense you paintin' up for war," Lothrop told him. He's gone. You might's well sit down. I sent him off to Socorro."

"You would!"

"Did you think I wanted to see you put a chip on his shoulder an' get yore light blowed out?"

"Humph! It'll take more'n a blankety-blank Smoke-wagon Kid to blow it out!"

"That's a wranglin' subject," Lothrop said, "an' we ain't here to wrangle. Time may come when that fella will be worth more to us dead than alive. But right now ain't exactly that time. You string with me an' let my brains do yore thinkin', an' you may be something better than a saddle bum when they plant you."

He waited until Moelner had sullenly resumed his chair. While he waited, the sharp eyes beneath his sleepy lids roved over the faces of his men. A few were not there, but Keldane was, and Purdin, Rafe, Tombstone, Daggett, Suggs, Moelner and Hildermin were, also. They were a hard-faced lot, and tough as mesquite. A more scoundrelly crew would have been hard to imagine, and yet these men, despite their hard leathery faces, for the most part were accepted on this range as honest men. Suspicion attached to a few, such as Moelner, Tombstone, and Hildermin, yet nothing had ever been proved against them, and Lothrop did not believe that anything ever would be—so long as they trusted themselves

293

to his guidance, and played their cards at his direction. Of course, they might be killed in some nefarious enterprise. But they would entail no special risk for him, and while they were alive he felt fully capable of extricating them from any situation, however grave it might appear.

He did not believe himself infallible, but considered that he was more so than any of his opponents—and a damned sight more adroit. Scanning the present members of his crew, he mentally picked a number for the things he had in hand. But before he could get on with these plans, Purdin asked:

"When you reckon them two new hands will be comin' in?"

"Not for quite a spell. I've given 'em a job over in another section—a special scouting job," Lothrop answered, and grinned to himself. In truth, the only place those fellows Purdin referred to would be doing any scouting now was hell. Lothrop had taken them with him to cache a big haul just taken by the gang. Indeed, he had signed the fellows on with that very chore in mind. When it had been completed, he had ruthlessly shot the pair and thrown their carcasses into a gully for the buzzards to finish off. It was the sort of adroit step in which Stone Lothrop took a deal of pride.

He cleared his throat and turned to Suggs. "Pete—you recollect Stumpy's lynching?—D'you reckon you was seen around that park by any of them valley outfits?"

Suggs grinned, and blinked his squinty eyes. "Hell, no. They damn well heard me, an' I won't say they didn't, but as fer reco'nizin' me—cripes, they didn't get no chance. An' besides, it was gettin' pretty dark when I quit that hangin' bee."

"Hmm." Lothrop ran a tongue across his heavy lips and put a lazy half-smile on them. He looked at Mitch and Purdin. "I expect it's about time we got after Jones an' that yeller-bellied Corner. You swore that warrant out for them, didn't you, Black Jack?"

"I put that over slick as bear grease, Boss."

"I heard you did. Just wanted to make sure there hadn't been any hitch. Was talkin' to Thatcher, the other day—he runs the Star, over east of Rincon. Told me you'd sworn it out an' wanted to know if I reckoned Jones an' Corner really was on the rustle. I told him I would hate to think so."

The men sniggered their appreciation.

"I expect the stage is set enough by now. Rafe an' the other boys have been passin' the word around through influential quarters. By now, half the men who count in this country have got a vague idea that Jones an' Corner really are up to some ornery business. We'll smash them outfits flatter than a leaf. Then we'll lay pipe for Stewart."

"Why didn't yuh aim to bust that ol' hombre with the others?" Moelner jeered, "You'd of saved us boys a lot of time an' energy that way, not to mention the savin' in lead. When we take after them pals of his, he's goin' to grab the tomahawk sure as hell!"

"I guess not." Lothrop looked his lieutenant over coldly. "Like I've said before, the trouble with you, Mitch, is that you haven't got any savvy. You're a reg'lar hell-bender when it comes to spoutin' lead, but every time you open that trap of yores you put your damn foot right in it. If I'da gone after Stewart same time as Jones an' Corner, a number of hombres around this stretch of cactus would have smelled a powerful strong odor. We'da stirred up a hornets' nest that all the lead in the Territory couldn'ta quieted. When I lay pipe, I look ahead. An' I look careful. You should know by now I don't pass up any bets."

He let his glance rove over the men once more, wondering if better hands could be picked for his purpose. It seemed unlikely. These were tall men, of a characteristic leanness of body in the aggregate, and a squintiness of eye. They were garbed in more or less traditional style, wearing similar boots, vests, pants, and wide-brimmed hats. They had a characteristic woodenness of face and watchfulness of glance. They were tough, and ready for any deviltry; they were skilfully shaped to his touch and would, he believed, go through hell for him, despite their constant wrangling. One or two perhaps—if the price offered were big enough—might sell him down the river. A recollection of Ruidosa drove a fleeting scowl across his cheeks. He would take care in future to keep less trusted men where their weaknesses could be discounted.

"We're ready," he said abruptly, "to open up the ball. The first thing to be opened is Stumpy Harker's grave. Tombstone, you an' Keldane here go out an' stumble across it, accidental-like. Keldane better find it. You go with him to the county seat to help him break the news an' to swear to the identity of the body. I want this thing done right. Me an' some of the other boys will happen into town three-four hours behind you."

Suggs and Moelner began to grin. Someone sniggered. Keldane said, "What's the rest of it?"

"When I get in an' hear yore news about findin' my missing puncher," Lothrop smiled, "as man an' sheriff I'll get out a prompt reward for information leadin' to the arrest of Stumpy's murderers."

George Hildermin stirred restlessly. "Ain't there somethin' I can do?"

Lothrop nodded. "Yeah. This is your part, George. When that reward goes out, you step forward to claim it. I'll question you as to why you hadn't come forward sooner, if you knew about this lynchin'. You'll say you were scared of the lynchers an' their friends. I'll ask you if you could swear to their identity. You say yes; the men who swung poor Stumpy were Hootowl Jones an' Lefty Corner and their outfits. Got it?" Hildermin's repulsive countenance showed he had. He looked well pleased at the part he'd been picked to play. His huge jaws spread his wide lips in a grin. "You bet!" he said emphatically.

"How come I didn't get a rung in on that job?" Suggs asked. "I'm the gent that ackshully saw the lynchin'."

"Yeah, an' you work for the Two-Pole-Pumpkin. So did Harker," Lothrop said. "That wouldn't do at all. Folks would get suspicious quick. Now Hildermin, here, ain't known t' have no connection with this outfit. He's a outsider, plumb entire. You get the picture?"

Chapter XV

SAUCE FOR THE GANDER

Before the Grand Hotel a crowd was breaking up as, on the following afternoon, Guy Antrim rode his tired horse into Socorro. Antrim cast a searching glance across the solemn faces of such men as chanced to pass him. He remarked a certain determined kind of gleam that had not entirely faded from their eyes. He grew aware of a paucity of words; most of these men were silent, tight of lip, and he discerned that as they caught his gaze the eyes of most grew wary, focusing inscrutable looks upon him, and upon his dusty horse. He turned these things over in his mind as he nudged his horse on slowly. He deduced from his cogitations of these things that something serious was afoot, and came to the conclusion that his errand here might not be quite the waste of time he had been deeming it. The very air seemed to hold a sense of tension, of reserved turbulence that recalled to his mind other scenes like this from the past—scenes that made of sleep a restless nightmare, scenes of ominous calm that boded trouble—

He saw a man he recognized, and beckoned him over; waiting with one knee crooked about the horn while he rolled and lit a cigarette, careful to break the match before he tossed it in the dust.

"What's goin' on?" he asked as the man came up.

The fellow shook his head. "The devil's doin's, Kid," he said, and spat disgustedly. "They've organized a Citizens' Protective Association—vigilantes, I call 'em. Stewart's been elected leader."

"Ed Stewart? The owner of the Crazy L, over in Gawdforsaken Valley?"

"That's him. I say he's takin' a lot on himself to come over here stirrin' up trouble. There'll be some vacant saddles come out of this now, I can tell you. I've seen these things in Alder Gulch. Only reason them fool miners at *Santa Rita del Cobre* ain't organized is on account of Fort McLane bein' so close.

An' there's talk of a vigilance committee gettin' under way at Silver City. Imagine that! An' with them soldiers at Fort West bein' practically over their damn noses!"

"I expect maybe those Fort West troopers are plenty busy, what with keepin' their eyes peeled for redskins an' keepin' down mortality at that *Pinos Altos* gold camp," Antrim surmised.

"Mebbe so," the fellow said dubiously. "But it looks to me like this country is gettin' ready t' go t' hell. I reckon I'll cut my stick an' drift to newer pastures."

Antrim observed that it "might not be a bad idea," and earned a hard stare from the man, who growled:

"Them that sows brambles better not be goin' around with bare feet!"

Antrim looked down at his dusty boots. "I still got two-three miles of cowhide under me," he chuckled mirthlessly, and urged his horse toward the Pinto Bar.

When Antrim entered the resort, bent on washing some of the alkali from his system, a lank, rawboned man at the farther end of the bar was keeping savage time with his glass to a raucously howled:

> *"Brigham Young is the Lion of the Lord.*
> *He's the Prophet and revealer of his word.*
> *He's the mouthpiece of God unto all mankind,*
> *And he rules by the power of the Word!"*

"Mormon Joe" abruptly stopped and left his music hanging in the air. Nearly every man in the Pinto Bar turned to see what he was peering so ludicrously at. It appeared to be the man who had just pushed inside the swinging doors: a beardless youth, at least six years Antrim's junior, who was clad in blue "store duds" of some Eastern cut. His feet were encased in bright yellow shoes and his head was topped with an elegant light beaver hat, tilted jauntily to display his yellow curls. He was a handsome young fellow, and very nattily dressed.

He looked about the room good-naturedly, bowed to all the company, and started toward the bar. He had almost reached it when his progress was blocked rudely by Mormon Joe, who lurched in front of him with a drunken swagger. Joe's bloodshot eyes surveyed the youth as though he were some new dance hall girl.

"Well!" he exclaimed, planting hands on hips. "Jes' whar in hell did yuh blow in from?"

The young stranger said, "Why, I just come down from Santa Fé."

"Didn't raise yuh thar, did they?"

"No, indeed. I was not reared in Santa Fé. I came from the East, originally."

"Yuh don't shay! Well, I don't savvy nawthin' about that there East yuh talk about, but I'd allow yuh shure come 'original,' all right." He laid a derisive glance upon the stranger. "I allow that East yuh brag about is some place round the ocean whar they jerks the sun up like they does a anchor. Ain't that right?"

"The sun never sets on Boston, sir."

"Huh? Say! How would yuh like to fight?"

"I don't believe I'd care to," the young stranger replied politely.

The broad grin on the face of Mormon Joe grew huge and wicked. "Listen," he snarled, "I'm the 'riginal wild lobo of the fair Cibolas. When I says 'Fight!' no man in pants denies me!" He glared at the youthful stranger, affecting a ferocious scowl. "I'm the orneriest man in this whole damn country! I'm a bob-tail wouser, than which there ain't no worst any-mile in the whole Apache Nation! I've drunk blood with Victorio; I've spit on Geronimo; I taken more scalps'n Dan'el Boone an' Davvy Crockett rolled inter one! I killed me a depity three months back, an' defied the sheriff t' take me up. I ain't killed no man in this stinkin' hawg-waller yet, but I'm a-goin' to kill yuh if yuh jest open yore mouth!"

The stranger placed a hurried hand across his lips, and Mormon Joe guffawed. Sobering, he snarled as he glared around at the watching faces. Then he swung his glance again to the stranger and gritted: "I'm thinkin' o' feedin yuh to the ants. Yuh better cut a caper quick! Serve up one o' they eastern jigs, an' cut 'er proud. Hey, Mex—strike up that guittar?"

Antrim was minded to step forward and put a stop to this dude-baiting. Anyone acquainted with Mormon Joe knew that only one thing amused him as much as his *singing*—getting a laugh on some stranger. Neither were particularly popular with Socorro's better element. But Antrim was aware that up till now, few citizens among the latter element had ever dared come between Mormon Joe and his amusement. And for good reason: Mormon Joe was suspected of belonging to the hard case crew who ran things. So now Antrim was minded to interfere in this youthful stranger's behalf.

But as he would have started forward, he caught a curious glint in the young man's eye that made him decide to wait a bit. The stranger seemed no speck perturbed by the bully's threatening bluster. Indeed, Antrim thought, he appeared to relish it.

"If you are intending to use that pistol you are

301

holding, please be careful where you fire. I would hate to have my shoes or clothes damaged."

"You *what!* Damn my eyes, I'm a sight more apt ter puncture yo' mortal tintype! By cripes, I'm a Spanish lobo from the burnin' Jornada. I cut my teeth on Satan's gun barrel. I'm a killer from the headwaters of Bitter Crick, an' by Jericho, I'm like t' kill yuh while I'm at it! Yuh fling a fancy hoof, an' fling 'er quick!"

As Antrim eyed the youth he began to doubt the accuracy of his recent impression. This business should be stopped before someone got badly hurt. He shoved free of the bar and told Mormon to pull in his horns before they got knocked off.

The stranger looked wonderingly at Antrim. He bowed politely from the waist and thanked him for his good intentions. "But," he said, "this fellow isn't bad. He's just a big overgrown boy that wants to play. A bit full of animal spirits, of course, but—"

Mormon Joe swore loudly. "Git outer my way!" he bellowed. "I'm a-goin' to shoot me a man!"

A headlong charge, on the part of the patrons, was instantly precipitated toward open windows and swinging doors. The only ones to hold their places were Antrim, the four members of the vigilance committee, and the youthful stranger.

Antrim's lip curled as he stared after the departing patrons, who were leaving in such precipitous haste. Such scenes as this were nothing new in his experience; he had witnessed many. But his sneer abruptly ironed out as he noted the proposed victim still standing indolently in his tracks, not having budged a fraction. This *was* new! And there was another difference, he found. The vigilantes were still there and showed no signs of leaving. Well, well.

Antrim hunched his shoulders more comfortably against the bar and waited.

The stranger stood quietly, a faint smile on his mouth, watching the cursing Mormon Joe. Nor did he so much as move until the bully's weapon began to focus. In the twinkling of an eye, then, he took a long step forward, with his left hand seizing the desperado's gun-hand at the wrist while his right presented a large-calibred derringer whose muzzle he planted firmly against Joe's quailing stomach. It was swift work and efficient.

In this pose the stranger, as though about to ask a blessing, said, "My dear fellow, stand fast and release your pistol or I shall spill your life blood like dirty water—and just as quick."

Reluctantly Mormon Joe let his gun drop to the floor.

The stranger stepped back a pace. "Now take up your position again at the far corner of the bar where you were when I came in."

As Mormon Joe, muttering abortive curses, obeyed, the stranger beckoned the barman and asked for a cigar. Quietly lighting it, he began to puff enjoyably. The crowd, noting the lack of fireworks, had returned as far as the doors and windows, and from these vantage points stood looking in. Ignoring them, the stranger said:

"Mormon Joe, if you move from there till I call you, it'll not be long until you are shaking hands with Saint Peter—or the keeper of another place."

For several moments longer the stranger puffed appreciatively. Then he strode down the bar and halted before the scowling badman. "Shove your hands above your head and keep them there. I am going to shove the fiery end of this up your nose, my friend, and if you value your life you had better leave it there till it goes out."

He did so and stepped back, presenting the muzzle of his derringer at the bully's stomach in a deadly aim. His eyes were cold as flint, belying the gentle smile upon his lips.

Mormon Joe went pale as ashes. Sweat broke out upon his face and ran down it in great streams that mingled with his tears. But he dared not move his hands.

A great cheer went up from the onlookers, in which was mingled a number of hoots and cat-calls. Antrim saw a few scowls among the audience, but when the eyes of the four vigilantes swept that way, the scowlers vanished.

Antrim passed the vigilantes on his way to the swinging doors. "Who is that young fellow?" he asked guardedly. As guardedly, one of the four said, "That's Ted, ol' Stewart's son. Jest got back from College. Looks like a education can be right handy, sometimes, don't it?"

"If he's wise," Antrim answered, "he'll lose no time in gettin' outa town. Joe's friends'll make mincemeat out of him for this."

The vigilante smiled bleakly. "I don't reckon they will, Kid. A new day has dawned for Socorro. We're aimin' to make this town a place where men won't be scared to bring their wimmen an' kids. Hard cases has run this country long enough. Their number's up, an' if they don't pull stakes right quick, they're not goin' to be in any way to travel."

Antrim shrugged. "Their number's up, but they won't be travellin' yet. It'll take more'n this to scare them out. There'll be blood spilled a-plenty before this country's tamed."

LOTHROP READS THE SCRIPTURES

Lounging on the porch of the Grand Hotel, Antrim, awaiting supper, observed a pair of determined-looking riders jogging their dusty ponies up the road. The drooping sun hung low above the southern shoulder of that yonder mountain, and flung their bobbing shadows on ahead. Antrim watched them absently. His mind was turning over the latest news from Lincoln County, retailed to him by a drummer with "plenty of tongue oil." This news tallied rather closely with that disclosed by a letter from Santa Fé which he'd been handed by the Grand's proprietor half an hour before. He had been wondering, too, why it was he had never met but three of Lothrop's riders during his visits to the Two-Pole-Pumpkin; he'd met Mitch, Suggs, and a man named Rafe. He'd not seen Lothrop's foreman, Purdin. But the Lincoln County matter had been uppermost in his mind when he spotted the pair of riders. "Poor Axtell," he mused, and shrugged. "Middle of a stream ain't what I'd call a rightful place to swap horses."

He dismissed his musings and conjectures then and turned a more careful attention on the two approaching horsemen. He had his badge pinned plainly in sight, and he saw the two men's eyes flick towards its gleam, swing their mounts and make directly toward him. With that canny ability he possessed to feel out latent values, he sensed a veiled excitement in these newcomers.

The elder was a pale cadaverous man with sunken eyes that were dark and brooding, and great hollows in his cheeks. His companion was a dark-faced man with heavy sideburns and a close-cropped black moustache. Both were hard and capable, efficient-seeming men. He watched them dismounting before the hitch rack. They swung under it and came to a stop at the edge of the three steps leading to the porch.

The elder said in a flat, challenging way, "You the sheriff of this here town?"

"Well, not exactly," Antrim smiled. "Im one of the deputies. I reckon you'll be findin' the other at the office—it's up the street a place. The sheriff's name is Lothrop."

"That so?" the younger said. "Now I'll be damned if we didn't cover one dusty smear of territory plumb for nawthin', pard. That is, onless the sheriff's here?"

"No, he isn't here right now. Expectin' him, though, in a coupla days."

The pale, cadaverous fellow seemed to be sizing him up. Now he said, as though weighing his words, "I expect you'll do, like enough. You are one of his depities, you say?"

Antrim nodded. "What's up?"

The elder looked at the younger, then both took a guarded glance about. "Well, I'll tell you," the gaunt man said. "Buck here's found a stiff."

Antrim regarded the dark-faced man with a closer interest. "A dead man? Where?"

"Well—" the dark-faced Buck appeared to hesitate. His roving eyes flicked round suspiciously. "Mebbe we better take a walk over towards yore office, sort of. What we're figgerin' to tell hadn't ort to be overheard."

Antrim shrugged. "Just as you please, gents," he

agreed, and swung into step beside them as he came out into the still-hot smash of the sun. "My name's Antrim," he said conversationally.

"That so?" Buck asked.

The cadaverous man said, "Glad to meet up with you, Antrim," but did not offer his hand.

These men were cagy, Antrim thought. And yet they seemed to have ridden far to pass on their information; possibly from the neighborhood of Gawdforsaken Valley, judging from what the younger one had let fall. Of course, he could not blame them for being careful; plenty of gents were filling unmarked graves because of a careless tongue. He studied them covertly with a sidelong glance. There was something—

"This dead man," Buck said abruptly, "had been under sand about ten-twelve days. You know what kinda climate we got here. There was some rocks piled atop his body, but a coyote or some such varmint had got one leg out for a meal. We stumbled across the place accidental-like—I did, rather. It was in what you might call a out-o'-the-way sort of stretch. Seein' that leg sort of roused my itch for nosin'. I pitched off them rocks an' took a look."

He squinted reminiscently into the sun-flecked distance. When he turned back to Antrim his face was sober. "My pard, here, had been out huntin' some strays. Fact is, we both was. In different direckshuns. When we met up, I told him about this stiff, an' he allowed as how he'd like to take a look. We went back to the place an' I showed 'em. He took one squint an' swore. Why, that's—"

"Ease off," the cadaverous man snapped testily. "Only a fool would be so plumb brainless as to go shootin' off his mouth in the middle of the street!

307

Think I wanta play target to hard case lead? What yuh got t' say will keep till we git to the office."

A dull color flushed Buck's cheeks and he shut his mouth.

The journey was completed in a stilted silence. Reaching the adobe building serving as sheriff's quarters and jail, Antrim shoved ahead and led the way inside. Farley, he saw, was still behind the desk where he had left him almost an hour before. Farley was the Socorro deputy; a kind of spineless sort to all appearances.

He roused himself sufficiently to glower at Antrim. "Yuh back again? Cripes! I sh'd think you would be ashamed to show up here after refusin' t' serve that warrant—"

"I," Antrim cut in coldly, "didn't refuse to serve the warrant; I suggested that the matter could wait till the sheriff got here. An' we wore that subject out some while ago. Right now we're figurin' to talk about a dead man. You better listen."

Farley had been a sullen lump against his chair, but Antrim saw him straighten with a swift alacrity when the words *"dead man"* struck his ears. He shot a startled, probing glance at the two men who had followed Antrim into the office. For an instant he seemed paralyzed. Then he gulped and swept a moistening tongue across his lips. "I got t' go uptown a spell," he muttered, getting up. "Got to see Jess—"

"Jess can wait; these strangers mebbe can't. Sit down," Antrim said, and turned his shoulders to the man Buck. "Proceed."

Buck, with an unflattering look at Farley's whitened face, said, "It was like I told you, Antrim. After I'd stumbled across that grave an' got a squint at the stiff's mug, I got to thinkin' mebbe my pard might want to have a look-see, too. He did. He'd been through this country before, two-three years back, an' allowed it might be some fella he knowed. So I took him to the place. He took one look at that stiff an' says, 'Hell! I know that jasper! That's Stumpy Harker, what used t' work for the Two-Pole-Pumpkin brand.' "

"Just like that, eh?"

"As Gawd's my witness, jest like that exackly."

Antrim swung a probing glance on the gaunt man's face. "You couldn't be makin' a mistake, by any chance?"

"Not a chance, Mister. I played stud all night with that gent in Rincon oncet. Two years back come grass, it was. He darn near took my shirt."

The silence thickened with unspoken thoughts, while Antrim weighed the statements carefully. If this tale was true, Lothrop could quit fretting about Stumpy's extended absence; in fact, if this tale was true—Antrim left the thought there. "Two years is quite a spell," he suggested.

"If you ain't figurin' to take my word for it, why that's yore business, I reckon, Antrim. It was Stumpy, though. Come on, Buck, let's get outa here. We was fools t' waste our time."

"Keep your shirt-tails in," Antrim's voice reached out to stop them. "Whether it's Stumpy, or not, it seems like you found a dead man. In which case, you fellows are apt to be needed as material witnesses—"

"To what?" Buck snapped out instantly.

"A coroner's inquest. The law is aimin' to take hold round here an' put a end to some of these killin's. Whenever it gets half a chance, it likes to do things accordin' to Hoyle. You better—"

"To hell with that," the gaunt man growled. "We

done our duty as honest citizens by reportin' our find. Whatever else is up t' yuh. We got work of our own to tend tuh. C'mon, Buck."

The pair started for the door, but stiffened to a halt with the muzzles of Antrim's guns against their bellies. Their faces paled and they stepped back a pace or two. Buck jerked up his chin. "What the hell you mean by that?"

Antrim said, "Just this: You gents are goin' to stay right in this office till Lothrop passes the word that you can go. Better sit down an' make yourselves to home. I ain't expectin' him before tomorrow."

A rousing anger flashed a touch of color into the pale man's cheeks. His bony hands were resting on the crossed gun belts that circled his skeleton hips; gun belts whose holstered weapons were slung butt forward for a cross-arm draw. "Look!" he growled. "I've come more'n fifty miles outa my way across a damn' part of that blisterin' Jornada jest to pass on that information. Do you think I'm goin' to be kept from my work another day jest to favor a loco starpacker that ain't got savvy enough to recall he's only the people's servant?"

"That's about it. You an' your friend are goin' to wait till the sheriff gets here."

"By Gawd, we ain't! Yuh can't hold us here like this!" Antrim gave them stare for stare.

"Can't I?"

"The law don't give—"

"The law," Antrim said with a hard and instant grin, "has been altered."

Sheriff Stone Lothrop, accompanied by a number of other men, among whom were Moelner, Rafe, Daggett, and Suggs, rode into town about two hours after dark. They dismounted and racked their horses before the sheriff's office, and observed that there was a light burning inside. They strode to the door, and Lothrop pushed it open. He stopped with indrawn breath upon the threshold. "Well," he drawled. "Well!"

Deputy Sheriff Farley was a sullen lump in the chair behind the desk. Across from him, on a bench against the wall, sat two men in dusty range garb, their faces screwed in scowls that plainly advertised ill-humor, their eyes a-smolder with resentment. Across from them, against the opposite wall, sat Antrim, with a rifle across his knees. There was a lurking gleam of capricious humor in the glance with which he favored the newcomers.

"Howdy, Sheriff," he said, "an' the same to your friends. Come in an' set awhile."

The cadaverous man started to spring to his feet. The crack of Antrim's rifle whipped across the silence. The would-be riser sank back on the bench with a stifled curse. He put a hand to his ear and it came away red. He stared at the blood with bulging eyes.

"You ain't hurt," Antrim told him soothingly. "I just clipped your ear to remind you that orders is orders in this country—especially when they come from the law. You was told to set till the sheriff give you leave to go. I ain't heard him countermand the order."

The lazy half-smile parted Lothrop's heavy lips. "Hmm," he drawled, "you was prepared to keep 'em quite a spell, I'm thinkin'."

"I was prepared to keep them till you came. They've found a dead man that's like to interest you a heap—they've found the corpse of Stumpy Harker."

311

A dark flush ran across the bulldog grip of Lothrop's features. His big, rocklike figure seemed to swell and heighten. "They've *what!*"

"They stumbled across the grave of Stumpy Harker," Antrim told him evenly. "Leastwise, they claim it's Harker's body they've found. Allowed it has been under sand ten-twelve days. In this climate, I'd say recognition was easily possible that long—providin' wolves an' buzzards was busy elsewhere. But I figured you'd be wantin' to talk to them yourself."

"You figured right." Lothrop's tone ran wickedly even. He rolled his shoulders round on Buck and Buck's companion. He stared at them, and the smoke-grey surfaces of his eyes showed a hard opacity. "Names—let's have 'em quick!"

"Keldane," said Buck, without reluctance. "My pardner's known as Tombstone."

"What you doin' in this country?"

"Huntin' hawsses. Strays. We work for Cachildo. He runs a hawss ranch beyond Black Mesa."

"An' what makes you think this stiff you found was Harker?"

Antrim, while Buck was explaining, looked at Mitch Moelner's pitted countenance, just in time to catch a peculiar look that passed between the gunman and Buck's pardner, who had been occupying his leisure by tying his neckerchief over his bullet-nicked ear, and grimacing mightily.

Lothrop seemed to be weighing the details of that poker game in which Tombstone had claimed to have been trimmed. A change rippled across his heavy cheeks suddenly and he drove a suspicious glance at Tombstone that put a cloud of caution across the latter's restless gaze.

"What," Lothrop demanded softly, "terminated

that friendly game of draw?"

Tombstone stopped fiddling with his neckerchief abruptly, and the lamplight seemed to accentuate the sunken hollows of his cheeks. The jade green of his glance took on a brighter sheen that hid his thoughts entirely, but did not relax the tautness of his pose. He watched Lothrop with a risen vigilance, Antrim thought.

"Come," Lothrop said. "I want an answer. If you played draw with Stumpy one night in Rincon two years ago, the game must have wound up some way. How?"

"Why, like he told you," Tombstone said, as though surprised at such obtuseness. "Stumpy damn nigh took my shirt."

"Let's see," Lothrop mused. "There was you, an' Stumpy, an'—who else was in that game?"

A slow wind stirred the hair that fell to Tombstone's open collar. He shoved his hands in his pockets, then pulled them out. The lines of his graveyard face etched deeper and a pulse throbbed against his bony forehead. "There was a couple saddle tramps. I don't recollect their monickers."

"One of them was a big fella, wasn't he?" pressed Lothrop, smiling. "A big Mex known as Concha? A fella that was gettin' trimmed even worse than you was an' that made a ugly sug—"

"Great Gawd!" Tombstone gritted, and his frame slouched lower and tensed.

Lothrop's grin licked a thin line across his mouth. "I thought so. Well, it's past an' gone. No need to go into it now. I just wanted to be sure you was the fella I had in mind. I reckon you would know Stumpy if you seen him. I'm acceptin' yore identification of the corpse. I s'pose you buried him again?"

"Yeah," Buck answered, when it seemed his partner was too amazed. "We covered 'im over an' piled rocks atop to mark the spot. Tombstone whittled a little cross of greasewood. Said it wasn't right that a gamblin' fool like Stumpy should be forgot."

Details, Antrim was thinking. Corroborating details; the little things that a less careful mind would have overlooked.

"That's right," Lothrop told Buck grimly. "He ain't goin' to be forgot. How was he killed?"

"There was marks on his neck," Buck said, "that looked like rope scars. We figger he was dragged by a rope from wherever they caught him to where they aimed to plant him. There was little bits of sagebrush in his clenched hands— There was a bullet hole between his eyes an' no gun in his leather. We figger they shot him after they'd dragged him into the gulch."

Antrim could picture perfectly Stumpy's outthrust hands clawing at bushes, rocks, prickly pear—anything, in the fierce agony of that awful progress at the end of some skunk's rope. He could visualize the murderer, too, as with a sneer the fellow put a Colt's slug between his moaning victim's eyes. The pair had been well drilled.

Lothrop's lids dropped dangerously at the corners; the eyes beneath his heavy lids were bitter bright. "By Gawd," he swore hoarsely, "this killin's got to stop! We'll see whether lives can be snuffed like guttered candles! *Farley!*" The change in Lothrop's tone made that deputy jump. "You go get that damned printer out of his bed an' have him run off a bunch of handbills. We're offerin' five hundred dollars for any information that'll lead to the arrest or death of Stumpy's murderers. If the county won't stand for it, I'll foot the bill myself. *Jump!* damn you! I want action!"

Chapter XVII

THE HAIR ON A FROG

Keldane and Tombstone were told that they might consider themselves at liberty so long as they stayed within the confines of the town. But Lothrop warned that if they attempted to leave Socorro, and were caught in such an attempt, they would be placed under immediate arrest and locked in jail for safekeeping. They were, he said, material witnesses, and as such he proposed to have them handy.

Farley had been gone on his errand ten minutes when the rest of them filed from the office. They gathered by the hitch rack where a man in merchant's garb stood facing Lothrop enquiringly.

"I expect you are the gentleman I'm seeking," this stranger said. "You're Sheriff Lothrop, aren't you?"

Lothrop made a high and bulky shape where he stood beside the soldier-straight erectness of the merchant. The light from the office windows lay strongly on the latter's face, while Lothrop's was in the dark, and was made even more unreadable as to expression by the downpulled brim of his Stet-hat. But Antrim guessed at the close scrutiny Lothrop was giving the man, and was not surprised when Lothrop nodded with a sort of saturnine indifference and started toward his horse.

The merchant laid a detaining hand on Lothrop's

arm. "Just a moment, sir," he said politely. "I have a little matter I'd admire to discuss with you, if you can spare a moment for a stranger. I'm Thaddeus Fischer. I own the Freighter's Exchange over to Carrizozo."

Lothrop turned his big shoulders slowly. The light played across his features now, and Antrim could see the lazy half-smile on his lips. But his sleepy lids were lower and effectively concealed the expression of his eyes. "Sure," he said tolerantly. "What can I do for you, Fischer?"

Fischer faced him earnestly, and Antrim now saw that he had a small carpet bag tucked under his off arm. "Lothrop," the merchant said, "I've been told that the life of a man with money in this town ain't worth the flick of a bull's tail. I don't know whether some practical jokers have picked me as a gullible sucker or not, but I think it best to take precautions. I've got twelve thousand dollars in this bag that I'm figuring to take to Santa Fé."

Lothrop's face was inscrutable, the half-smile still fixed upon it. "Well," he admitted, "I expect this town may seem a little wild, perhaps, to a stranger. But it ain't so bad to folks that know it. I do my best to keep it civilized. I expect you'll be all right."

"Maybe so. But you are the sheriff, an' I'd take it as a mighty big favor if you'd condescend to take care of this money for me till I'm ready to leave."

Lothrop massaged his bristly jaw with one big hand while eyeing the merchant dubiously. "I'll tell you, Fischer; I'd like mighty much to oblige you, but I'm not expectin' to be here overlong. I'm hopin' to start out on a manhunt right soon."

"No matter," Fischer said with perseverance. "I'm not expectin' to stop here overlong myself. An' I'd feel a heap easier in my mind if you'd take care of it for me."

Lothrop studied him briefly. "Well, shucks," he said. "If you feel that way about it, I'll oblige you. You'll want a receipt, I guess?"

Fischer laughed. "No, let's not be bothered with a receipt, Sheriff. I'm not reckonin' a writing will be necessary between you an' me. I couldn't imagine any gent with gall enough to try stealin' it from you."

Lothrop chuckled, tucked the bag under his arm, and started down the walk. "Any time you want it," he called back over a shoulder, "just let me know." Moelner, Suggs, Rafe, and the others started after him. Keldane looked at Tombstone, Tombstone shrugged, and they too turned and went striding after the others. A number of onlookers stepped out of the shadows and clustered about Fischer. Antrim heard one of them contemptuously call the merchant a fool. He saw Fischer grin. "Oh, I don't know," the merchant said, "I couldn't think of no other place where t'would be as safe. He'll hand it back, all right. I can go get some sound shut-eye, now."

Antrim breakfasted early the next morning, then headed for the sheriff's office to learn what might be scheduled for the day. As he dragged his big silver spurs along the plank walk, his roving eyes saw how the bright metallic sunlight washed the walls of the frame and adobe buildings, and provoked sharp contrasts of white and black.

He paused on his way to enter the Pinto Bar. The place was deserted save for a half-asleep bartender and a swamper who was lethargically resting on his broom. The air in there was close and sultry and contained a sour smell that was disagreeable to

Antrim. He went out and continued toward the sheriff's office. There were three horses hitched to the rail before it; Moelner's, Lothrop's, and a strange piebald mustang. "Lothrop must be huntin' the proverbial worm," was Antrim's saturnine thought.

He entered and lounged against the wall beside the door. Lothrop's thick wide chest made a heavy shadow against the opposite wall. On one corner of the desk sat Moelner, thinly smiling. A stranger stood between them and turned curiously at the sound of Antrim's entrance. He was not a prepossessing man; he had pale, watery eyes that were bulgy and a mouth whose width was like a sabre slash across his wrinkled face. His jaws were truly massive, and when the fellow spoke Antrim decided that "repulsive" was the kindest term one could apply to him.

They had evidently been awaiting him. Lothrop said, "I told Mitch you'd be along here any minute. Knew you wasn't the one to laze yore life away in bed. Too much get-up-an'-go about you, Kid. Look, I want you to meet this gent. His name's Hildermin. He saw Stumpy's killin'."

Antrim pulled his attention from Lothrop, laying it on Hildermin with a cold, deliberating insolence. "Some folks take a long time to realize a thing," he said.

"All fellas ain't as quick on the trigger as you are, Kid," Lothrop murmured soothingly. "Besides, Hildermin was scared if he talked the killers' friends would blow a winder through his skull. You can't hardly blame him for that."

Antrim's mouth took on a thin, sardonic curve, and his red brows lifted mockingly. "Is the five hundred bucks reward goin' to stop them?"

"You're kinda proddy this mornin', ain't you,

Kid? Somebody step on yore pet corn?"

"I got a notion someone's fixin' to," Antrim's drawl rolled back an answer. "This town's full of fools." He crossed to the desk and sat down on the corner opposite Moelner, stretching his lean frame forward, hooking his bootheels over an open drawer, resting his sinewy arms with their long slender-fingered hands across his knees. Hunkered there, he flicked a cynical upward glance at Hildermin's face. "Who you claimin' downed that puncher?"

"Lefty Corner an' Hootowl Jones between 'em."

Antrim made no answer to that for the moment. He sat there quietly, his hands idle and his head inclined toward the floor. In that position he asked, "Where's Farley? An' Suggs an' Rafe?"

"They've gone down to swear out a warrant—two of 'em in fact. No use puttin' this off. I've still got that rustlin' warrant t' serve," Lothrop muttered, slapping his pocket. "It goes against the grain, sort of, to think yore own neighbors could be that kind of skunks, but facts is facts. I reckon Jones an' Corner have gone plumb bad. Tell him, Hildermin, what you told us."

"I was ridin' through Gawdforsaken Valley, twelve days ago come tomorrer, on my way back here from Fort Craig. I guess you know where Stumpy was buried? Well, I was ridin' along the far side of a ridge. Jest as I toped 'er, I seen two fellas down in a gulch on the other side heatin' a iron in a little fire. They had a calf hog-tied close by. I was screened from their sight by a handful of dwarf pines, so I decides to watch awhile an' see what's up. Them fellas was Corner an' Jones.

"All of a sudden, Jones drops his iron an' wheels, draggin' at his gun. Corner pops offn that calf's head

319

an' reaches for his rifle. I'd been watchin' 'em so plumb interested I hadn't heard a thing. But now I hears horse hooves comin' hollity-larrup. It was Stumpy—yuh could see his elbers flappin'. He had a way o' ridin', Stumpy had, which was all his own. I reaches fer my long gun an' then recollects that I'd left the fool thing to home. A six-gun, at that range, wouldn'ta been no more effective than a pea-shooter! I seen there was nothin' fer me t' do but watch in the hopes o' bein' able to bring them devils to their just reward later."

Hildermin cleared his throat and looked slanch-ways at the others to see how they were taking it. Lothrop and Moelner seemed impressed.

"Them rustlers was layin' lead all around Stumpy now. Seemed impossible they could miss so frequent. I was beginnin' to wonder if they was only tryin' t' scare him when his horse took a sudden stagger an' went end over end, throwin' Stumpy clean away. I figgered t'see Stumpy up an' givin' 'em tarnashun fury, but he never moved. Just lay there stunned-like. I reckon he musta struck a rock or somethin'. Jones an' Corner comes runnin' up with their guns held ready. I couldn't hear a thing they said, but they was sure doin' a pile of talkin'. Then Jones goes over to Stumpy's dead nag an' gits his rope from the saddle. Corner grabs it outen his hand an' slips the noose round Stumpy's neck, Stumpy never liftin' a finger— which proves t' my mind he wasn't conscious. Jones goes an' gets their broncs then an' they climbs aboard 'em an' heads on down the gulch, draggin' poor Stumpy after 'em. They hadn't gone ten steps when they stops an' Corner turns round in his saddle. He looks back at Stumpy an' laffs. Then they kick in their spurs an' off they goes again. Stumpy

320

had come to by now, all right—yuh could tell it by the way he was clawin' at anything that come within his reach. It was pitiful. I can tell yuh, gents, an' it fair made my heart bleed for him. When they got down by that place where them two fellas found him, that damned Corner draws his pistol an' lets him hev it!" Hildermin dragged a grimy sleeve across his face. "Only the distance kep' me from goin' down an' revengin' Stumpy then an' there. I tell yuh gents, that scene's been hauntin' me ever since!"

Antrim stared long at the floor. When he looked up there was a frosty, ironical glint in his hard blue glance. "For sheer hauntin' power," he remarked dustily, "I'd say a fat reward had it all over a scene like that."

Hildermin's face bloated with anger, going red and white by turns. Yet, seemingly, he hadn't the guts to show an active resentment, though his right hand rested not three inches from his holstered weapon.

Uncurling, Antrim slid off the desk. His lean, hard shape made a high presence in the room. Moelner's gaze was on him, returning his mocking look sneer for sneer.

Lothrop's high blood laid a dark flush across his cheeks. His burly shoulders tautened visibly, and a savage restlessness stirred his heavy lips. Yet he did not speak at once, and when he did his tough face smiled thinly and the expression of his eyes and mouth changed instantly.

"Shucks, Kid," he said, "because this fella didn't do what you or me mighta done under them circumstances is no reason for us to go on the prod. You an' me see too much alike for us to fallin' out over some other hombre's peccadillos. Go take at ride an' cool yoreself off. What you are needin' is time for reflection. You meet us here at ten o'clock. I'll have a posse rounded up by then an' we'll be ready to go."

Mockery swam in the hard glance Antrim swept across the three of them. Then he turned his back contemptuously and went striding through the door and out into the hot morning sun.

When the clank of his spurs had died away, Mitch Moelner snarled, "I'm goin' to gut-shoot that cocky son yet!"

Lothrop said, "You talk too much, Mitch. Keep still now for a minute while I think—"

"He's onto us," Hildermin growled, but Lothrop shut him up with a heavy look. He had seen Antrim's temper burning like a white flame in his eyes, and he had suddenly realized the utter recklessness of this man he had to deal with. He had sought originally to align Antrim with his purposes as the safer of two dangerous courses. It was patent that if Antrim was not for him, the youthful leather-slapper would most certainly be against him. It had been recognition of this fact that had caused Lothrop to make a deputy of him at the outset. As to his identity Lothrop had had no reliable knowledge, nor at that time had he cared. Now, however, he was beginning to wonder. In the last few hours he had seen that in Antrim he had to do with a two-edged tool, a powerful weapon that might cut either way. And without warning. Antrim was a man, he found, who could not be led, and a man whose latent antagonism was now become a visible thing. Was it born, he wondered, of jealousy, or of some deeper thing?

"We won't be breakin' with him just yet," Lothrop said evenly.

He swung his big shoulders to the door as Rafe came in. There was an excited glint in Rafe's keen eyes. Rafe said, "Them damn things are takin' hold, Stone. Thirty of the law-an'-order fools in this town subscribed to an obligation of mutual support an' protection yesterday afternoon in front of the Grand Hotel. That means—vigilantes! They've adopted resolutions an' call themselves the Citizens' Protective Committee. An' Ed Stewart has been elected leader! Stewart's kid an' four of the members of this precious gang made a monkey out of Mormon Joe in the Pinto Bar, an' he's pulled out of the country—left last night!"

Lothrop's laugh had no mirth in it. "So they want law an' order, do they? All right, we'll give 'em a bellyful!" He lifted his chin from his chest, and his glance was filled with a hard determination. "We'll kill several birds with the same shot. We'll get Curly Ives an' show him men can't hold other gents up in public an' then beat their heads in with a gun barrel because their pockets didn't have enough change to satisfy. We'll get Ives an' see him hung; it'll discourage competition an' win back the public trust. We'll make an example of him, an' mebbe by then I'll have thought of a fitting way to deal with the Kid."

Rafe said, "What is it, Chief?"

"I was thinkin' of a number of things the Kid has let drop in his palavering with me," Lothrop answered with a chuckle that came from deep inside him. "Mitch jogged my mem'ry when he mentioned Ruidosa. I reckon the Kid's packin' some grudge he hasn't advertised— Yes," he nodded with a definite satisfaction, "I believe I've got that hombre pegged."

"I can wind him up right now, if you'll give the

word," Mitch said with a harsh malignity.

A slow humor mellowed the bulldog grip of Lothrop's features as he rose, adjusting his gun-belt. "Well, well, there'll be time enough for that when we get these other matters tended to. Go fetch the boys, Rafe. We're goin' after Curly Ives."

"How you figgerin' to come up with him?" Moelner sneered. "Goin' to spread salt around?"

Lothrop laughed in a pleased manner. "I can find an' *get* anythin' I want in this country, Mitch. What the hell do you think I've been payin' spies for?"

Striding past the public corrals, Antrim sought the rear of the livery stable owned by Clem Holt. There he found a weathered bench against the wall and sat down, placing his broad shoulders against the hot wood to take advantage of what little shade the eaves afforded. The burned-dry air held the mingled and familiar odors of dust and hay and horse manure, of harness leather and gun oil. He folded his arms across his high chest and squinted his eyes against the glare of the baking desert. He considered the things that were in his mind.

He recalled what the man in Rincon, the rancher from Lake Valley, had told him concerning Smith's Train and the Lothrop rider who had been seen around Silver City and Fort Bayard. Smith's train had not arrived in Socorro, nor had it reached Engle even. He had made discreet inquiries of a man just recently come from there. It was not hard to put fact and fact together now, in the light of what the Lake Valley rancher had told him. Smith's Train, beyond a doubt, had fallen either into the hands of the gang that was terrorizing this country, or had been ambushed by Geronimo's warriors. Antrim did not consider the latter possibility more than two seconds.

He recalled the chase of Moak, and Moak's screamed, "Gawdlemighty, Stone! Don't shoot!" *Stone*—a kind of familiar form of address that seemed to Antrim as he turned it over in his mind. It savored of past association—

The mutations of his exploring thoughts next took his mind to that scene of half an hour before when Keldane and the gaunt Tombstone had told Stone Lothrop of their finding of Harker's body. When recounting that episode to *him*, the game Tombstone had played with Stumpy that night in Rincon had been *stud;* but when going over it for the sheriff's benefit the game, curiously enough, had become *draw*. Yet the pair had been well drilled—he gave them credit. The whole thing had run off as smooth as butter. The only real mistake that any of them had made had been the over-thoroughness of the precautions to effect an air of disinterest on the part of Tombstone and his partner.

But why should they feel the need of being clothed with an air of disinterest?

With suspended judgment he proceeded to the matter for Purdin's accusation of Jones and Corner. Purdin was Lothrop's foreman—did that hold any significance? Well, whether or no, the accusation appeared to have been well bolstered by current rumors. And Purdin had sworn out a warrant; Antrim had seen it there on Farley's desk.

A part of the testimony concerning Harker's death had definitely involved Jones and Corner—not alone in a killing, but in rustling, too. And rustling was what Purdin accused them of.

Antrim slid off the bench with a queer look in his suddenly narrowed eyes. He was well aware of how the practice of "sleepering" calves was carried on, and knew that it required no altering of brands. Nor did the gentle art of mavericking. Such practices were indulged on animals which had never worn a brand. He understood that a sleeper was a calf which had been ear-marked with its owner's proper mark and left to run with its herd until after the round-up when the thief would cull it out, slab his own brand upon it, alter the earmarks and drive it off to some spot where his own critters ranged. And a maverick, he knew, was an overlooked and therefore unbranded critter whom the first gent that came across it was very apt to regard as his own property, and so mark it. That many a man mislaid a maverick on purpose was common knowledge. But such practices, in that country, although unpopular, were not considered downright rustling.

Purdin had called Jones and corner rustlers. And his charge was borne out of Hildermin's testimony—if a man could put any faith in it. Which Antrim did not. But it was Antrim's notion that none are so quick to point the finger of guilt at others as the guilty.

Squatting on his bootheels, and still with that peculiar glint in his squinted eyes, he sketched four brands in the sand with an index finger: a Long H; a Cinch Ring; a Two-Pole-Pumpkin; and a Crazy L. He regarded these marks for some time in a thoughtful silence. Then, leaning forward, he superimposed one brand upon the other three. None of those brands would cover Lothrop's, but—as a result of his alterations, Antrim now had not four brands before him, but four more or less perfect specimens of a single brand.

Slowly, as he got to his feet, a sardonic grin twisted the width of Antrim's lips. "I reckon," he muttered softly, "I better go take a look at Stumpy's corpse."

Chapter XVIII

THE LONG H JAMBOREE

Two weeks passed; two dusty, hot, and busy weeks through which the tempers of men flared high and frequently, and their nerves drew taut as bow strings, and the wicked violence of their acts increased almost in proportion with the numbers of newcomers to the Territory. Chuckwagon fires lit the nights in forty places as the fall round-up gathered beef for market and branded late calves and those overlooked in the spring work.

Each passing night saw more reps and straymen, as the riders from distant outfits were called, cutting their drifts from the day herds, catching up their strings from the remuda, packing camp beds and personal plunder, and "dragging it for home."

While the round-up progressed, old friends would meet and yowl at each other; pranks and horse-play were common, despite the seriousness of the occasion and the shortness of the men's tempers. Bad blood boiled with irritating frequency, and gun fights were not uncommon. The outfits moved on from place to place, leaving behind their blackened campfires, their tin cans and broken bottles, and the ground deep-cut with the scars and furies of the chore.

Lothrop and his posse were off scouring the country for sign of Ives; they found much "sign," but Ives proved as elusive as the rainbow's end—or the pot of gold supposed to be in its vicinity. Always the posse would arrive upon the scene of his latest adventure after the wily renegade had yanked his pin.

The rancher had gotten his bag of money from Lothrop and departed with three companions on the trail to Santa Fé. Along that trail two days later, he had been found by a freighter with his head bashed in, the bag gone, and a bloody axe laying across his body. The bodies of his three companions were also there, and likewise.

Antrim, on his way to have his look at Stumpy's corpse, found a dead man hanging to a cottonwood at the valley's edge. A note had been stabbed to the tree with a bowie knife: "We don't savvy how many examples are goin' to be necessary to learn gents to keep their irons off other gents' critters, but all will be provided that are needful."

Antrim had cut the man down and buried him, leaving the rope hanging from the limb and the knife with its grizzly message still impaled. He piled rocks atop the grave to mark it. When he mounted, then, he headed straight for the Long H of Hootowl Jones.

Antrim said, "Jones, you been losin' any cattle?"

The rancher gave him a long cold stare. His voice came light and frosty. "It's none of yore damn' never-mind, but you might's well know. My tally shows I'm short six hundred critters."

Antrim listened beyond the words for those things Jones wasn't telling. He could feel unseen eyes boring hotly on him, and guessed they peered above the sights of rifles. He let his glance drift casually about and observed many places where a man—or men—might lie concealed with a long gun cuddled to his shoulder.

There was a rider coming across the flat at a steady lope, but Antrim's glance hung fixedly on Jones. "Been hangin' any cow-thieves lately?"

Jones faced him stiffly, hands at sides, his fingers spread; his gaunt form threw a dark, foreshortened shadow on the hard-packed ground. Smoke stirred in the sulky brilliance of his gaze. "I don't do fool things, Mister."

"Meaning you ain't been 'tendin' any necktie socials?"

"Meanin' I ain't answerin' any questions," Jones said drily.

Antrim heard the approach of a horse behind him, but did not turn. Not even when he heard its hoof-pound cease, nor when its rider growled:

"Yuh want I should pot 'im, Hoot?"

Jones appeared to consider. "No," he said, "Not yet, I guess. Know him, Lefty?"

The newcomer wheeled his bronc around the horse of Antrim. He sat his saddle, a fat tub of a man, eyeing Antrim insolently. "No. What's he doin' here —who is he?"

Jones' eyes flicked the question straight at Antrim. Antrim's left hand drew his vest apart. The sun smashed reflections from the metal there. He watched the narrowing of Jones' thin lids. "The name's Antrim—if that means anything to you."

Corner snorted, "The hell it is!"

On Jones' forehead, a vein pulsed heavily. He said, "That piece of tin you're packin' don't mean a thing to us. I never did cotton to one-man law—particular the kind Stone Lothrop stands for. It's time this country got a new deal—an' it's goin' to get one."

"I expect you mean a vigilante deal," Antrim said, and caught a blur of motion off to the left. He turned deliberately in his saddle and sent a long keen stare in that direction. The bunk-house door was standing open. In it lounged a big man, a man almost as big and tough and solid as Lothrop. A man who met his stare and returned it, smiling grimly.

Antrim said, "You might as well come over here, Ed." Like that; then he added with slow irony, "An' bring your friends—they won't want to miss this."

Stewart came trotting across the yard, his big shoulders rolling heavily. Six others came behind him: dark clad fellows with sombre faces and a cold, efficient look. Stewart halted to the left of Antrim, and his men deployed to either side.

Jones said with an audible touch of insolence, "Get on with it."

"I guess that warrant ain't been served."

Corner growled, "What warrant?" and stood eyeing him suspiciously.

"The warrant chargin' you an' Jones with swingin' wide loops."

"Rustling!" bellowed Corner. "Who the hell says we been?"

"Purdin—the Two-Pole-Pumpkin foreman."

Corner swung with an oath. "I told you fools that outfit wouldn't take that lyin' down—"

"Slap a latigo on that dam' jaw!" Jones snarled and Corner subsided sullenly.

Antrim grinned. "No sense takin' his head off. I know a sight more than he could tell me, now. Anyway," his eyes swept the ring of watchful faces as he paused to get their full attention, "this rustlin's a side issue now, as far as you're concerned. A warrant's been sworn out chargin' you with murder. I kind of reckoned you might be surprised."

All at once the stillness of those men went thick

330

and curdly; there was a feeling there that scraped the nerves like a rasp. Antrim felt it, and a cold grin fired up his face and made it reckless. "You don't cotton much to that, I reckon."

Behind the spiralling smoke of his cigarette, Jones' eyes stared sharply from angular, squeezed-down lids. He snapped the butt away, and his mouth showed a stiff, grim line. "That's a hell of a joke," he said.

"Yeah—ain't it?" Antrim swung his grin on Stewart where he stood with half-closed eyes. "Some gents found Stumpy Harker. Found him buried about two miles from here. There was a window in his skull."

That startled them. Jones' sombre face went blank. Corner's mouth fell open. The glint in Stewart's eyes changed, and changed again—brashly. The forms of Stewart's men slumped lower, the muscles flattened along their jaws.

"So you come here figurin' to trail us in." There was dust in Jones' tone; there was smoldering flame in his brittle glance.

Antrim said evenly, "I don't condemn a man until I have the proof. But you haven't got the picture yet. Harker's neck showed a rope burn— An' his neck was broke. In fact, he was dead when that bullet struck him."

Antrim's face raked each tautened face with close interest. He caught a risen vigilance in Jones' pale eyes. Corner's jaw had closed, but his cheeks were ashen and there was a tremor in the hands across the horn. Stewart's men were steady, watchful, depend-able—they were waiting for Stewart's sign. Stewart's glance at Antrim showed a grim amusement.

"Well?" Jones grunted.

Antrim's glance had been on him with a covert

speculation. But with Antrim's words, the expression of his eyes and mouth changed instantly. Corner let out a frightened bleat. With a vicious oath Jones drove a curling hand to his hip.

Antrim's voice struck the stillness with an impact: "First man touchin' leather'll take on lead poisonin' 'fore he can yell 'Jack Robinson.' Now go ahead an' draw!"

The men's eyes dropped from Antrim's face to the guns staring wickedly from his hands. No man had seen them shucked from leather, yet there they were, coldly naked and darkly gleaming.

Antrim jeered, "C'mon—draw, if it's a fight you're wantin'."

"I guess it ain't just now," Stewart drawled.

"You show good sense," Antrim murmured as, with a swift blur of motion, he returned his guns to their holsters. A grin streaked across his lips. "May interest you to know that Lothrop's got a witness to Stumpy's killin'. A man who claims to have been watchin' Jones an' Corner taggin' a calf with a runnin' iron when Stumpy came chargin' hellity-larrup onto the scene. This gent claims Corner an' Jones opened up an' downed Harker's bronc, throwin' Harker clear an' stunnin' him. He says Corner then slipped a noose round Stumpy's neck, then they got aboard their cayuses an' dragged 'im down the gulch a piece. He claims Stumpy came to durin' the process an' begged for mercy—that Corner just laughed an' shot him through the head."

"That witness is a liar!" Jones snarled.

In the subsequent hush, Antrim watched the men's faces toughening up, saw the turgid rage that lay behind each narrowed pair of eyes, felt the tempestuous surge of the hot blood roaring through their arteries.

He saw Jones' eyes gleaming through a scarlet fog, and heard Steart's soft, "An' so?"

"So I'm hankerin' to know," he answered evenly, "why you boys hanged Stumpy."

After a pause during which the tension slacked a little, Stewart observed, "That means you ain't puttin' a heap of store by Lothrop's witness."

"Might mean that."

"An' since you ain't," Stewart went on, ignoring his interruption, "I'd admire to know just what give you the notion we hung Stumpy."

Antrim's slow smile uncovered a gleaming line of hard white teeth. "You ain't denyin' it, are you?"

Stewart cleared his throat. "Right now we're fixin' to get at how you got the notion that we did. From what things did you draw that opinion?"

"Stumpy's dead, ain't he?"

Stewart's shoulder stirred impatiently. "Quit dodgin', Kid, an' give me this thing straight—"

Jones broke through his words with a sudden curse. "Did *I* hear you call him '*Kid?*'" Jones' tone was brittle. "Kid *what?*"

"Smoke-wagon Kid," Antrim said, and matched the closeness of the other's glance.

Jones' face went a little greyish under its deep bronze; sweat gleamed suddenly along his cheeks, and his eyes were full of a straining care. His lips went firmly shut, and he kept them that way grimly.

Antrim's gaze swung to Stewart. "Is it a trade?"

"I'll swap," Stewart said, and reached up his hand as he stepped in beside Antrim's horse. Antrim knew that old trick of the Texas gunmen, but he believed he'd measured Stewart correctly and did not hesitate to grip the rancher's hand. Stewart stepped back and Antrim explained:

"Two gents came into Socorro couple of weeks back an' handed out a fancy line about stumblin' over the grave of Stumpy Harker. They found the grave; I've checked up—seen it myself. One of them swore to the corpse bein' Stumpy, an' to prove his point—him being more or less a stranger to this country—mentioned having been trimmed at poker by Stumpy some two years ago. They told the story to me the first time, an' the game this fella played with Harker was stud. When they recounted it to the sheriff, the game had become draw. The sheriff threw in some substantiatin' incidents to bolster the thing more. All three of 'em was razor-slick in their parts. An' all three of 'em," he finished dustily, "was lyin'."

"It wasn't Stumpy?" asked Corner.

"It was Stumpy. I buried him deeper, but you can look if you've a mind to. The point is, I knew Stumpy myself—an' I never knew him to play cards."

Stewart nodded thoughtfully. Jones breathed, "An'—?"

"I kept my suspicions to myself. Lothrop puts up a reward of five hundred bucks for information leadin' to the arrest or death of Stumpy's killers. Next mornin'," Antrim's eyes met Jones' with a cold humor, "a fella named Hildermin comes to the office to claim the reward. He tells how he witnessed you an' Corner polishin' Stumpy off."

Jones' mouth twisted and the sulky brilliance of his half-closed eyes sharpened up. Stewart chewed at his moustache. Corner snarled, "The lyin' polecat!"

Stewart said, "I'm surprised they ain't had a posse here to serve their warrants."

"They're busy chasin' Curly Ives right now. After

they get Ives they'll be comin' after you boys. Leastways, that's what Lothrop's plannin'."

Stewart eyed him shrewdly. "You think different?"

Antrim scowled, and shot Stewart a keen look. He drew a long breath. "Lothrop's goin' after Ives first because he's a thinkin' man who keeps an uncommon sharp eye for details. He's got pipe laid pretty well for you gents. But he wants to be certain there ain't no hitch or kick-back. He's goin' after Ives now because he figures that destroyin' Ives will discourage competition, and because it will win over to his side a large measure of the public trust. He's got to have that behind him if he's goin' to stay in business."

"Business?" Stewart's gaze was quizzical.

Antrim's lips streaked a smile. "You know well as I do what I'm talkin' about, Ed. A leader of vigilantes has got to have a head on his shoulders. Now look—in catchin' up Ives—"

Antrim let his voice trail off as Jones grunted, "Rider comin'."

"Let him come," Stewart snapped testily. "Go on, Kid, you've got my interest up."

"In catchin' Ives," Antrim repeated, "Lothrop figures to have a hangin'; it's the only way to put the fear of God into the hard-case crowd that's runnin' things. Lothrop don't want competition. He aims to run the Socorro bunch to hell-an'-gone. He aims to get the public confidence with the same move."

The rider Jones had seen arrived. His horse was lathered—half out on its legs. The rider himself looked as though he'd been dragged through a knothole; his face was grey with alkali, and his clothes were powdered with it. He slid wearily from his horse.

"What is it, Happy?"

The rider drew a grimy hand across his cheeks. "Lothrop's caught Curly Ives! There's goin' to be a lynchin'."

Stewart's glance met Antrim's. There was admiration there.

Antrim said, "We'd better ride. Lothrop's goin' to overreach himself sure as God makes little apples. He don't know the temper of that crowd."

Stewart asked wonderingly, "What crowd?"

"A crowd of honest ranchers I've advised to be in Socorro," Antrim answered shortly. "Just let them fellas get one bad actor hung, an' they'll get the fever quick."

He lifted his chin from his chest and saw Jones watching him narrowly. There seemed a new boniness to the rancher's dark face, and in the cooling wind flowing off the San Andres his gaunt form looked as tough as saddle leather. He was leaning forward on the balls of his feet, and the pale eyes beneath his puckered brows were keenly searching. "Who the hell are you, anyhow?"

"Just a fool that's hell for justice," Antrim drawled.

Corner sneered. 'There ain't no justice!"

Antrim's voice was as light as down. "That's why I drew cards in this game."

Stewart said briskly, "Get your broncs, boys. We'll trail along."

"Just a second." Antrim looked at Stewart carefully; widened his gaze to include the others also. "You fellas haven't answered my question yet. That was part of the bargain."

Stewart said slowly, "We found evidence that Two-Pole-Pumpkin was rustling our cattle. There's a coupla hides inside the house now, if you are interested. We caught Harker off his range; we

336

found a cinch ring on his saddle that was pretty warm. He wouldn't spill his guts, so we hung 'im as a warnin' to the rest of them."

Antrim knew the penalty for rustling was hanging. He found no fault with that. It was the fact that Stumpy had been hung without a trial. He said, "Stumpy never rustled a critter in his life. He wasn't built that way."

Corner rasped, "He sure showed pore judgment in pickin' his companions, then."

"So your smart jokers hung Stumpy because you figured his outfit was on the steal—"

"Yuh fool," Jones broke in hotly. "Yuh don't reckon a square waddy would be beddin' down on the Two-Pole-Pumpkin, do yuh?"

"Well, Stumpy was," Antrim observed, and slid coldly from his saddle. He started slowly toward Jones; there was a sultry anger in his glance that told plainly of the rising turbulence in his blood. Jones didn't lose his nerve. But Corner did—and his left hand went streaking hipward. Jones caught the move. With twisting lips he followed suit.

Twin bursts of flame rolled out from Antrim's hips. The reports banged loudly on the chilling air. They shook the powder smoke stretching across that interval, and smashed against the yonder buildings flatly.

Corner was down, grotesquely writhing, tiny whines of sound dripping from his drooling lips. Jones was staggered back, his twisted face a fish-belly white, his gun discarded and the hand that had momentarily held it now clutched to the stained shoulder of the limply hanging arm. A malignant hate glared from the squinted eyes above his clammy cheeks. Stewart's men stood stiff and silent. A cold amusement showed in Stewart's eyes.

"The next time," Antrim told them dustily, "you boys see to it that you hang a guilty man, or I'll come back an' give you somethin' to remember me by." His glance flashed briefly to Stewart. "You'd better get to Socorro an' keep your bunch in hand. I'll be seein' you," he finished, and broke from his rigid stillness, backing watchfully to his horse.

No man spoke while he got aboard; there was no sound save for the creak of saddle leather and the monotonous whine of Corner's groans.

Chapter XIX

"THEM WOLVES ARE OUT FOR BLOOD!"

Yolanda had definitely made up her mind. She had thought about this thing carefully, and had weighed each step that she must take, each lonely mile that she must cross. She had balanced the discomforts and likely dangers of her plan against the slavery, abuse, and close confinement of her life with Lothrop; and freedom—not matter what its price—seemed utterly desirable. Antrim wouldn't have her; that much was patent and showed her plainly the folly of longer staying there. There had been a time, after his shooting of Ruidosa, when she had again begun to hope. But too many days had now passed without sign from him, and hope was gone back into the dust from which it came.

She had in these past months been given many an opportunity as good as this, for the opportunity was really so in name only—a mockery from which

Stone Lothrop drew sardonic amusement. Neither he nor any member of his tough-faced crew was now on the ranch; that constituted what semblance of opportunity there was. Many times she had witnessed Lothrop's smile when, on returning after some protracted absence, he had found her there. She had found its smugness maddening, the suaveness of his greeting a fiery irritant, and the blandness of his suggestion that perhaps time had hung a little heavy on her hands and had made those hands itch with the desire to curl their fingers about a gun. His compliments on her looks on such occasions had been both unctuous and oily, and his compliments on her culinary art accursedly fulsome. She was determined to surprise him truly this time.

It was impossible for her to leave the valley without crossing some small portion of the terrible Jornada; it doubled the risk she ran in leaving, and was the thing that had thus far discouraged all thought of flight. But she had weighed her chances well and had counted the cost. Death on that burning desert was infinitely preferable to living there longer.

She would go northwest from there, pointing her way across the lava beds by the yonder sombre outline of Black Mesa. There, somehow, she would manage to ford the Rio Bravo's muddy waters and reach Fort Craig. There, she would see the commandant and demand an escort to Socorro.

Her pack was made and her water bottles filled. All that now remained before her on the ranch was the capture of one of those half-wild mustangs in the big corral and, once captured, the getting of a saddle on its back.

She returned to her room for one last look at the

spot where Antrim had stood when he'd shot Ruidosa. She knelt upon that spot and prayed. She stumbled blindly down the *sala*. In the living-room she wiped the mist from her smarting eyes, hoisted the pitifully small bundle of things she wished to keep, and stepped out into the sunlight of the *patio*.

It was at a panicky pace that she left the gate behind, moving hurriedly across the open yard toward the watching horses in the pole corral.

It was a dim starlit night and a lantern was a necessity if one would see the path before one's feet. It was a wild and blustering night, and a crisp, dank air flowed off the *Manzanos* and whirled in bitter gusts about the corners of Socorro's buildings, plastering the shirts and vests of the gesticulating throngs against their torsos, and flapping the wide brims of the men's sombreros, and driving grit and dust into their savage faces.

Yesterday afternoon Stone Lothrop and his tired but triumphant posse had succeeded in bringing their man back alive, and at this very moment he was awaiting trial in the ramshackle county jail. If appearance counted for anything, it was a trial that bade fair to be short and potent.

The name of Curly Ives had become synonymous with evil; the fellow had truly run amuck and was definitely known as a heartless killer. No man could leave his house without leaving anxiety behind while such a menace roamed the streets unchecked. Yet only Lothrop had dared take steps by which Ives' suppression of destruction might possibly be encompassed. Through entirely personal motives, Lothrop had done more; he had caught the renegade and locked him up in jail.

Lothrop, as he saw the rising temper of the crowds now swarming before the Grand Hotel, smiled to himself and considered his work well done. Everything was running smoothly. As soon as this particular episode should be relegated to the past, he meant to take such steps as would bring the Smoke-wagon Kid to heel. And after that he would crush the valley outfits that had dared dispute his rise to power. Yes, events were shaping nicely.

Antrim, idling into the Pinto Bar, observed the mob's growing agitation and nodded wisely to himself. This was what he had suspected. Lynch law was about to be put in operation—and this time, with Lothrop's sanction.

Yet he was definitely surprised when he saw the sombre group of horsemen start uptown from the jail. They were coming too quietly and too determinedly to be any part of that gesticulating, raucous, swearing mob. As they approached nearer he observed that they rode in such a manner that their three-deep ranks formed a hollow square, and he saw that in the hollow rode a solitary horseman, with arms bound behind his back.

The cavalcade rode straight up the center of the street, the cheering pedestrians moving from their path, and closing in again behind to follow. The crowded spaces resounded to the gusts of noise; then all that turbulence fell away as the cavalcade of black-garbed horsemen halted before the Grand Hotel. Antrim saw men hurriedly approaching the spot with lanterns to dispel the gloom, while other men came up carrying packing-boxes and other burnable waste. This latter was swiftly made into a growing pile and ignited to furnish additional light. In the comparative quiet which now obtained, he

341

could distinctly hear the rumble and rattle of an empty wagon. He swung his glance about and saw it. Four men were propelling it toward the gathered company.

Antrim left the resort. Mingling with the crowd, he gradually threaded his way forward till he held a spot of vantage close beside the now opened front of the horse-formed square. He saw a man unlashing the prisoner's arms. He did not see Lothrop, though, nor had he expected to; the sheriff knew better than openly to appear at such a proceeding. But several of his crew were there. Two men whom Antrim recognized as Mitch Moelner and Tombstone stood among the watching throng not far away. He found a place where they would not be too apt to notice him in the event they glanced his way.

Stewart seemed to be in charge of operations. The wagon was drawn inside the lighted square and its tongue upended. Ives was dismounted from his horse and sitting at a packing-box table facing another and bigger box which served Stewart as a platform.

"Wonder where the Great Seizer is at?" a man near Antrim muttered.

The man's neighbor said, "I hope yuh ain't fool enough t' think he'd come pokin' round here at a time like this. He ain't nobody's fool—not Lothrop! An' yuh mark my words, kid; there's more t' this than meets the eye!"

A man across the way shouted, "Let's git a-goin'! I hone t' hear thet slat-sided son gurglin' on a rope!"

But mostly, these men watched in silence. They seemed satisfied to let the vigilantes do their work in their own way, just so the work was done.

Ives, while things were warming up, conducted a

facetious chatter with those members of the crowd who stood nearest, and even had the gall to exchange repartee with a number of his captors until sternly bidden to keep silent or suffer the indignity of a gag. Antrim, marveling, thought him the coolest man among the crowd.

Curly Ives was a hard one, and continued outwardly unmoved throughout his trial. Not once could Antrim catch a sign of worry on his sardonic features. He seemed as unruffled as an eleven-times widow contemplating matrimony, as the man next to Antrim told his neighbor. Ives must have known his fate was sealed, yet no sign of the fear such knowledge might have been expected to engender ever touched the weathered roughness of his cheeks. Staring out across the stern and frowning visages of those men gathered to determine his guilt and punish it, his gaze was caustic and defiant.

But his wasn't the only nerve apparent; Antrim could not help but admire the cool, self-contained manner in which Stewart with quiet simplicity was conducting the desperado's trial. His uncompromising yet dignified bearing was bound to earn the respect of all discerning honest men. No man could guess how many of that assembled company might any moment decide to rush the vigilantes and, in bloody carnage, attempt to free the prisoner. The true test must come when Ives' fate should be announced.

The time came. Stewart cleared his throat and a guard touched Ives' arm. "Brother, you had better take this standin'," the guard advised. "An' you'd better be lookin' forward to another world. You are played out in this one, sure."

Ives got to his feet with a sneer. "This business is

goin' t' make yuh uncomfortable as a camel in the Arctic Circle."

"That's my lookout," snapped the guard. "Button yore lip; the boss is goin' to pronounce yore sentence."

"I'd like a couple of burnin' sensations first."

"You'll get all the burnin' sensations you are lookin' for in about five minutes," the guard predicted grimly.

"Hell," Ives snarled. "What kind of trial's this, where a gent's last request don't git no damned attention?"

Many persons in the crowd appeared shocked by the demand, but the drinks were sent for and Ives put them down with evident satisfaction. It was possible he was seeking in this manner to bolster up a failing courage, though Antrim did not think so. The talkative man next to Antrim said, "Ol' Stewart looks solemn as a tenderfoot trapper skinnin' his first skunk!" This fellow's friend grunted, "I reckon he's thinkin' of what Ives' cronies is goin' t' do about this business if Ives gets hanged. I'm sorta wonderin' along them lines myself."

Stewart said, "Curly Ives, the jury has turned in its verdict. They have come to the considered opinion that you are guilty—"

The rest was drowned in sudden uproar as the crowd shouted its hearty agreement with this just verdict. But as the tumult subsided there could be heard from the shadows along the fringes of the mob guttural curses and vicious maledictions, and abruptly several sharp *clicks,* as of pistols being made ready, were plainly audible. Someone shouted, "By grab, the stranglin' murderers'll never dare to hang 'im!"

An unwonted quiet followed on the heels of this threatening remark. There was a momentary lull in the progress of Ives' trial. He smirked suggestively at the expressions of anxiety he discerned upon those faces nearest him. To Antrim it was apparent that this critical moment held the necessity for prompt action. His face expressed approval as Stewart raised a hand and, as he got the crowd's attention, said, "It is this jury's recommendation that Curly Ives be now hanged by the neck until dead."

A blur of motion to one side swung Antrim's glance in that direction. He saw Tombstone struggling to raise the gun his fingers gripped. And he saw Mitch Moelner's sinewy hands exerting pressure to restrain him. Even as Antrim watched, he saw the tension drain from Tombstone's frame, saw the man's malignant features smoothed by returning caution; saw the pair of them abruptly wheel and unobtrusively leave the crowd. But if those two did indeed adjourn, there were many others who did not, and everywhere Antrim could see the flash of naked weapons in the red glow from the roaring flames of that pile of combustibles gathered in the center of the square. The crowd began to bellow approval of the sentence, and through that upward surge of voices hoots could be detected and not a few outright threats and jeers. The dark-garbed horsemen held their double-barrelled guns in readiness and presented a determined front. Stewart said coldly through a lull:

"The first man moving a finger to obstruct the ends of justice will get a load of buckshot through his guts. I reckon most of you know me well enough to sabe that when I say a thing I mean it." Then to his aids: "Proceed with your duty, men."

The wagon tongue was broken off, and one end of it thrust into the ground. The other end rose slantingly across the wagon body, projecting above the packing box by the side of which Ives stood. he was ordered to stand atop the box.

"If you hang me, you'll be hangin' a innocent man!" he cried. "Gawd, I'm innocent as a babe unborn! I never killed no man, nor woman, nor child—why, I'd swear to it on a Bible!"

Stewart took a Bible from his pocket and handed it to one of his men, who strode to Ives and offered it. The renegade grasped it eagerly and kissed it. Then, with owlish solemnity, he repeated his denial and called upon every saint in heaven to witness his absolute innocence.

Stewart said disgustedly, "You had better save your breath, Curly. We've got positive proof of your guilt in connection with the deaths of three men. You are going to stretch hemp. Have you any last words?"

"All I got to say," snarled Ives, "is that I'm innocent. An' I hope every last one of you rots in hell for this!"

Hardly had those words left his mouth when two burly vigilantes hoisted him ungently onto the box. The noose was adjusted swiftly. Stewart said:

"Do your duty, men."

A lariat snaked the box from under Ives. Death took him with hardly a struggle.

Moelner, followed instantly by a panting Tombstone, entered the sheriff's office and shut the door. His eyes went at once to the girl who stood against the wall; then they went to Lothrop inquiringly, sternly. "What's she doin' here?"

A ripple of sardonic humor disturbed the heavy

set of Lothrop's cheeks. "Get tired of waitin' for me at the ranch, I reckon, an' come to town to hunt me up. She come across Daggett an' he brought her here."

Yolanda met his mocking glance with frigid composure and cold indifference. She did not speak.

Daggett snickered from his place beside the desk. Black Jack Purdin frowned uncertainly. Lothrop said, "Feelin' her oats a little. But I'll sure take that out of her when I get her home." And a sour grin crooked his heavy lips.

"Where's the rest?" Moelner grunted.

"Down at the corral, ropin' out fresh broncs. We're goin' to leave pretty quick."

"You are damn' right we are," Moelner said. "We're goin' to leave quicker'n that."

Lothrop eyed him with a risen vigilance, his big shoulders hunched a little forward. "Ain't they hung Ives yet?"

Moelner said, "They've hanged Ives—" and was checked by Lothrop's curt:

"What the hell's gone wrong? If they've hung Ives we've got Stewart where we want him, ain't we? What the hell's gone wrong?" he repeated wickedly, and there were flecks of flame coalescing in his eyes.

"They've got necktie fever," Moelner gritted. "Tularosa lost his nerve an' tried t' bolt. Some of that crowd recognized 'im an' them vigilantes piled all over 'im. You've overreached yoreself, Stone. You furnished 'em with an example, an' now them wolves are out fer blood!"

Lothrop, with his glance on the brightness of Moelner's slitted eyes, drew one long breath and swore.

"But yuh ain't heard—" Tombstone started.

"Heard what!"

"They put another box alongside Curly's danglin' body an' made Tularosa sit there while they tried 'im," Moelner snapped in a wire-tight voice, "An' Tularosa's squealed!"

Chapter XX

THE VIGILANTES STRIKE

While the jury was off to one side determining the fate of Tularosa, Antrim saw the tall, gangling figure of a frock-coated frontier sky-pilot step up to where Stewart stood with arms folded across his high chest. The parson gestured toward Ives' dangling body with a bony hand. "To hang a boy that age!" he spoke indignantly. "It is an outrage, sir, I tell you—it is an abomination in the eyes of the Lord. Two wrongs never make a right. The Scriptures bid us turn the other cheek—"

"We've run plumb out of other cheeks to turn!" shouted an irate merchant.

The parson ignored the interruption. "Didn't you sympathize with that poor lad? Didn't you feel for him?"

"Well, yes," Stewart answered, eyeing the man solemnly. "The boys felt for him more or less—they felt for him round the neck."

Those men who had been especially selected to form the jury of the impromptu court now filed back into the square and returned a verdict of guilty.

Tularosa's cheeks were as white as snow. He

turned to Stewart composedly, however, and said quietly, "I know that my time's arrived. You are figgerin' to hang me, an' I deserve it. I've got no kick. I knew what I was doin' when I got into this. The gang's a black-hearted bunch of vultures an' I'll be glad to see it broken up. I come of decent people, an' should ought to have gone straight."

Stewart nodded. "I'm sorry about this, Tularosa. But I've got to do my duty as I see it. The law here—what we have had of it—has been corrupt. It is time the folks of Socorro County got a new deal. You have been found guilty of participation in a number of infamous robberies, two of which affairs compelled the killing of honest citizens. You will have to die."

"I know that," Tularosa said. "But I would like to tell you about this gang so you can clean it up proper. I'm not saying this to get off, either."

"You have information for us as to the identities of the men belonging to this gang that has been terrorizin' this country?"

"Yes. Lothrop is the leader. He organized the gang and runs it. I hope to hell you get him. I know most of the other men who are important. They are Black Jack Purdin, Tombstone, Mitch Moelner, Ruidosa, Rafe, Mormon Joe, Brazito, Daggett, Suggs, Hildermin, an' Buck Keldane."

A man pressed forward from the crowd as Tularosa finished. He said, "Mr. Stewart, I been prospectin' over in the Sierra Caballos. Five-six days ago I seen some buzzards flyin' over the canyon I was workin'. They was further down. After a time I got curious an' headed that way. I found a bunch of skeletons an' some papers in a bag. The papers were addressed to Craig Smith at Silver City. I allow them skeletons is what's left of Smith's Train."

The crowd surged forward with a roar; only the levelled shotguns of the mounted vigilantes held them back. When some measure of quiet had been restored, Stewart demanded of Tularosa, "What do you know about Smith's Train?"

"Plenty—it was our gang that stopped it."

"Where? An' when? We must have names."

"On the night of August 13th," Tularosa said without bravado, "Stone Lothrop, Purdin, Moelner, myself, Tombstone, Keldane, Daggett, Rafe, an' a couple others whose names I never heard jumped Smith's Train near the top of the divide where the trail overhangs Cripple Canyon at Dead Man's Drop."

"Where did you put the money?"

"Stone Lothrop took those two fellows whose names I didn't know an' the three of 'em went off some place to cache it. Lothrop came back alone an' allowed he'd sent the others off to another section on a job."

"Do you know where they went?"

"I got an idee," Tularosa admitted drily, "that they went to hell. I'll look 'em up pretty quick."

"Did Lothrop's gang kill the whole crew of Smith's Train?"

"Yes. We killed Craig an' the other two others. Laidley an' Shinkle. We was scared to leave any man alive."

"Who are on Lothrop's ranch aside from those men you've named?"

"There was a puncher named Stumpy Harker, a feller what limped. He was a pretty square hombre. I reckon you know what happened to him, Stewart."

"Yes," Stewart said. "What happened to Harker might be described as the fortunes of war, an' the

350

result of bein' found in bad company. Was there any other person besides Lothrop's wife?"

"Hell—she wa'n't Lothrop's wife! Nor yet his 'woman' even," Tularosa said, and spat. "Only reason she was on the spread at all is cause Lothrop tricked her into comin' to the valley, an' once there wouldn't let her go. She might have tried to clear out when no one was on the ranch. But you know that stretch of the Jornada, Stewart. You couldn't hardly expect a woman t' brave that all by her lone self."

The revelation slipped like a knife's cold blade up Antrim's back, and the firelight, striking his eyes, showed a dark fierce glitter as he wheeled; showed his high flat cheekbones pressed rashly against the tightdrawn skin. His glance, as he ploughed his way through the muttering groups, struck back with a brittle hostility; the wicked turbulence in the Smoke-wagon Kid unsteadied him, made him blind to the danger of the crowd. He did not wait for a path, but made one, his broad sloping shoulders deliberately smashing men aside with an utter indifference that did not heed their after movements, and that registered through that assemblage like a trumpet's blare. No man staged nor tried to stem that cannonball progress.

He put the trial behind and strode deliberately to the hitch rail fronting the Pinto Bar, where he jerked loose his claybank's reins and swung into the saddle. He swung his cold-jawed bronc around and sent it toward the sheriff's office. Dismounting before that building's darkened windows, he went up its steps and kicked the door wide, flattened himself against the wall with both guns drawn.

But nothing happened, and only the echoes of his thumping bootsteps and the door's loud striking bang came back. He slipped one gun in leather and struck a match, shielding its flame with cupped hand. "Lothrop," he said with a frozen clarity. "Lothrop." But no man was in that building, nor in the jail; not even Farley, as he found upon inspection. Lothrop and his men were gone.

He holstered his other gun with a sleek, grim motion and retraced his steps, his hard teeth gleaming in a white, cold line. He swung into his saddle and sent the claybank toward the desert in a fast run.

It was half an hour before Antrim's rage cooled sufficiently to allow for clear reflection. He knew, then, what he had to do. The vigilantes would be onto Lothrop's trail by daybreak, and they would stay with it until they ran him from the Territory or left him and his followers strewn across that harsh land in unmarked graves. They might even attempt to do the like for him, yet this he doubted, for Stewart and many of the others were too keenly aware of what they chose to consider his love of justice and marked adherence to fair play. He had been ever known to give his men a break. His danger now, he knew, must come from Lothrop's men, and from such other turbulent souls as might wish to claim the doubtful glory of having "downed the Smoke-wagon Kid."

Antrim's desire now was to come up with Lothrop's riders before the vigilantes. Not that it would make a great deal of difference really whether those desperate men were wafted from this world of lead poisoning or by way of hemp. But the tempestuous surge of his roaring passion had abated, and he could view all things again in their true perspective.

The pounding of his quickened pulse had slowed to a wicked smoothness, to an evenness of tempo that revealed his determination as fully as did that unswervable stubbornness that lay along the forward throw of his jaw. He was again cognizant of his mission in that country, and was recalling the bitter fact that he was not a free agent now, as he had been while courting the impulsive Yolanda those long nights ago in Santa Fé. Freely, as he rode through the blackness of the night, he damned both Axtell and those others—"includin' that scribblin' nitwit, Wallace!" Because he'd been uncommonly fast with his lead-dispensing, he'd let them persuade him against his judgment. Well, they need not worry: he'd perform to the letter this chore they'd set him. Then he would put that country behind him, and try to wash its odious taste from an outraged memory.

Hardly had the hoofbeats of Antrim's buckskin faded beyond the edge of town when three vigilantes swung down before the sheriff's door. They mounted the steps and pushed inside the office, exploring it even as Antrim had done before them, and with equally barren result. "Looks like the bird has flown," said one.

"Well, I dunno about that," replied one of his companions drily, "but I'll hev to admit that he sure is on the wing."

In another part of town four roving members of the Committee came upon the trail of a citizen whose stealthy movements roused their instant suspicion. Called upon to halt, this citizen opened fire, downing a vigilante. The other three took after him with a stern determination that shortly landed him upon one of those boxes in the center of the square. A rope was swiftly noosed and the noose fitted to his neck.

At another place, Chips Dorado, a tinhorn gambler, was hailed by a pair of dark-garbed riders.

"Hello, Chips," said one. "You had better come with us."

"What for?"

"Well, we are conducting an investigation in front of the Grand, and we'd like for you to be there."

"What have I done now?" demanded Dorado testily.

"We aren't sure. But we know what you've done in the past, and I am afraid you must consider yourself under arrest."

Quick as a flash, Dorado drew a derringer. But a swinging vigilante boot knocked it from his grasp before he could fire. "If you make another move like that," softly purred the owner of the boot, "we shall shoot you where you stand. Come along now; you're not the only pebble on this beach."

"I'm awful cold," Dorado muttered. "Do you mind if I get my coat?"

"No need to bother. You'll be warm enough directly."

Chapter XXI

GAWDFORSAKEN VALLEY

The noonday sun was slanting brightly down across the colored adobe buildings when Guy Antrim reached the Two-Pole-Pumpkin. Its lazy yellow warmth gave them a slumbrous, deserted appearance—a suggestion of having been vacated in a hurry which the ten solidly motionless horses in the big corral bore out effectively. But Antrim had trailed too long with danger to put any faith in appearances, and he approached the place with high caution. Behind the angling smoke of his cigarette, his eyes stared sharply with a close attention for the minute details of this scene. But he could discern nothing of an alarming nature.

He swung from his horse by the big gate guarding the *patio,* and threw one keen swift glance at these smaller buildings' backs. No single thing was moving, yet he could not shake the feeling of menace which had fastened on him with his entrance to this place. The ranch was too quiet—there was a brittle quality to its hush that dragged like a file across his nerves.

His lean-sinewed shape throwing its long shadow across the ground before him, he strode into the *patio* with a springy step—and stopped. Then he knew. His breath deepened and the fingers of his tapering hands splayed out to either side. His blue glance beat hard against the toughened features of the big man lounging in the nearest doorway. And he stood there that way, knowing that one further move might betray his purpose in returning to the ranch. "Howdy," he drawled. "I guess you are Purdin, the foreman, ain't you?"

"I guess I am," the big one said, and told Antrim by his tone that longer subterfuge would be wasted effort. Somehow he felt a little glad. He said:

"Well, Purdin, I've come for—" and was checked by the range boss' oath.

"What you've come for," Purdin snapped, "an' what you'll get is two different things, you slat-sided, sneakin' b—!"

And with the words the foreman's fat right hand slapped downward.

The adobe walls batted the echoes of those shots back and forth with a hellish racket. Purdin's knees buckled and sprawled him forward across the sill.

Antrim's glance raked brightly round, and he did not break from his rigid stillness, nor did he raise the muzzles of his lowered pistols. Each doorway into the *patio* framed a watchful man, and each man's hand held a levelled weapon.

A cold grin curled Antrim's wide lips saturninely. "I guess that is it."

"You are wrong," Mitch Moelner jeered, striding toward him. "Shootin' would be too easy, an' I never was keen on firin' squads. Don't think yo're passin' out that neat—though you will wish you was before we're through, I shouldn't wonder. Toss away them peace-makers."

Antrim said, "I'll lay them down," and did so, carefully.

"All right. Now back away from 'em, smart fella."

Antrim backed half a dozen paces. "What's the big idea of all this?"

"You know well enough what the idee is," Moelner growled. "But just to refresh yore mem'ry I'll say that we heard from Santa Fé."

Antrim's face showed a study in bewilderment. Moelner thrust his thumbs inside the armholes of his vest in a way that made its silver buttons flash. His lips cracked in a hard and instant grin. "We heard about that letter you got," he jeered. "You ain't kiddin' no one. Farley had some talk with the Grand's proprietor yesterday mornin'. They're great friends—Farley puttin' him in the way of makin' some quick money off an' on. He told Farley all about them fancy seals that was on yore mail."

The sense of impending disaster spread a shadow

across that interval. The silence grew thick and clogged. His hard restraint put an ache in Antrim's muscles. He relaxed them suddenly, and let his breath out, too. He swung his sloping shoulders toward where Lothrop's form made a broad and solid shape against the wall. Lothrop's face hung like a black cloud in the sun.

Antrim laughed. The sound was a shocking thing in all that curdled stillness. He poured rash words after it recklessly:

"Why, you bunch of imitation badmen! You wouldn't scare a three months baby back where I growed up! Just let me get my guns an' I'll take the whole yellow-bellied crew—one at a time or all together. Makes a fella laugh to think of you saddleblanket coyotes settin' up to be like them hard cases in Lincoln County! It's a joke!"

The muzzles of Tombstone's guns tipped upward viciously. But Lothrop's cold words rattled across his intention like chunks of ice. "You fire them guns an' I'll smash every bone in yore body!"

Sweat gleamed on Tombstone's hollowed cheeks, but he put his guns away and stood with his lank arms folded across his bony chest.

Lothrop watched him a moment longer, then his glance swung back to Antrim and his lids slid up a fraction and a sour grin curled his lips. "Almost, Kid—but not quite good enough. You ain't goin' out that easy, bucko. 'Landa," he said sharply, raising his voice. " *'Landa!*"

The girl came, and her slender form made a long, willowy shadow in the door. "Ain't this," Lothrop asked, "the curly wolf I took you away from in Santa Fé?"

Yolanda did not answer, but her eyes met Antrim's

squarely.

It was as though, in that one instant, a veil had been stripped from his eyes, and for the first time he saw her clearly as she really was—tall and slim and straight and proud. He discerned the reckless slant of her cheeks, and marked the rash impulsiveness of her nature that at last she'd learned to check. He recognized the fine generosity that was in her, and the stalwart courage, too. He observed how her lips with their fierce, proud lines were in scarlet contrast with the whiteness of her face. Then he looked into her level eyes—and caught his breath. All the gravity of his strict countenance softened as he looked at her, and the cynical mocking twist left his mouth.

For that one moment he was like a boy; like that boy she'd known back in Santa Fé. Then Lothrop's lazy drawl broke the spell with insolence. "Take a good look at him, girl. He won't be so much to look at next time you get a chance to see him . . . if there is a next time, which I doubt."

He tipped his head at Antrim, and his sleepy lids squeezed down with a sly, sardonic humor. "I've a hunch that you're not goin' to be around this Territory much longer, Kid. The Apaches are pretty expert at redressin' their wrongs. I've thought a lot about them redskins lately. I've learned a few of their tricks . . . Like their ways with burnin' splinters, f'r instance. An' with knives. An' ants, an' such-like. I've been wonderin' if them tricks would work as well for me. You said a minute ago, Kid, that it makes you laff to think of coyotes like us settin' up to be like them hard cases over in Lincoln County. Seems like you said it was a joke." His long smoke-colored eyes were filled with a sulky brilliance as they rested on Antrim probingly. He said:

"I'm goin' to give you time to find out if the joke was worth the laff."

Lothrop, Moelner, Daggett, and Tombstone lounged in the room Lothrop used as an office and waited while Yolanda fixed up a snack of grub to cut their hunger. Lothrop seemed unable to make up his mind whether to quit the country quickly, or stick around a spell longer and clean up a few loose ends that were left in his business, brought about by the sudden sense of civic conscience he had unwittingly roused in the breasts of Socorro's citizens. His effort to trap Stewart had been ill-timed. His plan had succeeded far beyond his expectations—too damned far, in fact. He had not even dreamed of such an outcome. He had thought to get Stewart to hang Ives for him, and then make Stewart pay the price of such an illegal lynching. Like his successful plotting against Jones and Corner, the position into which he had maneuvered Stewart held no advantage for him now.

He well realized that once the vigilantes got on his trail he'd have to pull his pin and drift. He had not sufficient men at his disposal successfully to defy Stewart's swollen force. But he did not expect any move from Stewart yet; the man would be too busy cleaning up the county seat and its environs. As long as he kept away from towns, Lothrop decided, he'd be safe enough for another week, and much might be done in the length of seven days.

But he was not figuring on passing up any bets. He had Suggs, Farley, and Hildermin out scouting now with orders to report immediately if they saw any dust in the direction of the Jornada. He considered that should any such dust be sighted, he would still have a leeway of time in which to get himself and his men away on the fresh horses that were saddled and ready inside the 'dobe stable.

Tombstone swung his cadaverous shape completely around and started for the door. After him Lothrop drove a cold, "Where the hell you goin'?"

"I'm goin' out an' see that lobo suffer!"

"Keldane can watch him without yore help."

Tombstone pivoted with a sultry curse. There was a cruel and glittering balefulness in the slitted eyes he flashed on Lothrop. "That may be so. The ants won't be needin' my help, neither. But I like t' watch 'em workin' an'—Hell! What's the sense in spread-eagling that smokeroo a-tall, if a gent can't watch him squirm?"

Lothrop drawled coldly, "You may be needed here. An' anyhow, I'm not trustin' you out of my sight, Tombstone. I'm goin' to take a look at him myself, soon's I eat. You can go with me."

Chapter XXII

"WALLACE"

Lothrop looked up from his plate abruptly, and his intent stare fastened on Daggett and instantly drew that burly ruffian's gaze from his food. "What's up?" he growled, wiping a greasy hand across his moustache.

"You sure you locked that filly in tight?"

"Hump," Daggett said. "I reckon I know how to bar a door an' block a window. Seems like you're gettin' kinda nervous, Chief."

Lothrop grunted. "Mebbe I am," he agreed, and resumed his eating. But a few seconds later he looked up again. "Seems like I keep hearin' sounds," he muttered, sending a sharp glance round the room.

"Sounds? What kinda sounds?"

Lothrop scanned the faces of his men with the probing intentness that was becoming a habit with him lately. The language of looks and signs and movements was as familiar to him as a printed page, and in these men's bearing he had discerned since early morning that his leadership there was at an end. His men now appeared to trust him no farther than he trusted them; distrust had begotten distrust. One opportunity was all they'd need; his name was written on their lead, and they meant to use it if they could. He read the intention in their covert looks and furtive stares, in their visible restlessness and tautened cheeks. The vigilantes had cast the shadow of the noose upon them, and they were blaming him. He found it significant that Mitch Moelner's eating was being done with his left hand, while his right lay conspicuously idle on the table's edge. It was like a shouted warning. From now on, Lothrop knew, unremitting vigilance would have to be the price of his life; not one beat of these men's pulses must be allowed to escape his notice. He had witnessed the mercurial temper of these savages far too often ever to dream they'd leave him quick and bolt. No—they'd leave him dead, or not at all.

Once again his thoughts were scattered by those elusive, grim, deceptive sounds. A repetition of those sounds he'd heard before; as ghastly as the hollow pounding of a man nailing down a coffin lid, and quite like it.

Lothrop felt a shiver run through his burly frame. Lifting his chin from his chest, he found Moelner watching him. The gunman's eyes were sharply suspiciously on him and with a strange intentness. The laden knife his left hand wielded was poised midway between his mouth and plate. The fingers of his right began a nervous drumming of the table's edge.

Lothrop snarled, "Stop that, Mitch!"

A wildness threaded the air of the room. Moelner stopped his drumming, but his eyes returned Lothrop's scowling stare with a sulky brilliance. The hollows of Tombstone's gaunt, cadaverous cheeks looked sinister in the failing light.

"I heard them sounds myself this time," muttered Daggett irritably. "What you'spose they are, Mitch?"

"Hell, I ain't no mind-reader," Moelner snapped. " 'F you are so damned curious, you better go out an' see."

But Daggett was not, apparently, that curious. He shoved his chair back a bit from the table, but he did not get out of it. Lothrop flicked a slanchways glance through the window at his side and remarked how the shadows were long across the range. The rough and distant shoulders of the Elephant Buttes were turning purple; a sure sign that dusk was near. That business with Antrim had taken longer than he'd thought. The sun wouldn't have done the fellow much mischief in such a short while. But those ants . . .

Lothrop jerked his eyes around to Tombstone immediately when that man moved a hand. Tombstone brushed the hand across his bristly, bony jaw and gave the watcher a snaggly-toothed grin. Reaching out that skinny hand, he picked up the chew of tobacco he'd deposited on his plate edge at the commencement of the meal and thrust it into his mouth. He masticated with a sort of bovine pleasure that grated on Lothrop's wire-taut nerves.

Yet, despite the crazy fluttering of his pulse, Lothrop kept outwardly calm and placid; only the glittering sharpness of his glance showed the strain that he was under.

Then a faint, far spatter of sound drifted across the desert's silence and collected in the room, laved against its walls like the ripples of a pool disturbed by some tossed rock.

"Gunfire!" Mitch Moelner's tone was cold.

Tombstone and Lothrop each shoved back from the table and paused; the eyes of each watched the other with a straining care. The danger in that place would come from Tombstone—Lothrop knew it. Moelner was the worst antagonist to be faced among his men, but Tombstone's was the more erratic temper. Tombstone would be the first to crack.

Moelner said, "We better get outside. That sounds like trouble."

Daggett grunted and rose, the eyes of every man upon him. "I'm goin' to get them broncs from the stable. We better have 'em handy."

Lothrop thought, "He's goin' to try a sneak an' cut for the timber." But aloud he said, "Yeah. Bring them into the *patio*. No tellin' what that firin' meant, but it sounded off toward the southern end of the valley—off towards Corner's place. We'll wait here."

"You can wait here," Moelner said. "I'm goin' outside. If that's trouble an' it's comin' here, some of us ought to hole up in these other buildin's. We'd hev anyone who came between a crossfire then."

"Wait," Lothrop breathed softly. "Listen!"

To the ears of all was now audible the far fast flutter of drumming hooves. Rapidly they neared, growing to a thunderous rolling beat as they swept into the yard and ceased. The rider's boots hit dirt, thudded across the hard packed ground of the *patio* and came toward the door.

Daggett backed to one side, his attention divided between that opening and the men about the table. A man came through the opening, breathing fast. That man was the dusty, leather-faced Rafe. "Boss," he said, "I passed Hildermin, Suggs, an' Farley up the valley a half-hour back. Then I damn near run into a big crowd of riders from the Long H, the Cinch Ring, an' the Crazy L. You heard that firin'? I reckon Suggs an' Farley an' Hildermin is out of luck. I—" he broke off short as the strangeness in the men's attitudes became apparent to him. "What's up?"

"Nothin'," Lothrop said. Then—"Daggett's goin' after fresh broncs. We've got 'em saddled in the stable. You better . . ." His voice trailed off and each man tensed as the vibrant drum of many sand-muted hooves came floating through the swirling dusk. With an oath Rafe bounded to the window. They could see him start, could see his fingers tighten on the window ledge. A foul tide of curses came spilling from his lips. He wheeled and put his back to the wall; his face was grey. "Too late," the words came bitterly. "We're cut off. There's dust bulgin' in the north pass. By Gawd, I don't see why I ever joined this gang!"

Moelner sneered. "Get hold of yourself. We ain't licked yet. Get out of the bunk-house an' gather all the rifle fodder you can find. When that crowd comes pourin' in, you let 'em have it for all you're worth. Daggett, you do the same, an' hole up in Purdin's shanty. That way we'll have them night-ridin' vigilantes right where we want 'em—we'll send the whole damn crew to hell on shutters!"

The two men went out, and when the sound of their dragging spurs had faded Lothrop said heavily, "Boys, we'll never cut it. Stewart's got too many—"

"Hell!" Moelner sneered. "You never let odds worry you before. You've lost yore grip, Stone. Yo're saggin' like a ol' man in his dotage. You—"

"By grab," Lothrop drawled, "I don't have to take that kind of talk off any man, Mitch. An' I ain't takin' it from you."

Mitch Moelner jeered, "What you figgerin' t'do about it?" and got out of his chair.

Lothrop rose, too; and Tombstone. Tombstone seemed to see his chance and took it. Both clawed hands flashed hipward in a vicious cross-arm draw. But only Lothrop fired. Flame spurted from his thigh and the room glowed redly. Tombstone smashed backward across his chair; both struck the floor in a jarring impact whose sound was lost on the rolling echoes of Lothrop's shot.

Lothrop turned his smoldering gaze on Moelner. "You was sayin', Mitch—?"

Moelner's lips cut a tight grin across his teeth. "I was wrong," he said and, crossing to the wall, he got a box of cartridges and took a rifle from the rack. "Which window shall I take?"

"I reckon it won't make much diff'rence." Lothrop slipped a fresh load into his gun and thrust it back in leather. "We can't stand them fellas off long. Take any one you want."

The approaching horsemen made a heavy sound

in the night outside.

From his aperture across the blackness of the room, Mitch Moelner grunted, "My cartridges are gettin' low, Stone. How many you got left?"

"Damn few," Lothrop muttered heavily. "Not more'n a handful. We've done well to last three hours. Flashes still comin' from that bunk-house window?"

"Not for haff an hour."

"Daggett's still on the peck," Lothrop said. "But he's usin' his six-gun now. He won't last much longer."

Moelner pumped a whining slug at a blotch of movement behind the gate. The shadow jerked larger, then flattened with abrupt finality. "I guess I got one that time," Moelner growled with satisfaction. "No, Daggett can't last much longer, an' I reckon we can't, neither. You was right. There's too many of 'em for us."

What caused him to turn then must have been that sixth sense given by an all-knowing Providence to men who have ridden long on the gunsmoke trail. Standing in the open doorway like some dark ghost in the smoky murk stood a hatless shape.

A startled oath leapt from Moelner's lips. "Stone! You got yore hat on?"

"Sure," came Lothrop's voice from the other window.

"Then—Gawd! *It's Antrim!*" Moelner shrieked, and let go his rifle, his right hand flashing to his belt.

The room rocked with the roaring jar of thudding weapons. Moelner half rose from his crouching posture, then seemed to be leaning forward as though to meet the twin bursts of flame that bulged from the middle of that door-framed figure. Then his body pitched forward, crumpling.

Lothrop's ripped-out oath was a thing hurled in fury: savage! Flame tore from the upswinging muzzle of his pistol in a livid arc. Then the pistol clattered from his hand, its fall as unheard as the strangled sob that came welling from his throat as his burly shoulders sagged back against the wall.

The shape in the doorway crossed the room, found the unshattered base of a lamp and struck a match, applying it to the oil-soaked wick. The yonder firing dropped away to a vast, enfolding silence as the wick flared up. That wavering light showed Antrim in Keldane's trousers, his upper body bare and raw and swollen, as were his face and arms. His wheeling figure sent a crazy all-chest shadow gyrating across the raftered ceiling, and his cracked lips streaked a wicked grin as his eyes met Lothrop's glance. His eyes took in the latter's figure where it sagged in a sullen lump against the wall, and the grin showed satisfaction.

"I reckon you'll live to hang, at that."

Antrim found Yolanda where she had been fastened by Daggett in her room. She had no words to offer him, nor had he need of words when he saw and interpreted the light that was in the brightness of her eyes. He said, "Yolanda, I've been the biggest fool in this Territory. I—I've treated you worse than dirt. I been a stiff-necked damned coyote an' I ain't fit to wipe the dust from your boots. If ever a man deserved nothin' better than a hidin', I'm the man, an' I want you t' know that my eyes are open now to all these facts I . . ." His voice trailed off, and a higher color came into his bloated cheeks.

She came toward him then and stopped before

him when only the breadth of one hand could be placed between them. "I know, Guy. You are all those things you've called yourself, and more." She looked up at him and smiled through sudden welling tears. "We've both been the worst kind of fools, Guy. But, oh, my dear—!"

And then she was in his arms.

At noon, on the fourteenth day after their marriage, Antrim received a wire from Santa Fé:

Guy Antrim
Socorro New Mexico
Good work all round have spoken favorably of part played by you in higher channels appointment as U. S. Marshal following by post
Congratulations
Wallace

THE END